PORTALS

Junctions Murder Mystery Series

Book Three:

PORTALS

L. E. Fleury

The reader should be aware that the characters in the *Junctions Murder Mystery Series* are fictional. While most of the historical locations and events are accurate, the writer has taken artistic license on certain issues to enhance the plot or to paint a more beautiful mental picture. Enjoy the books!

I dedicate this book

...to the Father: Thank you for giving us eternal life.

...to the Son: Thank you for your Blood Covering that gets us back Home.

...to the Holy Spirit: Thank you for enriching our earthly sojourn.

"For we wrestle not against flesh and blood, but against principalities, against powers, against the rulers of the darkness of this world, against spiritual wickedness in high places."

Ephesians 6:12 (KJV)

CHAPTER ONE

Families

"He come in, drunk as usual, smashing the front door wide open so's to scare us. He'd done this a dozen times before, so we was prepared, but this time he had a baseball bat in his hand.

"She peered back at us two kids with the message: 'Do what I told-cha' and then she gave him that look: a steel-blue look he had never seen before.

"Mind you, he stood a good two feet taller than her, but that chilling look in her eye brought him to a sudden stop. I remember he snuffed up a lot of snot before he began to talk all crazy, like always. But she stepped toward him with her head down, like a mama fox defending her kits from a drooling bloodhound.

"'Now you listen to me, Willis P. Bigelow: You better just think twice before you swing that baseball bat at me, or anybody else in this house. Are you listening, mister? Are you hearing me, loud and clear?' She moved even closer. 'You jes' go ahead and take a swing at me with that thing. Matter of fact, take a swing at any one of us… it don't matter. Know why? Huh?' She moved in close enough to breathe into his face. ''Cause whoever you miss, is gonna kill ya.' She nodded into his stunned face. 'That's right.'

"We could see his eyes shift slowly from her to each of us kids. Of course, we was doing what she told us to do:

standing on chairs and glaring at him for all we was worth. Let me tell ya, our knees was shaking, but our nostrils was quaking. Oh, yeah, he knew we wasn't kiddin'.

"Then she lets him have it. 'Go ahead, Willis, take your best shot. But I can gar-an-tee you better never fall asleep in this house from that minute forward, 'cause you ain't never, ever, gonna wake up again.' She nodded slowly and walked away."

"Oh, my gosh," Connie Collins declared. "Did your mother really say that to your father? I've never heard that... such strong... sort of thing, and I've been a counselor for many years." She turned to her friend, Laura Wilson. "Are there really people still like that in Vermont? I mean, it's the nineteen-fifties, for Pete's sake."

"'Fraid so," Laura smiled.

The rest of the Swift Street Quilters nodded their heads in agreement.

"Don't mean to shock you." Lou Bigelow grinned at the woman. "But me and my brother, Bud, learned a good lesson that night." She shook her sand-colored curls in a reassuring nod. "We don't take no guff, offa no-body."

Connie put her question together carefully. After all, she and Laura were brand new to this quilting club, having met at the Maple Leaf Sewing Circle up there in Essex Junction, then also joined these quilters at the Swift Street Pentecostal Church, located near the southern limits of the city of Burlington. This was only their second time at these Sunday afternoon gatherings. The group had opted for the Sunday crafts time, in order to accommodate the schedules of work-week ladies. Saturdays were too crowded, and the meetings only occurred twice monthly, so these strong-willed women chose Sundays, whether the legalists in the congregation liked it or not. That's how it was. So, Connie was cautious, pausing long enough to preface the query with a fairly neutral comment: "I'm guessing this worked for you. You didn't have to do anything drastic, did you?"

"Nah. He threw up in a bucket, then fell into bed."

"And that was the end of it?"

"Nah. Ma took the bat and swung it hard into the headboard right above where his head was on the pillow." She smirked. "He sat straight up and yelled."

She laughed out loud this time. "Ma pushed him back into the pillow and leaned over him. 'Jes' so you don't ferget,' she says."

The rest of the women politely stifled escaping murmurs.

"Time to break for a snack," one of them announced.

As the two women traveled back toward Essex, Connie couldn't help but bring up the subject again. "They wouldn't really have killed him, would they?"

"Umm, probably not." There was a short pause. "Maybe just broke his legs, or something."

"Oh, you can't be serious, Laura."

She was chuckling, but had a point to make. "Hey, we have a whole lot of survivors in this state, that's a fact. And they don't always have access to counselors like you and Don. They have learned to handle things for themselves, and it isn't always pretty. And believe me, it is still happening in the here and now."

"In the present? In the state of Vermont?"

"Ay-yuh. Right now in the wonderful state of Vermont."

***

The Swift Street Pentecostal Church was located a few hundred feet away from the busyness of the quilters that particular Sunday afternoon. Its history included a rich legacy of dedication: the faithfulness of seven stumbling souls, trying their best to take a little territory for Jesus, the Christ, the only Way to Heaven. It was a thriving little house church, begun in what was now the parsonage, and location of this Sunday's quilting activities. Many hours of potlucks, prayer meetings, and general fellowshipping had strengthened the bonds over the years. They built the congregation up to thirty people, before the plans to construct an actual church building were birthed. In the next ten years, they had converted the old dairy barn into a real sanctuary; a place of worship. Every plank, every nail, every broken ankle from a roof-fall — all of it was for the glory of God.

The broken ankle — long-since healed — belonged to Lou's older brother, Bud, who was sitting in his truck in the parking lot waiting for her to finish up the quilting gig. They were born eighteen months apart, looking so much alike, they could have been twins; he was built like a solid totem pole, topped off by wavy brown hair. At barely five-foot-six, she was a more feminine version, with a small bosom accenting the barreled chest, and brown curls draping gently down upon the very same type of squared-off shoulders.

They also shared a somewhat sketchy ethnic background, mostly because their mother seemed reluctant to discuss it beyond the fact that she, herself, had been born in Quebec and was an only child, but she seemed especially proud of her fair skin and blue eyes. Once married, the little woman immersed herself in the challenges of homesteading, but with a flair. She read pretty much anything she could get her hands on, listened for hours to classical music on the radio, and still managed to help her husband pound out tree stumps to clear the rocky Vermont soil. She cooked and sewed and cleaned like the rest of those hardy farm wives, but this diminutive lady could also split rocks and stack a stone fence with the best of them.

They were, in fact, a fine-looking couple; him being a tall redhead, and she a petite sable-haired thing with piercing sapphire eyes. And for a while, all went well for this pair. The hard work of building up a poultry farm out there in Hinesburg was softened somewhat when the two of them went square dancing every other Friday each month, and they were able to go to the movies in Burlington, at least once in that same time period. It was during these movie visits she became enamored of the comedy team, Bud Abbot and Lou

Costello. And it was the reason why, when she finally had her children, she chose to name the two innocent youngsters after this amusing duo. The siblings later decided that she did so, to keep life a little lighter, a little more humorous, and maybe, a little more removed from reality.

Sadly, Willis had undergone a dramatic change the summer of Bud's fifth birthday. The two children later surmised it was due to the family's involvement with what Ma called "the water witch."

"We need to do somethin'," she muttered to Willis. "We need a new well, or we'll lose every last chicken we own. Then what will we do for a living?"

The little ones were enthralled by the tall woman with the skeleton-bone face. Her name was Edith, and she was from the hills of Jericho, Vermont. Her thin frame was draped with gray clothing over a blouse with tiny blue checks all over it, and she breathed hard through her mouth while walking, no matter how slowly. She made it quite clear that she would only use a forked branch from a live willow tree, when it came to choosing a divining rod. The woman also made it plain that she was a dowser, not a witch. But the youngsters weren't all too sure about that.

It was a good thing there was a live willow on the property, because it took her three days and three divining rods to finally come up with some water. The family watched in fascination as she asked the wobbling fork yes and no questions: "Should I walk left to find water?" The stick would wiggle and Edith would either move that way, or ask if she should turn right, instead. Try as they might, however, the children could not discern just exactly what that wiggly willow thing was doing. The parents went along with it, probably figuring that as long as the witch knew what she was doing, it would all work out. At one point, Willis even walked along with the lady as she dowsed.

And it all worked out. Late on the afternoon of the third day, the point of the fork slammed downward, pinpointing the source of ample ground water. Ma paid the lady her twenty dollars, and the next morning, the two grownups started to dig.

It took a few days, but they hit water about twelve feet down. After digging another three feet, they had enough flow to start flooding the hole. They came up, wet and smiling, proud owners of a new well.

"Not bad, for a week's work," Willis had said.

The loose dirt was packed into a protective ridge around the top of the hole, and he topped it off with a cover made of heavy planks but before he dragged it into place, she jammed the dowser's willow branches into the cracks of the underside's reinforcing boards. "For good luck," the little woman had declared.

Edith came back the next day to survey the whole project, and then she muttered something as she scattered some kind of sugary-looking powder over that wooden top. When the children reached out to touch the dusting for a quick taste, she glowered and stamped her foot at them. "Don't touch that," she whispered hoarsely. As she turned to wobble back to her car, she called out to the adults: "Don't touch anything, and, whatever you do, don't drink the water until the tenth day."

But five days later, things went completely dry on the farm. Willis had to haul water from his neighbor, Walter's, place, but it wasn't nearly enough, and the friendly fellow, who had a large family of his own, was hesitant to give away any more of this scarce commodity. By the sixth day, Willis Bigelow had to make a hard decision.

Ma objected, but he insisted. "I'll drink the well water, myself. If I get sick, we'll know it won't work; if I don't, then we have a chance to save the flock."

He hauled up a bucket of the stuff that afternoon. Ma wanted to boil it first, but that wouldn't have worked in trying to water a hundred or so chickens, so she bit her lip and watched him take a full glass. They waited for an hour, and then he took another full glass. As the evening came on, he decided to take one more glass before going to bed.

In the morning, he was feeling fine, so he continued to quaff down several more glasses that day. Again, he arose in the morning feeling just fine. That was encouraging, because the hauled water supply was nearly gone. "If I get through tomorrow, that will make eight days, right? And that's close enough so I can use it for the chickens. But you and the kids go ahead and finish up the hauled stuff."

Willis's plan seemed to work well. The clucking flock survived the eight-day water, and he, himself, seemed none-the-worse for having broken the water witch's stern word of caution, until sometime around the end of October.

He was staring out into the cold night, pressing his face quite close to the bedroom window so that he might get a better view of the full moon. Its white glow lit up bare trees along the ridge above the long roof of the henhouse. She was watching him from under the patchwork quilt, curious about this unfamiliar behavior. Suddenly he shivered. "Come to bed, before you catch a cold in front of that window."

"Not tired."

"You sick or somethin'?"

He turned and sighed impatiently. "Nah. I just don't feel like sleeping." His hands went deep into the overalls pockets. "Just bored, I guess." He raised his brows. "Think I'll go down to Sam's Place and have a swig of homemade jack."

She sat up. "Really? Applejack?" She gave him a questioning look. "You don't even *like* that stuff."

"I… do… now."

She waited up for him. When he stumbled in by the back door, the blue light of morning lit up the sky behind him. She stood up and said, "Time to feed the chickens, Willis."

By Halloween, he was past the applejack and into the hard stuff, and things only got worse, until they finally culminated that night with the baseball bat. By that time, the children were nine and ten years old, in public school, and clueless about keeping family secrets. The teacher called the sheriff, who paid a visit to the Bigelow home, and managed to make a deal with the parents: No citation, on the condition that the whole family starts counseling with a clergyman immediately. Sheriff Max Duncan even gave them the phone number of a reliable pastor over there on Swift Street.

That was how they started attending the Swift Street Pentecostal Church, and how Willis seemed to get the drinking under control. Now, six years later, Bud was waiting to pick up his sister in the parking lot.

She yanked the door open and crawled in, pulling her crafting bag in behind her. "Sorry I'm late. I brought you some cookies."

"Aw, it's okay. I was just sitting here, thinking about Pastor quitting."

"I know it. We was *all* surprised when he told us this morning."

"Not all of us, Lou-Lou. Those guys on the board had to know. Least, that's what Pa said." He turned the key in the ignition. "And that's not *all* he said." He took a long look at the church building in front of them. "He said we need to watch out for some stuff. Bad stuff." He checked on his sister. "Lock that door so's it don't pop open on you. Not picking you up off the road again." As soon as she pushed the button down, he shifted into reverse.

"What bad stuff, Buddy?"

"More like, 'bad people.'" He had raised his voice to be heard over the engine.

"What bad people?"

"People who would like to break up this whole church family, sis." He pulled the truck out onto the road, heading for Hinesburg.

"Who would do that?"

"I don't really know," he lied. But of course, he wasn't going to tell her such a thing. He had heard about when the church had finally been completed, a scarce ten years ago. It had all come together on Easter Sunday of 1943, and the congregation of thirty thankful saints were in earthly heaven. They had done it. It was a real church building. The church family sang songs of praise and thanksgiving. They hugged joyfully. And then they hugged again.

But now, Pastor James suddenly resigned to go help his elderly father run the family farm. That left a certain fellow to move on a long-standing goal: make this Pentecostal church into an elder-run church. It would be a difficult task, given that most of the parishioners had put their backs and hard-earned money into establishing this place of worship — this place where decisions were made in a democratic form of government. But Lou didn't have to know all that. This was a man's business, not to be involving the women. The men in this church would have to handle that schemer.

***

They had gone north from Bible school to take over a tiny church on a remote island off the most northeastern point of the continental United States, this young man and his new Swedish-heritage wife. He was full of hope, and his tall, blonde spouse was ready to follow this starry-eyed man to the ends of the earth, if necessary. They had jumped in with both feet. Folks were welcoming, for they truly wanted a local church. But two years later, he got sick, and things fell apart. It was a struggle to keep a church family together, let alone support a church building. After that, Leo Spencer fell into fits of deep depression — so dark that he did not even respond to Heidi's tender exhortations. In the spring of 1953, the couple was living in a tent on the south end of the island, where Leo was eking out a living as a fishing guide, although he was careful not to go out too far or too long in his rented boat. This timidity would make him the perfect patsy for a certain Mr. Suree.

Michael Suree (pronounced "Sue-_ree_" after the French version) liked to refer to himself as "an old pugnacious pugilist." In reality, he was more of an actor/boxer, a fast-talking showman who helped sell boxing as a major attraction. Although a small man who topped the scales at 147 pounds, he imagined himself a champion in his own weight category, prancing around in gold-colored satin trunks, a shimmering red robe flowing with his every movement. He recited bad poetry for the press, and winked shamelessly at the ladies. For a while he was the darling of the boxing world, making his fortune before reaching the age of thirty and not without some risk; there were two bad cuts on the face, shattered teeth, and even a broken nose, on the road to success. The scars made permanent worry lines on his forehead, the teeth were replaced by a dental partial plate which looked like an ivory overbite, and the nose collapsed into a pointy thing that twitched when he talked, but no matter the cost, the obsessed man would not, could not, abandon the goal of total success. He would be a winner, and he would never, ever, settle for anything less.

That was why he got involved with the powers-that-be in the boxing scene. When things got too sketchy, he retired to sell real estate in New Hampshire, but his bigger-than-life personality got him into more shady deals. Before long, he found himself up against a brick wall: get out of town or go to jail. Moving to New York State, he immediately found a lovely Christian girl from a solid Christian family. She was a slender beauty with dark curls and a sparkling smile and he met his goal to get "saved," and then married… all within six months. His new church, which sought out non-denominational churches it could take over, recognized the salesman in this new convert, groomed him carefully, and four years later, sent his family of four off to Vermont to accumulate a new church for this aggressive denomination. His target was the Swift Street Pentecostal Church, which, despite the name, was actually a non-denominational group. The fast-talking amicable fellow settled in, got involved, and waited for his chance. Meanwhile, he often assured his wife, "I'll get this done, or I'll die trying."

Over the next few years, Michael (known as "Mickey" by this time) set up a homestead in nearby Hinesburg. The property — resembling a small Vermont foothill — was accessed by a dirt road just off the county highway. This long driveway passed on its left, a large, tree-lined field and then an oversized pond, before rising slowly to the peak where an imposing log home stood like an ancient castle. From there, the road descended once again around a curve, to end at the north end of the pond and the guest house. There, he and Rita raised three boys, whom Mickey attempted to turn into fighters in every sense of the word. For Mickey Suree, there was no room for losers in that family, and slackers were quickly dealt with. By the time Pastor James announced he would be stepping down, these youngsters were approaching their teen years, and the Suree family was widely known. Meanwhile, Mickey started up the thriving Green Mountain Insurance Company.

Money, social position in the community, and the reputation of a do-gooder/host — all of these things were in place, it would seem, to facilitate the big takeover, whenever Pastor James signaled his retirement. Church membership was now at over seventy souls.

But there was one more piece of the plan Mickey had to work on and he was quick to respond when he heard about the unhappy pastor up in Maine. One of the Swift Street church deacons had been up there for a fishing trip, and was relating the success of the adventure — unwittingly opening the door for the charismatic insurance man to make a strategic move. Reservations were made immediately, and Mickey arrived in the Pine Tree State two weeks later, Bible in hand and a plan in mind.

When Mr. Suree arrived that early April, Leo's life took on a whole new meaning, for his client was quick to assess the situation, and take charge. Most of the original fishing trip was conversation, with probing questions and spiritual encouragement. At the end of the excursion, Leo was seeing God and the world in a much better light. It would be the first of three fishing trips for the two men, over the next three months, the third one being in late June. It was on that final trip Mickey made his move.

After more long conversations on the boat and around the campfires at night, the troubled couple slipped firmly under the mesmerizing influence of the charming businessman. They were convinced they should get back to pastoring, and it would not be happening where they were, but they lacked the finances to do anything about it. Things looked quite bleak.

Before that week was over, Mickey offered the couple an out: Let him find them a position in his church, to replace Pastor James. After all, Mickey was head deacon, and he could practically guarantee Leo would be the new pastor. "Take a couple of weeks to think about it," he urged them. "We could probably get you out of here before the snow sets in. Think about it."

Once back in Vermont, Mickey made almost daily long-distance calls to the remote phone set up for the fisherman's business. Every call updated Mickey's efforts to make this thing happen. Slowly, the salesman drew the patsy into the plan. Finally, the Spencers agreed to let him pay for gas and lodging in order for them to come to Hinesburg. "I would like you to meet the board," he said. "And of course, you can stay in our guest house, for as long as you like."

The hopeful couple arrived in Hinesburg in late July, their 1936 Ford truck panting its way at last up the long driveway. The Suree family was there to greet them, just past the curve in the road down from the main house. There at the guest quarters door, the young men unloaded four battered suitcases, two boxes of Pastor Leo's books, an insulated box of lobsters on ice, and a wire cage containing a yellow tomcat named "Crusty."

At the tall blue spruce right across the road from that guest house, a flock of crows descended with barely a wing-flap, where they went silent, every glinting dark eye taking its own mental photograph of this crouching feline form — its colored striping, its size, and the stark white flash of terror beneath its scruffy brows.

It marked the moment when these families — the Bigelows, the Swift Street Pentecostals, the Surees, the Spencers, and even that silent flock of crows — would become part of a sinister story.

CHAPTER TWO

Hair

On the Sunday after the Spencers' arrival, Pastor James officially resigned from his position at the Swift Street Pentecostal Church. The Surees had made sure the congregation knew there would be a potluck celebration at their homestead that afternoon, no quilting group meeting was held, for it was certainly expected that all would turn out to thank and bid a fond farewell to the man and his family. Indeed, Mickey had made sure things were ready: the swimming hole — a huge, spring-fed pond with a large statue of a seated prizefighter at its center point, the three yellow canoes, and of course, the volleyball courts. Meanwhile, the seasoned hostess, Rita, had commandeered enough women to decorate and serve from the food tables. The Suree boys led the sports activities, including supervision of the life-sized boxing ring in the south pasture. Everything ran full force until dusk, when a huge bonfire was lit south of the pond, and the gospel music began. For a good hour, heartfelt harmonies wafted across the meadow. As things wound down, the guests slowly departed. At ten o'clock, Mickey, his sons, Pastor Leo Spencer, and the other four board members closed things down. The Suree boys left as soon as they had permission.

"Well," Don Collins remarked as he joined the deacons around the dwindling campfire, "that was a great success. I think Pastor James was touched by all that went on here today."

Mickey picked up a branch and poked at the fire. "Yes, gentlemen, I think we have paid proper tribute to one of the founders of this wonderful little church. But we now need to be prepared to protect its future. Pastor James is gone. We must be ready to keep his legacy, don't you agree?" The board nodded solemnly. "And we need to take careful inventory of where we are, and where we need to be, say, five years from now. Do you agree with that, also?"

When Brother Don nodded quietly, the other three men acquiesced.

Brother Suree breathed a heavy sigh. "I hope all will go well, but I must admit, I am quite concerned. Things may fall apart in a big hurry. You all know what a strong leader Pastor James was." There was a solemn pause, while Mickey poked at the embers, once again. He raised the stick and placed it in the dirt beside his log seat. "I must tell you, guys, that as head deacon, I feel a great responsibility to keep watch over his legacy." He looked sadly around the little curve of men. "I am going to need all the help I can get from you, to keep the future of the Swift Street Pentecostal Church on the straight path, to fulfill its purpose for the glory of God." He looked around, making eye contact with each of the four men. "I need to know I can count on you — each one of you — to help me live up to this task."

The other deacons, recognizing their support was being questioned, attempted to reply. The first one, Gerald Short, tilted his head to the side as he spoke: "I'm sure the congregation will be happy to support you and this board, as we attempt to do that."

Michael Suree drew a slow breath as he thought about how to answer this namby-pamby excuse for a man. A picture of this silly, sweet-smiling moron flashed before him: Here was a guy who had the backbone of a jellyfish, who gushed over every soul in that little church, but who could not even control that dominating, opinionated woman he was married to, and — God help us — she, herself, being the secretary of the church for the last five years. Nothing got by her. She knew all the doctrines and rules of this congregation, and she was exceedingly verbal when things were not exactly in order. She would have to be gotten under control, and her own husband, who should have been scripturally responsible to do that, was an ineffective member of that spiritual order.

"Thank you, Gerald. That is encouraging."

Sammy Black, a towering, large-boned, somewhat clumsy fellow, cleared his throat and looked at Michael for permission to speak. When he got the nod, he murmured softly that they could all depend on him, for sure. Then he looked down at his shoes.

Harold Taylor was more selective in his reassurance, being well aware of the head deacon's disdain toward him, concerning his standing in the church as a "seer."

"I would like to encourage you, Mickey, but I really don't think you'll want to hear what I have to say."

"Don't be foolish, Harold. I would very much like to know what you have to say."

"Do you, Mickey?"

"Absolutely." An irritated head deacon spit it out between his clenched teeth.

The slender stretch of a man leaned forward to peer around the half-circle at his church leader. "Mickey, I have had a dream."

Mr. Suree drew his legs up under him and leaned forward to confront this prophet of God. "Better be good, mister."

"Oh, it's not good, Mickey." He waited until he saw the defiant gleam in the fighter's eyes. "Yeah, that's right. Not good, and nothing you can do about it." The head deacon's gleam got brighter. "Nothing, mister."

"Oh now, Harold," Don interjected, "it can't be all that bad."

"Well, you'll all have to judge for yourselves, and I really mean, *judge for yourselves,* okay?" He glanced again at Mickey, then lowered his head as he began to talk about it. "I'm calling it a dream even though it was kind of weird, and yet, it wasn't a vision. I can't explain it." He shook his head. "All I know is that somebody in this congregation will die before Christmas." He lifted his balding head and looked around at the board. "And it will be somebody who is tall and light-haired."

"What do you mean, 'light-haired'? You mean, like, blonde, or something?" Don's voice was just above a whisper.

"Don't know." Harold shrugged. "Just got the word, 'light-haired.'"

There was a moment of befuddled quiet. Then Mickey spoke up in a mocking voice: "Thanks for those words of encouragement, Brother Harold." He rose to dismiss his guests. "The Lord bless you and keep you. And drive home carefully." He turned to head for his large home just up the slope. "By now, our wives must be wondering where we are."

Off to one side, Leo Spencer sat quietly in awe of this artful leader. The man certainly knew how to keep command of a situation. Surely, he and Heidi had made the right decision to be a part of this man's admirable endeavor. At the last minute, he called out: "Hey, Mickey! I'll make sure the fire is out before I hit the hay."

The spiritual hero turned and gave him a thumbs-up. "Knew I could count on you, buddy!"

By the time he had done that very thing, Heidi came carefully through the darkness of the lumpy field. "You done there, hon?"

He reached for her hand. "Yeah, it's out, for sure."

They made their way back to the guest house, guided solely by the light of the stars. The grasses were already moist with dew beneath their feet. As they stomped and wiped their shoes at the doorway, he turned and drew her close. Their noses touched, even though she was wearing flat shoes. "You know what, my statuesque Swedish bombshell? I love you more than I could ever say."

"Why?" She pressed her mouth close to his. "I'm a girl, you know, and we need to know these things."

He leaned back and thought for a couple of seconds. "You're so soft and sweet and so ding-blasted smart." There was a quick kiss on her forehead. "And you have such beautiful, long legs."

***

The cool evening air buzzed through the open windows of Don and Connie Collinses' Studebaker sedan, whipping across where Laura Wilson sat in the back seat. The conversation was animated, with Connie turning in her seat to speak to her friend.

"And so I asked her for the recipe, but she was reluctant. Some people are like that, you know. They end up telling you no, or worse, they give you the recipe, but leave out a couple of ingredients." She looked over at her husband and laughed. "Some people, honestly."

He glanced at Laura in the rearview mirror. "Kinda windy back there. We can roll these up, if you want."

"I want!" She was holding her blouse shut at the collar. The task was quickly accomplished. "Thanks," she said. "It will be easier to hear you, too."

"Right." Even so, Connie turned around to speak. "So, things will probably be a bit different until we get a new pastor. It will be the board that's in charge until then." She glanced again at Don. "How do you think that will go?"

He dimmed his headlights for oncoming traffic as the vehicle headed along Hinesburg Road toward South Burlington. "Hard to say. We'll be dealing with a whole different personality, what with Mickey leading the flock."

"What kind of changes do you see coming?" Laura was fishing, hoping.

He switched the lights back on high beam. "Hard telling."

"You thinking about Jessie and Jack?" Connie ventured.

"Ay-yuh, I guess I am." A sad little smile crossed her lips. "Sure would be nice if they would start coming to church with me."

"Well, they're watching you, Laura, and you have to remember, it's only been a few months since you accepted Jesus. These things can take a little time; we simply have to be patient and pray, of course." She leaned back toward Don. "Isn't that right, hon?"

"That's right. But I can see where you might think Jessie would like Mickey's style. After all, Jessie is a successful businessman, as well." He quickly inserted the caveat: "Of course, Mickey is more of a fast-talker. Your husband is, shall we say, a bit more refined?" They all smiled. "But, yes, that might open the door for Jessie to get involved, get his spiritual life in order, and usually, the young men follow the lead of their fathers… if they respect them, that is."

"Oh, Jack dearly loves and respects his father, that's for sure," the proud mother responded.

"He's a really good kid," Don reassured her.

"Smart as a whip, too," Connie commented. "Graduated way ahead of his class."

"Honest as the day is long," Laura mused. "Don't know how all that happened. We just got blessed, I guess."

"He even knows how to pick a girlfriend." Connie was grinning. "Diana Bixby is not only pretty, but an intelligent young lady, as well."

"She graduates in a couple of years, did you know that?"

"Yup, I do, Laura. And she wants to go to McGill University in Canada the following fall." The counselor had a sudden thought. "I wonder how Jack will handle that."

"That's a good question. I guess we'll *all* have to handle that when it's time." The mother turned her attention to the outside landscape. "Whoa! We're at Williston Road already?"

Don steered the car across that main road and headed for the back way to their home in Winooski. Lime Kiln Road was not lighted nearly as well, so the ride changed to a slower, winding pace. Don made that part of the ride more interesting with his question for Laura.

"As a fellow Vermonter, I wonder if you have any information about what they used to call a 'poor farm' that was supposed to be located somewhere along this road. I think it was in the twenties. Anyway, it was a real farm, with everybody pitching in."

"Um, I think maybe I have heard something about that. Where did *you* hear about that place?"

"From my grandmother. She said it was a big farmhouse, where whole families lived together. I guess it was sort of like communal living, with a common area and kitchen, and each family slept in their own bedroom."

"That must have been crowded — a whole family in one bedroom," Connie noted.

"Better than sleeping in the woods," the blonde lady remarked.

"Or worse," he said. "Anyway, back in high school, I tried to do a report on that place, you know, for Vermont History class. I had to give up on it, because I couldn't find any verification."

"Ay-yuh. I guess we might find some kind of information on it, if it really ever existed, in the archives at the state capital."

"Probably so. But I was merely a green freshman; what did I know?" He looked sideways at his wife. "But I *was* handsome, so that counts for something."

A mental picture of this pixie-faced fellow as a high school freshman brought soft laughter.

When they reached the intersection of State Route 15, right in front of St. Michael's College, Don took a sharp left, and three minutes later, the Studebaker purred into the driveway off Florida Avenue.

"It's been a great day." Laura thanked her friends as she moved her lanky form out of the back seat and into her own car. Before she backed out to head for her own home in Essex, she saluted a goodbye with a touch of her pointer finger to her platinum bangs.

***

The Suree boys were exhausted and headed straight from the picnic to the dorm-like room they shared on the second floor of the big log house. Their father believed that "men are made to do battle and sex," and it was his aim that at the end of each day, those three boys were too darned tired to get involved in either one. While he was successful on those two counts, the micromanager still couldn't cover all areas of all three brothers' lives. It was because of that, Paul, the oldest son, dropped a bombshell that night. He was the last out of the shower, slipping into his bed even though his abundant hair was still damp.

"Hey," middle brother, David, piped up, "Mom hates it when you get the pillow soaked like that."

"Mmmm." Paul had other things to think about.

Twelve-year-old Matthew rose up on his elbow to punch his own pillow. "You're gonna catch shee-it," he squeaked.

"Shut up, pipsqueak," David admonished as he reached for his own towel at the foot of his bed, and threw it to his big brother. It landed with a plop, right in the middle of his face.

"Shee-it! Cut it out!"

"You guys need to quit swearing so much," the fifteen-year-old cautioned them. "People will think you're stupid, or something."

"You can shut up, too, Wavy-Davey."

The sensitive one sat up and swung his feet down the side of the bed. "What's up with *you*? You got something stuck up your butt?"

Paul snorted and turned his face away, but David persisted. "You in trouble?"

Pipsqueak lifted his head far enough to peer across the room. The tall form of his big hero shifted under the covers. "Paul?" When no answer came, the youngster slowly swung around to sit on the side of his bed, also. "P-Paul?" This time there was a hint of fear in the voice.

The two younger boys waited for what seemed a long time. Finally, Paul heaved a heavy sigh, rolled over, and sat up to address the wary pair: "You know those guitar lessons I've been taking for a year?" Two heads nodded. "Well, I've gotten pretty darned good at that." They nodded in agreement, for he really had. "But I've been doing something else, when I went to those lessons in Burlington." He bit his lip. "Mom and Dad don't know about it." Two sets of eyes widened. "I've been playing in a rock and roll band."

"Wooo!" they cooed together.

"Um, so, we kind of thought we would have somebody record us, and see if we could… you know… be a real band."

Another cooing duet, this time with little smiles.

Encouraged by the response, he went on: "So we did that, and a guy called us an agent. He wanted to send it in for an audition, and the next thing we knew, he was telling us to name our band, because we are booked to go on TV in New York City in October."

"Whoa!" David was standing up. "A TV show? What's it called?"

"*American Bandstand.*" He put in a qualifier: "I guess it's pretty much local, and so I don't know if it will go out over the whole country. I mean, it's just starting up. I guess they want to see if it will be popular enough, or something. But anyways, we're actually going on the show, whatever happens."

"That is so neat-oh! Your band on TV." A sudden thought hit. "The name! What's the name of your band?"

Paul was on his feet. "It's called Trouble. Isn't that a great name?"

"That's neat, too!" Matt's eyes reflected his enthusiasm. "And you'll have the flashy clothes, right?" He was already picturing shiny suits with the turned-up shirt collars. "And you need to cut your hair in a duck's a— , um, I mean, a D.A., just like on TV."

Paul was finally into it. "And that's not all; I'm going to bleach it to a movie star blond." He grinned. "Can you see me in that whole get-up?"

"Yeah! It will be so, I mean, your own family won't even know you." The youngest boy went for a hug, and Paul bent down to scoop him up for a swing around on that very spot.

But when he stood the boy back on his feet, Paul came face-to-face with the sensible one.

"Dad will never let you do this." David's serious look pushed his brother into a virtual step back from that reality. He quickly focused on the floor.

"He can't stop me." He looked up at David. "I'm eighteen. I can go do whatever I darned-well please." His gaze intensified. "I really want to do this."

"He wants you to go to college."

"I know." He looked down at the youngest one, who was suddenly staring at his hero, the joy of the moment before, now subdued. "I don't want to make trouble, guys. But sometime, sooner or later, we have to start being who we want to be, and I know I can really play that guitar." He was determined. "Before Dad settled down, he did what he needed to do. He made a lot of mistakes. Well, maybe I need to do the same thing. I hope he will see it that way, and let me go without any bad feelings."

"But Mom will cry," Matthew whispered.

***

"I have an early shift tomorrow," the Burlington Transit bus driver reminded his wife as they put things away from the Surees' picnic.

Connie looked up from filling the empty cake pan for an overnight soak. "I do remember that. Do you want a sack lunch, then?"

"No," Don replied. "I'll just grab something." He leaned back against the kitchen shelf, folding his arms across his chest. She knew he had something on his mind, so she turned the water off and waited.

"Howard had a dream, or something."

"He does that, I guess."

"Ay-yuh, he does, but this one is somewhat troubling." He made eye contact. "So it's probably best if you don't repeat this, alright?" She nodded, and he knew he could trust her. It took a few seconds to relate what Harold had told the board, but then Don got to the real issue. "He was talking about somebody dying before Christmas, and he's been right before, but this time, I don't know, the wording of the 'message' is confusing."

"Like how?"

"Uh, it was that this was going to happen to someone who was not only tall, but 'light-haired.'" He blinked slowly before he continued. "When I asked what 'light-haired' meant — you know, blonde or white hair or what — he couldn't answer me."

"Well, it could mean either one of those colors, don't you think?"

"It could. But it could mean something else entirely."

"Like what?"

"Um, it might not have anything to do with *color*, babe." He knew it might be a stretch, but went for it, anyway. "It might refer to somebody with light hair growth."

She blinked, weighing the thought.

"So what if it's someone who has very little hair on their head — like somebody who is balding or something?"

She nodded slowly. "I see what you mean, and it could be right on the mark, but where are you going with this? What's bothering you so much?"

"Don't you see? It's bad enough that such a prophecy would be given, that somebody in the church will be dead by Christmas, but what if that person turns out to be somebody who is simply tall and balding?"

For a few seconds, the only sound in the kitchen was the last gurgle of water down the sink's drain.

"Oh my," she said slowly, "Harold Taylor would have prophesied his own death."

CHAPTER THREE

Factoids

Although Monday was usually the pastor's day off, Mickey grabbed Leo and the two of them opened the church office, being careful to lock the door behind them. The office was located in an attached structure, like an afterthought, to the lower back wall of the parsonage. It was out of sight of most folk who might make an unscheduled visit to the pastor's quarters, and there was no doorway directly from the house itself, so the two men felt reasonably safe from discovery in the midst of their mission. They had managed to secure enough information on church member lists and committee members, amongst other things, before Greta burst in. As church secretary, she had certain duties to complete, before the pastor came back to work on Tuesday. Michael was not aware of that, which is why the two men got caught with their hands in the church cookie jar.

She was furious.

"What are you doing in my files?" She looked at her desk. "And why have you been into my private work area?" Her normally peaches-and-cream complexion suddenly turned to rosy velvet. "This is outrageous. This is absolutely illegal. You have no right, no authority, to be rummaging through the church office like this."

"Of course we do. I am head deacon, and I have it on good authority — and I do mean *authority*, Greta — that there are some serious allegations concerning church records, that you

— yes, *you* — are responsible for." He clutched a bundle of files to his chest. "The board will be reviewing this information. In the meantime, you are to turn in your keys, and will be in this office only by permission. Is that clear?"

Her eyes narrowed. "And when did the board get together and vote on this action?"

There was a smirk, then a twitch of the nose. "That's for me to know, and for you to find out." With that, he nodded to Leo and they headed toward the door.

She hit him with her three-pound purse, right between the shoulder blades. "Drop that stuff, mister!"

He turned and pushed his elbow into her bosom. "Don't make me have to get rough, Greta."

Her clasped hands came down on that extended elbow, sending the records across the floor. Before he could recover, she was in his face.

"Listen to me, Mr. Phony-baloney, if you need to beat up a woman, just so you can do whatever you want, then you're a sorry example of a man of God." She took a breath through her nostrils. "Now, you and your buddy get out of here, before I call Sheriff Max Duncan."

Maybe it was because he knew what the Chittenden County Sheriff was like, or maybe because he'd been caught with a handful of church cookies, or both, Mickey Suree slowly backed off.

Not that the fight was over.

In the car, he came down hard on the woman.

"Well, you see what we're up against here, Pastor Leo. As I have told you several times, the church secretary is a tyrant, and most certainly a part of the inner group that we will have to challenge and ultimately defeat, if we are to bring this church up to biblical standards."

He dropped Leo off at the guest house, then drove back uphill, where he joined his family for an early dinner. In a few minutes, he was listening to the chatter of the young people, enjoying Matt's question about the crows.

"Hey, Dad, the crows are still in the tree down there near the guest house. It's almost September, and I was wondering, do they fly south in winter?"

"I'm not sure about that, son. Why not look it up in the encyclopedia set we bought you guys a couple of years ago?"

"I know! I know, Dad!" David was glad to show what he had learned. "Sometimes they do, and sometimes they don't." He smiled, knowing he had made a few points with his father. "And we only have to watch our own flock, here on the property, to know whether they will stay, or go."

"Good job, David." Then, before leaving the room, the good husband kissed the top of Rita's head in a thank-you-for-the-meal gesture.

There was a boxing match on the black-and-white television, board games out in the cool of the patio, some popcorn, and all seemed right with the world. When the moon rose, the whole family yawned and all went to their beds.

But as Michael Suree lay stiffly upon his feather mattress, secretly, deep down, he was getting ready for his next move. Somewhere around midnight, his face relaxed into a smile and he drifted off to sleep.

The following morning, he showed up at the church property with a legal-sized tablet on a clipboard. It would be clutched to his breast like a sacred treasure, daily, throughout the next few months.

***

"I couldn't believe it, once I stopped and thought about it," the forty-ish secretary told her husband. "He said there was evidence I have mismanaged some kind of church records. God only knows what that means." She poured him a second cup of coffee to go with his blueberry pie. "They were stealing private information from our church office, and they got caught, so I'm of the opinion that he came up with something to threaten me with, you know, just to get me out of the way at the moment." She brushed the apron that fit firmly around her ample middle before she sat down across from him. "But what if he actually accuses me?" She lifted her own cup. "Although, I know very well I haven't done any such thing, at least, not on purpose." It was a quick sip. "And that's what worries me: That man knows exactly how to destroy people. I've seen him do it. There's a reason for the frequent turnover of board members."

Gerald's usually kind countenance grew hard. "Yes, I've been watching this man, and I must admit, I have had misgivings more than once." He placed his fork carefully on the edge of the plate, so as not to soil Greta's carefully starched and ironed tablecloth. His eyes conveyed the gravity of the situation. "Looks like you *are* going to be targeted, honey. We are going to have to be diligent, and very, very loving, whatever that man does." He reached for her hand. "And even that will probably not be enough. We're going to have to pray the Blood Covering over both of us."

"And over our church."

"Exactly." He managed a small smile. "That's my girl. Right on the mark."

Her hazel eyes glistened. "It won't be easy, we both know that. All he has to do is make the same allegations over and over and over, and pretty soon, it won't matter that they're not true. People will start to wonder, and then eventually, believe it."

"So that is an important part of our defense: Let him do all the talking. All we ask is proof, whenever those accusations come up." He smiled gently. "And there is no proof, because there is no crime. So we let him bury himself in the lie."

She nodded. "I guess."

She came into the living room, having done up the dishes and swept the kitchen floor, and slipped into her chair beside the lamp table they shared. The radio was broadcasting a program featuring a newly formed orchestra. Gerald's head was leaned back and his eyes were closed. She enjoyed the pleasant contours of his face accented under the lamplight, until the music finished. Before the announcer could continue with the hushed-voice introduction of the next piece, she turned the knob and silence filled the room.

He opened his eyes. "All finished out there?"

She nodded, catching his inquiring gaze. "Need to make one more point about our head deacon, if I may."

He sat up straighter in the overstuffed chair. "Sure."

"He is a relentless fighter, agreed?"

"Yes."

"But not necessarily for godly reasons or goals?" Her golden-brown curls shook gently around her soft, round face.

He looked confused. "You said, yourself, that you've had misgivings over the years. This man is not always on the up-and-up, right?"

"That's true." He turned his body slightly toward her. "So, what are you getting at?"

"Is lying and manipulating and destroying people godly behavior?"

"Of course not."

"Then, what kind of behavior is it?"

"Well, it's certainly not godly, so it must be ungodly. I mean, there is no real in-between. We are either doing righteous, uplifting things, or we are doing various degrees of not-so-godly... er... um..."

"Okay, honey, try to follow me, here: When a person pursues and bullies and lies about another person, that is not godly behavior, right?" His nod signaled permission to continue. "So, if it's not godly behavior, it must be some degree of ungodly behavior and what's the source of *all* ungodly behavior?" She waited for the light to come on, then said it: "The source of all ungodly behavior is evil — plain, rotten-to-the-core evil." She leaned into the circle of the lamp's light. "And what is the source of evil, honey?" Her small golden eyebrows lifted as she answered her own question. "Satan and all of his demons. *Period*."

"Greta, are you... are you saying that our head deacon is controlled by... demons?"

***

The next Sunday morning, Connie and Laura stood two rows back from Mickey and Rita Suree, during the worship service preceding the sermon. Connie nudged Laura. "What in the world is happening there?"

They watched the man pull his trembling wife to his side with a one-armed steely grip, as she sobbed gently. The two women exchanged a whispered, "Whoa!" Both of them closed their eyes, worshipping expectantly. After all, the temporary leader of the church's wife was obviously experiencing a special spiritual moment. The hymns rose, drifting through this place of worship, until the quiet of the moment signaled a time of teaching. Mickey Suree walked humbly toward the pulpit, where he paused, sighed, and slowly lifted his head to speak.

"My brothers and sisters in the Lord," he spoke sadly, "I come before you this morning with a message that I wish, with all my heart, I would not have to bring you." He waited until he was pretty sure he had most of their attention, then raised his voice in a serious declaration: "I am grieved to bring a warning to this wonderful congregation — something I have been confronted with, just this week." He rubbed his chin once before he continued. "I truly regret, that I must inform you that our congregation is being contaminated — I might even say, 'poisoned' — by a spirit of gossip."

The little congregation suddenly lost their worshipful joy. A chill settled over the sanctuary, as everyone waited for the next words.

"I am so grieved by this I can hardly speak of it." He stroked his chin one more time. "But we must address this mean-spirited invasion of our fellowship. We must." He stood tall as he went for the finish: "I am asking you today, as followers of Jesus Christ, to put aside all rumors and mean accusations against church leadership, no matter how these lying individuals may insist they have the truth. Lies are lies, and these murmuring people have an agenda." He suddenly became the wiser, older brother, leaning against the pulpit like a protector of the innocent. "We know how, when church leadership changes, there are folks who want to move in and take over. And believe me, I have seen this many times." He stood straight one more time. "I'm asking you today, don't let this happen. Don't listen to rumors and accusations against your church leaders. We have been faithful for so many years, you all know that." The voice choked up as he made the final plea. "I'm asking you to stand tall, be wise, and don't listen to gossip, vicious, vicious, gossip, that could destroy our wonderful little church." He bowed his head. "Now, Lord, we ask You to anoint this sermon, this teaching, that I am about to deliver this morning. May every word be a blessing to You, and may all of Your children be blessed by the hearing of The Word."

Connie and Laura were stunned. "What just happened, here?" Laura asked her friend.

"Something bad," came the answer.

Two rows in front of them, tears streamed down Rita Suree's cheeks.

***

Heidi Spencer was beginning to sense a disturbance deep down in her spirit. The events of last Sunday's service kept surfacing in waves of anxiety and confusion. Here it was, Wednesday morning, and the distress simply wouldn't go away. Even her timid approach to the subject with her husband left her with a nagging throb. Something was not right. She drew a long breath as she sat on the small porch of the guest house, taking in the colorful early-autumn view down toward the north end of the pond, stroking the back of her close companion, Crusty, who reclined languidly across her lap.

She had met her feral friend at the edge of the island's southern shore up there in Maine. The scroungy creature had been crouching amongst the rocks, looking for nourishment from dead crabs washed ashore from the Atlantic. She'd watched in fascination as he crunched and peeled whatever flesh he could from those crustaceans, marveling at the survival instinct that drives all living creatures. The next day, she returned to that spot, and found him there again. This time, he acknowledged her presence with a low growl before slinking away. That was when she fell in love with that little lost marmalade kitten. Four weeks later, she had enticed him all the way to the tent where she and Leo lived, with little tidbits of raw fish and milk. Somewhere along that journey, she named the gold-striped tomcat "Crusty," short for his usual main course, crustaceans. It took almost five months to get him inside at night, and another week before he would let them pet him. By the time winter began, he was wormed and healthy and settled in; a pet, but on his own terms.

When it came time to move to Vermont, they knew he could not be left behind; he had been exposed to the domesticated life for over a year, and to leave him on his own again seemed cruel. Leo fabricated a cage from a lobster trap, and the three of them made the transition to this autumn-colored meadowland in Hinesburg.

"Tell you what, Crusty," she said, "let's take a walk." She slipped him to the porch floor and stepped down the stairs. He followed, with a soft mew. Before long, he was ahead of her, knowing the routine all too well: It was a trip to the pond, and some Vermont "fishing" for the happy feline.

As they approached the placid pool, it was Crusty who, crouching instinctively, took note of the crows swarming in circles above it, and it was Crusty who cautiously moved toward the edge of the water, where a dead body lay wedged, face-down, in the mud.

CHAPTER FOUR

Containment

Mickey Suree did not like Sheriff Maxwell Duncan. The two had crossed paths several times in the last eight years or so, and it had not been pleasant. The problem seemed to be that the two men shared almost identical personalities — forceful and tenacious, hiding under a thin veil of backslapping, philanthropic activities. They both knew how to get what they wanted, and were willing to wait for as long as it took. The only difference between them was, to put it bluntly, one was a slick businessman, and the other was a slick cop.

So when the sheriff caught up with Mickey at the church that Wednesday afternoon, Mister Head Deacon was anything but pleased.

"Something going on down the road?" he asked the lawman.

"Not exactly." He pushed his official uniform's hat back on his head, then looked across the parking lot at the parsonage. "Pastor James around?"

"Nope. He's retired. Moved out last week."

Max nodded slowly before he cleared his throat. "So, no pastor or church counselors on the property at the moment?"

"No," came the impatient reply. "At the moment, I am the man in charge. What do you need?"

The sheriff tried to keep it professional: "I need to do my sworn duty to the people of this county." He paused just long enough for the concept to sink in, then turned to signal for Deputy Smith to join them. As the young man approached, the sheriff moved back around to address Mickey. "Mister Suree, I am here to inform you of your wife's death. I am sorry to have to do this." He drew back quickly as the little pugilist's fists flashed into boxing mode. Suddenly, the alert deputy was shoulder-to-shoulder with Max. The two towered over the frozen boxer and waited until that fierce face began to soften, and the hands slowly dropped.

"No."

Sheriff Duncan shook his head in sympathy. "We need to come in and sit with you for a few minutes."

"No."

"Sorry, sir. But that's what we do, until you have a family member or a friend get over here."

"No."

"Tell you what, you need to let us know who you want to come to be with you, and we'll radio it in." He waited for the answer that did not come. "Would you like for us to call somebody?"

"No."

Max scratched under the brim of his hat. "So, I could drive you back to the house in your car. Deputy Smith will follow in our vehicle."

The next "no" was muffled by the tires of Leo's truck pulling into the parking lot.

"Heidi told me," he murmured as he hurried to his friend's side. "Aw, damn, Mickey. Aw, damn." He glanced at the lawmen. "I'm Pastor Leo Spencer."

"You're a pastor?"

"Yes."

"Can you counsel and comfort this gentleman?"

He looked at Mickey's pale face. "Yes, of course."

"Then we will leave him in your hands." Max directed his next words straight to Michael Suree. "We will leave you for the time being, sir, but we *will* have to meet with you again. You need to remain in the area, so we can do just that. I need to be sure you understand that, and that you agree to cooperate." He waited for the nod of agreement, then turned to leave.

As Deputy Smith started the vehicle, Max grunted. "How about that, huh? The guy never even asked what happened to her."

The younger man snorted incredulously as he pulled out onto Swift Street. "Never even cried, either."

***

Don and Connie Collins were at the log house by four that afternoon. He finished a bus company day shift at three, rushing to pick her up from her teaching job at Essex Junction High School. Both being professional counselors, and him one of the board of deacons, they felt their presence would be beneficial. Connie went directly to the guest house to be with Heidi, who had discovered the body; Don was there to meet the two younger boys' school bus at the end of the long road into the property. The next few hours passed like a horrible dream; even Mickey's silent arrival and quick disappearance into the master suite on the main floor seemed surreal.

"He never said a word all the way home; I guess he needs to be alone right now," Leo surmised, as he took a seat in the spacious living room. Almost as soon as he sat down in front of the massive stone fireplace, he was up again. "It's going to cool down out there in a few minutes. I'll build a fire to keep the place warm, maybe even derive some comfort from the glow and the crackle."

The fire was just taking hold when the phone in the kitchen began to ring. Word had gotten out, mostly through the board, and people were calling to offer condolences and whatever help might be needed. At the end of an hour, plans were in place for meals to be brought, and a memorial service at the church, all of which had to be okayed by Mickey, himself, but he had not come out through that door.

"I wonder if I should check on him," Leo thought. He stood for a moment before he knocked, listening. No sound came forth. "Maybe I should peek in, in case he's sleeping." He tried the knob, which turned easily, allowing the door to swing slightly open. A peek around the edge revealed the empty bed and sitting area and a soft light from the little room off to the right. Knowing this was Mickey's business office's private back entrance, he stepped softly inside the doorway, just far enough to see the man sitting at his desk. He was slumped over with his head bowed into his hands.

"Lord God," Leo thought, "I don't know what to do."

Suddenly, Mickey sat back, reached down to his left, and slammed a drawer shut. Startled, the pastor drew a quick breath. Then, the weakness behind his knees drove him into a slippery-shadowed exit. As he drew the door carefully shut behind him, an old insecurity came flooding over him, chilling him clear to the bone. He moved quickly over to the warmth of the fireplace, where he wobbled down into the chair. The fear was overwhelming.

Was his strong mentor and the new pastorate both gone?

A movement at the head of the stairs signaled Don's soft descent. Leo waited until the man came across the room and stood in front of the flickering glow.

"How are they doing?"

"All three are sleeping, finally." Don shifted the weight of his pudgy body, lifting his hands out toward the heat. "Hell of a thing, losing your mother, especially like that."

"Yeah, face-down in the mud." He looked up at the man who was still rubbing his hands in front of the fire. "Um, do they know that, actually?"

"No. They just know she drowned."

"Yeah, that's all they need to know." He shivered. "My Heidi discovered the body." He looked toward the guest house. "Is your wife still with her?"

"I believe so."

The pastor stood. "I think I should go to her." He glanced toward the door of the suite. "Mickey is still up, sitting in his office." The tone was apologetic. "I don't think there's anything else I can do for him."

"You're probably right, Leo. You should go to your wife. She's had a terrible shock."

"You know, that woman has seen a lot, what with living out there on that island — dead animals, and who knows what else — but this one is beyond the beyond."

"She needs you, man."

Connie arrived as soon as she left Heidi in Leo's care. "I should have brought a sweater," she whispered.

"Come over here beside the fire."

As he put his arm around her, she reached out her own hands, spreading the fingers wide. "I think that lady is going to be a long time getting over what she saw today."

"Probably." He was curious. "Anybody have any idea what happened?"

"Heidi wasn't sure. Said somebody thought she drowned, but the coroner said it could have been suffocation." Suddenly, her head was cuddling into the curve of his shoulder. A sob escaped before she went on. "Our sweet, beautiful, vibrant Rita — gone, in such an awful way."

"I know," he murmured into her silvery hair. "It just doesn't sound like an accident, does it?"

She drew back, no longer whispering. "I know you, Don." She eyed him suspiciously. "What?" When his elfin face drew tight, she repeated the demand. "What are you thinking?"

He shoved his hands into his pants pockets. "Don't really know, babe, but the boys were talking."

"Talking?"

"Sure. You know how we encourage trauma patients to verbalize their emotions. We do it all the time." He turned to warm his back by the fire. "Well, they were unmistakably upset that the last thing they heard from their mother was some kind of argument with their father."

"When was that?" She answered her own question. "It had to be last night."

"Right. It was Paul, the oldest, who heard the front door slam, and when he went out to the top of the stairs, his dad was standing down here, looking at that door. He said he asked what was going on and his father told him, "Mom's having a hard time again. She's going to visit her sister, like always. When she gets back, she'll be fine. Now go to bed.""

"A hard time? What does that mean?"

"A hard time… again." He gave her that knowing look.

"Again. So that was an ongoing thing, that 'having a hard time' thing."

"It would seem so," Connie noted.

The nearly spent logs crackled and popped gently.

"You weren't in church last Sunday, were you, Don?"

"Nope. Had a day shift."

"Well, I was, and so was Laura. She went with me."

"I remember."

"Well, we were so surprised. I mean, we had never seen Rita in tears like that. We thought she was having some sort of spiritual thing going on. But then, after worship, Mickey got up and said something about a big, bad spirit of gossip invading the church." She leaned forward, clasping her hands just under her chin, making the point. "We were stunned."

"You told me about that."

"I know, but I don't think I told you that as he was doing that, we looked over at Rita, and the tears were streaming down her face." She put her hands on her hips. "Now, why do you suppose she was so grieved?"

"Good question." Suddenly he checked his watch. "But let's talk about it on the way home. I need to get some sleep before my next shift."

As they headed for the door, she was still asking questions. "Did the boys mention why their mom was having 'hard times'?"

"Actually, Paul had something to say about that," Don said, as they exited the lovely log mansion.

Across the room, the door to the master suite closed quietly.

***

"I can't believe it, I just can't believe it." Lou-Lou Bigelow rocked back and forth on the edge of the truck seat. "We're never gonna see that twinkling smile again." She wiped her runny nose on her sleeve.

"Sit back, will ya?" Bud tried to see the lock button on her door. "Push that thing down. We don't need anybody else dying, for gawd's sake."

"Stop your damned swearing," she sniffed indignantly. "You need to have more respect for the dead, Buddy, you really do. Ain't you ever gonna learn to be a gentleman?"

He rolled his eyes. "A gentleman. A gentleman." He looked down over his right shoulder at his sister. "And just who is going to teach me that, huh? My father? Huh?" He virtually spit out the contempt. "I swear, he's getting worse by the day."

She was quiet, knowing there was nothing she could say to smooth things over. After all, the man had been disappearing several nights every week, and no amount of questioning would get the fellow to even answer. He had plainly slid back into his old ways. It had been going on for the last month, and only getting worse. Ma had withdrawn, throwing herself into the poultry business, the garden, and reading books at night, until she fell exhausted into bed, only to rise the next morning, to repeat the ritual.

Lou attempted to get the subject back to the Surees' family tragedy. "I hope they like the macaroni and cheese casserole."

"Of course they will. Everybody likes macaroni and cheese." He tried to be careful as he asked: "Um, did anybody tell you what happened? I mean, did she fall in and drown, or what?"

41

"Nobody is talking about it, you know? I mean, it's like they don't want to, you know?" She scratched her arm. "I guess they need to wait for the cops to do an investigation, or something."

"Okay, that means there are some serious things going on, you know what I mean?"

"Most likely." She leaned back against the tattered upholstery. "I guess we can thank God that we, our family, ain't involved."

***

Mickey stayed isolated in the suite or his office until Thursday evening. Only the boys and a couple of the deacons were allowed entry. Plans were made for cremation and then a memorial service a week from the following Saturday, which would allow plenty of time for Rita's family to come from various points of the country. Finally, he made a quick call to Leo and Heidi, requesting their presence in his office the next morning.

The sun was well on the rise that Friday, when the two arrived, walking past the handsome sign identifying the home office of The Green Mountain Insurance Agency. They entered through the elegant double doors, where the business was attached to the west end of the log home. Deacon Sammy Black, an impressive hulk of a man, and full-time insurance agent for the company, welcomed them into the small waiting room, motioning toward two overstuffed chairs on the right. As the two sat down in the narrow space stretching across the room to a restroom and a coffee alcove, Sammy let them know there was fresh coffee while they waited for Mickey to get off the phone, then he shuffled through the open doorway of the heavy glass block wall separating the waiting room from the back hallway. They heard him tap lightly on the boss's office door and murmur that they had arrived, and then his towering figure disappeared quietly into its own office across the hall.

"Quite a place," Heidi whispered.

"Yeah."

She rose to look at the official licenses and awards that touted the fine reputation of the business, neatly arranged on the handsome logs of the west wall behind the two chairs. He rose also, but went to view the items on the wall space up over the coffee corner. A large framed photo of Mickey in boxing trunks, surrounded by gold-framed news articles and awards, were artfully displayed.

"Whoa! Look at this," he whispered to her. They were both still checking these out when the famous fighter spoke.

"Good morning."

He was pale, but looked stronger and more alert than they had expected. There seemed to be no time for condolences and hugs, either. He led them into his office with the usual quick step, waved them into two overstuffed leather chairs, and sat purposefully down behind the large desk.

"I have a proposal for the two of you." Seeing that he had their full attention, he went right into it. "Things have changed, for sure, but I would hate to leave you both in a financial pinch. I realize it will probably take a bit longer before we can get you on as Pastor Leo, but I think we can work it out."

The man was relieved to know he had not lost his shot at this position; he leaned forward as casually as he could. Out of the corner of his eye, he could see his wife take a slow breath. He waited.

"I wanted to get you started by doing a couple of sermons, anyway — you know, to commence a relationship between you and the congregation. It was my plan to inch you into place, over the next few weeks. We'll just start sooner than I had planned. So, I would like to see you do the sermon this coming Sunday. I know it's not much time to prepare, but I'm sure you have something you've preached on before, and this is a new audience, so I think you can pull it off." He cracked a small smile. "Of course, you will receive the usual guest preacher fee, so that will help with the finances."

"Thank you, Mickey." He broke a small smile.

"I will take the Sunday following the memorial service, that's the next one after you. Then we'll squeeze you in again the next week. How does that sound?"

"I would be honored."

"Good." He turned his attention toward the wife. "Now I need to talk to you, Heidi. I have a proposal for you, and then you'll have to talk it over with your husband, that's how it should always work, am I right?"

"Of course."

His demeanor softened a bit, as though he thought to speak differently to a woman. He looked to the floor, then lifted sad eyes toward her gaze. "As you can imagine, Heidi, losing Rita has been devastating to me and the boys. It will be a long time before we get our equilibrium back." He pinched his mouth into a shaky pucker. "But we also have a serious loss in another way: We have lost our nurturer." He moved his brows into "worry" mode. "There is no one to cook a lovely meal for us, to see that we have clean clothes and beds and bathrooms, to softly reassure the two younger ones. I could go on, but I'm sure you see what I mean." He glanced over at Leo. "Now, please understand, I would never wish to interrupt your own family life in any way, but, if I could hire her for a while, until we get our emotional feet under us." The attention went back to her.

"Here's what I propose: I hire you to cook one meal a day, and you start showing my boys how to take care of themselves — how to do laundry — that sort of thing. I promise you Wednesdays and Thursdays off, and on Saturday, a strong young lady to help with the more serious housekeeping." He quickly amended that: "Of course, you would be instructing the boys on that, as well. After all, they'll eventually have to take over all those chores."

He paused to let the couple exchange a look, then went on, "I want you to know that I have already contacted Lou Bigelow — you know her, right? She's the perfect one to help with the heavier cleaning on Saturdays — strong and willing, and anxious to make a little money." The brows raised again. "And it would help you two out, financially, at the same time. I promise, I pay very well."

"Um, I don't know. This is a really big house," Leo observed.

"Yes, but you don't heavy-clean the whole house every Saturday. You clean one area each weekend. It's just a matter of organizing your work load, right?"

Heidi looked encouraged. "I guess that's true. You place one brick at a time, Leo."

Michael picked right up on that. "And before you know it, you have a whole brick wall, right there in front of you!" He stood up, as though the conversation was over. "So, think it over, Heidi. The both of you need to hash out the details. Get back to me by tonight. I do have some people coming over to get things in order before all the relatives get here on that day, and it would be nice to have a couple more sets of hands to get all that done, and we only have a week to do it all."

"Are they all staying here at the house?" She was wary.

"So to speak. Most of them bring tents and trailers to camp in. We have to set up electric and water access all over the lower field." He managed another small smile. "Aren't we blessed that the trees down there are turning color so early?"

Leo suddenly got the picture: preparations involved more than a few beds being made up. "So, who is organizing all the details?"

"You're looking at him." He walked ahead of them to open the outside door. "I have it all under control."

And he did.

That night, the Spencers decided to accept his offer.

***

Laura Wilson hung up the phone. "So, the memorial service is a week from Saturday," she told her husband.

He grunted a reply and turned the page of his newspaper.

"Jessie?"

"I heard you, hon." He peered over the top of the page. "Guess she had a big family. There should be lots of people there." He shook the drooping sheet straight. "You have to make something for the potluck afterwards?"

Jack came into the kitchen, letting the back door slam behind him. "Somebody having a potluck?"

"Please don't slam the door, Jack."

"Sorry, Mom. I forget." He padded across to a seat at the table, having left his barn boots outside near the back steps.

"You might want to bring your boots into the wood shed; it's supposed to rain tonight."

The tall boy grinned. "Found a yellow leaf in my right one, this morning."

He picked up his fork. "What's for supper?"

"Meatloaf, right after you wash your hands."

Jack bent his head backwards. "Oh yeah, forgot that, too." As he went to the sink, his father chided him.

"You'd better start remembering these things, mister. What would Diana think if she knew you were such a slob?"

He laughed as he wet the hand soap under the faucet. "She already does. Has to tell me that stuff all the time." He rubbed his hands vigorously. "Still likes me, though." As he dried off, he added the fact that they were going to a movie. "It's Friday night," he reminded his parents.

The son helped his mother clear the dishes after supper, then disappeared for a quick shower.

Jessie picked up a towel to dry the warm, wet tableware. She smiled at him. "That's sweet of you, Mister Dairyman."

He winked at her. "I'll collect on the favor later, Missus Dairyman."

She winked back. "Promises, promises."

"Hey," he moved in to speak softly. "We'll be alone, remember?"

"O-oh, so we will." It was time to play the coquette. "You know, I only go out with guys who sing to me."

He was happy to play along. "I will sing to you all night, if you want."

Upstairs, they heard their son whistling in the bathroom. Suddenly, they looked at each other.

"Kind of makes you wonder," she ventured.

"Wonder? Um, you wondering something about our boy?"

"Well, he's a healthy, normal kid, wouldn't you say?"

Suddenly he got it. "Oh." He put the last spoon in the drawer. "Ay-yuh, I would certainly say that."

"So, have you had that talk?"

"Ay-yuh, a long time ago." He snapped the towel out before folding it in half, lengthwise. "But, maybe I should drop another friendly reminder." He slipped the dish towel over the swing-out rod inside the door beneath the sink.

"Right. You know, those two are crazy about each other." She stopped as Jack came banging down the stairs, wet hair poking out from under his baseball cap.

"See ya later," he yelled from the back door.

"Hey, Jack! Could you give me a hand with something for a minute?"

She was upstairs in the damp bathroom when he came back in.

"How did it go?" she called out, as he ascended to the top landing.

"Excellent. What a great kid, Laura."

"You know, the Collinses were just saying the same thing last time we rode home together."

"You mean, from church?"

"Yes." She stopped to watch him pull off the flannel shirt. "From church."

He could see it in her eyes. "Aw, Laura, you're not going to ask us to start going to that church with you again."

She lowered her face to untie the belt of her robe. "I'm thinking it would be nice if you could go to the memorial service, that's all."

"What for? We don't even know anybody."

"I think it would be nice if I could show off my great little family." She slipped the robe off.

He was down to his shorts. "I agree, we have a great little family." He tugged at the elastic. "And I want to keep it the way it is. No changes." He turned on the shower. "Hey, Missus Dairyman, we need to change the subject." He pulled her inside, under the warm water.

"Tell me, young lady," he smiled through the dribble, "have you ever sung in the shower?"

CHAPTER FIVE

Questions

The congregation was polite and compassionate toward the guest preacher who so graciously filled in for their grieving leader, Michael Suree. The sermon was accurate, though nothing new, and delivered by an obviously nervous fellow, but being the good folk that they were, they shook his hand and thanked him profusely at the end of the service. On the way home, Heidi told him how proud she was of him. "Did you see how attentive they were, hon? I think they really liked you."

"I wish Mickey had been there. He always gives me the bottom line, you know?"

"Well, today was *your* day, and you stood on your own." She smiled and patted his steering wheel hand. They rode the rest of the way back to the Suree homestead without conversation, letting the old truck do all of the chattering.

When they had turned off the country road and made their way up the winding direction toward the main house, however, their attention was caught by the two official vehicles parked in front of the insurance office. One was a dark-colored sedan, and the other had a Chittenden County Sheriff's Department logo on the side. As they drove slowly by, toward the guest house, Leo wondered out loud. "You think we should stop and see what's going on?"

Their answer came almost as soon as they pulled up next to their quarters; Sheriff Max Duncan and Deputy Smith approached rapidly on foot.

"What's happening?" Leo asked, as soon as they drew near.

"New development in the death of Rita Suree," the senior officer announced. "The coroner has some serious questions about how she died. You'll need to be available in a few minutes. Right now, Mr. Suree and his sons are being questioned." He glanced up at the activity in the crows' nesting place, then turned back, his arms akimbo, a posture of authority.

"Really?" she exclaimed. When she turned to her husband, his face was ashen.

"I need for the two of you to go inside and wait for the detectives to come down to talk to you. They're almost finished up there. Just make yourselves comfortable, hit the bathroom or whatever, and be ready for them when they get down here, okay?" Again, he looked up at the blue spruce, where the stirring was more intense. She saw his concern.

"It's just the crows. I feed them every morning, just me and my cat, Crusty. I've been told they will protect their food source, so maybe that's what's going on. Why don't you come inside? I'm sure they will settle down if you don't appear to be a threat."

The two lawmen exchanged amused smirks, but were happy to be invited in where they could at least sit down for a few minutes.

Sure enough, the investigators moved their sedan down to the front of the guest house not long after. However, they sat in conversation for a bit before they exited the car. As they did that, the sheriff and his deputy slipped out onto the little porch, allowing the Snoop Squad from Burlington Police Department to enter and do their job.

The question came quickly, and the detectives expected prompt answers, even though not even a whole week had passed since Rita's demise.

"How did you discover the body, Mrs. Spencer?"

"Did you touch anything or remove anything from the death scene?"

"The only footprints we found at this end of the pond were yours. How many times did you approach and re-approach the body? Or had you been there before?"

"Exactly where was the canoe when you first spotted it?"

"What did you mean when you said the crows were circling overhead?"

"Did you see any other animals or people in the area, either the night before, or that same morning?"

"What were you doing the night *before*?"

"What time did you go to bed that night?"

"Was your husband home at the time?"

"Where were you, Pastor Spencer, from the early evening to the early morning of that particular night?"

Suddenly there was a ruckus on the tiny front porch. "That's enough! You've been grilling them long enough."

Leo rose quickly to let Mickey inside.

"That's all for now, gentlemen. No more questions. If you want to talk to these people, you will have to do it through a lawyer."

"But we have nothing to hide, Mickey," she objected.

"You don't understand, Heidi. They can twist and turn everything you say and use it later in court." He turned to the inquisitors. "Enough. You need to leave *now*. If you don't, there's a Chittenden County sheriff right outside the door, and I will file a complaint. You guys have committed an egregious overreach." He pointed toward the door. "Now, leave."

As the law enforcement left, he reminded the couple that there was a lot to be done in preparation for the influx of trailers and whatnot next week. "We need to have a meeting this afternoon, to get it all finalized. Meet us in front of the fireplace in the great room — I'm talking about the living room — at one o'clock." And then he was gone.

"I wonder what they asked *him,*" Leo murmured.

"I wonder what they asked the *boys,*" she said, right out loud.

***

There were only four days to get ready for Rita's family's arrival. Posts were driven into holes all around the large field just south of the pond. Electrical cords and water hoses were strung up near mowed campsites, each of which had a number spray-painted at center ground. By the time all the work was completed, tire tracks had carved out a primitive road circling from the campsites, past the fire pit, all the way to the elevated outdoor fight ring, where lights were strung around the ropes. A couple of picnic tables were placed in the ring's center for socializing and the inevitable song fest. It would not be the usual atmosphere, but Mickey knew this singing family would not be silenced by grief, and it was crucial he make them comfortable. Very comfortable.

He even went so far as to hose down the statue until its glittering gray Vermont granite glistened brightly from the center of the pond. Resembling the famous "Resting Boxer," the ancient bronze piece by Apollonius the Athenian, the naked, muscular figure hunched forward in exhaustion, all the while looking over his right shoulder as though an opponent might rise fiercely up from the waters behind him. It was, Mickey thought, the perfect, final touch for the usual Suree hospitality.

Up at the log house, folding cots were brought into the boys' dorm, and two guest rooms — reserved for the older members who could not camp — were readied.

Heidi and Lou were thankful for the handful of ladies who helped get the place into shape — under Mickey's watchful

52

eye, of course. By Thursday evening, all was prepared, and not a smitch too soon, for the first arrivals showed up at dusk.

At that moment, Mickey became "Michael," the name her family had always called him, and the signature on every birthday and Christmas card over the years.

It was Michael and Sammy Black who directed them to the campsites, and the two men were out there early on Friday morning, ready to do it again. By late that afternoon, all guests had arrived. There were hugs and tears and the group stood across the pond to stare and pray over the taped-off site across the water, where their dear Rita had been found. Then they drew together at the boxing ring, and the singing began. It lasted until almost midnight.

The next morning, Heidi needed to head up to the house to make breakfast for the few who were staying there, but before that, she grabbed the bird seed and walked quickly over to the tree to feed the crows. As usual, Crusty followed, his tail raised straight up, anticipating the fun of a meal, even if it wasn't for *him*. He sniffed and puttered around the trays as she poured out the feast for her feathered friends. As she turned to leave, he started to follow her, but something distracted him, and he stopped in a sudden crouch. Heidi reached the porch, dropping the bag inside the cottage door, and left for the big house, without seeing the huge raven perched on the porch roof.

Crusty stayed crouched, watching the thing move back and forth on its perch, the head cocking left and right, eyeing the seed. The cat turned his own head, ever-so-slowly, toward the scattered cawing from the spruce branches above those trays. Then he started to creep along to the safest place he could, staying low to the ground. All that was near was a shrub at the base of the tree.

The raven spotted him and let out a loud squawk. Crusty broke into a full run for the shrub, but the swooping attacker laced claws through the furry back, flipping the frantic feline into an uncontrollable roll across the grass. Before he could get footing, the large bird came swiping by again, tossing the golden-striped body into another rotating tumble, but this time, it ended up close to the underside of the shrub. The third pass was accompanied by a rising crescendo from the tree itself.

The raven landed in front of the shrub and poked its beak threateningly into the ground several times before it pulled back, apparently satisfied that it could pursue its goal of breakfast, undeterred by a cat.

The noise from the tree was getting louder, awakening a number of campers, who proceeded to walk cautiously up the road past the big house, then down toward the ruckus. Their curiosity was piqued by the sight of a huge black bird swooping down and then back up to the porch roof of the cottage.

"What the heck is *that*?" somebody asked.

"Looks like a raven."

"What's it doing?"

"Must be after something… probably food. But we can't see around that curve."

"What's all the noise in that tree?"

"I'm pretty sure those are crows, and if they are, there's trouble ahead."

"What does that mean?"

"Crows and ravens are arch enemies. In fact, we should probably not get any closer."

"Why not?"

"Stand still and watch," came the answer.

The raven left its perch once again, even though a few of the crows were circling above the tree. It reappeared in a moment, hopping along the roof, emitting a raucous call toward the small things gliding above. Then it swooped forward once again, disappearing from sight.

Suddenly, the crows dropped out of the sky, followed by screaming comrades emerging from the depths of the tree. The racket increased as they also dropped from view.

"What's going on?" It was the camper who had spoken first, before.

"It's a bird fight. The crows are attacking, I think."

"We should get closer."

"That wouldn't be smart. They don't call it 'a murder of crows' for nothing."

The high-pitched din was attracting attention all over the property. Heidi went to the window and saw what was happening. "Crusty," she whispered. The woman bolted out the door and down the road, running right past the little crowd of campers who were frozen in awe. She was almost around the curve of the hill before the bravest ones took off behind her.

"Wait! Don't go down there!" they cautioned her. But she ran until she saw it, and the horror of it stopped her in her tracks. The others caught up to her, and then they, too, came to a halt, gasping at the sight.

The raven lay on the ground, as the crows flew to peck at the already-injured intruder. The wounds were mostly in the head and legs, disabling the bird to a point that it had no way to defend itself. It flopped and rolled helplessly as the attack continued.

"Crusty." She frantically scanned the ground.

"Who?"

"My cat."

"Um, is that her over there under that bush?"

The relief came out in a strangled sob. "Th-that's him." She started to go to him, but someone grabbed her arm.

"No, ma'am. The cat is fine. Leave things be. It'll be over in a few minutes."

It seemed much longer than that, but finally there were only a couple of crows on watch, hopping around the mortally wounded raven. A couple of times, it lifted its wing in desperation, only to receive another series of pecks into the empty eye socket. The screaming still came from the tree, not one bit diminished as long as there was life in the enemy.

The watchers stood stunned by the brutality of nature, none of them moving until the two final warriors inspected and pecked at the dead body a few more times, then lifted into the air and disappeared into the evergreen limbs.

Slowly, the noise began to decrease, as the crows started to settle down. At that point the cautious audience slowly approached the scene of the killing. Heidi called Crusty out into her arms, stroking his rigid frame.

The rest of the group could only stand and stare at the bloody body in the grass.

"Why do you think they killed the poor thing?"

"Probably protecting their food. See those pans of bird seed?"

"Or maybe they were protecting the cat. Look at him. He's petrified."

Heidi tried to smile. "They were protecting Crusty, because he's part of their 'feeding team.'"

"So, those two reasons go together. It could be one or the other, or both."

But in the tall blonde's mind, there was no question about it.

***

"So, where are you in line of the eight siblings?" Connie politely asked one of Rita's brothers. The memorial service was over, and they were all back at the Suree property, sharing a cold lunch on the house's spacious patio, outside the front door.

"I'm actually the oldest," the white-haired fellow replied. "I'm George."

"Nice to meet you, George. I'm Connie."

"I know who you are — you and Don. I just moved in a couple of houses down the street from you."

"Oh, my! How nice. And what brings you into the little town of Winooski?"

"I've been hired as a visiting professor at the UVM. I'll be here for the entire school year, if I behave myself." He grinned.

"So, what's your field of expertise, Professor?"

"I'm an archeologist, so that covers a lot."

"Well-traveled, I would wager." When he nodded in agreement, she went on: "That had to be hard on your family."

"It was." He looked down at his shoes. "But I've been a widower for the last seven years, and no kids, so that doesn't matter anymore."

"Oh, I'm sorry, George. I didn't mean to be so flippant." She gazed out over the little crowd, needing to change the subject. "So, which one is your sister, Tykie?"

"Who?" The athletic man looked puzzled.

"Tykie. The one Rita visited when she was needing a break." She leaned in closer. "The boys told us about her."

"Really?" He shuffled his feet a bit. "Don't know where they got that. We don't have a sister named Tykie, unless this is some kind of inside joke." He picked up a half-sandwich, sniffed it, then took a bite. "Of course," he mumbled through the ham and cheese, "in this family, that wouldn't be too far-fetched."

"Oh, I see." She smiled. "Well, all I know is that the boys call her that."

"So, if they know who she is, I'm sure they'll point her out for you." He winked playfully.

She smiled a polite thank-you and moved on until she was at her husband's side. At the first opportunity she inquired as to whether he thought she should ask one of the Suree boys to point out their Aunt Tykie.

He took her arm firmly and led her to a quiet corner. "Don't know if you have noticed, but members of the Snoop Squad managed to do a little mingling, and they asked me the very same question." He glanced around. "I told them the boys had never met the woman, and as far as I could figure out, they ought to get that information from Mickey." He took a sip of his fruit punch. "They weren't too fond of that idea, since they were crashing the party, so to speak."

"I can't believe Mickey is allowing them to stay."

"Oh, he spotted them and escorted them right out to their car. I couldn't hear what they were saying, but I could see there were some sharp words being exchanged. Those two detectives were mighty unhappy when they left."

Suddenly, the two were keenly aware of a conversation nearby. "So what's this about you guys having an Aunt Tykie?" the white-haired uncle was asking Paul.

"Mom's sister?" The tall Suree youngster shoved his hands into his pants pockets. "What about her?"

"I'd like to meet her."

"What? Why do you say that? She's *your* sister, for Pete's sake." He motioned around the crowd. "*You* show *me* which one she is."

The man wiped his hands quickly with the crumbled paper napkin. "I never heard of the lady. And I'm pretty sure I would know if it was a cute nickname for one of the girls." He tossed the napkin into the garbage can to his right. "So, I'm curious, you know? I mean, who told you that you even *had* an Aunt Tykie?"

Paul wasn't sure he wanted to answer that. "I don't remember. Maybe we just heard about her long ago, when we were little kids. What's the difference?"

"Seems odd, that's all." Uncle George gave it one last try: "So, your dad know about this mysterious aunt of yours?"

Paul pretended to hear his name called. "Oh, sorry. I'm needed out back." He strove to make a believable exit, turning to hurry away. "Talk to ya later."

The Collinses were quite sure this oldest son had some questions for his dad. They watched him move quickly toward the insurance office doors.

"Mickey must be in there," Don whispered. He grabbed her arm, steering her smoothly into the house, across the bustling great room, to the door of the bedroom suite. There, they turned their backs to the half-opened door, before stepping backward into the bedroom. For a second, they stood still to listen. When the voices grew loud enough from the open office door, they quietly moved closer in order to hear more clearly.

"Dammit, Dad, you lied to me. In fact, you lied to all three of us."

"I wasn't about to tell on your mother."

"Tell *what* on our mother?"

"About… about…" There was a hesitation. "Oh well, I guess you're going to find out, anyway. I had to spill the beans to those fricking snoops." Another pause. "They asked the same question: 'Which one is Aunt Tykie?'"

"So what did you tell *them*?"

"The truth. The whole, damned truth." It sounded like he flopped down into one of the leather chairs. "There is no Aunt Tykie. Mom and I just made her up, so you wouldn't know she was going to motels to get away from us, or maybe just from me." His voice seemed to be a bit muffled. "I'm a hard guy to live with, son, you know that. Sometimes she just couldn't take another minute." They heard a big breath before he dropped the final bit of information. "She probably went to a motel somewhere to hide and get drunk for a few days. I *think* she was by herself. I hope so."

It got quiet. Then the young man spoke up.

"What a couple of frickin' phonies." Then the boy was stomping toward the waiting room. As the outer office door slammed, the Collinses hurried softly across the room and back out to join the others, but the patio was suddenly nearly empty.

Down the road, the big family was slowly moving back toward the campground, to gather guitars and banjos and harmonicas. Pretty soon, they would start singing.

Most of the relatives left early that next morning, the others electing to attend the Swift Street Pentecostal Church's eleven o'clock service. The music was especially moving, what with Rita's kinfolk joining in, and then it was time for Michael to deliver the sermon. He shuffled his notes around on the tilted pulpit, then looked up.

"Yesterday, brothers and sisters, we said goodbye to our dear Rita. It was a loving and moving time, and I know, if God allowed, she was looking down and flashing that irresistible, sweet smile of hers. Oh, how sweet she was, and we will always remember that sweetness, will we not? But, oh, how grateful we are, to know she is resting at last in the arms of the Lord. She has no more worldly trials, no earthly tests, no worrisome moments. For that, I am personally grateful, for I know how much she had to endure at the hands of those who should have been the *exact* ones to love and support her, whose hateful attitudes and acid tongues brought so much grief to that dear lady." His gaze traveled slowly across the congregation as he continued. "As many of you know, I'm just an old fighter, and I've faced a lot up there in the ring, but I have to say, it saddens me beyond words, the terrible gossip and murmuring she had to endure, and for that reason, I have implored all board members to be especially careful to protect their wives from such torment. I put all those guilty folks on notice, here and now, that we will not tolerate such treatment of our spouses. Therefore, even the slightest offense against these board members and their wives will be dealt with in the most severe manner." He swallowed hard. "Maybe I did not protect my sweet Rita the way I should have, but I promise you, in her memory, I will be on guard to protect those other ladies."

Slowly, he spread the notes out in front of him, then bowed his head. "Now, Father, we ask you to bless this teaching from Your Word; may it reach down deeply into every soul, and glorify Your Name."

Connie looked up from her bowed head. Her eyes locked with Don's. "What gossip? What mistreatment?" she whispered.

He shook his own head in bewilderment, as he reached for her hand. *"This is calculated, nasty stuff to be coming from a preacher,"* he thought. *"But then, he's not really a preacher, is he? More like a poop-stirrer, and godly leaders don't do that. What this man is doing is out-and-out evil."* He glanced at Connie.

"She knows. And so do I. This whole thing is demonic."

CHAPTER SIX

Actors

The next day, Mickey made his move. He sent Leo to the church office to retrieve — ostensibly — a list of tithers, so an assessment of finances could be made by the board of deacons. Before the would-be pastor left, there was over an hour of instruction on how to handle the situation. "Remember, make sure you start by telling her that we need it for the meeting," he concluded at the end of the lesson.

She was seated behind her desk when he arrived.

"Good morning, Greta."

"Good morning." Her reply was cool, but polite. "What brings you here today? You know we are officially closed? It's Monday."

"I do, but Mickey sent me over to pick up some figures for our meeting tomorrow night."

Her eyes grew wide. "'Our' meeting?" She sat back in the spring-loaded office chair. "Are *you* actually attending a board of deacons meeting?"

"I was invited, yes."

"Who invited you? I mean, these meetings are open to observers, by invitation only. I'm curious, Leo, what are *you* doing at a meeting of the deacons?"

"I guess that's between the deacons and me," he replied, following the script he had rehearsed with Mickey. "I need to have a list of those folks who are regular tithers."

Her eyes grew wide again. "Oh, I don't think so. I'm not supposed to give out that information to anybody but the official board, or the pastor. Sorry."

"The head deacon has sent me to pick up that paperwork, Greta. I suggest you comply *at once*."

"Are you on the board? No. Are you the pastor? No." She waved him away. "Tell Mickey he needs to follow the rules."

"I'm afraid I must insist—"

"You can stand there and insist your head off, mister, but I'm not handing that kind of information to anybody but the board or the pastor." She slammed her hand on the desktop. "Now, get out. We're not open."

This time, he raised his voice, as instructed. "I'm asking you for the last time, young lady—"

"Oh, you are, are you?" She shot up from her seat and reached for the phone. "Get out, before I call Sheriff Duncan!"

"You can call whoever you want; Mickey sent me for that stuff, and I'm not leaving without it." He stood his ground, still yelling.

"Get out!" When she slammed the phone down, it missed the cradle, cracking sharply against the heavy paperweight next to it.

"You can't make me, and I'm not leaving without that information. Do you understand me, or do I have to write you a big fat note?" He snickered, right on cue. "Come to think of it, a fat note is probably what it takes to get something into your big fat head!"

"*What!?*"

"Yeah, that's right. Your big fat head — you know, the one that goes with your big fat butt."

The glass paperweight caught him on the right shoulder.

He was rubbing it when he reported back to Mickey.

"No paperwork, right?" the instigator asked.

"Nope. Just a physical injury."

"Okay," Michael Suree smirked, "mission accomplished."

The Tuesday night deacon meeting was held until well past midnight.

It took a lot of work, but he put the evidence out there over and over; when that didn't get results, he resorted to outright threats. "If any one of you doesn't get on board with this action, the rest of us will hold you personally responsible for any more damages caused by this woman, to this church body." There were uncomfortable shiftings in the chairs around the table. "I'm serious. There is no room on this board for any guy who would allow such outrageous behavior in the operation of this church. It is neglectful and unchristian shepherding, and that's the bottom line."

It was going on the half-past twelve mark when they took the final count. Gerald Short had to abstain, of course, but, over the objections of Don Collins, the board of deacons voted to fire Greta.

On the way out the door, Harold Taylor murmured into Gerald's ear, "God, I'm *so* sorry Gerald. We would have been here all night. But maybe we can fix this with a congregational vote at the annual meeting in January."

Don was fuming as he rolled into bed. Although he didn't want to wake Connie, he could not stop the tossing and turning. At three in the morning, she finally reached up and turned on the bed lamp that hung over the headboard. "Got something on your mind?"

The events of the evening came pouring out. At the end, he read the look on her face. "Yeah. Obsessive. Extremely controlling. Heartless. Like a pitbull in a dog fight, without any real blood."

But she said it more succinctly: "Demonic."

He laid his head back on the pillow. "We need to research this. I mean, we don't know what we're dealing with here. There are a lot of different kinds of demons, each group with their assigned roles in the big satanic drama."

"That's true, but we do have quite a library downstairs in the office. We should probably start there." She reached to turn off the light. "Meanwhile, you need to get some sleep."

He turned over, tucking his face into the pillow. "God help us," he prayed out loud.

***

On Wednesday, Greta was officially fired, and Mickey took over the church office. Little change was made in the two rooms; he claimed the pastor's desk in the back one, and Leo settled comfortably into the wobbling chair behind the former secretary's position near the front door. When asked, the two men replied that there were no plans to hire a new receptionist. "We need to get the books straightened out first," was the excuse.

When questioned as to Leo's presence in that position, Mickey expressed his gratitude for the way the man had stepped up to volunteer in the office. "He's had experience in running a church, and will be of great value as we attempt to get things back in proper order."

But by Friday, things took a turn for the man in charge. He was called in by the detectives at the Burlington Police Department. They got to the big question immediately: "You stated that your wife would occasionally leave home and go to a motel, where she would drink and hide until she felt like coming back home. How do you explain the fact that there are no records of her car being registered in any motels within a hundred miles of Hinesburg, Vermont?"

"I can't answer that question, any more than you can."

"Why not?"

"Because that's what she told me she was doing, and that's all I know."

"We have it on good information you're a man who manages people and projects right down to the last detail.

You mean to tell us, you didn't know what your wife was doing — and doing it — how many times?"

"Some things are better left alone."

"Oh yeah? And how many times were these things left alone — three or four? Or was it a lot more, Mr. Suree? How many years did this go on?"

The little man stood up to leave. "I'll let my lawyer answer that, gentlemen."

He made the call from a phone booth, before heading back to the church office. Hiring a lawyer was something he wanted to keep quiet about as long as possible. Meanwhile, he had a much more important picture to unfold to the general public.

***

Sunday arrived too quickly, what with the Friday interruption, so Mickey didn't have too much to say from the pulpit. He announced — ever-so-sadly — that Greta was no longer church secretary, and urged the congregation to give her a big thank-you hand clap for so many years of service. "And, again, I caution all of you: let's not slip back into gossiping and theorizing. Our church is being led with the greatest of care and we must stay in prayer, 'trusting and obeying,' as the old hymn says."

But that afternoon, the quilting ministry had a visit from the head deacon and his helper, whom he referred to as "Pastor Leo," as the two of them walked amongst the ladies, complimenting them on their work, and inquiring about techniques. The visit lasted for about seven minutes, and then they were gone, without so much as a "goodbye."

"Well, *that* was creepy." Lou let it slip. She looked around, uneasily. "Okay, no gossiping or whatever. But I feel like somebody just prowled around, looking for something."

"So, no gossiping." It was a voice from back in the corner.

"Not gossiping," Lou corrected her. "Just telling you how I feel. And I feel like we just got checked up on. So there."

"I have to admit, it struck *me* the same way," another voice whispered.

"Well, saying how you feel is not gossiping." This time it was Laura. "And that was no casual visit. That was weird. I feel like they wanted us to know they can come into our meetings and do whatever they want. It was like an overused plot out of an outdated, sorry example of a spy movie. That's how I feel, and I don't care who knows it."

"Be careful," the voice from the corner admonished. "They could shut us down, if they don't like what they see."

"Oh my goodness." Lou dropped her patchwork to her lap. "Can they really *do* that?"

***

Uncle George was waiting in his car in front of the Collines' home in Winooski, when they got back from church on that third Sunday in October. The couple recognized the man's football physique as he rose out of the car and waved for their attention. "I'm Professor George White, Rita's oldest brother. We met at the memorial service, remember?" He continued to approach for a handshake with Don. "I'm the uncle who spilled the beans about there being no 'Aunt Tykie'"

"Of course," the two of them responded.

"We need to talk." He glanced around, quickly. "In private, and I *do* mean private."

Once safely settled in the basement office, the three of them sat in silence for a minute. The counseling couple watched the brother, and waited.

"I want you to know that I have checked you both out." He was not apologizing. "I know where you met in Long Island, that you, Don, are a retired B-25 pilot, were stationed at Mitchell Air Force Base, and I know that's where you two were married. I also know where you both got your counseling degrees and where you both work, and that you're registered, licensed professionals." He raised his eyes to the ceiling. "Even so, I prayed a whole lot, before coming here today." He brought the gaze down to Don's eyes. "This could be very, very risky for me, and for my assignment."

"Assignment? Who do you work for?" Don kept that eye contact.

"Let's just say, an organization that is watching my family's church denomination very closely. My family pretty much grew up in these teachings, but it has bothered me for a long time, that these church leaders are up to some questionable, *evangelization*, shall we say?" He licked his lips slowly. "I got to the point where I couldn't condone this stuff, so I went to the big boys and offered to do an inside investigation. In short, I'm a turncoat — a plant — for those big boys." He licked, again. "May I leave it at that? It would probably be better, if you two don't know all the details."

"Oh, I don't know, Mr. White. We like to keep things above board." He was being cautious, of course, for the couple had previously worked secretly with other authorities.

"And that is commendable. But there are times when the less you know, the less you can be held responsible for. It's just common sense, but of course, I would make sure that you know what you need to know — to be safe — as we execute this investigation."

"Investigation?" they asked together.

"Tell you what; let's take a realistic look at what's happening in your church." He leaned forward, elbows on the knees. "Almost overnight, this wonderful little congregation has turned into a group of suspicious, wary people. Where, only weeks ago, there were happy brothers and sisters in the Lord, you now have church leaders monitoring and reprimanding honest inquiries. Am I right?"

They knew he was right, because Mickey was virtually everywhere on the premises, clutching the ever-present clipboard tightly to his bosom, except when he'd drop it down to scribble a few notes. He was showing up at key meetings, such as the missions' committee, the women's committee, the Sunday school program, and the benevolence ministry. On the other hand, he was leaving the minor groups — like the nursery ministry, the janitorial services, and grounds maintenance to Leo, who was spontaneously dropping in "to encourage" them with many questions and suggestions, then reporting the actual inner workings of each group directly back to Mickey. In short, every aspect of church function or outreach was being "supervised" in great detail, and all of them were being made aware that whether they liked it or not, they were all under the watchful eye of Mr. Michael Suree, their self-appointed protector and spiritual guide.

"And, I should add," Rita's brother continued, "I am aware there have been lights installed for night surveillance on the church grounds."

"And all of the church locks and keys have been changed," Connie blurted out.

"Okay, I wasn't aware of that one," George admitted.

"They just told us that this morning," Don mumbled.

"Alright," Mr. White surmised. "That's the way they do it; total control." He huffed a short laugh. "Only it usually is done inch-by-inch." The laugh was repeated. "Looks like Mr. Suree is in more of a hurry." He leaned back in the chair. "Makes me wonder why."

"So, what's he after, with total control like that?" She was going to get to the bottom of this.

"Oh, sorry. Should have made that clear." He lifted his hands to smooth an invisible territory. "An elder-run church."

"As opposed to…?" She waited.

"The current democratically run organization you now have." The professor blinked slowly. "See, they believe that no church should be a democracy — that such a thing is absolutely un-biblical."

"Wait a minute. We elect our deacons, and they pretty much run the church." Her brows pulled together. "So, if the congregation doesn't elect the deacons, what puts them in power?"

"Well, according to my denomination, the Word shows how it's done." He picked up a Bible from the nearby bookshelf. "Titus one, verses five through sixteen, for example, seems to teach that elders are to run the local churches."

Don read the scriptures out loud, then put the book down. "In other words, there's really no room in church *government* for deacons or pastors — are you following this?" The professor waited patiently.

"So, refresh my memory: What's the difference between a deacon and an elder?" she asked.

"Not all churches have both, but the comparison goes sort of like this: The deacons are more about manpower projects, while the elders are more like the spiritual leaders. If a particular church has only elders or only deacons, the job description of works and spirituality rest on the one group, regardless of whether the group is elders or deacons. At any rate, it's important to note that they both tell the pastor what to do, unless he has the guts to tell them to take a hike, and lose his pastorate." There was a soft chuckle. "But the Organization of Elder Churches of America, my denomination, doesn't want to bother with the sole position of pastor. They figure elders are already pastors and teachers, chosen by God to lead the church body."

The couple looked doubtful.

"So, like it or not, the OECA is adamant that the Bible says a church should be run by elders — so much so, they pursue that goal like a lioness on a hunt." He scratched his head. "That's not morally healthy, and this national oversight committee I'm working for is looking into it. Some churches may have legitimate legal recourse."

"Wow," she murmured.

Seeing reluctance on Don's face, Professor White went for the jugular: "This may not seem like something you want to get involved with, Don, but I need to ask you how you think these folks at Swift Street Pentecostal would feel about having their church stolen from them, because this is exactly what this situation is all about." He leaned in. "This guy is my brother-in-law. I've known him for a long time, and I haven't always liked what I saw. And now my sister is murdered. Yeah, that's what I truly believe." He sat up straight. "And I believe it was because of that dirty rat's role."

"Dirty rat?" Don's eyebrows lifted, just a little.

Laughing, the man asked the question: "Don't you know what his last name means?"

Don and Connie exchanged visual curiosity.

"It's pronounced 'Sue-_ree_', right?"

The couple nodded the affirmation.

"Well, that's the French pronunciation, and — guess what? Suree is the French word for mouse!" He let it sink in for a few seconds. "In other words, unless you folks work fast, your church is about to be taken over by none other than Mickey Mouse."

***

Greta was still weeping. "They lied out and out. I did _not_ retire, They framed me." She leaned her head on her husband's shoulder, right there in front of the kitchen sink. He held her firmly, speaking against her temple, fluffing the sandy-colored curls with his breath.

"This is not over yet, honey. God is still ultimately in charge. We need to be patient. Eventually, it will all work out."

"But it's not true… not true… not right." She drew back to blow into the tissue.

"That's right, Greta. But we know God will eventually expose this whole make-believe scenario." He drew her close again. "We only have to wait, that's all. God will draw back the curtain and expose this whole thing."

"But can't you see, honey? The next thing is to get rid of _you_." The tears came again. "They're going to accuse you of not having control of your own family, no, your own wife." She sobbed the words. "They're going to kick you off the board of deacons."

"Umm, probably, but that's not who I am, in God's eyes, anyway."

"What?"

"I'm not just a character in some earthly drama, Greta, I'm also a beloved son of the Most High God." He nuzzled into the curve behind her ear. "I am secure and happy in my role, my position, honey. Let them do whatever they want. It's a lot of foolish, soul-ish play-acting. My Father has this whole drama all under control, and when the final curtain falls, it will be a beautiful story with a phenomenal ending." He kissed the side of her neck. "So, let's sit back and 'watch the performance,' shall we? It will be an artistic triumph, directed by the greatest Director in all of creation." He brushed another kiss across her golden brow, and exhaled a huge breath.

"Let the show begin," he proclaimed.

Diggings

"I'm going to overlook that you even asked me that question, Al." Mickey leaned back in his office chair, holding the phone in the tuck of his shoulder and neck. "Of course I didn't have anything to do with Rita's death. Believe me, I really loved that girl. We had three kids together, for gawd's sake..." He waited while the lawyer apologized. "Okay, I understand that you had to ask, but I did not appreciate it." There was another apology. "So, okay, all you have to do is keep the snoops off my tail. Treating me as a murder suspect is a waste of their time, and mine. I have my hands full at the church." He listened impatiently. "What *about* the canoe?" His fingers tapped the desk's top. "Look, she never left the property. Her car, *with* her suitcase inside, was found off to the side of the road, right down there at the south end of the pond. Don't ask me why. But *something* made her get out and walk over there to the canoe rack, pull out the thing and put it in the water." He paused. "That's right. They found her footprints, and *only* her footprints, in the mud where she pushed it in and got into it. But it still doesn't make sense." Al asked the question. "Because she never got into those things, that's why." The lawyer inquired as to why not. "Because she..." Mickey closed his eyes and laid his head back against the soft leather. "Can you believe this? When you think of all the things that girl could do... she never learned to swim."

Ma Bigelow had been trying to keep track of the water witch over the last ten years or so, which wasn't easy, because the fragile tower of a woman isolated herself from people most of the time. Upon occasion, Ma would hear that Edith was coming to find water for one of the neighbors, and she would take a freshly slaughtered chicken over there to help celebrate the event. Folks enjoyed watching the frail dowser work, and there was always a party or picnic atmosphere to be enjoyed by all. But Ma was there for more personal reasons: She wanted to see what happened after the well was dug, when that strange woman would come back to inspect and "bless" the finished work. So, the poultry lady always made a double visit: One to bring a chicken for the party, and the other to bring a dozen eggs, just by chance of course, on the day of Edith's inspection of the well. Unfortunately, in all that time, she did not see anything unusual at those inspections. But on this particular October afternoon, she finally hit the jackpot.

The new well was located over the hill from the Bigelow property, in a field owned by Walter, the man with the large family. It had been a long, dry summer of touch-and-go for that family's water supply. Finally, it went bone dry. Returning the favor of ten years ago, Willis had allowed him to draw water from the Bigelows' well for over a week before Edith showed up to do her "bit of magic," as the townsfolk like to say. On the day of the actual dowsing, Ma brought the plucked carcass, and stood back with the small gathering of watchers, chatting amicably as she kept watch out of the corner of her eye... and this time, there was something different about that woman.

It was almost imperceptible, but there it was... a little twinkle, the hint of a smile, a flutter of eyelashes coming from the boney face, directed toward the man who had hired her. At her request, Walter was walking along beside her, hands in his jacket pockets, glancing quickly at her and then at the path before them. Ma took a sudden breath. "Where did I see that before?" The words were hardly out of her mouth before she remembered.

Willis had done the same thing, all those years back. Just walked along beside her and talked — very softly — just like what was going on right now.

"Did she ask any of those other guys to do that?" Ma recalled there had been maybe six other times she had witnessed this lady dowser in action. "Who had hired Edith all those times?" Quickly, she remembered: "Three were women, and three were men." She closed her eyes, in order to see the past more clearly. "And none of those three men were asked to walk with her." She double-checked. "No, because one of them was crippled, in a wheelchair, and the other two... no, they stood with their wives and drank beer." Her eyes were opened on that late-September day. What she saw was greatly intriguing.

She made sure of the day Edith was scheduled to inspect the finished well, and was there, eggs in-hand, before the water-seeker arrived. She talked the wife into walking to the site, just for fun, to watch the "blessing." When the water witch arrived, she motioned them away, impatiently. They moved back a few feet, admonishing the rowdy children to stand back. When they turned around to watch her, she had already muttered something, and was tossing handfuls of gold-colored crystals over the top of the well cover. The children could not be held back. With squeals of delight, they reached for the powdery treat.

"Stop! Stop right now!" the short-winded figure whirled between them and the shimmering layer of granules. "Don't touch that," she croaked down at them. The two women pulled the young ones back, but Edith continued to shoo them away, gasping for air as she stumbled to and fro, protecting the dusted well cover. Finally, she glared at the women. "Don't let them near this well, and whatever you do, don't drink the water for ten days." She stopped and looked at the wife. "Ten days. You got that?"

"Yes, ma'am."

As Ma walked back over the hill toward home, she had another revelation: She had not sprinkled gold dust over the wells of those other six people, and certainly never told even *one* of them not to drink the water for ten days... only Walter... and Willis.

***

"I'm telling you, there will be a suicide in this church body, sometime next spring!" Harold averred. "It will be about a cleansing of some sort." He glared at Mickey, whose seated figure was silhouetted by the mid-October sunlight through the window behind him. "I don't care whether you believe me, or not. It is going to happen, and I am supposed to let you guys know."

"Fine," the board leader replied. "Now we know. Let it go, Harold. We have other issues to deal with right now."

"We sure do," Gerald agreed. "We have a whole bunch of people who want some answers."

"We'll take that up at the next meeting. Right now —"

"Sorry, Mickey, but we're going to have to address this." Don knew he was in the majority, but the head deacon had his ways, and usually he got them, in the end. "As he just said, Gerald, Harold and I have heard complaints from so many folks in the congregation, concerning the restrictions and dictates — those are their words, not ours — and we could end up having a church split if we don't do something."

"A church split, eh? And what does that mean? I'll tell you: We get rid of the complainers and rebellious ones, and then we have a peaceful church body once again." Mickey Mouse's eyes were positively beady.

"We've always had little disagreements, you know? But we have always worked things out." Harold looked straight into the glistening beads. "We don't have to split this church body, sir."

"Sometimes that's exactly what it takes, to get things in biblical order." The pointy nose twitched over the slit of a smile. "If they are rebelling against God's Word, then they need to find another place to go on Sunday mornings."

"But these people have put literally thousands of dollars, not to mention, sweat equity, into this church. We owe it to them, and to ourselves, to at least talk about these issues," Gerald quietly asserted. "We need to talk, Mickey."

"I don't need *you* to tell me how to run this church, Gerald. God knows, you can't even run your own household. I don't know why you don't just resign, you know that? You don't even qualify for the office of a deacon, mister. You shouldn't even be sitting in this meeting."

"That's going too far, Mickey." Don could feel the color rising in his face.

"Well, *somebody* needs to speak the truth around here, and it might as well be me. After all, as leader of this church, I have to take all the heat, anyway." He held the pen in his hand like a small scepter. "I don't think half of you guys even realize the burden I carry, trying to bring this church through a change of leadership." Seeing the men avoid the intensity of his visage, he let them have it: "I take the heat, so I call the shots… got that?"

"I don't think so." Harold leaned forward. "May I remind you, sir, that arrogance is unbefitting behavior for a church deacon? Maybe you should sit back and think about that for a while."

"I don't have to think about something that does not exist, mister." He rose with a switch of his backside off the chair. "This meeting is over. I want you all out of here, *right now*."

"You can't do that, Mickey," Don said.

"Watch me." He stepped across the room toward the door, followed by his obedient shadow, Leo Spencer. "I'm on my way to the church office, around the back of this house. If, by the time I reach the phone on my desk, all of your cars are not on the way out of the parking lot, I will call the Chittenden

County Sheriff's Department, and press charges for —" The door slammed behind them.

The men looked at each other. Then Sammy Black stood up. "I work for the man. Sorry."

As he closed the door behind him, the other three sat there in shock. Finally, Gerald Short said it out loud: "We need to get rid of this guy."

"I'm afraid it may be too late." Don's lips squeezed tightly. "He's already gotten what he wants... a split church, and even worse, a split board of deacons."

"Surely, there's some way to stop this nonsense." Gerald was hopeful.

Don stood up. "Ay-yuh, but we'll need to make those plans in private."

"In private?"

"Yes, Harold. We can't do anything when we have a dictator throwing temper tantrums at our meetings." He motioned for them to follow him out.

"And, that's how he manages to stop us from accomplishing things he doesn't want happening... exactly like he did just now."

By the next week, Mickey had devised a plan that would shut people up, and still keep his tight grip on the leadership of the Swift Street Pentecostal Church. He would give them what they wanted: an intermediary consultant... but that consultant would have to be approved by himself.

And he knew just the guy for the job.

That afternoon, he called the University of Vermont, asking to speak to someone in Religious Studies. After a couple of tries, the operator connected him with a woman who asked how she could help him. He explained what he needed, and almost immediately she suggested someone. "We have a visiting prof who's joined us this fall. He is well-informed on church politics and practices, I can assure you. I don't know if he would be interested, but I can give him your number and he should get back to you sometime shortly after three o'clock."

The church phone rang at five minutes past three.

"Swift Street Pentecostal. This is Pastor Leo."

"Yes. Good afternoon, Pastor. I'm returning a call from Michael Suree."

"Oh yes. From the university?"

"That's correct."

"And may I tell him who's calling, sir?"

"Of course. It's Professor George White."

***

Suddenly, it was Halloween night. Ma Bigelow was ready. She watched her husband drive the family Ford away toward Sam's Place, not having bothered to try to stop him, because she knew better. He had had that look in his eyes, that blank stare that always preceded his autumn visits to that tavern. It was something that continued like clockwork, starting somewhere in the middle of October, and culminating, always, on this holiday for ghouls and black cats and witchery. No, she knew better than to raise any objections, for this thing had persisted, despite the months of counseling and years of church-going.

But this time, she had a plan, and it began at eleven o'clock, just as Buddy was headed up for bed.

"I need to borrow your truck, boy."

"Yeah, Ma? What for?"

"Got some unfinished business. That's all you gotta know."

He knew better than to poke his nose where it didn't belong. "Sure," he said, handing her the keys.

"I'll be buying your gasoline for all of next week, so's you won't come up short on cash 'cause of me," she promised, as she slipped out into the dark.

It was close to eleven-thirty when she parked the old truck on the edge of a pumpkin field, just up the hill from Sam's Place. She grabbed a flashlight from the glove compartment before stepping from the running board to the damp stubble of vines and leaves. The moon was bright enough to illuminate her off-road trek through the vegetation as she crept slowly along the slope, until she reached a sudden drop in the landscape. It was as though someone had scooped out a bowl-shaped setting right there in front of her. The small tavern was located at the bottom of the bowl, and on her side of the roadway. She could see the blinking lights along the roofline, flashing like sparks off the half-dozen cars in the parking lot. Ma paused, noting that Willis's car was parked right at the front door.

"This is close enough," she whispered to herself. A move toward the left put her behind some kind of shrub. "Hope you ain't poison ivy," she muttered at it. But to make sure, the woman shone a quick beam of light along its surface, then, satisfied all was well, squatted down to get her bearings.

It took a few minutes.

The gurgling of the brook that flowed behind this little drinking establishment covered the sound of her movements as she crept carefully to what looked like a steep drop-off to the constant flow below. Dropping to all fours, the nimble lady went forward, eager to see what else lay down there. When she fell flat and pulled herself to peer over the edge, a delightful surprise appeared below.

"Oh my gawd, will ya look at that…?" The blue eyes were wider than ever.

Deep yellow foliage glowed against the dark, slate-blue sky, quivering gently in the white light of the moon. Their soft gray tree trunks thrust in and out of the shadows that dropped to the other side of a steadily moving ribbon of shimmering water. Little ripples wriggled forth from both sides of glossy rocks that lay just below the surface of roiling glass. Moonlight sparkled off every little whirlpool, and illuminated the flickering edges of Lewis Creek.

"It's like a scene from a fairytale movie, or somethin'." She shifted her weight to avoid a couple of rocks poking at her ribs. When that didn't work, a quick tug moved the largest one —about the size of a tennis ball — which she just held onto, not thinking about it. After all, the entrancing view under her nose, was not to be ignored. Indeed, Ma Bigelow surrendered to the beauty of the moment, her attention falling, eventually, under the overhang where she lay prone, to a small stretch of rocky shore glowing like pearls in the moonlight. All in all, it was as though she had a prime seat on the top row of a gorgeous little amphitheater.

The creaking front door caught her attention, and she realized the tavern was in full view of her right line of vision. That's when she saw the man come slowly toward her general direction, then turn onto what seemed to be a path down to the babbling water's rocky shore. From where she lay, it was an unobstructed panorama. Being brought back into reality, she checked her watch.

It was three minutes before midnight.

The spry lady lifted herself to all fours and watched as the man removed his hat, dropping it behind him where the path commenced from the parking lot. A few wobbly steps later, he dropped his coat in the same manner.

"What the hail…?"

She couldn't believe her eyes as he pulled off his sweatshirt and tossed it into a nearby bush. In that moment, she recognized Walter, the neighbor with all the kids.

"What's that?" A glow caught her attention, down there in the center of the creek. It was like a column of shimmering droplets had lifted from the water, and inside was the form of a woman and… was she…? Yes, she was singing. The magical sight was entrancingly familiar, and Ma Bigelow couldn't take her eyes off it. So intense was her attention, she did not notice the man's slow, purposeful approach to the rocky spot beside the creek. When he came into full view, he was standing with his back toward her, staring at the shimmering tower, and completely naked.

"Oh my gawd," she gasped. She looked back at the singing seductress. "Oh my gawd," she said, again, "it's a *si-reen*!! An honest-to-gawd *si-reen*, just like in *The Odyssey*, or *The Iliad*, or somethin'." Horror gripped her as she saw the man step into the edge of the rushing water, for she knew what might well lie ahead. "No-o-o-o, Walter!" She was on her feet and throwing the rock as hard as she could. When it hit the back of his head, he dropped backward onto the opalescent rocks.

Suddenly, an ear-splitting shriek pierced the night, resounding from darkened slopes of the surrounding landscape... going on and on. The little woman covered her ears, and yet she could not stop watching, as the tower of glitter slowly collapsed back into the water, revealing a nude, feminine body. Finally, the last echo died somewhere in the nearby hills, as the nymph-like creature disappeared into the shade of the other side of the creek.

It was deafeningly quiet.

She stood there, stunned by what had just happened, until the men, alerted by the shrieking moments ago, came running down the path.

Willis came home shortly after she did. She was reading in bed, of course, so he had no idea.

"That damned fool of a neighbor was there at the tavern tonight," he muttered, "making an ass of hisself."

"Is that right? You talking about Walter, with all the kids?" She waited for him to tell the whole story. "My-oh-my. Who would believe Walter would do a thing like that? Must be the booze, eh? Beats me, why you guys even want to go there..."

"Ay-yuh... guess maybe I'm done with that place."

She smiled and kissed the carrot-topped head as he laid it on the pillow. Before she reached to turn off the light, she put a bookmarker into her book on Greek mythology, closed it, and tucked it into the bedstand drawer.

CHAPTER EIGHT

Revelations

In early November, Paul, being eighteen, was old enough to get his own share of his mother's life insurance, which left fifty thousand to each of the children, and another fifty thousand to Michael. The young man put it into his savings account and announced to his father that he would be leaving home immediately. There was a Burlington apartment to be shared with a couple of buddies.

"Oh, and by the way, Dad. I'm in a rock band, and we're scheduled to do a TV gig in two weeks."

"What?"

"It was supposed to be earlier, but there were some technical problems."

"When did you join a rock band?"

"Doesn't matter. I'm there now, and we auditioned and we got the gig." He was enjoying the baffled look on Mickey's face. "It's on *American Bandstand*, in New York City. Pretty special, huh?" He ignored the glare. "Anyway, I'm out of here in the next hour or so."

The flabbergasted father stood there with his mouth open, as his son climbed the stairs to pack.

Upstairs, the two younger boys hung around, watching Paul stuff his belongings into a couple of suitcases.

"You going to New York City, Paul?" Matt's twelve-year-old voice squawked under the stress.

"Nope, not yet. Got a place in Burlington." He avoided looking at the kid.

"Hey, that's not too far," David said bravely. "Don't worry, Matt. We can still bug him. Besides, you'll be back to see us, won't you, Paul?" There was a little worry there.

"Sure. But at first, I'll be real busy getting ready for the TV thing." He jammed a pair of high-top tennis shoes into the corner of the biggest suitcase.

"Oh." David went over to sit beside the youngest one. For a few minutes, the two watched quietly.

"You guys seen my green sweatshirt?" His head was down near the closet floor.

Both boys jumped up to help find it, but the older brother came up out of the depths, sweatshirt in hand. "Never mind." He sniffed it. "Pee-yoo! But, oh well…" It should have been funny that he stuffed it in beside the tennis shoes, but the younger ones sat back down, hands folded tenuously in their laps. He pretended not to notice. "So, what time is it?"

David glanced at the clock. "Eight thirty-four."

"Oh, hey… you guys need to start getting ready for bed." He kept it light. "Look outside! It's dark already."

Neither one of them moved. It was up to him. "Hey, Matt, come over here and sit on this thing so I can close it."

"I can help," David offered, following his little brother.

Paul made a big thing of it, pretending he couldn't get that thing closed, hefting both of the boys to sit on the cover, grunting as he finally flipped the clasps closed.

"Shee-it! I couldn't of done it without ya, guys!" He grabbed them both, one in each arm and swiped them off onto the floor. For a moment, there was the old, friendly scuffle, filled with macho punches and giggles, and then they lay there, looking at the ceiling.

"Okay, gotta hit the road," Paul shouted a little too loudly as he sat up and jumped to his feet. As his brothers rose, he grabbed the two bags and headed for the door. He let them follow him down the stairs, teasing them as they descended behind him. "Watch out, will ya? You want me to break my neck?!"

But at the door, he stopped them. "Okay, guys, this is it. I'll see you later."

David nodded, unable to speak.

"We're… we're still gonna be brothers, right, Paul?" Matt bit his lip, to stop the quiver.

"You're never gonna get rid of me, pipsqueak," he grinned. Then he picked up the bags and left.

The two boys ran to the window to watch their hero load the baggage, then drive away down the dirt road.

"You two need to get ready for bed," their father reminded them from behind his tall, wingback chair in front of the fireplace.

***

"We'll have to be exceedingly careful how we handle this," Gerald warned his wife, Greta.

"Right. But I think it is sweet how that young man wants to keep in touch with his brothers. Heaven knows, Mickey doesn't let things go, especially rebellion from his own son." She stared out the car window. "Looks like it might rain before we get to the church."

He glanced at the dark gray cloud to the southeast. "Looks more like it will get a little wet in Shelburne." He adjusted his speed to slip into the Route 7 traffic as they turned south from Flynn Avenue. Their modest house was a few blocks away from that Shelburne Road turn, and in earlier years, they had often walked the route all the way to Sunday service. Today, they were driving past the familiar neighborhood of similarly comfortable dwellings with their neat lawns and decorative window shutters, past the Children's Home and the Country Club Golf Course, to make the left turn down Swift Street to the church. They were almost as far as the Children's Home when he repeated the word of caution.

"We'll need to be on the up-and-up… right out there… no hiding it. If Mickey hears us tell the boys, he hears us. No sneaking around about it."

"I agree. After all, it's not our fault Paul doesn't trust his father to let the boys know when the TV program will be on." She patted the suede purse on her lap. "We'll tell them the truth: Paul called and told us that the show will be on TV… all the way up here in Vermont… this coming Saturday at eleven in the morning, and we are so excited." One more pat. "Not relaying any messages; just sharing how excited we are. That's all."

"Exactly. That should be fine. No confrontations necessary."

"Still," she sighed, "I wish we didn't have to walk on eggshells like this. It used to be a joyful thing, going to church."

"Greta, as long as I'm still on the board of deacons, we need to show up," he said as he made the turn onto Swift Street, "whether it's comfortable or not."

"Ay-yuh, I know."

The vehicle moved slowly down the slope to the church driveway, and then carefully into the parking lot between the parsonage and the church building. He set the brake, then got out to fetch the casserole for the potluck after service. They were headed into the house to place it in a warm oven, when big, fat raindrops came down to spot their clothing.

"Told ya," she grinned.

They took seats in the back for this second Sunday in November, to avoid eye contact with the head deacon as he opened the service. The usual announcements were more upbeat this time, however.

"Just a reminder, here, that our annual church business meeting will be coming up in a couple of months. We will be making some important decisions this year, not the least of which, is the approval of a candidate for our new pastor." He smiled. "On that subject, it is my pleasure to announce that the board of deacons has accepted the application of Pastor Leo Spencer, and will be asking for your approval of that appointment at the meeting in January."

Across the congregation, four deacons had the same thought: "*When did we vote on that?*"

Mickey called Leo to the podium and conducted a short interview, something like a newscast to introduce a candidate for President for the United States. It was apparent this was a scripted presentation, although the two made every effort to make it look spontaneous, with chuckles and feigned surprises — "Is that so? I never knew that about you." It ended with Mickey leading a prayer for the candidate and the future of Swift Street Pentecostal Church. Then Pastor Leo delivered The Word, spending twenty minutes on John 3:16, which contained, once again, no new insights. Everybody in that little congregation had learned that "God so loved the world that He gave His only begotten son, that whosoever believeth in Him shall not perish, but have everlasting life" — at least twenty times before. But they were patient, though still hungry for some real teaching, bearing in mind there might be some lost soul in the crowd who just *maybe* needed to hear that.

After the final hymn, the men moved chairs and set up tables, while the ladies hefted bowls and pans and colorful casserole dishes from the parsonage all the way over to the hastily assembled dining area in the sanctuary. Mickey and Leo were nowhere to be seen, so Don said grace, and the feasting began.

The elderly and infirm passed through the line first, followed by mothers with young children, and then the rest of the little crowd. They loaded thick, restaurant-style plates with a pleasing variety of offerings, then found a friendly place to sit at one of the tables. Talk was lively at the one where the Bigelows and the Collinses shared conversation with Gerald and Greta Short. The young Suree boys took the last two chairs.

"What the hail is that on your plate?" Willis stared at a strange, slimy thing tucked alongside Lou's garlic mashed potatoes.

"Pa, watch your language," the daughter murmured.

"No, but I mean, what *is* it? Some kind of cabbage?"

She put her head down. "I don't know. It looked interesting, so I thought I would try it." Her eyes asked the question of Greta, just to her right.

"Oh! That's an artichoke!" She smiled. "Not everybody likes them because they have to be eaten a certain way." Seeing Lou move in closer to peer at the odd thing, she explained further. "It's a green vegetable. Look." Greta picked up one of those on her own plate. "Watch." Using her fingers, she held up what looked like a small cabbage halved down the middle. "I only take a half, because you have to peel off one leaf at a time." She glanced over at Lou's plate. "Oh, you didn't take any dip. Here, take some of mine." She scooped a spoonful onto the young woman's plate. "Now watch."

The whole table went into student mode, as she gently pulled the outermost leaf away from the bunch. After dipping the pale white bottom edge, she turned it over like a small umbrella and inserted that edge into her mouth, until her bottom teeth reached the fat center of the leaf. Then she gently closed her top teeth over it, and slowly pulled the leaf through the barely closed grip, squeezing the tender pulp from within. When she slipped the leaf out through her closed lips, there followed a short swish and swallow. "Mmmm," she smiled as she dropped the depleted leaf onto her plate. "Delicious!"

"Ooo! Ooo! Let me try it!" Matt exclaimed.

"Me, too!"

As the boys scrambled away to find artichokes, Lou chided her father. "You oughtta try it, Pa."

"I ain't no gawddim rabbit."

"Willis..." Ma's rebuke brought a polite inspection of the ceiling by the rest of the folks at the table.

Connie thought it was time to change the topic of conversation. She looked around. "Wonder where Mickey disappeared to? And Leo, for that matter." She spotted Heidi, deep in conversation at another table. "Well, *she's* here, anyway."

For a couple of minutes, the six diners focused on their plates, humming approval between bites, enjoying the din of the potluck. Connie, secretly regretting her remark, was relieved to see the two boys finally swing back onto their chairs, plates heaped with artichokes. A chuckle made its way around the table.

"Wow!" Buddy remarked. "By the time you get all them things et up, you'll be ready to take on the fanciest restaurant in New York City."

Another chuckle made the rounds.

"So," Gerald took the opportunity to bring up the subject, "has anybody heard from Paul?"

"Not a word." Don was enjoying a piece of chocolate cake. "Guess they should be there by now." He licked the frosting from between the tines of the fork. "You folks heard anything?"

"As a matter of fact, we have."

And that was how Gerald and Greta got the message to the two boys. The youngsters were excited, forgetting about the artichokes for a couple of minutes, long enough for Greta to suggest they keep it as a surprise for their father.

"You know, tell him just before the program comes on. I bet he'll enjoy seeing Paul on TV."

Connie was giving Don an "uh-oh" look, when the two men came bursting into the room. Mickey headed for the first group of young men he could find, shaking hands and slapping backs and doing the mentor thing. Leo was not far behind, landing on another group of men, these being older, to pump and slap and make male noises.

"Look at those two, working the room like a couple of politicians," Don muttered to his wife. "It would be comical, if it weren't so sinister."

"Yup, you're right… just like politicians looking for votes." She shook her head.

"That's exactly what they're doing, babe."

***

Monday, the Burlington Police Department's Snoop Squad finally tracked Mickey down at the church office. Leo had stepped out, so the man had to answer his own phone. Once he did, there was no way out.

"Yes, this is Michael Suree. What can I do for you?"

This time, it was no foot soldier; it was the inspector, himself. "The coroner's report is in, sir, and we need to talk to you… in person. It would be best if that interview took place in the next twenty-four hours."

He was there, with his lawyer, the next morning. The room was small and filled with cigarette smoke from the chain-smoking Inspector McDonald. The tall boss of the detective squad leaned back in the straight chair, pushed his rimless glasses back up onto his nose, and shook out the three-page report with the other hand.

"This is quite a report, Mr. Suree. Not that we haven't been surprised before, but this one pretty well takes the cake."

Mickey never moved an eyelash, but the lawyer snorted. "We don't need dramatics. Just get on with it."

"Well, let's start at the beginning." Another shake of the paperwork. "It seems conclusive that she died by drowning. Lungs full of pond water, so it happened right there. Footprints matched the shoes she was wearing, and those were the only prints we got, where the canoe was pushed into the water. No paddle found, but the canoe was tipped over, so it may have fallen out. Six paddles found in the canoe storage rack, though, so how many paddles do you have, sir?"

"Six."

"Six." He lit up a cigarette, blowing the smoke toward the ceiling. "So why would she get into a canoe, without a paddle, do you think?"

"I have no idea."

"No?" He stared at Mickey for a moment. "Your boys told us that their mom couldn't swim." He paused, to let it sink in. "Is that true?" Mickey's affirmation allowed the next question. "So, why in hell would she have even gotten into that thing?"

"I have no idea."

This time, he blew smoke out through his nostrils. "Any chance she was suicidal?"

"If she was, I sure didn't see it."

"What do you mean, you 'didn't see it'?"

Al leaned toward the inspector. "Watch it."

"Look, Al, we know this man probably oversees how many times a day his dog pees, okay? Seems odd that he wouldn't be aware of his own wife being upset."

"That's an assumption, designed to lead my client into some kind of a corner, and you know it." His large dark eyes fixed tightly on the policeman. "Just watch it."

Another puff of smoke went forth. "Well, let's just look at the fact that the body was found at the other end of the pond." He peered at Mickey through the clear lenses. "According to our measurements, the deepest water is in the center, where the big statue is located, and it's only twelve feet deep. The depth decreases quickly to five feet only a couple of yards away from the statue… and your wife was five feet three, correct?"

"She was."

"So, if the canoe tipped over in water too deep for her to stand up, she should have been able to get a couple of yards to safety, don't you think?"

"Inspector…" the lawyer warned him again.

"Look," he hunched toward the two across the table, "we *must* know if she could have even *done* that because, if she could have, then we might have a case that somebody was already out there — maybe somebody who could swim — and maybe they tipped the canoe and prevented her from struggling those two yards." He stopped to take another drag, then spoke through the smoke to make his final point. "We need some input, here. We need some help."

The little man looked sideways at his lawyer. "I guess... maybe that would make sense. Yeah, she probably could have made it that far."

The warning look from Al brought an almost-apology. "Thanks, Mr. Suree. That helps, because we can now consider the reason the body ended up in the mud at the other end of the pond." He punched the glasses, again. "We can theorize that the killer would have dragged her there and anchored..." He reconsidered his words. "So, that person would have had to go back through the water and exit on the west side, where there is a grassy drop-off." He shook his head. "You can't get footprints off of long, wet grass."

"No." The widower suddenly seemed intrigued. "No, you can't. But did you see footprints or indentations in the water near her body?"

The inspector took a look at the report, flipping the pages carefully. "Nothing here about that. Why do you ask?"

"It seems... odd, that's all. Not normal." He felt Al touch his shoulder. "No wonder you said this one 'takes the cake.'"

"Oh, that's not the part that takes the cake, Mr. Suree." He flipped to the back side of the second page. "Ay-yuh, here it is." He looked up. "Did you know your wife was pregnant, sir?"

The head dropped, so the lawyer stepped in. "You don't have to answer that, Mickey."

"Come on, Al. He *had* to have noticed a bump that big." He turned to address the bowed head. "Men see their wives naked all the time. You sure had to know about this."

"Yeah, okay. We just didn't want to tell anybody yet."

"No? Why not?"

"She was scared... wanted to have an abortion."

"Lots of women get scared, but this lady had had three babies, and she wasn't that old. What was she afraid of?"

"I couldn't get it out of her. All she did was cry."

"So she was crying a lot. Didn't anybody else see that?"

"They thought it was because of all the changes at the church, or something, and I just let them think it."

The cigarette was smashed into the dirty ash tray. "Alright, Mr. Suree, your wife was pregnant… seven or eight weeks, according to the coroner."

"Oh no, it was a lot longer than that."

"How did you know? Had she seen her doctor yet?"

"No. We guessed, from how big she was."

"But the coroner states here, the baby was only in its seventh or eighth week of development."

"That can't be right. She was showing. She had a real bump there."

"I know, sir, and that's what 'takes the cake' in this report."

"What?"

"The baby was in its seventh or eighth week of development, alright, but it was twice as large as it should have been."

CHAPTER NINE

Lists

"Aha! Just as we thought." Don held the opened book closer for his wife to get a look. "It's a Jezebel spirit, pure and simple." He beckoned her away from the bookcase, pulling his rolling chair around to the front of the desk. As he sat down next to her, she peered at the page where his finger was pointing. "Look. It's a list of characteristics of a Jezebel spirit. Not sure I would agree with all of them, but this is a malady that has troubled the organized church for a long time." He let her take the book. "Those two pages cover it pretty well." He leaned back in the desk chair, where he pushed a one-footed, squeaky rhythm disturbing the quiet of the basement office.

She reached out to steady his movement. "Sit still, would you?" Then she started to read the list. "One: Threatened by those with a prophetic gift; over-whelming need to control those who show such gifting."

"Mickey can't stand it when Harold has a dream, or whatever. He's derisive toward him, insinuating the man is a fraud."

"Okay, I assume you have seen this?"

"The whole board has witnessed this dismissive attitude on Mickey's part."

"Okay." She went to the second characteristic. "Actively seeks favor with the congregation and the community, by philanthropic activities... always in the open." She shook her head. "Well, he certainly has done that. I can name at least ten things in the last few years: sponsoring sports events for children, donating his time to supervise the new parking lot at the church, and God only knows how many times that family hosted picnics and youth rallies and weddings and showers — all at their beautiful homestead." She shook her head again. "And all in the open, and hey — how many times were these events covered by the newspaper, huh?"

"A *lot*."

She went back to the list. "Three: Often confides to key people in their church about a vision for the future of that congregation, even claiming, humbly, that they felt it was a message from God, but were too fearful to say so because it might cause a problem in the church body."

"Thank God, Pastor James saw right through that one."

"He did?"

"Oh yeah." Don's pixie smile told the whole story. "Pastor thanked him for being wise enough to keep these revelations to himself."

"How do you know that?"

"It was at a campfire a couple of years ago. I was leaned back, hat over my eyes, like I was asleep. I guess the guy thought I wasn't listening. Anyway, it was just him and Pastor, as far as he was concerned. I was quite impressed with the way Pastor James handled that."

"Mmm." She went on to the fourth characteristic. "They will make strategic moves in the governing of the church. If caught overriding the authority of the pastor or the board, they justify their actions with such excuses as, 'I was only doing what God told me to do, to protect this church.'" She looked at her husband as she relayed the last quote. "'By this time, they will have the favor and backing of some, if not all, of the congregation.'" She held the book to her chest. "Okay, I'm not sure *that's* true."

"Oh, it's true. This congregation is backing this guy, by not doing anything to stop him. They're supporting him, by *default*, Connie." Seeing that she agreed, he went on. "Yeah, they aren't doing anything to stop him. It's like they are too unsophisticated to handle this stuff." He shrugged. "Have you heard even *one word about canning this guy*, from the women — let alone, the men — in Swift Street's congregation?" She had no answer. "There you go. If the congregation doesn't speak up, the leaders will herd them like sheep to the slaughter."

She blinked a worried look, then addressed the list again. "Five: Exhibits a poorly disguised obsessive-compulsive behavior in private and business lifestyle."

"That's a 'yup.'"

"'Six: Honestly believes they're on a mission from God, and if it doesn't work in one place, they will move on to another location in pursuit of that goal.'" She closed the book. "Well, he doesn't seem to be moving on, does he?"

"Nope."

"Even so, I have to ask… can a *man* have a Jezebel spirit?"

"Yup. That's on the next page."

Her shoulders slumped. "So, what are we going to do?"

"We're going to get some expert advice, babe."

***

"The ladies have put me in charge of the Christmas pageant," Laura announced to her husband and son at Tuesday's suppertime.

"Hey, that's nifty, Mom. You're good at that sort of thing."

"Ay-yuh. Good at bossing people around," Jessie joked.

"That, too," the young man added. "But making costumes and hanging tinsel on coat hangers… well, she's *really* good at *that stuff*." He pulled a chicken leg off the platter. "I still remember the Halloween costume I had in the fifth grade: Frankenstein. It was totally gruesome. Made the girls throw up."

She smiled. "Maybe it was a tad too graphic, but you insisted, so I went along with it."

"No kidding, Dad. The teacher pulled me to the side and asked me to wash off some of the blood around the pegs in my neck." Male laughter filled the kitchen.

"Anyway," she continued, "I really need to get started on this. It's getting pretty hectic for everybody, what with all the stuff going on in that little church right now."

"Like what?" the dairyman wanted to know.

"Oh, for one thing, the quilting ladies are finishing up lap robes for the old folks' home out there on North Avenue in Burlington. We need twenty-three of them by December fifteenth. Then there's the special Christmas music for the first two Sundays in December — that means people in the sanctuary trying to practice while we are putting together the pageant program, all at the same time. And, as if that wasn't enough, Mickey has started Sammy Black distributing a questionnaire to every single family and all of the unmarried folks, working up a survey on how they all feel about the leadership of the church."

"Must be some murmuring going on, or he wouldn't have to do that."

"I think you're right, hon." She poked her fork into a golden-brown chicken thigh. "Word is out, he's hired a professional mediator to come in and smooth things over. In fact, he told us we needed to complete this survey, and have the numbers ready for this guy, by the last week of November, no less."

"Let's see... didn't you say there would be a church meeting in January?" He tilted his head thoughtfully. "The annual business meeting, right?" Her mouth was full of chicken, but she nodded. "Well, not too hard to figure that one out. He wants to make the leadership look good." He picked up the glass of cold, raw milk. "By the way, isn't that when you folks are supposed to vote on that new pastor?"

"Mmm-hmm," she hummed through the mouthful.

"What are you getting at?" the boy asked his father.

"The numbers will be rigged, I guarantee."

"Huh?"

"Listen, son, anybody can twist statistics and get the results they want. It's done all the time." He took a quick swig of the milk. "And I find it hard to believe that someone so controlling would allow a survey of any kind to go on in his church, unless he was sure he could tweak the results."

"So, Mom," Jack looked straight at his mother, "it's a sham. What a waste of time, and so unnecessary, with everybody being so busy."

"Or, maybe the timing of this survey and mediation have been deliberately staged… to keep folks focused on one hand, while the other hand is doing the trickery." His smile was ironic. "It's a diversion, Laura."

"Oh, I hope that's not true, hon."

"Sorry. And that's not all: Has anybody considered what Mr. Suree will do with all the information he's collecting on every single soul in that congregation?" He reached to touch her hand. "That guy is going to know who his friends are, and more importantly, who his *enemies* are, once that so-called survey is completed."

She lowered her head. "I suppose you're right, Jessie." The sadness came not so much from the truth in her husband's statement, as it did from the fact that he had just found something else to add to his long list of reasons *not* to get involved in the Swift Street Pentecostal Church.

***

On Wednesday morning, Mickey caught the boys as they each quickly downed a bowl of cereal. "You two ready for the school bus?"

"Got ten minutes," David mumbled.

"Takes that long to walk down there." He looked at his watch. "Okay, I'll drive you down."

They looked up in surprise.

"I need to talk to you for a minute, anyway." He slid onto the stool at the breakfast counter. "Got to make sure we get things coordinated." He seemed a bit pleased with himself. "Got something arranged for you two guys this weekend."

"This weekend?" It was David mumbling again.

"Yup." The father grinned. "Guess where Sammy's taking you?"

The brothers exchanged a wary look.

"To the movies?" Matthew ventured.

"Better than that." Another grin. "To the rifle range. You have a ten o'clock reservation." He stood up, motioning his sons toward the door. "You can hug me later. Right now, you have a bus to catch."

"We gotta tell him," the father heard Matt whisper to his brother in the back seat.

"Tell me what?"

"Uh, Dad...," David spoke slowly, "we actually had a surprise for *you* on Saturday morning."

"Really?" They saw the curiosity reflected in the rearview mirror.

David cleared his throat. "It's about Paul, Dad. He's gonna be on that TV show, you remember?" The eyes in the mirror were no longer focusing on the boys.

"Well, guess what, Dad? The program is going to reach all the way up here in Vermont, after all. Isn't that great, Dad?"

"Sure." The voice was cautious.

"So, it's going to be on at eleven o'clock on Saturday morning."

"I see."

"It's called *American Bandstand*."

"Oh, that's why I missed it; the TV listings in the paper didn't have that one in there.

"Yeah... So we were gonna surprise *you*."

"Yeah, we were gonna surprise *you*, Dad," Matt parroted. "Are you surprised?"

"I certainly am, Matt."

"So, we *do* want to watch Paul on TV." A pause allowed for an answer, but none came. "You want to see him, too, don't-cha, Dad?"

They watched the back of his head bend slowly forward, then back. "Oh, I certainly do, son. You bet." He drew the car to a stop. Down the road, the yellow school bus was grinding its way toward them. Michael Suree turned to smile reassuringly at his two young boys. "You can do the firing range any old time, but it's not every day we get to see Paul on television, right?"

The Suree brothers waved happily from the window as the bus pulled away.

***

Leo didn't seem like himself. She noticed him slipping back into the old, familiar darkness that had plagued him up in Maine. Leo was definitely insecure, too easily upset if Mickey was upset. There had been too many incidents interfering with the plan to make him pastor of this little church, and Leo didn't handle such things well, at all. It was time for her to start shielding him from stress. That was why she began to hover.

This was not easily done, because she was kept busy in the big log house, cleaning and fixing the daily meal, except on Wednesday and Thursday. In addition, she spent extra time with the boys, helping them to become more proficient in their own realm of daily chores. This required her presence every afternoon when they got home from school, even when she had the day off. It was the least she could do, she thought, to keep some sense of normality in the Suree household. But on this particular Friday afternoon, Leo needed a hot bath and a rubdown. By the time he dozed off, she was going to be very late in getting to the Suree kitchen.

At about four-thirty, the boys went from the school bus to the mailbox on that same side of the road to gather the mail, as they always did. But this time, there was a large manila envelope addressed to *them*. They read and reread their names several times, hardly able to believe their eyes.

"Is it really for us two guys?" Matt finally spoke it out loud.

"Darned right," David said, as he carefully tore open the top of it. "Here." He handed a couple of other small envelopes to his brother, freeing up his hands to tear as carefully as he could. When the top was opened, he gently pulled a piece of flat cardboard through the slit, almost dropping two 8 x 10 photographs to the ground.

Hastily, he pulled them back into view, then gasped.

"Oh… my… gosh, Matt. Look at these."

The pictures were identical: Black and white glossies of the band, Trouble.

Five guys in glittering suits, ruffled shirts, and pompadour hairdos, flashed smiles at the enthralled Suree lads.

"Aw, jeez, look!" Matt grabbed a copy. "Look at Paul's hair." He wrinkled his nose in delight. "It's almost white. Look at it!"

"Yeah, I see that." David looked down at a scrawled message near the bottom of the photo in his hand. He read aloud: "'To my brother, Matt. Love ya, Paul.'" He made the correction. "Wait a minute, this one is for you. Here. Gimme mine."

They hurried home, but Heidi had not yet arrived, and there was no one in the insurance office.

"We can show them later," David said.

They sat on their beds and stared at the pictures until Heidi called them down to supper.

"Your father has a late appointment," she explained as she served up a couple of hamburgers.

"We wanted to show him these," they said, holding up the glossies.

"Oh my…" She stood still for a moment, obeying the check in her spirit. "*This is not good; Mickey will not like this.*" Leo would know the same thing when he came up for a hamburger later, and that would lead to another dive into the pits of despair, so she made a careful suggestion. "Tell you what… why don't you keep them in your room so they don't get soiled here at the dinner table. Accidents happen, you know." Then, for good measure, she made sure they kept those photos under wraps for as long as possible. "As a matter of fact, you should keep them hidden until you and your Dad have breakfast tomorrow morning. That would be a great way to start your day, don't you think?"

***

By ten forty-five on Saturday morning, the little audience had assembled in the television corner of the large living room of the log house. Mickey made a big production of turning the rabbit ears, first one way and then the other, until the fuzzy images appeared on the screen, at least identifiable. He had asked Heidi to forego the weekend "deep clean" until noon, so there would be no interruption during the telecast, but she and Leo slipped in at the last minute anyway, because the worried, would-be pastor wanted to show support for his mentor… whatever that might be. David and Matt had front row seats, but when the magical hour of eleven o'clock drew nigh, they pulled their father into the privileged seat, right there between them. Their faces glowed with anticipation, and each one held the autographed photo on his lap.

The show's logo flashed onto the screen as rock and roll music blasted forth from the television. The booming voice of the announcer introduced the premier of *American Bandstand*, "…brought to you by…" — the boys in Vermont could have cared less — "and featuring the Nightliners as guest band for today! Go, man, go!!!"

The five-piece rock band, dressed in white suits, fell into a full, thumping-twanging-grunting mode, as teenagers took to the small dance floor, gyrating slowly, slumping and flopping through — apparently — the latest dance crazes. Boys in jackets and front-pleated pants threw their heads into endless, lazy gyrations, while plaid-skirted girls pushed the air around with their arms, for the first five minutes of the show.

"Where's Paul's band?" David asked nobody in particular.

"Oh, this is only the opening band, most likely," his father suggested. He took a handful of popcorn and leaned back into the comfort of the sofa.

The show's host took over to announce "the most popular song in America." It was a slow-dance, with the youngsters leaning onto each other, as though dying of thirst in a burning desert. At the end of that one, Michael looked around and commented, "So, what was *that* all about?" He drew his two sons close. "Am I missing something here? What is so great about this show?" He gave them a squeeze. "*You* tell *me*."

By the time the show was over, the two boys were hitting bottom. The rock band, Trouble, had not appeared on the program, not for one minute.

"Oh, you have to remember that television is still new; there are a lot of glitches. Not all things work right, all of the time." He tousled David's hair. "Try not to take it personally, son." He caught Leo's eye. "You know what? Pastor Leo is free this afternoon. What do you say, the three of you take in a movie?" His brows indicated this was not an idle request, so Leo responded with enthusiasm.

"Let's check the movie listings, fellas!"

Mickey's office phone was ringing off the hook by noon that day. He finally answered it, knowing all too well, who it would be.

"You gawd-damned son-of-a-bitch! You lousy piece of crap! I *know* what you did, you bastard! My agent told me." The fury increased. "You call yourself a father, a man-of-God? Huh?"

"Cool down, Paul."

"Stuff that crap up your butt! This is another example of the shee-it you have plastered people with — not only your working buddies, but your very own family, over and over and *over*! You're a real piece of scum, you know that?"

"Cool down."

"Who the hell are *you*, to tell *anybody* to cool down? You... you have shown me, finally, who you really are, you know that? I mean, who would do such a thing to his own son? Who would buy off a producer, to keep his own son from making good on TV? Who would *do* that? *Who*?"

"Maybe... a desperate dad?"

The laughter was almost hysterical. "Desperate? Hell yes, desperate to keep it all under control, you weirdo... so desperate to win, that you cheat and cheat and cheat." There were sounds that could have been sobs. "Well, I am done with you, you two-faced bastard! I don't believe you represent Jesus Christ... not now, not ever." The voice faded into a muffled dialogue. "...coming back to Vermont, telling everything I know... finding out who murdered my mother...you son-of-a-—"

Mickey hung up, and coolly turned to an afternoon of consuming tasks. Shortly after the violet shadows of that November day descended, he took a few minutes for a sandwich at the supper hour. There, he patted the two disappointed youngsters on the head, reassuring them that they would probably see their big brother very soon. Then he went back to his office to prepare for a meeting with George White.

The professor was on time, having navigated the dark, icy road through the property, for the seven-thirty meeting.

"I have the statistics you asked for," Mickey said, as he handed the paperwork to the man.

"Thank you, Michael. Although, I can't guarantee they will support your agenda."

"Who said I have an agenda?"

"Everybody has an agenda, Michael. Call it what you may…" He glanced quickly over the checklist. "So, I am to use these figures to support your leadership of Swift Street Pentecostal."

"Something like that," the head deacon smirked.

"…bringing you closer to turning that organization into an elder-run church." He leaned back into the leather. "Tell me, Michael, doesn't it ever bother you? This assignment?"

"What? Are you kidding me? I take this whole thing very seriously, mister. In fact, I will not even consider stopping, until I have accomplished that goal. I think that's what the Organization of Elder-run Churches of America have trained and assigned us to do, and as far as I know, our assignment has not been changed." He cast a suspicious eye toward the scholar. "*Has* it been changed, George?"

"It has not." The professor tucked the list into the inside breast pocket of his jacket as he rose. "How long before you need this so-called mediation plan?"

"Yesterday."

Mickey closed the office door behind his brother-in-law, and retreated to his bedroom, where he took a long, hot shower, then retired for the night.

The phone in the kitchen was ringing persistently. Mickey's alarm clock told him it was three in the morning. It seemed like a long trek from his bed to the breakfast counter, with the insistent jangle marking every step through the darkened house.

"Hello?"

"Mr. Michael Suree?"

He answered through a fog. "Yes."

"You have a son, Paul Marcus Suree?"

"Uh, yes."

"Birth date…?"

He caught only the gist of the rest of the conversation: The drive back home had been interrupted by a sudden winter storm. Somewhere north of Rutland, Vermont, the vehicle carrying the rock band, Trouble, had flipped off the road and rolled down a steep embankment.

There were no survivors.

CHAPTER TEN

Idols

The news hit the folks of Chittenden County like an earthquake that would not stop. All five boys had come from the same general area — Burlington, Colchester, Hinesburg, and two brothers from Winooski — where the aftershocks rumbled incessantly throughout the days leading up to the memorial service. The grief was so overwhelming that several of the pastors involved with these families had made the guarded suggestion of one service for all five boys, in hopes that these families would be able to comfort each other. It took place on the first Saturday of December, at Burlington's Memorial Auditorium, kitty-corner across from the grounds of that city's Edmunds High School. On that day, cars lined the snowplowed margins of Main and South Union Streets, as hundreds of mourners climbed the gray-white stone steps to pay their last respects. Inside, the crowd took seats under the steel-framed, opaque glass windows on the south and north sides of the spacious auditorium.

A heavy floral scent filled the inside atmosphere as Don and Connie took their seats beside Leo and Heidi. Don looked around, trying to spot the other deacons, but this extended family section on the main floor was packed, and he didn't want to appear disrespectful, so he turned his attention to the notes for the service, printed on yellow-edged paper. Across the front, beneath the stage, five white coffins formed an extended half-circle, each one draped with yellow chrysanthemums, shiny gold ribbons trailing through the white lace of baby's breath blossoms. Leo noted under his breath that the caskets were all closed.

"Probably just as well," Heidi whispered back. She nudged his arm. "Oh, look at that." On each side of the line of floral-draped coffins, a huge photo of the rock band, Trouble, was grandly displayed on large, white easels. "They sure looked like rock stars."

Connie, who was sitting beside her and heard the exchange, tilted her head toward the lady. "Even though they never really got to do that thing."

"What thing?" Don looked up to see what she was talking about.

"I was sharing with Heidi about the photos on the sides." She nodded back and forth in their directions. "They never got to be rock stars."

"Yeah. Kind of ironic, isn't it?" He motioned to the rows of flowers lining the front of the stage, and the backdrop lighting behind the speakers' chairs.

"You'd never know that, by the looks of this place." He clucked his tongue softly. "What we're really doing, is mourning the death of five young, ambitious, and probably greatly misguided youngsters." He leaned back in his metal folding chair and focused on the iridescent glow of the ceiling, which was illuminated by the ambient light of the five windows on each side of the facility. "This is a great gathering site," he murmured. "Every town in America should have a meeting place like this. Too bad it has to be used for this kind of occasion."

Even as he spoke, the music started, ever-so-softly, over the loudspeakers high above each side of the stage. The last of the seats were being hurriedly filled, and then the doors were closed. A respectful pause ensued, before the line of immediate family members began to emerge from some lower level door, sedately guided by the funeral director staff, to their respective seats at the very front.

Heidi spotted Mickey steering his two sons along, somewhere in the middle of the procession, and nudged Leo before nodding in that direction. Connie caught that and nudged Don. All four watched, until the father and sons were seated, then turned their attention to the beflowered podium up on the stage. Three men in dark suits filed in and took a seat, where they were silhouetted by the pale blue backlighting.

A young girl in a long, black dress approached the podium microphone, a shiny, gold guitar in hand. She slung the instrument into place, and hit a couple of chords before moaning out a mournful dirge that had no references to God... only words of unfulfilled dreams and the mystery of life.

"Oh, brother..." The Collinses knew, right then, that this was a side-show.

When it was finally over, the immediate families exited toward the South Union Street doors, where they could receive words of kindness from the exiting crowd. The Spencers and Collinses waited patiently on the other side of the receiving line, watching as Michael Suree and his boys stood there for a good forty-five minutes, until the last person paid their respects and left. During that time, they couldn't help but note that the woman to the left of Mickey, the single mother of the boy from Burlington, kept shooting dark looks toward him.

"Come on," Don suddenly whispered to Leo. As the two men moved forward, he signaled for the ladies to get David and Matt out of the line. "Get them out of here, if you can. They don't need to hear this..."

They reached Mickey just as the woman was spewing her hatred.

"You lousy, rotten phony. I know what you did. My son called me — collect! He told me everything." She moved into his face. "You did this! You killed my boy, as sure as we're standing here."

Matt and David looked back at their father as the two women shuffled them along.

"I hope you rot in Hell, Mister Sue-ree!!"

Don and Leo moved in between the woman and Mickey, ushering him quickly out the door.

They were out on the cold street before David stopped in his tracks to ask, "What did you do, Dad?"

"Just tried to help, son."

"What does that mean?"

"We'll talk about it later. Right now, we have to get to the cemetery."

Over the next few days, the boys slowly put the picture together, their respect for their father dwindling with each piece of the puzzle that fell into place. It was the beginning of the end of life at the big log homestead for David and Matt, for things would never be the same between the three of them. By the end of the year, they would leave, taking up residence at a boarding school in New York State. Their father felt it would be best for all concerned.

***

If there were any regrets on the part of Mickey Suree, they were not on display. He threw himself into his assignment, more focused than ever. The annual church meeting was only weeks away and there was still much to do, including tweaking the statistics George had provided — oddly enough — just hours after the funeral at Memorial Auditorium. By the second Saturday in December, the head deacon figured that the majority of the congregation not only approved of the current church leadership, but would gladly accept these same individuals in the new governance of an elder-run church. Of course, only Leo was qualified to be an elder, but Mickey could handle that small matter. All the little pugilist needed was to get Leo in as pastor, in order to set up the knockout punch that would take all the other contenders out of the race for the championship.

He just needed enough votes.

Meanwhile, the boys had not left for New York yet, so Heidi was still at the main house almost daily. Days off seemed a moot point, seeing as how her employment was probably going to end soon, anyway. So Mickey's routine continued much as before Paul's death, and he would have played out every single minute of it, if Heidi and Lou hadn't done that one, last deep cleaning.

It happened on that same second Saturday of December.

"So, this one is going to be a little harder," she remarked, holding the door to the bedroom suite open for Lou, who was carrying a metal pail of warm, soapy water. "Go ahead and put that down over near the bathroom, because I'll get *it* done first, while you move across the bedroom toward the office door." Her blonde head poked into the doorway at the ivory-colored tiles around the wall of the tub and shower. "Take down the shower curtain, would you, hon? I can manage the rest pretty much on my own." She glanced around at the personal items Mickey had carefully placed on shelves and cabinets, glad that he wasn't at home at the moment. "Feels weird enough to handle all that stuff when he *isn't* here," she muttered.

Lou dropped the shower curtain into the tub. "Want me to soak it?"

"No. I'll take it from here. You go ahead and get the windows and under the bed, like we did in the other bedrooms. Don't soak those wooden floors with that hot water. Wipe-wipe-wipe, quickly, just damp enough to clean. No puddles, okay?"

The young girl grunted her acknowledgment, then focused on her chores. Heidi went to work quickly, getting most of the room done before Lou poked her face through the doorway. "What about the sitting area? There's a rug there."

"Move the coffee table off, then vacuum the rug, then roll it up so you can wipe the floor underneath."

"It's round."

"What's round?"

"The rug. How do I roll up a round rug?"

"Start on one side and roll it up like a pie crust."

"Oh!" The light went on. "No problem, but I have to get some clean water first. I still have all that floor all the way over to the office door."

Heidi was done with the bathroom by the time the light blue Oriental rug was vacuumed. Lou bent down to roll it up. "Hey!" She tugged at the edge several times. "It's nailed down, or something."

"I can see that from here." She approached to kneel beside the girl. "Yup, looks like carpet tacks or something." She sat back on her haunches. "Guess we need to leave it alone. Probably that way to prevent them from catching a toe on the edge." She rolled her hips to the right, swinging her legs out to where she could stand up… and tipped the pail of hot suds completely over onto the rug.

Lou let out a cry. All Heidi could do was yell, "Towels! Towels! Towels!" But by the time they had grabbed a half-dozen of them from the bath cupboard, the rug was thoroughly soaked. All they could picture was the huge puddle of water, soaking into the wooden floorboards beneath. They sponged and patted and sponged some more, but the rug was still full of water. Suddenly, Heidi ran for the kitchen junk drawer, coming back to hand a bottle opener to Lou. "Pry those tacks loose. Hurry," she commanded, as she turned the claw of a small hammer over, to do the same thing. They worked feverishly, until half the circular thing could be lifted. "Grab hold!" They both bent forward. "Lift!" It came up with a sucking sound, dripping great drops onto the colorful paint below.

"Whoa! What is *that*?" Lou's eyes were wide.

"Towels-towels-towels!" her fellow-worker shrieked. "You get the floor; I'll get the underside of the rug." For the next few minutes, the priority was getting rid of the soaking that could do so much damage. When it finally appeared to be under control, the two ladies looked at the flashy-colored design on the floor.

"What *is* that?" The tall blonde stood up to get a wider view.

"I think my ma could probably tell us." The girl had been eyeing it as she dried it with the towels. "Yeah, I think she could."

"Well, never mind it. We need to dry out this rug." She reversed the vacuum's sucking motion to a blowing one, then turned it full force upon the damp underside of the rug. Meantime, the girl went to the kitchen, returning with a pencil and tablet."

"What are you doing, Lou?"

"Making a drawing. My ma will know what this is."

"Never mind that. We need to get this rug dried and tacked down again, before Mickey gets home." When the girl continued to sketch, she grew impatient. "For Pete's sake, Lou! At least open a window so the place won't smell of wet wool."

But Mickey smelled it, the minute he came into the house, and so did the boys, who were huddled at the top of the stairs.

***

Harold Taylor, the balding deacon who seemed to be a seer/prophet, was on the phone with Don Collins. "Lord, I'm almost sorry I was right... this is all so tragic... but it *is* important that I be right in these prophecies."

"Of course." Don was removing his bus driver tie as he spoke. It had been a long day of guiding the cumbersome vehicle through the snow.

"Maybe a certain gentleman will stop with the sarcasm whenever I speak up about these things. In fact, I am reminded of the next incident: Next spring, a suicide, of a cleansing type, it would seem. I hope he stays aware."

"So, he could actually prevent these things, if he wanted to? I mean, could any one of us even *do* that?"

"Don't know. That's not my gift. But God can do anything, right?"

"Right." He sat down on the side of their bed, to let Connie get past on her way to the closet. "So, Connie *said* you would call me back after I got home. Said you had something bothering you."

"Ay-yuh." He took a long breath. "You familiar with that survey Mickey took of the congregation?"

"Ay-uh. Didn't approve of it, but my opinion doesn't always matter."

"Same here. But what definitely bothers me, is who it was that tallied up all those answers."

"I… don't know who that was, Harold."

"It was one of Mickey's relatives — can you believe that?"

"That right?"

"None other than one of Rita's brothers. His name is George… George White, I think."

"Really???"

"Yup. You know him?"

"Connie and I know who George White is."

"Well, there you go. I tell you, I don't know how Mr. Suree gets away with this stuff. That's got to be illegal, or at least immoral."

"Mmm," Don hummed.

"So, what do you think? Should we challenge those statistics? I mean, the annual meeting is just around the corner." Another big breath. "For all we know, he's even stacking the deck to get votes."

"Be aware, Mickey is, in fact, wanting to change the bylaws at an emergency meeting this week. He wants the voting age down to sixteen, and no requirements for membership, whatsoever. Anybody could come in off the street and vote however he pays them to vote." He caught the shocked look on his wife's face. "Of course, I wouldn't advise accusing him of such a thing, but I would advise that we not allow those bylaws to get changed, even if he tries to keep us there until three in the morning."

"I agree with you, one hundred percent." Still another breath. "So, how do you feel about my contacting Gerald Short about this?"

"By all means. And remind him that a stacked vote could also mean Leo gets in as pastor. Nobody I know wants this guy for our pastor, regardless of how experienced he may seem. He's a puppet for Mickey, pure and simple."

The call ended, and Don hung up. From the other side of the bed, she asked, "What about George White?"

"Well, it seems we have more than only Jezebel spirits to talk about with the prof."

***

He didn't actually fire either of them, but after he sent Lou Bigelow home with what would be her final check, Mickey insisted on walking Heidi back to the guest house. He was pulling on his jacket as they started carefully down the hill on the icy road. The sky was dark with the promise of more snow, providing the perfect opening for his conversation. "Wow, look at that sky, and it's only one o'clock in the afternoon."

She glanced at it, too nervous to reply.

"So, was it like that, up on that Maine island? Dark skies out over the Atlantic?"

"Sometimes." She pulled her collar up, pretending to bend into the wind.

He took a couple of steps before he approached the subject. "I imagine you would hate to go back to that freezing, bleak place, young lady. After all, it was almost a death sentence for your husband." He didn't look at her as he continued: "And I'm assuming, you *do* love your husband, don't you, Heidi?"

"Absolutely." She kept her head down, waiting for the rest of it.

"And I'm also assuming you would never do anything to destroy his opportunity to pastor such a great little church as Swift Street Pentecostal." The pause was intentional. "Am I right?" Seeing the short jerk of her head, he kept the narrative going. "Bearing all that in mind, then, it would certainly be prudent for you to rethink what has happened in the last few minutes." He slipped ahead of her, just far enough to stop her in her tracks. "The floor under the rug was deliberately painted to protect the wood in case there was ever the very same type accident as what happened this morning. Rita and I hired some whimsical artist to do the job, and — lo, and behold — she did some kind of design for the fun of it." He had his hands on her shoulders, looking intently into her face. "That's all there is to it… but do you think, for one short second, the general public would believe that?" He gave her shoulders a shake. "Do you?" Not waiting for an answer, he stepped to the side, continuing the slow, careful steps across the crunching ice.

Overhead, the deep blue-gray sky was gently disturbed by a black flock, returning from the winter morning scavenging. Their descent into the blue spruce was orderly and quickly finished, even before she could look up, but she knew. "The crows are back," she murmured.

Mickey searched the horizon. "Where? I don't see them."

"Um, they come in, little-by-little, sometimes. I don't always see them, myself."

He let it pass, concentrating on the other issue, entirely. As their footsteps crackled through the crisp of the curve in the road, he finally made his pitch: "Listen, Heidi, I need to know I can trust you. Leo belongs in this church. I know that as sure as I'm standing here, begging you. And I *am* begging you… please don't misread this situation." He reached out to touch her arm; her offended reaction was the give-away.

The man's face went hard. "Okay. Okay, I see you have made up your mind." He snorted a puff of cold air from his nose. "So now I have to get tough." His body shot forward, stopping her again in her tracks, but this time, he was nose-to-nose with the terrified woman.

"I have proof that this paint job under the rug was done by a local artist, and that she, and she alone, did her own thing. I have *proof*, do you understand that? And if you *ever* even so much as *infer* anything otherwise, I will personally destroy you and your husband." He stepped back. "Do I make myself perfectly clear?"

The dam broke.

"Get away from me!" The push against his chest was a gut-level reaction, sending the man down on the ice, where he slid across shards that cut into his face. She saw it, and tried to run for the safety of the guest house. She fell, more than once, before she looked back and saw him heading back to the main house.

"Oh, God," she moaned. "Oh, God." At the foot of the little porch stairs, she could go no farther. Hot tears came above the frosty breath. She did not lift her head to see it, but quietly, softly, there came a single ebony-winged creature, perching on the roof of that small porch. And then, another, and then another…

When Leo came home twenty minutes later, she was still there.

And so were the crows.

***

"Oh sure, I know that symbol. It stands for Lady Luck, as we would say in this day and age, but in the ancient times, she was a goddess called Fortuna."

"I *knew* you'd know what it was, Ma!" She turned to her brother. "It was under this round rug in their bedroom, Buddy, all nailed down around the edges."

"Yeah? Like they were hiding it, or somethin'?"

"Kind-a looks like it. What do you think, Ma?"

"Don't know." She studied the sketch again. "Not that it really matters, but what colors were… are in this thing?"

"The wheel is red, and the background is yellow."

"Mmm. Just curious. It don't… doesn't really matter." She turned the paper sheet a half-circle to the right, then once more. "Yup. It's the eight-sectioned wheel. Supposed to stand for Fortuna's full basket — a corny-co-pee-a, I think it's called." Her eyes focused on the living room ceiling as though it were a movie screen. "See, she was a popular Greek goddess, all over Greece and Italy and all them places. Everybody liked her, because she blessed the harvest — you know — the gardens and the wheat fields and the cows and the chickens… things like that." She blinked slowly. "'Course, she could also take away good luck, if somebody was gettin' greedy, so there was the judgin' side of her, too. Sort of like them weigh scales you see that shows us how justice is blind. She could do them good, or take it all away."

The children weren't exactly following the storyline, but waited patiently for her to finish. "I'm thinkin' we need to tell somebody about this." She glanced quickly at her daughter. "So, what does this Heidi person think about all of this?"

"Well, it don't matter anymore, Ma, 'cause I think Mickey fired her… and me… when he got home and smelled the rug we was trying to dry." She shrugged. "Wasn't a whole lot we could do about it. We saw something he didn't want us to see, right?"

"Mmmm." She studied the drawing again. "But the thing is, you two *have* seen it, and you can't *un*-see it." The paper was laid down across her lap. "Somethin' tells me, that man will fix your wagon if you open your mouth, either one of ya."

The siblings exchanged a troubled look.

"So-oh, I'm thinkin' you need some kind-a protection… like maybe an expert opinion and proof that it was a mistake, an accident that you two saw the bloomin' thing, and meant no harm." She patted the sketch firmly. "You need some friends, Lou. In fact, so does this Heidi." One more firm pat. "Who do you trust, to cover your butt? Huh? Think about that."

Willis was at the back door, coming in from chores. His wife lifted a finger to her lips. "We need to shut up about this stuff. Your pa don't do too good with this kind-a problem."

It was just before the little family headed up for bed, when Lou drew her mother aside.

"It's the Collinses, Ma. They know how to keep a secret, and they help a lot — people with this kind-a problem."

"Alright. You and me, we'll make a phone call in the morning." She leaned closer to whisper the final word. "I want to be in on this, if there's any more information about Fortuna, okay?" There was a little hug. "You know how I love to study this stuff, right?"

***

Leo was pouring a hot cup of tea for his wife, as he tried to reassure her. "He told me what happened. Said you two probably got the wrong impression about the painting under the rug." He set the cup on the end table near where she was cuddled in a warm blanket. "Now listen," he murmured as he slid alongside her, "it was something Rita commissioned, and had no significance for Mickey whatsoever. He never gave it a second thought."

"Did he tell you he insisted on walking me back here, and then threatened me about jumping to conclusions, or whatever?"

"He was almost back to the house as I drove in. His face was bleeding a little, so I stopped to see if he was alright."

"His face was bleeding?"

"Yeah. Said he fell on the ice."

She snorted. "I pushed him."

"You what?" He sat up straight to look her in the eye.

"He was blocking my way, and yelling in my face."

He stood to his feet. "Okay, he did say he may have gotten a bit intense. But you know Mickey — he's an intense guy. He gets like that with everybody, Heidi." He moved a few paces away before turning back toward her. "I'm thinking you were really upset, spilling water on an expensive rug, not being able to fix things before he got back home. You were probably upset before you even left the place." He shoved his hands into the side pockets of his pants. "Maybe, *both* of you overreacted." Suddenly seeing the tears moving down her face, he went back to the sofa to pull her into his arms. "Heidi, I hate to see you like this. You're the one who's been so strong. Please don't stop being the strong one, honey. I need you to be there when things don't look so good."

She knew he was right.

At that moment, she knew she would have to apologize to Mickey and… suddenly, she remembered that the boys were upstairs while all this was going on. *"I wonder if Mickey knows that,"* she thought.

***

"Thanks for coming over," Don said, as he motioned George White to the only recliner in the living room.

"Oh, no, this is probably your favorite chair," the white-haired man objected. "I'm perfectly fine on the sofa." As he moved to that seat, he glanced around the room. "Nice place you have here." He looked to Connie for the next answer. "Did you decorate, or was it a two-sided project?"

"More like a fling-it-together project," she smiled. "We kind of live in the moment, not knowing where God will direct us next."

"I can relate to that."

She was pouring the coffee as she opened the subject. "Well, we know how busy you must be at the university, so we appreciate that you're taking the time to come by."

"No problem. I wanted to get back to you two, anyway."

They sat back to listen.

"I can't believe… well, I can, because it had to be God… but Michael asked me to work up a survey to be done in your church. I mean, it was right out of the blue." His shoulders hunched up, then down. "It was the perfect 'in,' to get involved in the stuff that's going on at Swift Street Pentecostal."

"Okay, so I need to know just how you figure?"

"Sure. Well, Don, I know how to rig surveys, and that's what Michael is counting on. He thinks the congregation will believe whatever we put out there, and really, he's almost right." He brought the steaming coffee up under his nose, without sipping it. "But what he's not ready for is something I'm quite familiar with: it's something I call 'the silent, secret element' — the folks who are not going to go along with his agenda when it comes to the vote." There was another quick sniff of the aromatic brew. "I've seen it happen, many times."

"So, you think this survey propaganda may not swing the vote for Mickey?"

"Can't promise you that, Don, but," he did a thumbs-up, "it sure seems to work out that way, more often than not."

"So, no promises as far as the voting next January."

"Nope. But I wanted to make sure you knew what I was doing. I have not abandoned my assignment." This time he took a small sip. "I am still answerable to the big boys."

Don took a long breath, then let it out, slowly. "Okay, thanks for the update. We will trust you with that whole thing." He glanced at Connie, looking for her approval of the direction he wanted to take the conversation. She nodded. "So, George, we are greatly concerned about the spiritual aspect of this thing with Mickey."

"And you *should* be."

"Uh…" The surprise threw him off subject. "We should be? What do you mean?"

"What's going on over there in that little church is, well, really very unsettling."

"What do you mean, Professor?" She slid to the edge of her chair.

"I think you two already know, this is a spiritual battle, not a political one."

He paused, pressed his lips together, then let the words come out. "You are probably... no, almost certainly, dealing with a Jezebel spirit."

Don and Connie were astounded.

"We were, uh, were going to ask about that exact subject," Don said.

There was a small space of silence, before George spoke. "Thank you, Holy Spirit. We have the same insight. That's good. That's really good, because we three — at least we three — know what we're dealing with here." He rubbed his hands together, thinking. "So then, I need to know how much you two know about this spirit, and how it operates."

A few minutes later, the three of them found themselves in complete acknowledgment as to what they were dealing with. The agreement was made to impede the working of this destructive entity, as much as possible, since — and they all knew this — there was no way to stop it, except to remove the source of power it operated from. In this case, the church, sadly, would have to disappear, be disbanded, so there would be no longer any base from which this wicked spirit could wreak havoc.

They sat quietly in the living room, dealing with that sad reality. A clock could be heard ticking, somewhere on that main floor of the house. Outside, a chilling wind whispered against the windows behind the sofa. The soft swish of the professor's rise to leave brought the evening toward its close. "I'm so sorry," he whispered.

"Sure. We appreciate... everything," she replied. But then, Connie suddenly remembered something else. "Um, Professor White, would you, by any chance, know anything about Greek gods?"

He smiled. "I do. Better yet, I know people who know a lot more about that subject, than I do. Why do you ask?"

"Well, there's this young girl in our congregation — Lou Bigelow — who came up to me, privately, and said she had a sketch of some kind of symbol... a symbol that was hidden under a rug in the Surees' bedroom suite." She swallowed hard. "I don't know if it's even important, but Lou's mother likes to read about Greek gods, and that sort of thing, and *she* says, we need to check it out."

"Really?" He seemed intrigued. "Is there a picture of it?"

"Just a sketch."

"Oh."

"But the mother is saying she recognizes it as... uh, let's see... uh... oh, yeah, as some kind of symbol of a Lady Luck goddess, or something like that."

George White's eyes glinted with interest. "I would certainly like to meet with that mother. Could you arrange such a thing? Remember, it has to be done in secret, as much as possible."

"We can do that," Don piped up. "I'll call you, as soon as we're ready."

CHAPTER ELEVEN

Illusionists

The Christmas pageant was only days away when the Bethlehem village backdrop was badly botched. The attempt to use sheets as canvases for the water-based Tempera paints resulted in a washed-out skyline with grossly bleeding edges.

"What a mess," Laura moaned.

"Looks kinda eerie," Lou Bigelow commented.

"Like a ghost town somewhere out West," her brother added.

"We should start over," somebody else suggested.

"Not enough time. It took two days for the glue to dry." Buddy shifted his weight in the folding chair. "Unless... we could try stapling new sheets onto the cardboard this time."

"Would staples really hold all that weight?" Laura sounded doubtful.

"Prob'ly not," he muttered.

The front door to the sanctuary opened. A gust of cold air accompanied Mickey's entrance. He took one look at the backdrop and smirked.

"We obviously have no art students on this paint job."

"No, sir." Laura blushed. "As you can see, we're stumped on how to fix this." She cleared her throat. "Perhaps we should forget about a backdrop entirely. We can make it work, I think."

As usual, the head deacon didn't give up all that easily. He approached the spoiled landscape slowly, clipboard held tightly to his breast, then came to a pregnant pause. They waited.

"You know," he said carefully, "I might be able to fix this." Again, they waited. "Yes, I believe something can be done." He turned to Laura. "You really do need professional help. That's exactly what you need... somebody to sketch in the edges, like some kind of abstract style. Yeah, I can see that working very well." He smirked once more. "I have someone who owes me a favor, and she's a professional artist." He patted the board gently against his chest. "She lives pretty close. Let me give her a call." Then he was out the door.

"Okay, we might as well finish up these angel wings 'cause, if she can come, it will probably be a while." Laura headed for a couple of folding tables, both covered in white crepe paper.

A few minutes later, Leo poked his head through the front doorway. "Got a message from Mickey! Your lady artist will be here in forty-five minutes."

A cheer went up from the little crowd, and then they went to work. It took almost that long for the seven of them to get six sets of floating fringes glued around the wobbly wire frames.

Suddenly, the doors opened again, and a lady stomped the snow off her boots as she pulled a scarf from her head.

"Hello, I'm Edith," the boney-faced artist squawked. "I'm here to clean up your mess."

Off to the side, Lou Bigelow gasped. "Oh my gosh! It's the water witch!"

***

"As a Christian, you probably don't believe that the so-called goddess, Fortuna, is real anyway, right, Mrs. Bigelow?"

The professor had caught her completely off guard. "Oh... of course not." She smiled weakly. "That would be stupid."

"You'd be surprised how many Christians argue about that," he commented.

The meeting was being held in the basement office at the Collinses' home. George had headed out as though to take his regular evening walk, then cut quickly around to the back entrance of the house. After making sure that only Ma Bigelow had been allowed to attend, he'd descended the stairs and sat down with her and the Collinses.

"I will get to your question about Fortuna, but we need to review a little background first — specifically on the subject of fallen angels." He opened the Bible he had brought with him. "We need to go to the Book of Genesis, the first chapter, to address an odd space of time between verses one and two, where the earth was 'without form and void' and 'darkness hovered over the waters,' along with the Holy Spirit." He tapped the cover of the book. "Some scholars believe there had been another civilization before this time, their reasoning being that God would not have created anything 'without form and void,' let alone without the glorious light of His presence. After all, He is God, the Creator of all things, and why would He have created something so dreadful in the first place? They reason God was actually rebuilding something that somehow got lost under that layer of water that was still covering the entire globe." He glanced quickly at Don. "I mention this because we do know that God could have spoken a new creation, without it having to be first, a place of desolation." Don appeared to agree with that, so the teacher put the rest of it right out there: "Scholars theorize that it was a flooding of the whole earth… maybe for the first time."

"Why would God do that?" Connie asked.

"Same reason He did it the next time — you remember Noah's flood?"

"People were so wicked?" she volunteered.

"So wicked, He had to start over," George confirmed. "But, do you recall *why* they had become so wicked?"

Don grimaced. "I think we're getting to the subject of Watcher angels, who left their heavenly assignments (watching over God's people) because they lusted after the human ladies." He folded his arms. "So, they did… uh… marry these ladies and that's where the nephilim came from."

"Tell us more about those." Ma was curious for details.

"Giants, actually," Don replied. "Hybrids, in fact: half-human, half-angel."

"I've heard that, but…" The little woman looked skeptical, so the professor stepped in.

"Consider this: The nephilim are mentioned in the Bible, and there are ancient hieroglyphics indicating the existence of these giants — some found right here in a United States desert. Have you ever heard of the lost nation of the Anasazi, that disappeared mysteriously from the four corners region of western New Mexico? There are drawings of small, five-toed footprints, being chased by larger, six-toed prints. Yes, that's right — more than one, by the way, scattered throughout the ruins of those cliff dwellings. And, also by the way, they resemble hieroglyphics found in Mediterranean ruins." He pressed a knowing smile. "So, they're well-acknowledged amongst the scientific community, as well as by Bible historians."

Don scratched his chin. "If I understand the story correctly, Noah's flood was initiated by God because the human race had been so polluted by this hybrid race, that it needed to be rescued from any more desecration." He frowned thoughtfully. "And there was something else…"

"I think you're referring to the Blood of Jesus, that would save the lost."

"But Jesus had not yet come, not yet made that sacrifice," Connie noted.

"Right. But the plan was there," George said. "Only, it wouldn't happen — it *couldn't* happen — if the human race was corrupted by being half-angel." He paused to make the point. "Think about it: The Blood of Jesus covers the sin of human beings, not angels." Another pause. "So, when the nephilim died, as does everything else on this temporary planet, there would be no way to save them from Hell. Why?

Because the Blood does not cover the sin of angels — only humans."

"Oh my gawd," the little woman murmured. "So what happened to them when they died, those things?"

"They had been living creatures, *spirits*, like you and me, which never die. They went into limbo, if you will, at least for the time being." He added proof of that for her. "The Bible refers to them as 'shades.' We know them better as 'demons.'"

"So, all those giants, the nephilim, that drowned in the flood, or floods, they never died; they became demons." Connie had never thought about it like that.

"By the way," George focused on Don, "those drowned nephilim… those demons? That's where your Jezebel spirit comes from." He glanced at the women. "But it gets worse: There are actual *legions* of demons all over the world, and very hard at work."

It was quiet while Ma Bigelow took in this new information. She wasn't ready to deal with still another weird entity, "Jezzy-bell" or not. "So, what does this have to do with the goddess, Fortuna?" Her voice was a bit shaky.

"Yes, of course. We need to get to that, and now we are ready." He leaned forward, the white hair glistening under the overhead office light. "We know that the stuff about Greek gods is pure nonsense, but we also know why the ancient civilizations invented them. You see, Mrs. Bigelow, there were gigantic, violent beings ruling over them, only — and here's where it all comes together — they were none other than those fallen Watcher angels."

"But… but what about… I mean, there was Titans and Olympians and there was wars and everythin'. What about all that stuff?"

"Fallen angels become evil, ma'am. They fought each other, for sure. How do you think the Titans got defeated and ended up in chains in Tartarus?" His eyes twinkled, just a little. "It was probably with the help of God, but the Olympians did that to them." He almost laughed. "It was like, well, think gang wars in New York City, with God, Himself, giving the odds a little nudge."

She blinked slowly. "So yer sayin' Fortuna was never a goddess?"

"No, ma'am." He went further. "Wasn't even a female, either."

The eyes went wide. "But she must have looked like a woman. Why would these old-time people be calling her by a female name?"

"Some angels have the power to take on forms, shapes, identities, whatever. The Bible warns us to be kind, for instance, because we may not know if we are entertaining angels. I'm sure you've heard that."

"Um, I think so." A cloud passed over her face. "So-so-so," she stammered, "ain't there no female angels, *at all*?"

"All references to angels in the Bible concern *only* male angels, ma'am." The teacher waited, sensing a breakthrough.

"But-but-but," she stammered, again, "why would God only make *male* angels?" She was baffled.

"I guess that's one question you may have to ask your Heavenly Father, when you get to Heaven, because I sure can't explain that one, Mrs. Bigelow." Wanting to be more of a help, he got back to the basic question. "In the meantime, I believe you had a drawing you had some questions about?"

Her visage brightened, and she handed him the sketch. "Could ya just tell me what'cha think?"

A darkness crept over his face, as he recognized the symbol. "Definitely the mark of the capricious Fortuna." He glanced at her. "Where did you find this?"

"Under a rug in Mickey's bedroom."

His eyes went back to the drawing. "Do you happen to know how large this thing is?"

Don remembered the rug. "About six feet across, I would say, and it's a circular rug, by the way."

The professor's mouth went into a thin line. "When it's that big, it usually means it's a place for performing rituals or ceremonies."

"Oh no," Connie's voice was little more than a whisper. "That would mean...?" She peered into the man's face. "Satanic rituals, right?"

"Right." He handed the sketch back to Mrs. Bigelow. "And you're saying Michael caught the two ladies looking at it?"

"'Fraid so."

"I can see why you feel they might need some kind of protection." He folded his arms, thinking. "I assume these two ladies are born-again Christians?"

"Yup, they sure are, mister."

"So, we only need to bind all demonic activity, in the name of Jesus. That would include anything that Mr. Suree, who *could be* demon-possessed, would attempt to do." He looked at the man. "Don, would you lead us in that prayer, so we can all stand in agreement?"

"Hey! What about *me*? I need protection, too, 'cause I seen a si-reen."

When she finished telling the short version of that experience, the other three just stared at her.

"What? Don't'cha believe me? I'm tellin' ya, it's the gawd's-honest truth."

"But that means those fake goddesses are still around," Connie noted. "So, does that mean there are nephilim still here, too?"

"Demons are demons, and they're not above impersonating a false god, even changing their physical appearances, and creating strange atmospheric phenomena," Professor White assured them. "We know fallen angels have come and gone, and then fallen angels have shown up again during another era. Why wouldn't they be around today? I believe they could be, but more likely, what we are dealing with here are probably scheming demons, masquerading as ancient gods. Yeah, just nephilim spirits, shades, demons, whatever. We call them 'powers and principalities' that rule over certain geographic areas on this planet. And, for good measure, don't forget they are organized, even to having their own royalty and serfdom." He lifted his hands as if to push it all away. "Listen, try to remember that we blood-bought Christians now have great authority over them, and yes," he took Ma's hand, "we will pray for you, too..."

A few minutes later, the professor had one more point to make, before leaving.

"About your Fortuna, Mrs. Bigelow... I came across some interesting information as I went back to renew my mind on that particular character." He had her attention. "Seems she was descended, or devolved, from the original goddess of fortune — a Titan, it turns out — by the name of 'Tyche.'" He paused, then repeated the name slowly. "Her name was '*Tie-key.*'"

Don and Connie spit it out together: "*What???*"

"Yup. I'm not sure how all of this fits together, but it would seem we may have stumbled upon the mysterious 'Aunt Tykie.'"

***

Nobody was telling who squealed, but the Burlington Police Department's detectives found out about the Lady Luck painting, and the rumor that Rita may have had a gambling problem. Inspector McDonald's first reaction was relief — that it was all so simple, after all. He immediately decided not to let Mickey know they were aware of the symbol under the rug. "We can get access to that when we really need it."

"Yeah, if he doesn't destroy it before we get to it."

"That would be a pretty complicated process. He'd have to use paint remover and do some scraping, and there would be fumes and all those paint peelings — not the perfect indoor project for winter months. We have some time." He lit another cigarette. "Besides that, we have two eye-witnesses who will swear in court that they saw it." Then he had a second thought: "I guess we'd better make sure we get signed statements, just in case."

"In case, what?"

"In case they suddenly disappear, or something."

***

The Christmas pageant was presented the Sunday before Christmas, to a packed church. The two Suree boys were excused, but all of the rest of the children — six grade-schoolers, and two teenagers — were recruited for the presentation. That took care of six angels and Mary and Joseph, all of whom paraded into place to the Christmas standard, "It Came Upon a Midnight Clear," sung by the congregation because there was no church choir. The last little angel approached the manger, crepe paper feathers rustling in the breeze, and placed the Baby Jesus doll in amongst the straw, bowed to Mary, then went to his place at the end of the line of angels across the back. He had to give a small push to fit onto the platform, so the whole flock rustled into an undulating shift to the right. That done, the shepherds came forth, two well-disguised men draped in hooded bathrobes and carrying shepherd's hooks that seemed a little short, but it didn't matter because everybody was looking at the little, white lamb they were herding ahead of them. It bleated and wobbled down the aisle to the strains of "Angels We Have Heard on High" until one of the men picked it up and the two shoddy sheepherders took their places to the left of the manger.

The wise men came next, two tall ones, and a short, chubby one who, if one didn't know better, could have been a woman. The stately chords of "We Three Kings" ushered them up the aisle, each one swishing along in satin and velour robes (borrowed from some gracious ladies) disguised in fake fur and numerous foil diamonds and rubies. Only one of the kings lost his crown, and that, just for a moment, since the cardboard was lightweight and easily swooped back into place. They laid their gifts at the manger and took their places on the right. During the finale, the overhead lights went off, as somebody beamed a flashlight behind the star which Edith had sketched in, high above the misty Bethlehem rooftops. At the last refrains of "Go Tell It on the Mountain," the lights came on, and it was over.

The applause was loud, with shouts of "Bravo!" scattered throughout the sanctuary. Somebody brought a beribboned poinsettia plant to Laura, who turned and signaled a final bow from the whole team. Then, in a flurry of crepe paper and discarded costume parts, everybody got ready for the special Christmas potluck.

This time, Mickey and Leo got right into business, working the room instead of helping set up the tables and chairs. They had been at the door, before the actual pageant, greeting and chatting with certain individuals and now, they were right back at it with the same people. Don saw it out of the corner of his eye as he and the other deacons were setting up.

"Campaigning, even during a Christmas event," he muttered.

Soon, the tables and chairs were in place. Two ladies topped them with more poinsettias — make-believe, this time — and the food began to arrive. A few minutes later, Mickey tapped a fork smartly against a water glass, to get the crowd's attention.

"I need to take a brief opportunity here, to thank you all for coming today. We have enjoyed every minute, and I can tell you, this is what it's all about: Being in a wonderful, loving church family. For you who are visiting, if you like what you've seen this morning, we want you to know you're more than welcome to come and join us at any time. As a matter of fact, we're about to have our annual church meeting in January, and it's open to the public for the first time, *ever*. So, if you want to learn more about us, please feel free to join us." He brushed the air with his hand. "But that's enough from me. Hey, I can smell that food, too! Let me lead out with grace, and then we'll head for the buffet tables, okay?"

When most of the folks had filled their plates, Don fell into line behind Harold Taylor. He gave the man a small poke in the middle of his back. "So, just when was it that we voted to open up our annual meeting to the public?"
The prophet/seer snorted and muttered back over his shoulder. "In one of his dreams, that's when."

There was no longer any doubt; the two of them knew they were watching a nightmare: Mickey was stacking the vote, pure and simple.

CHAPTER TWELVE

Delvings

Inspector McDonald leaned forward in his chair and grunted. Here it was, the fourth of January, 1954, and still no real progress in the Rita Suree case. For the umpteenth time, he flipped through the notebook on his desk, hoping to find that buried clue somewhere in amongst the scribbled names and notes.

"There has to be something," he muttered. But after turning a few pages, he leaned back, discouraged. He was pushing the glasses back up in place, when a smart-aleck meandered past his desk.

"Want me to draw 'ya a picture, Inspector?"

When the snickering had finished making its rattle around the room, the man got a grin on his face. "That's probably not a bad idea, mister. Come back here and diagram this thing for me." He tossed the notebook to the smart-mouth. "I want tags for all individuals who are working or living on the Suree property, and connecting lines drawn between them — each labeled, mind you — and then you show me where we're missing it."

"Like we did with that other case last year? That was kind of fun, boss."

"You have fun, my friend, while I take a lunch break."

When he got back from lunch, he was surprised to see all four of his team involved in the weaving of this case's 'picture' on the huge bulletin board covering the south wall of the office. Tacks held names in place, while different-colored strings stretched between them, each noting significant connections between all six people, gleaned from information collected earlier by the Snoop Squad. The list was quite short: Mickey, the three Suree boys, the Spencers, and Sammy Black. These were, indeed, the only persons who had a daily presence on the property where the death of Rita Suree had occurred.

"These connections seem to be running in circles," he noted. "Anybody got any ideas why?" When nobody answered, he ventured a guess. "Probably because we don't have a polarizing point."

"Like what?" somebody asked.

"Something that stops the circles; pulls them all into a point of interest."

"How about the fact that there was a death?"

"Maybe. Anybody else got something?"

"Better yet, sir… how about a *murder*?"

"Okay… anybody else?"

"Or… maybe a *suicide*, Inspector?"

He tapped a cigarette out of the pack. "I don't think that happened, and here's why: Why would anybody who can't swim and is *afraid* to drown, want to drown herself? Think about it — she could kill herself with pills, just fall asleep, and not be scared, right?" He lit the cigarette, blowing a puff of smoke into the air. "No, it probably wasn't suicide."

"Maybe she owed a lot of money, what with having a gambling problem. That could be more scary than drowning."

The smart-aleck spoke up. "Her husband is loaded. She probably wasn't that desperate. Maybe she was just playing around with a cult or something…"

"What kind of stuff is on that mark under the rug, anyway?"

The other three detectives spoke at once: "Gambling… Lady Luck… Yeah."

"More like a supernatural genie or something," the inspector noted. "That's nonsense, of course, but I *am* thinking more along the lines of cult activities."

"So, you think we should be concentrating on that, boss?"

He pointed at the string picture. "Let's try using that symbolic circle as the connecting point in your nice little piece of artwork." He stood up. "Who, of those four on-site groups knew about the symbol, *before* Rita Suree died?" The detective still holding the notebook tossed it to him, and he quickly scanned the notes. "The Spencers knew nothing about it. We should have known that, because Mrs. Spencer was one of the ladies who discovered it by mistake." He flipped a page. "And... mmm... the two boys only knew about it, after hearing the ruckus of Lou and Heidi trying to dry the rug."

"What about the fictional 'aunt,' boss? Anything there?"

"Don't know." He turned to Sammy Black's interview. "Nothing in Mr. Black's statement, either. But then, he just works in the office." He took a quick puff as he turned back to the first page of notes. "That leaves... Mr. Michael Suree, my friends." He closed the notebook. "How about that?"

"Think he did it, sir?"

"Might have." He sat back down at his desk. "Let's think this through, again." He flicked ashes into the butt-filled ashtray. "There's only one way to get into that pond without leaving footprints, and it's on the west side, where a grassy area drops off, oh... maybe a foot down into three feet of water. That's just deep enough to swim, and leave no footprints. Somebody could have coaxed her out in the canoe, then tipped her out and kept her from getting a few feet away into shallower water. Then, when she was dead, could have dragged her body to the north end of the pond, and stuffed it hard into the mud."

"That's where he would have had to make footprints, boss."

"Not if he pressed the body into the mud by walking and stomping on her legs, back, and head, then turning and shuffling out the underwater footprints for a few feet, before swimming back to the west bank. Once he got there, he could have waded, shuffling the prints away again, before crawling up onto the thick grass."

"Wouldn't there be mud tracks as he walked away?"

"Not if he took his shoes off." Another drag on the cigarette. "Or maybe he didn't wear shoes when he was in the pond. That makes more sense."

"So, he probably did it?"

"Don't know." He peered at the rest of the Snoop Squad. "What would be his motive?"

"Insurance money? I mean, the guy *does* sells insurance, so..."

"Nah, we checked that out. The policy was over ten years old, and the man has all kind of assets. Money is not a motive this time. Besides, she was crying all the time. That means there was some other kind of trouble, don't you think, sir?"

"Well, she was pregnant; we know that." The boss watched the smoke curl up toward the dusty ceiling. "It appears that no one else knew it yet."

"Think he killed her to stop that?"

"Don't know why he wouldn't allow an abortion. He could afford that." He took one last draw. "So, gentlemen, it would seem we have no motive."

It was quiet in the room before the smarty-pants spoke up. "We need to put the squeeze on those two broads who found that thing under the rug."

"Oh man, you're something else. Where did you learn to talk, anyway?"

"Okay, okay, I'm not Abraham Lincoln, but there was a reason why that rug was nailed down. My take is that somebody was hiding something, and if that's the case, I can guarantee you, that Suree, or whoever, had to pay those gals off, or threaten them, or something. They might have a couple of leads, for gawd's sake."

The inspector smiled. "This young man just might have something. We need to get some signed statements anyway.

Let's set up some kind of 'casual encounter,' shall we? We don't need to tip off Suree."

***

It was George White who took David and Matt Suree to the boarding school, an elitist institution populated by privileged youngsters, far enough from New York City to allow weekend visits. The Suree boys, however, were a long distance from their Hinesburg home, so there would be no such thing happening for the two of them. On the sad drive back to Vermont, their Uncle George was having a hard time with the situation, until he finally settled it in his head that it was all strictly temporary. "Surely, in a family of seven more siblings, there must be room for a couple of great kids," he muttered. "*Somebody* has to love those guys."

Although the daylight hours were getting longer, it was dark by the time he passed through Rutland. Once he left the lights of that bustling little town, he slowed down, searching the area along the roadside. When he spotted the dented guardrail where Paul's car had gone over the edge, he slowed the vehicle even more.

"Paul... I'm so sorry, kid. I'm so sorry it had to be like that..."

The earth shook, followed by a piercing blast from the snowplow's horn, as it came barreling toward the back of his car. He zipped back to reality and stepped on the gas. The wheels spun on the ice. Once more, he hit the pedal, moving the vehicle ahead, just before the flashing lights filled the rearview mirror.

As he got back out onto the road, he was shocked at how quickly that all had happened. He could have been dead, like Paul, because of a few seconds of in-attention; that quickly, and that dead.

The professor was a good mile up the road before it hit him: "Nobody would have missed me. I don't have a wife, or kids, or even a dog, for Pete's sake."

The car rumbled along through the snowy furrow of U.S. Route 7, its driver deep in thought. At last, the city limits sign for Burlington whizzed by the window. By then he had made some serious assessments on the life of George White.

"Life is too short and too fragile," he told himself, "for any more of this nonsense with Michael. He has fouled up almost every precious thing he has ever had, and that includes his family." He shook his head. "In fact, it's doubtful the man even has a family any more. Those kids probably will never be as close to him as they should be." He was driving across the Winooski Bridge when he made up his mind. "I'm going to put that louse out of business, and then I'm going to take those boys, and have a family myself."

Halfway up East Allen Street, he made the left turn onto Florida Avenue. When he passed the Collinses' house, he noted a couple of cars in the driveway. For a second, he thought about checking things out, but it was already January fifth, and classes would be starting at UVM the next day.

"Nah, I'd better make sure I have all my ducks in a row."

***

Inside the Collinses' house, the basement office was busy again. This time, only Connie was there, hosting Inspector McDonald, Lou Bigelow, and Heidi Spencer. None of them were aware of the professor's car passing by at this seven o'clock hour.

"Thank you for allowing us to meet in your office," the head of detectives said. "It was important that we have some privacy, as I said on the phone, to each of you." He turned to Heidi. "Your husband is at the usual Tuesday night board meeting, am I right?" She nodded yes. "He was aware that you were coming here?"

"Yes. I didn't lie, though. I brought a skirt that I need to have the hem let down, and Connie is going to pin it for me."

"I didn't lie, either," Lou smiled. "Me and Ma just told Pa we was goin' shoppin'."

His eyes asked the question before he did: "Where is *she*?"

"Waiting in the car."

"I invited her in, but she seemed to think it wouldn't be right," Connie said.

"Well, this probably won't take that long, anyway." He flipped open the paper file he had brought with him. "I have here some paper and pens, and all I need is for you two to each write down exactly what happened when you found the painting under the rug." He looked right at Lou. "Did you bring the sketch, miss?"

"Yup." She handed the folded paper to him. "Jes' so you know, I made another copy of it, in case this one gets lost, or somethin'."

"Exactly the same?"

"Yessir."

"Okay, now each of you find a spot here and write down what happened. And it's fine, if you want to talk to each other, but only about what happened when the two of you were together; sometimes one will remember something that the other forgot." He pulled a toothpick from his pocket and stuck it inside the corner of his mouth. "But anything that Mr. Suree said to you, alone, in private, you each put that down at the end of your statement."

Surprisingly, both of them were finished in fifteen minutes, so the detective read them over right there. The discovery of the painted symbol was recalled by each of them, right down to the smallest detail, so the man was more interested in what Michael had done when alone with each of them.

"Like I said on this paper, he was mad. I could tell. But all he said was, 'Here's your check for today. If you ever want to work for anybody else, you had better remember that gossip is the one thing that will stop you from getting that job.' Then he said, 'I hope I never have to report that you have spread stories about the Suree family.' So I said, 'No, sir. You don't have to worry about that.' Then he patted me on the shoulder and said, 'Good girl. See that you remember that.'"

"You got that all down on that paper?"

"Yessir."

"Then, please sign it with your whole name, and date it. That's all we need from you at this time."

Heidi handed him the paper. "It's kind of long, so maybe you should take the time to read it."

"Mmmm." He read quickly. "Threatened your husband's job. Screamed in your face. Manhandled you. You had to defend yourself. Your husband found you crying on your own porch, right?" He asked her to make that clear with a little asterisk note at the bottom of the page, then went on. "So, he told your husband he had fallen on the ice, when he knew you had pushed him. So, he lied, right there." The toothpick moved to the other corner of his mouth. "Makes you wonder why he thought he needed to do such a thing, eh?" He held the pick steady at the edge of his lips as he continued: "Mickey, as you call him, also told your husband that Rita had hired somebody to paint that thing on the floor?" He looked up to watch the affirmative nod, again. "Got any idea who that was?" She waggled a no. "Your husband also reminded you that Mr. Suree was an intense person, and was like that with everybody, so you were forced to apologize to the man." He raised his eyes to look her square in the face. "Mrs. Spencer, are you *afraid* of Mr. Suree?" He watched the tears start to well up.

"Yes. I really am. I want to get out of that place."

"I see. I see. Well, I'm sorry, Mrs. Spencer, but would you please write that down... right there, as your final statement?"

The three guests departed. Connie watched from the living room window as each vehicle disappeared in the falling snow, beyond the glowing streetlights. "Oh Lord," she whispered, "those three may have some idea of the *man* they are up against, but they have no inkling of what *powers* they're dealing with." As she went downstairs to air out the cigarette odors of the inspector's clothing, she came, once again, to an indisputable conclusion: "In order to get rid of this wicked Jezebel spirit, we have to get rid of its *source of power*, which means we oust Michael, or we close down the church, or both."

On the other hand, there was one thing she wasn't sure of: What was the connection between that Jezebel spirit and the Thyce symbol on the floor of the Surees' bedroom? It seemed an improbable partnership, because she knew demonic spirits did not often cooperate, since they were filled with hate, even for each other. The only reason for cooperation was for a mutual goal, perhaps the removal of some barrier, especially anything that kept them from destroying God's followers. On the other hand, they were competitive, in the most evil ways, fighting amongst the different principalities being one of the most common occurrences.

So, there was a real dichotomy there: Were these two demonic beings helping each other, or competing with each other? All she knew at this point, was that both Jezebel and Thyce were from Satan's kingdom… that was for certain.

***

That same Tuesday night, the seven o'clock deacons' meeting became a battlefield. After the usual "old business" was dealt with, Mickey went right into action, pitching the case for allowing new members and non-members to vote on church issues. At the end of what felt like a long half-hour, he stopped talking and called for a vote.

"Wait a minute," Harold Taylor objected, "we haven't discussed the other side of this situation yet."

"I think I've made an excellent case for approving this change in bylaws, gentlemen. I hardly think you can refute my argument, so why bother?" Mickey smiled and leaned back in his chair.

"Oh, I think maybe we might have a couple of good points," Harold stated.

"It will be a waste of time, Harold, but go ahead… I have all night."

"Well, first of all, this church doesn't belong to somebody just off the street. We have worked hard to make this a viable, organized part of the Body of Christ. To turn it over to the general public, would be a disaster."

"If you're absolutely serious about being a viable body, you need to be open to the input of some new opinions. What we have now, is a stale bunch of old fogies. We need to expand, and this is one way to do it… but I already said that. Were you not listening?"

"We were *all* listening, Mickey," Don asserted, "so the real question should be: Are *you* going to even listen at all, to what *we* have to say?"

"What do you think I'm doing? Hey, take your time; I have all night." He was still smiling confidently.

"Okay then, listen to this:" Don leaned forward. "I, for one, will not vote in favor of changing those bylaws… and by the way, I also have all night. Tomorrow is my break day." He returned the benevolent smile to the head deacon. "I can dance all night, sir."

"So can I," Gerald Short grinned alongside his friend.

"Likewise," Harold added.

The smile became a smirk. "We'll see about that." There was a twitch of the pointed nose. "We need new blood, so we can grow. Changing these bylaws is necessary."

"Not an acceptable answer," Harold objected.

"I agree. Indeed, a largely flawed one, to be frank." Don folded his arms.

"I respectfully agree with Brother Don," the soft-spoken one murmured.

"Nobody really cares whether you agree or not, Gerald. You're on your way out, anyway."

"Ah, but I am still here tonight, and still have a vote, brother."

"Listen, Mickey, we need to deal with your trying to get rid of Gerald, so you can get Leo on the board to replace him."

Don turned to the would-be pastor. "Sorry, Leo, I don't mean to be disrespectful, but Mickey has this all lined up, and we know it." His gaze went back to the mouse-face. "We've been watching these shenanigans for months, mister, and we've had enough."

"I don't know what you're talking about."

"So let me explain it: You've been campaigning for months, to stack the vote at next week's annual meeting. We know that you're stacking the vote in every way you can, so you can get Leo in as pastor of this church, and on the board of deacons. You're bullying Gerald to resign so you can get Leo on board, thereby shifting the voting power in your favor on this board of deacons."

The beady eyes flickered. "That's quite an imagination you have there, Don."

"It's more of a collective imagination, Mickey. There are at least two other deacons here who agree with me." He looked at the silent Sammy Black. "But then, we don't work for you, do we?"

Sammy glowered at him, but blinked back as his boss raised a hand of caution. "So now you are attacking these two men, who just happen to agree with me? What kind of Christian love is that?" He feigned shock. "I thought you were a more godly man than that, Don."

"I'm not the one stacking the vote in order to take over this church, Mickey."

More make-believe hurt feelings. "I can't believe you're inferring such a thing, Don Collins. Do you have any idea how long I have worked to build up this congregation, this church?" The eyes appeared to be tearing up. "I love this church family, and I always hoped they loved me back… me and Rita, and the boys." He sniffed through his dry nasal passages, twice.

"And we all know how loyal you've been, waiting patiently in the wings."

His mouth went hard. "Just what do you mean by that, Don?"

The pudgy bus driver waited a bit before he answered. "Just a gut feeling. After all, none of this activity started until Pastor James retired."

"That is sad, do you know that? I don't even want to respond to such nonsense." He twitched in his chair. "As head deacon, I would direct us to the next question, which is...?"

"Whoops!" Harold held up a pointy finger. "We haven't finished with the first one, and for the record: It's not a question, it's a discussion."

"Right," Gerald reminded the leader of the meeting. "We need to make it very clear." He rose higher in his chair. "We three are a majority in this matter, and we refuse to vote to change these bylaws."

"It's us three against you and Sammy, Mickey," Harold was pleased to point out. "And that's the way it is, so you might as well call for the vote, and save us all from a long night."

At twenty minutes past two on Wednesday morning, Don Collins moved that the issue of changing the bylaws be tabled until the next meeting. It was seconded by Gerald Short, whereupon, Mickey Suree declared it passed. The head deacon did not pronounce the usual blessing at the end of the meeting. Instead, six weary men brushed the snow off their vehicles and headed home.

CHAPTER THIRTEEN

Disenfranchised

Classes had started at Essex Junction High School and Diana Bixby was on a special project.

"You won't believe what I found out about the poor farms in the state of Vermont!" Her bright blue eyes sparkled as she spoke to her boyfriend's mother.

"Really?" Laura had not been aware that the girl was even interested in the subject. "Uh… and why are you even, I mean… interested in this?" She put down the holders that had shielded her hands from the steaming casserole.

"Jack told me that you were asking about it." The teenage girl was curious. "Um, do you have a special interest about this part of our state's history or what?" She lowered her eyes. "I mean, I don't want to poke my nose into where it doesn't belong." Her hands folded respectfully across her lap. "I… I have to do this paper for social studies, and Jack told me you were kind of curious about it."

Laura dug the serving spoon deep into the dish of macaroni and cheese and attempted to explain that she really wasn't, but Jack cut in. "Aw, Mom, you talked about this stuff last fall, or something. Didn't your friend, the bus driver, ask you about this?"

"Oh, I see where you're coming from." She sat down at the table, looking over to her husband, hoping he would offer a blessing over the meal. It did not happen.

"Hey," she pushed through the moment, "Don and I remembered a couple of references about poor farms. They probably were real, but most folks don't talk much about that, for whatever reasons."

"But there are records, Mizz Dub-ya! Lots of them!" The use of her nickname for Mrs. Wilson reflected the girl's enthusiasm. "They started way back in the sixteen hundreds. I guess the reason people don't like to talk about those places, is because they eventually had mostly old, crippled folks and just plain crazy people in there. Did you know that? And — oh, thank you." She helped herself to the string beans held out in front of her. "And, we still have a poor farm, right over there in Burlington. Did you know that?"

"Really? Where is it?" the woman wanted to know.

"It's up off of North Avenue, I think. The place is on another street... um... no, wait. It's a road. Yeah, it's on Goodrich Road."

"I never knew that," Laura said.

"Neither did I," Jessie murmured through a mouthful of candied carrots. "On Goodrich Road, huh?"

"Yes. I have a picture of it. It's a huge, brick building."

"My goodness, you actually have a picture? Where did you find *that*?"

"*Burlington Free Press* did a story on it, years ago, Mizz Dub-ya. I got it from their files."

"I'd love to see that," came the reply. "And I know Don Collins would *really* like to take a look at it, too. He was asking if I knew anything about a poor farm that he thought was located on Lime Kiln Road." She stirred her coffee. "I guess he heard about it from his grandmother."

"That could very well be, because Burlington had a whole series of those places, sometimes more than one at the same time." She stopped eating, holding her fork in midair. "Why's he so interested in poor houses?"

"Seems he tried to do a report on them when he was in high school, but gave up on it." She smiled. "Talk about history repeating itself!"

"Except this time, my smart girlfriend got all the facts, and she finished the report." Jack stabbed a couple of beans. "When do you turn it in?"

"Tomorrow morning."

"And who is your social studies teacher?" He stuffed the long beans into his mouth without cutting them first.

"Oh, it's still Mrs. Collins."

Jessie laughed out loud. "I predict you'll get an 'A' on that paper," he chortled.

And he was right.

The next night, Connie shoved a photograph under her husband's nose. "Take a look at this!"

"What is it?"

"A report on the history of poor farms in the state of Vermont. That's a picture of one that still exists."

"No kidding." He was pleased. "Some kid did my report for me, after all these years." He looked at the photo again. "Huge place, huh?"

"Huge. Yes." She was waiting.

"Solid. Made of brick, no less." He looked up. "So who would have thought?" He started to hand it back, but she pushed his hand toward his chest.

"You need to take a closer look."

"Oh-ho-kay." He peered more carefully. "What am I looking for, babe?"

"People. Look at those four people standing on the left side of the porch."

"Which porch? There are two..."

"Sorry. It's the left porch. Take a good look. Tell me what you see."

"Oh yeah, there they are. So, I see an older woman in an apron, then a man in overalls, then a tall woman in a long-ish dress, and then a man — even taller — in a rumpled jacket."

She waited, again. When he didn't react, she whipped out the magnifying glass from her pocket. "Try this," she urged him.

He started with the woman in the apron. "She looks like maybe the caretaker's wife… and the guy in the overalls is probably the actual caretaker. Don't see anything unusual about the lady in the dress, but she's probably one of the poor folks, 'cause she's terribly skinny. And the tall guy is probably one of…"

He stopped and moved the glass closer, then back, then closer again.

"See somebody you know, Don?"

"Maybe." He looked up. "That guy looks just like Sammy Black."

"*Deacon* Sammy Black, right?"

"Deacon Sammy Black, for sure."

***

The annual church meeting took place a couple of hours after the Sunday morning service. Dishes from the potluck were cleaned and back in the cupboard in record time, for all the ladies wanted to attend this one. They scrambled into the sanctuary, just as Mickey stood up to call the meeting to order. This time, he had a microphone.

The usual business meeting agenda was pursued, and then somebody raised his hand and asked the forbidden question: "How come you deacon guys tried to change them bylaws to allow new members and people off the street to come to this meeting and vote?" Mickey squinted and focused in on Willis Bigelow.

"Where did you hear that nonsense, Willis?"

"That ain't the question, mister." He lifted his left ankle onto his right knee.

The head deacon leaned forward onto the podium. "Well, in the first place, it would be good if you — and whoever filled your head with this stuff — would take a good look at those bylaws." He sneered it out. "They are confusing and abstract and nobody could possibly run a church by adhering to them. I mean, they are so vague, there is nothing to adhere to." He let the guy have it: "You *do* know what I mean, when I say we cannot adhere to these so-called rules that nobody understands anyway, don't you, Willis?"

And, of course, Willis did not have a clue what the word, "adhere" meant, so he just grunted and let the man continue with his searing condemnation. "If we are going to have a real solid, godly church, we need bylaws that are clear and concise. I would think that our congregation would be grateful for the diligence of their church leaders, in correcting and updating the rules by which this wonderful little church should be governed."

When there was no further reply from the baffled poultry farmer, Mickey Suree decided to keep the boxing match going. It was time to vote on whether Leo would be accepted as the new pastor. The little pugilist took his time, one short jab after another, repeating all of the man's qualifications and urging the voters to put this good candidate into this position of great responsibility. At that point, hands began to raise across the room. It was the eighth round, and opponents were blocking the punches.

"Could you please tell us how this gentleman got nominated?"

The answer was short and to the point. "By the same rules all candidates are nominated. It's standard procedure," the head deacon stated.

"We were wondering who it was that brought him before the board as a possible candidate."

"Again, it was standard procedure."

"But who recommended this particular man, and why weren't there any others considered?"

"We found no others who measured up like Pastor Leo."

"Could you give us the names of the others… the ones who didn't measure up?"

"What does it matter?" Mickey was getting fed up with this unknown advocate. "You have a board of deacons to take care of these things; there is no reason for any concern on your part."

"But we *are* concerned, and we would like to know how this particular gentleman got nominated, and who brought his name before the board in the first place."

"Look, mister… I'm sorry, I don't recall your name — must be old age catching up with me. Is that happening to anybody else?" He laughed and slapped his forehead, in an artful deflection.

The man didn't reply. Instead, he took his seat again, letting the feeble laughter fall into an uneasy silence.

"Are there any questions about the voting procedure itself? Everybody all set to do this thing?"

This time, Harold, the seer, spoke up: "I think we would like to hear you answer the gentleman's questions first, Mickey, if you would, please."

"I believe I have done that, Harold. The simple answer is that this church body needs to respect the integrity of the board of deacons, and let matters go at that." He patted the back of the clipboard that shielded his chest from some unseen punch to his midriff. "So, if Deacon Black and Deacon Short would please step forward and distribute the voting ballots, we'll get on with this."

The two men began passing the forms down each row, from the center aisle, as Mickey continued his persistent punches. "It is *crucial* that we stick together as a congregation. We need a pastor, and here we have the ideal person to fill that need. I trust that each one of you will do the logical and godly thing." He held up the clipboard, again. "I can only reassure you of my own good motives in backing Leo Spencer for our new pastor position, and I know in my heart, that my darling Rita would have stood firmly on that matter, right beside me, as I fight, fight, fight, to bring the best for this precious church body."

This time the unnamed man stood up and spoke loudly: "How can we hang together, when we can't even get a straight answer from the head deacon?"

"I believe I have answered your questions, sir. It's time to vote."

"Who says?" He looked around. "Are you people really going to vote this guy in, without knowing at least *some* of the details?"

Mickey directed his attention to the back of the sanctuary. "I believe all the ballots have been handed out, sir." He delivered what he thought was the winning punch. "So, by the rules, we can no longer lobby over this issue. It is time for each one of us to vote, without any further harassment from any more ungodly dissenters and troublemakers."

"*Really?*" the man's objection rang forth with bell-like clarity. And then he shrilled it again — "*Really?*" — before he sat down heavily onto the folded chair.

A solemn quiet came over the place, disturbed only by the shuffle of ballots and shifting bodies. Mickey scribbled a mark on his own ballot, then waited until he saw all of the faces raised and ready. "Please collect the ballots, and retire to the parsonage to count them. Deacon Collins, you will be the third person in the room, to verify, and announce the results of this vote."

As the three men left, Mickey suggested a break, whereupon most people moved to the side tables for coffee. There were few conversations going on, other than the occasional innocuous remarks about the January weather and the upcoming basketball finals. At length, the three men came back into the building and folks scrambled back into their seats. The results were announced by Don Collins.

He read the numbers loudly and carefully over the microphone. It was as though his voice was resounding out into a vast auditorium, and then he made the results clear. "As you all can see, we do not have a quorum, and that means we do not have a new pastor." Leo Spencer shrank back in his chair, shaking his head in resignation. It was over for him.

As Don went back to his seat, Mickey stepped forward, nose twitching upon a pummeled countenance. He looked around, going from one face to another, and another, for what seemed like a long time. Then, leaning on the podium, he spoke humbly: "I have to apologize to all of you. This has been a confusing issue for so many of you, and I should never have asked you to vote under such trying circumstances. Yes, this has been an emotional vote… a *very* emotional vote, and as such, I feel I must declare it an *invalid* one. We certainly cannot allow this kind of vote to stand. It is invalid, for sure, and I'm therefore going to take this matter before the board, and we will arrange for another vote, to be taken under more settled, calm circumstances. That is the right thing to do."

A murmur went through the room.

"Oh, no you don't!" The nameless man stood to his feet. "Look, *all* votes are emotional. What kind of crap is this? This was a legitimate vote, buster. Don't think you can pull that stuff on us."

"Sir, if you continue to make threats to your church leaders, we will have to remove you from this meeting," the indignant deacon declared.

The man picked up his hat. "This is not a meeting, this is a failed, rigged election, that's what." With that, he and his wife stomped out of the building. A goodly number of heads were bowed, not wanting to give away their feelings, as well.

"I'm sorry you all had to witness that," Mickey sadly murmured into the microphone. He took a moment to bow his head, as if in silent prayer, then cleared his throat. "We have one more bit of business to do, before we adjourn today." He cast a benevolent look over at where Gerald and Greta Short were sitting. "Deacon Gerald Short has something to tell us." He motioned to the man. "Gerald, would you please come?"

Deacon Gerald Short came quickly to the mic, an envelope clutched in one hand. He looked out over the gathering, breaking into his usual gentle smile. "My message is quite short." He waited for them to get the pun, but few did, most of them being still in shock from the loss of their vote. He tilted his head to convey a bit of sympathy. "Yeah, it is what it is, folks." Then he got down to business. "As most of you know, I have had the privilege to serve on the board of deacons for the last seven years, and it has been a rewarding experience. Greta and I have been blessed many times, as we both did our best for this great little church, and we want you all to know how much we love you." His mouth collapsed from the smile into a tight-lipped grimace. "But the time has come for us to move on. God has other things for us to do. So, at this time, I am submitting my formal resignation from the board, and, sadly, from our church membership, as well." He held the envelope up for all to see. "But we want you to know how much you all still mean to us, and we leave in love... no hard feelings."

As they made their way home through the violet shadows of that late winter afternoon, most of the members knew that it was a turning point. The demise of the Swift Street Pentecostal Church was, surely, not far off.

***

"We never should have gone to that meeting," Heidi thought. *"It was bad enough that he didn't get voted in, but to sit there in front of everybody, a loser."* She glanced across the living room at her husband, bent forward in the chair, his head in his hands. *"And for the head deacon to dismiss the vote. Lord! That probably made people even madder... and not just at him, but — by association — mad at Leo, as well."* Bitterness began to well up within. *"That man is not a nice person. He's a bully and a cheater and a liar. And to think that I actually had to apologize to him for something that he did. If I could ever allow myself to hate somebody, Mickey Suree would be the one. But I can't sink that low; that would be a victory for the devil, for sure."* A sigh escaped before

she could check it, but the discouraged spouse across the room did not seem to notice. *"You know what, Lord? I bet I can tell you that man's next move."* She folded her arms in disgust. *"Oh yeah, his next move is have the board vote Leo in, without the approval of the congregation... and why would they ever honor him or respect his position, then?"* She shuddered under the reality of the vacant seat on the board of deacons. *"Of course! Leo will be voted in as the replacement for Gerald Short, and that means Mickey will have a majority vote every single time."* She added it up: *"Sammy Black, Leo, and Mickey against Don Collins and Harold Taylor. Oh yeah, as Gerald had said, 'It is what it is, folks.'"* She was brought back from these thoughts when a tear trickled to a stop at the bottom of her nostril. "I need to talk to my husband."

He was startled when she touched his shoulder.

"We need to puzzle this thing through, honey." His eyes revealed a deep vulnerability, so she dropped slowly to sit submissively, strategically, at his feet. "Please just listen to me for a minute," she asked quietly. "I can't imagine the embarrassment you've been through today." Her hand reached for his. "How could Mickey have ever thought that you should be there? To even insist on such a thing!"

"I guess he was that sure it would be a winning vote. I mean, he had that survey done, and everything looked good, you know?"

"Well, he was wrong, and I hate to say it, hon, but this isn't the first time he's been wrong." She stroked his knuckles with her finger. "Don't you think we'd better draw back from all our blind trust in that guy?" Seeing the futility flooding into his gaze, she made an effort to enlighten him. "Look what he's done to you, and to me on the 'bedroom rug' thing. He's so driven, he runs roughshod over anybody who gets in the way."

"He's just intense."

"That's a pretty unhealthy intensity, wouldn't you say?"

He drew his hand away and leaned back. "That's not what I see, Heidi. I see someone who could balance my lack of focus, who could be the perfect business... er... ministry partner for me. We balance each other out, don't you see that?"

"Umm, no." She slipped down onto her bottom. "I see him leading and you following... him using you and you letting him..." She blinked back the moisture collecting around the rims of her eyes. "I don't like seeing my gentle, kind, loving husband becoming a tool for an ambitious character like Mickey Suree." She drew her legs around and stood up. "You are the love of my life, Leo Spencer. I refuse to let that man make you into someone I don't even know anymore."

"Heidi, please don't cry. Don't do this. I can't take another punch in the gut today." He rose to embrace his sobbing wife. "I'm no different than I have ever been. I'm still me. Here," he tilted her chin up toward his face, "Look at me. Do I look any different? Huh?" Her eyes were still closed. "Aw, Heidi... please don't do this to me. I need to be a pastor, to be a good husband, a good provider... for once in my life." His own shoulders began to heave in grief. "I... just... need... to... do this. It's the chance I've been praying for." He held her close. "Please don't give up on me again. I don't think I..."

"What are you talking about? I have never given up on you, Leo." She leaned back. "Whoever told you something like that? When did that notion enter your head?"

"I... don't know." He thought for a moment. "Up in Maine, I guess."

"Up in Maine? Who were you talking to about being a failure as a pastor, a husband, or whatever?" She frowned. "You never talked to any of the locals about such things, did you?"

"No. No I didn't. Not ever. I promise you."

"Well, I certainly hope you never said anything like that to any of your fishing customers."

He immediately remembered, but didn't want to tell her. "Uh, I didn't get into discussions like that with those guys. We only talked about fishing and sports."

She stood still, the addition going on in her head. "Except for…?" His eyes focused on the floor. "Oh-kay, Leo. He talked with both of us. As a matter of fact, that man hardly shut up, on all three visits now, did he?" She shook her head at the absurdity. "We told him everything except how often we made love, for Pete's sake." He silently continued to look at the floor. "Wow… how much more gullible could we have possibly been? I can't believe we opened up to him like that." Her hands went to her hips. "You know what he told me about you?" Her eyebrows went up. "He said that all you needed was the right break, and you would become a successful preacher. Almost his exact words, by the way. And that would cure your terrible bouts with depression, he said. Of course, I would go along with that; I wanted you to be happy." She stamped her foot. "That jerk talked us into coming down here to Vermont, to help put his big plan together, don't you see it, hon? We've both been used!"

"No. No, I don't see it that way. I see it as a move of God, an answer to my prayers." He held his hands out, palms up. "It was a miracle! The man kinda dropped into our lives, and offered us exactly what we were praying for."

"Or maybe he got enough information out of us, with all that friendly advice to entice us, and then he put out the bait. And we took it! We actually took it!" She flopped down on the sofa. "And so, here we are. I feel like we've joined the mafia."

"Why is that?"

"We are in over our heads, hon, we really are. I don't know how we can get back our respectability, you know?" She wiped her nose with a tissue. "We've sold out, and we can't get out."

"What do you mean, 'get out'? What do we need to get out of?"

"We need to distance ourselves from this man and his schemes. I don't see anything good coming down the road, if we stay associated with him." The tissue touched the end of her nose again. "Add it up: His wife is murdered and we don't know how it happened; he's lied his way into power over that whole church; there's a creepy symbol hidden under his bedroom rug; and then there's one other thing that nobody seems to be informed about... where did he come from, and what is his background?"

He moved over to the sofa and sat down beside her. "Aren't you overthinking this thing, Heidi? Remember, there's no such thing as a perfect person or a perfect church or even a perfect human life. We have to work with what we have, right? And I think we have a pretty good opportunity here, and I think we should take advantage of it." He patted her hand. "Try to enjoy the blessing, hon."

"Blessing, my foot," she muttered. She would have continued, but the phone rang. Leo picked it up.

"Oh yes, Mickey." Heidi pulled the phone away from his ear, to listen with him.

"Oh my god, Leo. I was so proud of the way you kept your composure all through that ordeal today. It just tells me, I've picked the right guy for the job. You're going to make a great pastor, man. And you will be pastor of Swift Street Pentecostal, probably by next spring. You know, those folks are clearly good people, and they'll come around, once they get to know what a great guy you are."

"Oh, you think so, Mickey?" There was hope in Pastor Spencer's voice.

"Give it some time, my friend. In the meantime, we need to vote you in at the next deacons' meeting. I will make that happen, and then you'll be on the board automatically. And then we can get some things done, finally." He chuckled. "All we need to do is be very, very patient. It will all happen in good time. Meanwhile, I know you're going to be the best pastor this church has ever had, no question about it. And that lovely wife of yours will be the ideal 'first lady' of this church, and she can do an excellent job of it, I know."

Leo took the opportunity to encourage his wife, since she was listening in. "You think so? How come?"

There was a tiny pause before the artful pugilist made his move. "Oh, just because she has proven herself to be faithful and obedient."

The faithful, obedient woman moved away from the phone, and out into the deep blue twilight, to sit down on the snowy steps of the little porch. Pulling the hood of her coat up over her head, she let it all out, shaking her fists into the air, moaning and bawling like a frustrated child.

Across the road, an uneasy stirring rippled throughout the shadowy branches of the tall blue spruce.

CHAPTER FOURTEEN

Hauntings

Don and Connie Collins finally caught up with Diana Bixby, some two weeks after the girl had turned in her report on the history of poor farms in the state of Vermont. Church matters and high school activities had curtailed the meeting, more than once, but here they were — finally — sitting in the second story study hall at Essex Junction High School.

"So, tell me about the report," Don urged the pretty, blue-eyed student.

"Well, maybe not the whole report," Connie interjected. "Mostly, my husband is interested in the photo you got from the newspaper files." She smiled. "If you wouldn't mind, though, I'm sure he would like to read the whole thing, at a leisurely pace, at home, maybe on a day off from work. Would that be all right with you?"

"Oh my goodness! Of course! I'm flattered you would like to do that, Mr. Collins."

"Just need to know what I missed, when I tried it, like, a hundred years ago..."

"I've read the report, and it was full of historic details, so it occurred to me that you may have had a plethora of notes." Connie was hopeful.

"Oh, you bet I did. A whole notebook-full."

"Great. You wouldn't happen to have that still available, by any chance?" the teacher asked.

"Yee-ah... but I don't know that you'd be able to decipher them. They're all mixed up." She perked up at the next thought. "Of course, I might be able to help you on that. Is there something you're looking for?"

"Actually," the man responded, "we are most interested in the photo we just mentioned." He looked to Connie, who drew it forth from Diana's actual report folder. "It concerns the identity of the four people on the front porch."

The girl took the photo and peered closely. "Yee-ah. I remember something about them, but it didn't seem relevant to the report, and Mrs. Collins limits us on how many words." She grinned at her social studies teacher. "Which is probably a good thing, because I can get pretty wordy. My English lit teacher tells me I might have the makings of a writer." She enjoyed that thought for a second, before dropping the real gem. "I'm pretty sure I kept the whole article, and that would probably tell us who these four people were."

"So, how long do you think it will take you, to find that particular information?" Don liked to get folks to commit to a project; it was easier on his impatient nature.

"You know, it might not take all that long, because it was an actual newspaper clipping. A story, if you will." Her eyes sparkled again. "I should be able to spot that thing pretty easily."

"Wow! That's really encouraging." His elfish grin registered the pleasant possibility of getting some answers, very shortly. "So, call us as soon as you find that clipping, would you?"

"Or, how much time do you have? Because I have that notebook right here, in the school newspaper room, down in the basement."

"Really?" Mrs. Collins was surprised.

"Yee-ah. I made copies of my report, just in case. I like to do that. Anyway, my notebook is down there, on a shelf near the mimeograph machine."

"Can we get to it?"

Two senior class students were in the office of *The Commentator* working on a rush job for the 1954 yearbook, so the trio were able to get in, grab the notebook, and get back up to the study hall, where there was relative privacy. Diana flipped carefully through the notes, until the copy of the faded article slipped from between the pages, landing in a slow glide, right at Don's feet. He picked it up carefully.

"It won't crumble," Diana laughed, "it's only a copy." Then the two ladies waited for Don to read it out loud.

"The dateline is October — something. I can't read the day, but the year is nineteen thirty-eight." His eyes moved down the page. *Who is Singing in the Woods?* He glanced up. "That's the headline."

"Okay, babe, just read the article," his wife murmured.

"'In keeping with our series on haunted houses in Chittenden County, this week's story features the strange activities on the Burlington poor farm, located on Goodrich Road.'" He looked up. "So, this is a part of a series being done — obviously, around Halloween."

"Gotcha," his wife verbally waved him on.

"'The property,' he continued, "'is centered between two wooded lots, with several small cultivated fields stretching from the back of the institution, all the way out to Nameless Creek. Caretakers, Ivan and Anna Knight, verified the occurrence of strange music and apparitions over the whole eight years they lived there, noting that the residents had expressed fear of going out at night, especially around late October, and particularly at Halloween.

"'The caretakers reported that another family, the Schwarzes, have lived there, off and on, as long as they have, and the Schwarzes agree.

"'This reporter did verify that information in a brief interview with two of the older Schwarz children, who both claimed to have witnessed these phenomena more than once. Asked why they thought no one did anything about these complaints, they replied that "Most folks just think we're crazy." The young man also stated that it was hard to get and keep work, once a person had lived at this facility. "That's why we have to keep coming back," he said, "ghosts and all."

"'His sister was adamant about the existence of several special ghosts that hovered around the property, singing mournful-sounding songs in foreign languages.

"'Authorities have acknowledged the complaints, but cite the lack of proof as the main reason for no decisive action. Furthermore, the official response has been low-key, a spokesperson from social services said, "In order to protect the privacy and dignity of these residents, many of whom are elderly, or handicapped folks who are struggling just to make it through another year."

"'Meanwhile, those strange events continue to reoccur, with frightful regularity.

"'Next week: The Ghost at Fort Ethan Allen.'"

Don looked again at the photo that led into the article. "Oh, there was a caption under the picture. You didn't copy that part, Diana." He read it carefully.

"'Caretakers Ivan and Anna Knight, Schwarz family residents, at haunted poor farm.'"

"May I see that again?" Connie turned it, so the light hit it more directly. "So those are the Schwarz kids. They look to be in their late teens."

She turned to Diana. "That Schwarz boy looks an awful lot like somebody we know, so we are curious about any relationship that might be there. I wonder if we might get some more information about this young man."

"Maybe there are records. You could pay a visit to the place, Mrs. Collins. After all, it's still there."

"Those places are notorious for being closed-mouth about their residents," Don noted, "and we can understand that; people have a right to their dignity."

"Well, I can tell you something about that guy right now, sir." She smiled. "I took *Introduction to German* for a summer course, last year, and I can tell you that that guy has a German name."

"Well," he chuckled, "I guess that's a start. So, he's of German heritage." He humored her. "Anything else, young lady?"

"Yee-ah, Mr. Collins. Do you know how the name Schwarz translates into English?" Her eyes twinkled.

He grinned, then winked at Connie. "Surprise me," he said to the girl.

"Schwarz is the German word for a color."

"Oh? And just what color would that be?"

"Black," she replied.

***

Somebody turned off the loud music just before Sheriff Maxwell Duncan made his entrance. Two men lay on the floor, one bleeding from the mouth, the other writhing in pain from a badly-sprained arm.

"Aw, for gawd's sake," the lawman muttered. He looked around. "Alright, what happened *this* time?"

"These two — all of a sudden — went at it," the bartender declared. "Don't really know why. Just right out of the blue."

"Yeah, surprised the hell out of the rest of us," somebody remarked.

He moved to stand over the two. "Can you stand up, either one of you? Because, if you can't, I'm citing you both for public drunkenness... and that will be on top of the disorderly conduct charges." Catching the bartender's eye, he inquired, "Any damages?" The fellow shrugged it off.

An amused little crowd watched as the pair struggled to their feet, yelping with each painful move. The sheriff shook his head. "You can't even walk. But I'm going to give you the benefit of the doubt, and say it's because of the injuries." He looked around again. "Deputy Smith was called home for an emergency, so I need a couple of good Samaritans. These guys can't drive themselves home, that's for sure." He waited.

When there were no takers, he sweetened the pot. "No offers? What a shame, because it would be a favor I would probably remember…"

"I can do that, Sheriff, and you don't have to do me no favors."

Max turned at the sound of that familiar voice. It was Walter-with-all-the-kids.

"Man," he said to the farmer, "what are *you* doing in a place like this?"

"Just having a beer, Max," came the sheepish answer.

"You sober, Walt?"

"Ay-yuh. Just got here a few minutes ago."

"Well, okay then. You know where these guys live?"

"Sure."

A few minutes later, the sheriff was steering his vehicle along the snow-packed road toward Route 7. Moonlight sparkled on the rolling fields, where occasional gusts of winds lifted and dropped wraith-like images. It was, indeed, a beauty that only came on a clear, cold night like this one. But the defrosters were working overtime to keep the windshield clear, and the snow tires clung precariously to the icy road. So, the lawman was not surprised when he spotted a pickup truck ahead, nose-first in the ditch.

Approaching on foot, he noticed the footprints leading from the driver's door up onto the road, where they disappeared in the sheet of ice. "Okay, they left it." A quick look told him that was probably a wise move, for the battered truck wasn't coming out of there without a tow truck… or a friendly neighbor with a tractor. Taking out a pen, he jotted down the license number and vehicle make, then called in to dispatch.

"Two-oh-one to dispatch. Two-oh-one to dispatch. Over."

A voice crackled back almost immediately. "Two-oh-one. this is dispatch. Over."

"Got an abandoned vehicle here. Stand by for license and vehicle info. Over."

"Ten-four." The airways hissed for a couple of seconds. "Go ahead, two-oh-one. Over."

Max gave the information quickly, then waited for the dispatcher to get back to him. It wasn't long before the radio rattled back to life.

"Two-oh-one, this is dispatch. Over."

"Two-oh-one. Over."

"Vehicle is registered to one Mr. Bud Bigelow, of Hinesburg. Over."

"Roger that, dispatch. I'll follow up right now. Over."

"Ten-four, sir. Uh, what's your ten-twenty, again? We got a replacement for Smith, waiting to meet up with you. Over."

"Couple of miles to Hinesburg Road. That's a good place to meet. Over."

"Ten-four. Dispatch over and out."

He caught up with the kid, who was slipping across the road to enter his own driveway.

"You okay, Bud?" he called through the halfway-down window.

"I'll get my truck out of there as soon as I can, Sheriff!"

"Get your butt inside, before something valuable freezes and drops off…"

The youngster grinned and went into a heavy-booted slip-slide toward the house.

Coffee break was at Howard Johnson's Restaurant on Shelburne Road, north of Flynn Avenue. Max was glad to be back on sanded road again, although the parking lot was glazed over pretty badly. Deputy Smith's replacement went to the phone booth to make a personal call. Inside, the warmth hit Max in the face.

"Hey!" Don Collins gave him a wave from one of the brightly upholstered booths along the south side of the establishment. "Come on over; I'm buying!"

Sheriff Duncan remembered the man. This was the counselor who had worked with… who was it? *Oh yeah, the*

Essex Junction High School cheerleader, who turned out to be a whole lot more than that."

The handshake was strong. "For Pete's sake, I haven't seen you for some time, uh, *Don*, right?"

"You've got it, Sheriff." The impish smile washed across his face. "It *has* been a while, but then, seeing as how you are the law, that might be a good thing."

The waitress, who had heard the greeting, placed a steaming cup of coffee in front of Max, who immediately wrapped his cold hands around it. "So, what in the world are you doing out on a night like this, Don?"

"Another board meeting. I tell ya, it's getting to be something else, since we lost Pastor James."

"Hey, I understand. I've met your noble leader." He lowered his voice. "Understand he's a suspect in his wife's demise."

"Not officially. But it wouldn't surprise too many people, if it's true."

"That guy is… not normal. That's all I think I should say," Max said.

Don's grin was entirely gone. "And that's the big problem — people are often afraid to stand up to that kind of treatment." Watching the sheriff take a sip of the warm brew, he noted the fatigue. "So, how's your shift going? A lot of cars off the road?"

"Not on my beat. Just one truck. One of your fellow church members."

"Yeah?"

This was his turn to grin. "The Bigelow boy. Had to leave his truck in a ditch. I caught up with him when he got to his driveway, so he's fine."

"That's good. And it's good to have no big problems during a shift, that's for sure."

"I wish." Sarcasm oiled his words. "Now, if we could just stop all those bar fights, a lawman's life would be a lot simpler."

"Had one of those tonight, did you?"

"Ay-yuh. A broken tooth for one guy, pretty painful sprain for the other. Mind you, I've seen worse, but none of it's pretty." He leaned back. "And you know what really bugged me about this particular fight?" Seeing Don's interest was piqued, he let him have it. "The damned bar is owned by one of your church buddies."

"What?"

"And the S.O.B. is, as I heard it, one of your noble leaders. In fact, I wouldn't be surprised if he was at the meeting you just left."

"You got a name for me?"

"I wouldn't want to be accused of any unethical tattling, Don. But I can give you a hint, and you can go from there, okay?" Don blinked in agreement. "First, you should know, we've had some reports of spooky stuff happening on the property... things we can't nail down, that don't sound normal. We have our eye on that little bar. So, bear that in mind when I tell you that the name of that beer joint is... Sam's Place."

***

"Um, Mom, you don't have enough kids in your church, to be having a vacation bible school." Jack pulled a luscious slice of pepperoni pizza loose from the side of the circular treat.

"The ladies tell me that doesn't matter, because these VBSs always attract kids from other churches, and the community at large."

"I guess the real question, Mizz Dub-ya, is, 'Will you have enough help?'" Diana wiped the sauce off her lip with the corner of the large paper napkin.

The three of them were seated in a favorite hangout at the Y of White Street and Williston Road, in South Burlington. It was Jack's eighteenth birthday, and with his father, Jessie, busy at the dairy farm, the little celebration was all the young man wanted. He was more interested in taking Diana to a movie, and then a stroll through Church Street, just the two of them.

"You know, I've already gone down the list, and it seems pretty well taken care of. I have people for games, snacks, Bible lesson, and music. Of course, some of us will have to double up, but," she smiled, "I think we can do this."

"Well, if it gets too tight, I can help." The girl took a long draw on the straw of her Pepsi. "I don't start summer classes until July."

Laura tilted her head. "That's so sweet of you, Diana." She tapped the table with her forefinger. "But, I have almost all of it planned... except... I guess it would be nice to have some kind of setting."

"You mean, like a puppet theater or something?" Jack hunched forward to check out the next slice.

"Hey!" his mother exclaimed. "What a great idea, Jack! Puppets!"

"Like sock puppets?" Diana suggested. "Kids love making those things."

"Sure... sure. That's a great idea." Her eyebrows drew together a bit. "Of course, that means we'd need a theater, for sure." She looked at her son. "We'd have to make something, I guess."

He sat up straight. "Hmm. I guess we could talk to Dad about it. I mean, just the basic thing, though, Mom. Dad and I are not into the fancy stuff; you'd have to find somebody to decorate it, or whatever."

"Yee-ah. Not my thing, either." The blue eyes glanced out the window at a passing truck, then back to Laura. "Do you have any idea who could do something like that?"

"Uh, maybe. We did have that lady artist who helped us fix the backdrop for the Christmas pageant. What was her name?" The two waited for her to ponder that. "Can't think of it right now, but I guess I could ask Mickey." She looked at her watch. "Oh-boy. I'm supposed to meet with the ladies at two." She pulled her purse up from the chair beside her. "I need to get going, and you two should be on your way before too long, if you're going to make the three o'clock show."

She was glad to see that someone had plowed the church parking lot. A couple of cars were already there, indicating the meeting would start shortly. Still, she took a minute to check in at the church office. Mickey wasn't there, but Leo was at the front desk.

"Hi, Pastor Leo." She surveyed the littered room. "Is Mickey coming in today?"

"No, he's seeing customers at his insurance office today. Is there something I can help you with?"

"Uh, well, maybe you can," she said, thinking it was worth a try. "Do you, by any chance, remember the name of that lady artist who helped with the mess I made of the pageant backdrop?"

He blinked rapidly. "I don't, but I *do* have her in the file." He reached for a little box on his desk. "Let's see, that would have been in December."

"Right."

"December, December… yes." He pulled up something that looked suspiciously like a recipe card. "Here it is. Had to call her, so we do have her name and number." He drew out a piece of note paper and wrote it down. "Edith," he murmured as he scribbled it out. "Mrs. Edith Schwarz."

***

The quilting club finally started to meet again, on the last Sunday in January. The ladies were happy to be back, and there was even a new member, Lou's mother. She insisted everybody call her "Ma," because that was what she was most comfortable with. It was one of the things that made her immediately likeable. The fact that she was outgoing and full of stories about music and history and what seemed like countless other subjects, added to the afternoon's bonding. "They like *you* better than they like me," the pleased daughter whispered to her ma just before it was time to clean up and go home.

"Oh, pshaw," the woman replied. "I ain't *that* special."

From across the room, Laura and Connie were having pretty much the same conversation. "We should take a minute to make sure Ma likes it here, and will come back next week," Connie suggested.

"Good idea, and I have the perfect way to do that," Laura replied. She picked up a couple of patches and walked purposefully over to the lady. "Ma," she inquired, "would you take a look at these colors for me? I'm not sure…"

"Oh, they're real pretty. Go together real nice. So, what-cha makin'?"

"A quilt for my son, Jack."

The little face lit up. "Yeah? That's real nice, Laurie. Ain't… aren't you jes' the nicest mama, doin' that?"

"She sure is," Connie slipped alongside her friend. "All mamas should make something for their boys, you know? I mean, the daughters usually learn how to do their own quilts, and sometimes better than their moms, but the boys, well, that's another thing." She threw out a little bait. "Have you ever thought about making a quilt for Buddy?"

"Oh-my-stars-and-garters!" The woman was genuinely shocked. "I'll be lucky to put together a few blocks, or somethin'."

"Really, Ma?" Laura chided. "I have an idea you've a lot more talent than you might think." She pushed around the colorful squares that the little woman had been working with. "Look at these, Connie. What do you think?"

"She has a good eye." Her gaze met Ma's. "You've done something like this, before, right?" Her forehead wrinkled with the thought. "Nobody puts hues of blue together like this, unless they've done something with color and texture before." She worked the wrinkles again. "Are you a knitter, or a dressmaker, or what?"

"She's a dressmaker, for sure," the daughter spoke up. "I have the nicest clothes in my whole classroom, and that's no lie."

"Aw, people learn how to do things, when there ain't much money."

"That's true, but not everybody pulls off dressmaking without the thing looking like a flour sack with a belt." They all laughed, so Connie continued: "So, your mama knows how to put together a nice-looking outfit, huh?"

Lou-Lou swiped the space across her ample figure. "Hey, if she can make *this* look good, she can make a quilt for her son, right?"

"Absolutely!" the two conspirators chorused.

"So, think about it," Laura urged the mama. "If you want to do this, we'll be right there with you… not that you really need us, but we can give you a few pointers on the actual quilting process."

"Who knows? Maybe you'll have a special birthday or Christmas present for your boy," Connie encouraged the concept.

"Aw, I don' know…"

The front door of the parsonage opened, issuing the frosty entrance of the so-called pastor of the church. Leo slapped a stack of notices on a nearby table. "Hey, ladies! Got some guidelines about the VBS next summer."

An awkward silence was interrupted by Laura. "Uh… wow!" She looked around. "We've only had one meeting, so, what's all this?" She watched him pat the stack of paperwork.

"Just keeping things within the doctrines of our little community," he reassured her.

"Oh, sure," she murmured.

"Say," he suddenly remembered, "did you get in touch with Mrs. Schwarz, all right? Will she be helping you with the puppet theater?"

"Not yet," she replied. "I'll give her a call this week. Thanks for the information, though." He waved a "you're welcome" at her as he went out the door.

"Who's Mrs. Schwarz?" Connie inquired.

"The lady artist who helped fix the nativity backdrop," Laura said, matter-of-factly.

Lou's surprised registered in her question. "You ain't talkin' about the water witch, are ya?"

"Well, her name is Edith. Does that mean anything?"

"Yup, it does, and I was here when she showed up to fix the background for the pageant." The young girl turned to her mother. "Ma, is that right? Is she married?"

"Not that I know of. I mean, that's her last name, all right, but as far as we all knew, when we hired her, she was a single lady. An old maid, if you will." She directed her inquiry toward Laura. "So where did ja hear that, anyways?"

"Oh, it was Pastor Leo who wrote it down for me. Should I double-check on that? I wouldn't want to embarrass her — oh my, no."

The little woman laid her blue patches neatly inside a small box. "I would get that figured out, if I was you. But don't worry none about embarrassing that one; she's long past that."

"Sounds like an interesting character," Connie commented. "Why do you call her the water witch, Lou?"

The mother answered for her. "She's whatcha call a 'dowser', a person who finds water on your land, or wherever. You probably have heard of people like that, 'cause there used to be lots of them around. But now, she's all we got in this part of the state… God help us." She stuffed the box into Lou-Lou's quilting bag. "She's one big piece of work, that one."

The would-be VBS director frowned her concern. "I probably should get information on this woman before I get our church too involved with… whatever." She remembered suddenly: "It was Mickey who brought her in, though, for the pageant repair."

"Oh… so Mickey knows her…?" Ma's words seemed carefully chosen. "How?"

"I'm not sure."

"Wait a minute. Ma, remember when the Surees turned that little fresh water spring on their property into the huge pond?" She squinted to remember the details. "Yeah, they had to dig down deeper to set the underpinnings for that heavy stone statue, remember?"

"Right." There was a glimmer in the mother's eye. "And they had a dowser come out to test that whole hollow, before they done all that work." She smiled. "It had to be her. That's the connection, I'll bet." She was following Lou out the door as she reached the conclusion. "So those two must be old acquaintances."

"Wait-wait-wait!" Connie hustled out behind them. "You're saying Mickey and Edith are old acquaintances?" She drew to a stop in front of Ma. "So, wouldn't that mean Rita would be in that same circle?" She glanced around, then lowered her voice. "Do you two have time for a cup of coffee and some pie… at Ralph's Diner? It's just down the road." Her eyes relayed the urgency. "I think we need to talk, privately."

"I… guess we could do that," Mrs. Bigelow whispered.

Laura was riding with Connie, but that wasn't the only reason she joined the other three in the booth farthest from the diner's front door — she needed to know who she was working with on this puppet theater project. From the chrome-trimmed counter a waitress asked if they wanted menus. "No thanks. We just want pie and coffee," the VBS leader answered. After placing four pieces of lemon meringue on the table, the frilly aproned lady filled the coffee cups and made a discreet exit into the kitchen, leaving the four lone customers all the privacy they needed.

"Please tell me all you know about Edith Schwarz," Connie commanded.

"Why? Is she in trouble?" Lou asked.

Ma held up a silencing hand toward the girl, and then proceeded. She laid out the most recent dowsing jobs the woman had performed, including the fact that only two of the men had received "special attention" from this water witch as she executed the search for water on their property. "Two things happened with these two 'fellas': They each had some kind of gold dust scattered over the top of the completed well, along with the usual murmured 'prayer' Edith always muttered under her breath, and then both of these men's families were instructed not to drink the water for ten days."

"You witnessed all of these... uh, six sessions, performed at six locations, for six families... over the last few years?"

"Yes, ma'am."

"Oh, Ma... just call me Connie."

"Yes, ma'am, Connie. But there's one more thing; something happened to those two men that didn't happen to any of the others." She waved her fork like a pointer at a blackboard. "They both started going to Sam's Place on a regular-like basis, even though they wasn't doin' that before."

"Mmmm," Connie mused. "So, Ma, you saw something on the night you slipped down to Sam's Place, I believe. Would you mind refreshing my mind on that Halloween night experience?"

Laura, who was seated right next to her friendly driver, bent forward.

"Nah, I don't mind." She looked at the tall blonde. "I seen a si-reen."

The story took only a few minutes to recount. By that time, Laura's jaw had dropped open.

Connie reached over and patted her friend's hand. "Hang in there... there's more." She jabbed at the point of the fluffy slice. "You all know that I teach a social studies class at Essex Junction High School, right?" Three heads bobbed. "So, I have this student who did a paper on the history of poor farms..."

Nobody was eating pie.

Pieces

"So, here's the deal," Mickey said to Willis Bigelow, "I haven't seen my boys since they left for school, and so I'll be gone for about three days, the first week of February. That's the perfect time for you to remove this painting from my floor. All you need to do, is open the windows and keep a fan going, and it should be fine."

"Sure, sure. I've done this before, when they changed the markings at the school gym." He nodded solemnly. "But this is smaller, so it won't take no time a-tall. Three days would be about right."

"And, like I said, I would appreciate your keeping this quiet. It's embarrassing that Rita had the thing done. It was her idea, but I'd like to keep her memory as sweet as she really was." He had conveniently forgotten Mr. Bigelow's impertinent question at the last church meeting. There was a chore to be done right now.

"Yessir," the redeemed man replied.

The deacon reached out to shake the poultry farmer's hand. "Thanks, Willis." As he escorted the man to the church office's exit, he turned to give a grateful pat upon the farmer's shoulder. "That's just a week away. I should leave next Tuesday morning, and you can start on that same day, okay?"

"That'll be fine."

As Mickey closed the door, his mind went back to the urgent phone call from the school's director. The message was delivered in a high-pitched command: "These boys are going through something above and beyond the usual culture shock of suddenly being in a boarding school. We're going to have to take another line of action, or, Mr. Suree, your sons will be phased out by the end of February. And, quite frankly, sir, I have a feeling they are not cut out for our rigorous program."

"Why do you say that?"

"They have had almost daily counseling, to keep them grounded. They are nearly physically ill, sir."

"But they have lost their mother, *and* their older brother, all within a few months. *Of course*, they're upset; their world has been turned upside-down."

"We're well aware of that Mr. Suree. That's the point. This program is more than they can take right now." The pause was short. "That's why we think you need to come, as soon as possible, to see the situation for yourself." He cleared his throat. "Like tomorrow, if possible."

"Tomorrow is Thursday. I… can't do that… that quickly. I have serious responsibilities here; I can't just pick up and go." He tapped the desktop with one finger. "I could get there by next week, if that would be acceptable."

"Not acceptable, Mr. Suree. Definitely not acceptable. These youngsters need a fatherly hug, if you will, and they need it *right now*."

"But I can't… do that right now. I can't drop everything over here and take off."

The director cleared his throat again. "So, what can we conclude here, Mr. Suree? That not only have these youngsters lost a mother and a brother, but — it would seem — a father, as well?" The silence on Mickey's end was like a black hole. "I think we need to do something, don't you agree, sir?" The man drew a long breath. "I don't suppose there is someone else whom the boys are close to? That would come immediately, I mean." He gave the father time to think, by laying out a possibility. "Then, you could come a couple of days later, and at that time, we could strategize — work this thing out, for the boys."

Professor George White left for New York State, right after his last class on Friday morning. He met with the boys that night, and spent all day Saturday with them before his departure at noon on Sunday. "Your dad will be here on Tuesday," he reassured them.

***

The little group was already gathered, this time in the living room of the Collinses' residence, due to the number of attendees — five being too crowded for the tiny basement office. They waited patiently, making idle conversation, until George came in via the kitchen door, head still buzzing from the long trip back from the boarding school. It was seven-thirty in the evening.

"Coffee?" Connie offered.

"Coffee-ed out." He sat down and surveyed the room. The Collinses were hosting both Ma and Lou Bigelow

"So, what brings us together this evening?" Professor White asked.

"We've discovered some interesting... no, let's say 'alarming' things about Deacon Sammy Black," Connie said. "He and his family were apparently residents of the poor farm out there on Goodrich Road, back in nineteen thirty-eight, or so.

Don quickly explained, as he handed the photo to George. "These look like both Sammy Black, and Edith Schwarz, but are identified as members of the Schwarz family. As you can see by the article, that family was living there, off and on, for years. And there was paranormal activity all during that time. And we have other issues with Mr. Black... like, he owns a bar and there are paranormal things going on there as well."

"Okay, one thing at a time," the teacher said. "First of all, I take it you want to know if these two are members of the

180

same family. Obviously, the reporter says so." He looked up. "So what's the problem?"

"Sammy, if that *is* him, has a different surname." Don glanced at Connie. "We're told, his last name, 'Black,' is the English translation of the German word, 'schwarz,' which refers to the color, black."

George smiled. "Hey! Pretty clever."

"But why would he do that?" Connie asked.

He shrugged. "Could have changed his name for a number of reasons. I would venture a guess that he needed to shake off old labels, or something." He tilted his head to the side. "Not the first time that's happened, right?"

Don agreed, moving on to the next point. "There was also the issue of whether or not Edith is Sam's sister, or just has married into the family." He glanced at Connie. "My wife's friend was told by Pastor Leo, that Edith was married."

"Ah-huh," George grunted.

"And maybe that is important... I don't know," Connie said. "But I'm more concerned about what that article says concerning the strange goings-on at that place. My question is, 'Did the Schwarzes *cause* the spooky stuff, or did the spooky stuff *infiltrate them?*'"

"Oh!" The professor seemed surprised. The drop of a pin could have been heard, while he absorbed the concept. It was Ma who finally spoke up.

"Damned if that ain't an interesting thought, Connie, ma'am." She looked at George. "You remember, Perfesser, last time we met, how we was wonderin' about why there was a Fortuna goddess symbol on that floor, and how that there was a goddess named Tyche that lived before the Fortuna goddess, and how that you, yourself, maybe had come across the mysterious missing Aunt Tykie?"

"Right." He tried to pull it together. "So you gals are thinking there's a connection between the Schwarz family background, and the present 'spooky stuff' going on in

Hinesburg — and maybe even an Aunt Tykie somewhere in the mix?"

"Um, I was thinking it was kinda interestin' how it was Edith, the water witch, who painted that symbol thing on that floor, and how it was all covered up like that," Lou offered weakly.

Ma jumped right in. "Well, it just looks to me like there musta been some weird things goin' on in those two's bedroom. If you ask me, they both knew this Edith Schwarz, and maybe even who this 'aunt' really was." Her eyes narrowed. "And maybe *still is*."

"Right. And if either Mickey or Rita — or even both of them — were involved in some kinda cult," Lou ventured softly, "then we might find out who's the *real* Aunt Tykie, and maybe even how Rita died."

"See, us ladies went for pie and coffee a week ago, and we got to talkin'." Ma shifted her bottom on the chair. "Afterwards, on the way home, me and Lou started puttin' two and two together, and we come up with a little theee-reee."

"Alright," the white-haired professor bent forward in full attention.

"Well, you was talking about how them kinda fairytales about Greek gods got started and then passed on over the centuries, ya know?" The sparse eyebrows wiggled. "What if the goddess Thyce kind of disappeared... um... in chains, I think ya said, Perfesser, and then — poof! — there's a whole new version of the same goddess, only with a new name." She grinned.

"Yeah! Think about it!" Lou exclaimed.

"Like, maybe a demon pretended to be the new version of that goddess with a new name like, 'Fortuna'?" Connie added.

"Listen," Don suddenly spoke up. "Rita was supposedly visiting this Aunt Tykie, every time she had a problem." He shrugged. "What if she *really was* doing that?"

"Although, I don't see how that could happen, when there's no such goddess in existence these days," Connie mused. Then her countenance darkened. "Unless… there *is* some other demonic being, impersonating her."

The professor's interest intensified.

Connie attempted to reach a conclusion. Her eyes rolled up to the right, then came back to focus on George White. "So, we added it all up, and this is what we came up with: Edith and Sammy are brother and sister, and so they have to know pretty much what each other is doing."

Lou swallowed hard. "So, the water witch knows about the bar, Sam's Place, and he has to know about her painting that symbol on the Surees' bedroom floor."

"Wait." George wanted to be sure. "So, you know for certain, that Edith really did that?" His smile was more patient than approving. "After all, you have already changed your mind about her being a married woman, right?" He leaned back in his chair. "I guess you've checked the public records, to be sure of that fact, right?"

"Um… no. We went ahead and assumed the detectives at the Burlington Police Department would already know if she was married. I thought we should ask them, but maybe they wouldn't want us sticking our noses into this case." Connie had a moment of doubt.

"Are you sure about them being brother and sister, Connie?"

"No," came the subdued answer. The little gathering shared a thoughtful moment. "We didn't dare check on that, either. We thought, like you did, that the reporter's word was good enough."

"Sorry. I'm kind of tired. I shouldn't have made that assumption." He stood up to stretch. "So maybe you folks have some facts to verify, before you go any further with your theory." His hands slid into his front pants pockets. "Am I right?"

"You certainly are." Don rose to his feet. "Thanks for some fresh input. It was exactly what was needed."

"Yeah, we need to verify some things, before we jump to conclusions." Connie studied the back of her hand. "I guess we need to check some public records."

The mother and daughter exchanged a disappointed look.

Suddenly Connie chuckled. "You know, if somebody came in off the street and heard our conversation, they would probably think we were all loonies, with all this talk about demons and gods and spooky stuff."

"Yeah. Probably," Lou admitted.

"Your wife just made a good point," the professor noted, as he and Don moved toward the back door. "People are more likely to believe in aliens from outer space, than they are in demonic activities." It was an ironic smile. "Right now, we have stuff going on in Nevada, some kind of a new base, and from what I hear, highly secret. That comment is more relevant than Connie knows."

"What do you mean?" Don's tone was guarded.

"Again, from what I hear, there was some kind of incident in nineteen forty-seven... a crash of an unusual craft, and there may have been aliens piloting the thing. The word is, those pilots, whatever or whomever they were, died, and the U.S. government did autopsies on those bodies."

"Uh-huh, I did hear about this," Don replied. "I was a B-25 pilot and we heard rumblings about that situation." He shrugged. "Of course, we never got any real answers. The CIA is still sitting on that one, I think." He addressed the prof: "So, what's *your* take on that?"

"My take — and that's all it is — is that if those dead pilots were aliens, they would have been more correctly identified as fallen Watcher angels, like the ones who mated with human women. They had flesh, of course, so they had bodies." He touched his temple with a finger. "Think about it: The devil is the prince of the powers of the air (Ephesians two). Satan is the head honcho, calling all the shots. I'm guessing that not only demons, but fallen angels come and go between Satan's realm and earth, all the time. Furthermore, they actually have portals where they do just that, in high places… often burial grounds or the like, where idols have been worshipped for years." He hastened to add a caveat, "Although, I have heard of portals which were shaped like a bowl. Archeologists are well aware of these sites, and they're all over the world."

"Wow!" Ma Bigelow, following the two, had heard that last remark. "So, do ya think maybe we got a portal over there in Hinesburg?"

"No-no, I wouldn't jump to any conclusions. Again, we need to check the facts, Mrs. Bigelow, before we get ahead of ourselves."

"Oh, right," Ma conceded.

"Meantime, I would appreciate it if you would keep my name out of all your investigations, whether it be with the city or state public records, or the Burlington Police Department's detectives' office."

"Yessir. Oh, and many thanks for taking the time to talk with us." She turned to follow Lou out the front door.

Don stepped outside the back door with George White. "Looks like this is going to be a lot more complicated than I thought."

"Oh yeah. And a lot more dicey." The professor laid his hand on the counselor's shoulder. "Make sure you pray over this little group; considering the spiritual angle on all this, they're going to need all the protection they can get."

***

Willis only intended to get a "leg up" on the job, by taking a look at the work area the night before he was to start. Mickey had given him a key to the front door, but he decided to knock, even though the lights were out in both the insurance office, and the main part of the house. He tapped lightly, waiting for an answer, since it was only six o'clock in

185

the darkening February evening. When there was no answer, he noted the empty parking spaces out where he had parked, then concluded no one was home. It never occurred to him there was parking near the back door of the big log house.

He turned the key in the lock, then felt to the right for the light switch. The large chandelier of the great room glowed softly to life. Having been in the house many times for various celebrations, he strode confidently over to the bedroom suite's door and opened it.

He was surprised by the low light of a bedside lamp, which revealed a rumpled bed and items of clothing strewn recklessly about the room. *"He must have left early, and in a real hurry. I hope the boys are alright."* The thought was cut short by thudding and moaning from the bathroom. "Oh my gawd," the man whispered, "he's fallen in the bathroom." He hurried to the open bath door and poked his head inside.

At first, all he could see was the steam coming from the shower, but a rhythmic movement behind the curtain revealed more than he wanted to know. A gasp escaped quietly, as he noted a large foot pushing against the wet floor, just outside the tub, as though to get leverage.

He was at the front door, switching the chandelier off, before he remembered to get the key out. The trembling hands could barely get the job done, still, he managed to get into his car and drive home.

When he got there, Ma was already reading in bed. He entered the room and fell heavily into the chair over near the window.

"What's wrong, Willis?"

"We gotta git outta that gawddim church."

A few minutes later, she was on the phone with Don Collins. "I know we decided to send you to talk to them detectives, but things just got a little more complicated." She paused to listen, then gave him the lowdown on what Willis had witnessed. Once again, she harkened carefully to the man's advice, then said, "Sure," before she hung up. When she crawled back into bed, the scruffy-haired redhead was already there. "What're we gonna do?" he asked.

"Don is gonna take care of it."

"We gotta get outta that place."

"Hmph. *Somebody's* gonna git out, and it ain't gonna be *us*."

He reached for her hand. "Listen, you don't know what we're messin' with here." Her eyes demanded an explanation. "I saw something really… weird. Really weird." He dropped her hand to extend his own, fingers spread wide. "On the outside of that foot… the one pushing on the floor… there was this… thing." He bit his lip, then said it: "That foot had six toes."

"Whoa! No kiddin'!" She seemed more thrilled than surprised. Jumping back out of bed again, she headed for the phone. "You should-a told me that in the first place. I gotta call Don back."

***

Tuesday, Don had a regular day shift, driving bus for Burlington Transit. He slipped into a phone booth during his lunch hour and called Inspector Liam McDonald.

"Sure," the man replied. "I'd be glad to meet with you all. Would you mind if we met at your home again? It seems the ideal setup, what with you folks being counselors; the neighbors probably don't think twice about it."

"No problem." He hesitated to ask. "I don't suppose it could happen this evening… we may want to move on some things while Mickey is still away, and he's scheduled to get back sometime Thursday."

"Like what things, Don?"

"Well, Willis Bigelow has a key to the house, and maybe we could get some photos of that thing on the bedroom floor."

There was a pause. "Excellent idea. It could take us days to get permission to do that, as a law enforcement agency."

"Okay, so we'll talk about it… tonight?"

"Absolutely. Is five o'clock too early?"

"Nope. Perfect."

"How many folks this time?"

Don had to think before he answered. "Connie and me, Ma and Lou and Willis Bigelow — that's it."

"I don't suppose we could get Professor George White to drop by, could we?"

"Wh-what?"

The head of the Snoop Squad laughed softly. "We know all about him, Don. The Feds have been watching that denomination for quite some time. We know George White is trying to get the goods on Michael Suree." There was a low chuckle. "That's sort of like having the fox protecting the hen house."

"Oh." He had underestimated the Burlington Police Department. That was more embarrassing than enlightening. "I guess that makes sense." He thought quickly. "I... guess I could ask him."

"Here's a thought, Don," the lawman suggested, "we could probably help him on his assignment, and he might very well have some historic expertise on all this weird stuff we need to talk about. It would be a win-win situation."

"Mmm, I don't know... I guess I could ask though."

"I can promise to keep his name out of this whole thing. He would be a 'secret witness,' of a sort. We can work something out, I'm sure." He sucked in a weary breath. "We're trying to find out who killed his *sister*, for Pete's sake."

CHAPTER SIXTEEN

Flames

Professor White was alarmed that his undercover status was well known by the Burlington authorities, but it turned out to be a blessing in disguise, for the detective may not have even listened to the angels-and-demons talk, if the man had not been there to interpret, backed by biblical history and archeological finds. Liam McDonald listened respectfully, then, without comment, switched to the more worldly oriented facts he knew these folks were seeking.

"Thanks for making your lists of questions, especially on such short notice." He shuffled through the collection. "It looks like you all have pretty much the same ones." He stretched a grin over the tobacco-stained teeth. "That helps, too." Pulling a pencil stub from a breast pocket, he made a check on each of the papers. "Let's start with the one about the two Schwarzes: Yes, they did live at the poor house on Goodrich, and yes, they are brother and sister. Some of you may already know they live together in a nice little cottage with a white picket fence, just outside the town square of Jericho Center." He looked around to confirm that. "Yes, that's good." He glanced at the lists, making more checks. "Next one is also pretty easy: I would be surprised if they didn't know each other's business. I'm sure he knows she painted the design on that floor, and even what that symbol means and she knows all about Sam's Place, which would include weird things like what Mrs. Bigelow referred to in her list, right here. How could they *not*??" He made a clucking noise. "I guess the bigger question would be, 'How could the Surees not know all this, as well?'"

"Oh, my goodness… of course." Connie shook her head. "They had to at least know about the symbol. Or maybe just Rita knew what it meant."

"Nope. Mickey Suree knew all about everything, all the time… and everybody in this room can attest to that." The detective drew out a toothpick from the same pocket, carefully pulling a bit of lint off the end. "He certainly knows about Sam's Place, because his company insures the place." There was a low hum from the group. "The owner of this little drinking establishment is — get this — a Mister Samuel Schwarz." Another hum, followed by more checked-off items on the lists. "Ay-yuh, the name change. So, that was done according to Mister Michael Suree's instructions." He brushed the next question away with one hand. "I'm not at liberty to tell you how I know that; you'll have to trust me on this."

"Wow! That pretty well answers all of *my* questions," Don concluded.

"Oh, there's more." The toothpick slowly slipped into the fold of the corner of his mouth. "On the day Rita Suree died, she was seven or eight weeks pregnant." He looked at Connie. "Would you happen to have a calendar from last spring and summer?"

"I certainly do. It's still on the kitchen wall." She returned quickly, handing it to the man. He flipped the pages back to the summer months. "Ay-yuh, here we go. Rita was killed on this day, so let's count back to seven or eight weeks." All heads leaned closer as he moved his finger over the pages. It came to rest on the last two weeks of June. "So, she conceived sometime during these two weeks."

Don reacted quickly. "No-no-no, that can't be. Mickey was in Maine, on a fishing trip at the Spencers' place. The timing isn't right."

"Oh, that's correct," Connie chimed in. "That can't be when it happened."

"The coroner was definite," Liam asserted. Then, as though he'd just thought of it, he said, "...unless she was with somebody else."

There was a quick little breath. "That's hard to believe, right?" Ma's eyes moved quickly from face to face.

"Nah," Willis said. "You're right, Ma. I don't see that lady doin' stuff like that." Connie moved her lips, in a silent thank you.

Suddenly, the professor cleared his throat so loudly that Lou, who was seated beside him, jumped nervously. "Oh, sorry, young lady." He cleared again more softly. "May I have a quick look at that calendar, sir?" He flipped the pages a couple of times, then sighed. "Well, I don't know what to make of this, but I might as well put it out there." He pointed to the twenty-fourth of June. "This is the date of a special night, a festival, dedicated to the goddess Fortuna."

"You prob'ly better talk about that, Perfesser," Mrs. Bigelow whispered.

"Ay-yuh," her husband twitched in his seat, "we got no ideer what that means."

"Well, it's... it's pretty much like most of those Greek god celebrations: food, libation, and orgies." He examined his knuckles. "Usually take place at a sacred, uh, sanctified place, with decorations and symbols that apply to that particular god."

The detective seemed like he didn't want to go there. "No signs of such goings-on, as far as the Snoop Squad knows." The toothpick wobbled as he made his point: "Probably more likely that Mrs. Suree had a boyfriend."

"Or... could it be her so-called boyfriend, was instead, the mysterious Aunt Tykie?" George was ready to present the rest of his theory. "Those Watcher angels, or Greek gods or whatever you want to call them, could morph into the opposite sex, or even animals, to do battle or indulge in malicious mischief, or even to copulate. They did it all the time." He opened his fist to examine the palm. "What if the so-called Aunt Tykie was actually none other than a Watcher, who changed into whatever form it needed to, to meet the needs of folks like Rita?"

"But all the Watchers are in chains in Tartarus, right?" Connie thought she had found a gap in that scenario. "If anything from the spirit world could have done such a thing, it would have had to have been one of the nephilim, posing as a god."

She waited.

"Nephilim are the giant children of fallen Watcher angels and human women," the teacher reminded her. "They are hybrids... and the last time I checked, hybrids cannot reproduce in-kind. It's like a horse and a donkey can produce a mule, but a couple of mules cannot produce a baby mule."

"Oh."

"So," he continued, "if this pregnancy was caused by a demonic thing, it would *have* to be a Watcher."

"Um," Lou's inquiry was timid. "Um, does that mean there's demons pretending to be Watchers?"

"Hold it!" The detective's hands went up, pushing the virtual garbage away. "Let's get back to reality, here." He glanced at the lists, once more. "Okay, Mr. Bigelow, it seems you witnessed some queer activities in the Suree bathroom, a day or so ago. I need to get a statement from you on that, but it may not have anything to do with the death of Rita Suree. I hope you understand that." He acknowledged the nod from the poultry farmer. "And, at this point, probably is not viable evidence, since you have no collaborating witnesses."

"I know what I saw."

"Yessir, and I respect that. I even believe you. But bringing up charges like that, right now, may not be a good idea."

"But what about them six toes?" Ma interjected. "That's got to mean *somethin'*."

Professor White bent toward Lou's father. "What's all this? I haven't heard any of this information."

"You can talk about this later, gentlemen," Liam said.

"No-no," George insisted, "this could be crucial."

"You have two minutes to convince me."

"But I need time to interview him, myself. This is not practical."

"Right." The head of the Snoop Squad leaned back in his chair. "I propose that you and I pursue this subject at another time, when we can be better-informed, and not rushed." He flashed his yellow grin once more. "How about it?"

The professor was a reasonable man, and he knew Inspector McDonald was right this time. "I agree. But," he looked straight at Willis, "I want... no, I *need* to hear all about this, understand, sir?"

"Alright." The detective took one last, quick look at the lists. "The last question is confusing." He glanced up at nobody in particular, then went right back to one of the pages. "Are Sammy and Edith involved in some kind of cult that makes all the spooky stuff happen?" He wiped a hand across his brow. "All we have on that, is what's in that old newspaper article, and what a couple of you have claimed to have seen, or whatever." His shoulder slumped. "I have no way in the world of knowing this stuff. I cannot answer you, because I don't know." The laugh was ironic. "Sorry. I don't even know *who* or *where* to send you for an answer." He shrugged. "That's it."

"Sure, Inspector, we understand." Don rose, signaling the end of the meeting.

Liam escorted Willis down to the basement office, wanting that interview before he left the Collinses' home. Connie took Ma and Lou into the kitchen. By the time the ladies brought forth a refreshing cup of tea and some peanut butter cookies, Don had filled George in on the whole bathroom incident which Willis had witnessed. George's face was white with rage. He did not stay for the refreshments.

Fifteen minutes later, the two men came up from the basement; Willis was quiet, and ready to go home. But the evening was not quite over.

"Oh!" the detective seemed to have one more thought, as he started out the door. "Just wondering. Is there any other person who knows the story about your encounter with the siren?"

The little woman stopped buttoning her coat, to think. "Uh, I guess that would be Laura... right, ladies?" There were two nods. "She was there at the diner with us, when I talked about it."

"Laura who?" he asked.

"Wilson," Connie said, reluctantly. "Why?"

"We should probably keep that kind of talk quiet. It may damage our investigation." He displayed that rusty grin again. "We want to find out who killed Rita Suree, now, don't we?"

The last vehicle pulled away, and Florida Avenue settled into a quiet peace. Night had fallen, and a little more snow. Windows glowed softly from the velvety row of cozy homes along the street. Don and Connie stood gazing out into that postcard-perfect scene.

"You know what, babe?" he finally asked.

"What?"

"This whole house smells like a dirty ashtray."

"That poor man has *no clue*, does he?"

"Right. Open every window and door, for at least a half-hour, and don't forget the basement windows."

"Right." But she wanted to give credit, where it was due: "Not that the man didn't help us. I mean, he brought up some interesting stuff tonight. Stirred up a few little fires, I think."

"Yup," he agreed, as he opened another window. "He did make us think."

She was on her way down to air out the office when she hit on the real point: "It's like that old saying: 'Where there's smoke, there's fire.'"

"Yeah?" He was opening the back door, so he turned and looked down the stairs at her. "And there was a real smokescreen, now that I think of it. I get the feeling the detective wasn't telling all he knew. I think that guy is onto somebody, or something, and it's likely something that is concealing a huge conflagration." He turned to stare out into the shadows of the backyard snow. "How do we get up close to that kind of information, I wonder?"

He heard her laugh softly as she got to the bottom of the stairs. "I guess we need to trust the Holy Spirit to get us through the smoke."

***

Because he had not started the job on Tuesday, as he had promised Mickey, Willis drove into the parking lot of the big log house, very early, in the soft glow of that Wednesday dawn. He had barely two days to get the job done, so he unlocked the front door and began to quickly unload the equipment. When all items were in place, he soaked the painted symbol with paint remover. It would have to remain in place for the recommended period of time, loosening the layers until they began to bubble up, ready for scraping. He worked feverishly, until he was satisfied the whole symbol was sufficiently soaked, then stood back, choking. There was no time to stop and open the windows, even if he had thought of it. To escape the fumes, he slipped out onto the patio, where he sat down on a bench, gasping for breath. Eventually, he relaxed, for the air was fresh and restorative, so he decided to linger for a little longer. It would be a while before the paint remover would work, and the view was pretty nice, as well, with it being daybreak, and all.

Indeed, for the next few minutes, he enjoyed a glorious sunrise. He marveled at the drama unfolding before him, moment-by-moment. Along the horizon, clouds floated like foam in a bathtub, glistening with yellow reflections from some unknown source. The fluffy surface dissolved and evolved, changing with each passing second. Suddenly, down toward the guest cottage, a flock of birds swooped upward, silhouetted by that iridescent bank of lemon-tinted fluff.

"What a pretty picture," he light-heartedly murmured to himself.

And then he remembered about the camera. "I was s'pposed to get a picture of that thing before I scraped it off." He wobbled over to the car, grabbed the camera, and popped a flash bulb into the reflector. "I only need one shot," he murmured as he swayed his way back into the house.

What happened next was the subject of speculation in Hinesburg for years. It was never definitely decided whether it was a camera flash, or a light switch, or even an accidental sparking of some sudden metal-against-metal. All that folks knew, was that something caused the explosion.

The reverberations were felt by the Spencers, who had just finished breakfast. By the time the fire department got there, half of the Suree bedroom was in ashes, and the surrounding areas severely damaged. Willis P. Bigelow was thrown out into the living room, his heavy canvas coveralls smoldering like a burnt log.

CHAPTER SEVENTEEN

Building

"Oh no, oh no," Laura whispered into the phone. Jack and Jessie watched her head bow low, before Jessie turned off the *Jack Benny Radio Show*. They listened quietly until she finished the conversation. "Yes. Yes, I will pass the word. Please keep me informed, will you, Harold?" She wiped the wetness away as she explained: "There was a terrible explosion and fire this morning at the Suree house. That was Harold, one of the deacons, alerting the prayer line. I'm the last one on the list, so he just got around to me."

"What happened?" Jessie pulled her down beside him on the sofa.

"Willis Bigelow was..." she suddenly remembered not to tell about the symbol. "He was removing paint from the bedroom suite, and there was an explosion."

"That's dangerous work, especially this time of year. You have to make sure to ventilate." He kept her hand in his. "Is the man okay?"

"Harold says Willis had his hands up in front of his face, and was wearing heavy clothing, so the burns weren't too bad in the covered places, but they figure he'll probably lose some fingers, or maybe even his whole hands."

"Aw, Mom, that's a rough one."

"Is there something we can do?" Jessie gave her hand a light squeeze.

"He's in the hospital, of course, and Ma and the children are determined to keep the farm going. But there are two things needed: Prayer for the Bigelow family, and *men* — workers to help put up temporary walls on the burn site." She looked at the two guys in her life. "I know you are both already too busy, but maybe we can find a way to help with that project."

"When are the guys going to do this?" The dairyman was already figuring out a way.

This Friday morning. Mickey is on his way back from New York tonight, and will be ordering lumber supplies tomorrow."

"That's Thursday," Jack noted.

The two Wilson men exchanged a look. "If we can get Kevin and Joseph to cover for us on that one day," Jack suggested.

"We'll have to give them overtime," his father said.

"I'll give up a day's pay, Dad. This is important."

Laura didn't know whether to laugh or cry. "Hey! You *do* remember that I know how to attach a milking machine, and scrape gutters, don't you?"

And so it was settled.

On Friday morning, the two Wilsons joined the whole board of deacons, Pastor Leo, and two more volunteers, who, though older, made up for it in enthusiasm. Don Collins managed to swap a shift with somebody who had an anniversary the following week, and that made a grand total — including Mickey — of ten men.

The fire department had finished its investigation by Thursday, so the men began to remove the rubble immediately. Handkerchiefs covered the faces of the determined clean-up crew, as dust and ashes rose under each sweep of the rakes and shovels. Don kept watch over the two older men, moving them to the perimeters, where there was less debris in the air. "Take everything off the desks and tables in those damaged offices, and place them in these boxes. They're important to the business, guys."

"What about what's in the drawers of this desk?" one of them asked.

He tugged at the bottom left drawer of Mickey's scorched desk, and, to his surprise, it slid open. "Just put each drawer's contents into a separate box."

The thing was right there, in front of him; a kind of handbook, rather old and tattered, but with the title still legible: *Rituals of Ancient Greek Gods*. Quickly, he grabbed a half-burnt newspaper off the top of the desk and dropped it onto the yellowed handbook. "Here," he said to the elderly gentleman, "let me help get you started."

A few minutes later, the drawer was emptied, whereupon, Don fan-closed the top of the box, and marked an "X" on the side. Not long after, he moved that box over next to what would be the new office entrance to the repaired house. Then, while the guys took a lunch break on the patio at noon, he flipped the box open and slipped the handbook under his overalls, sneaking it all the way to his own car. He knew he had made an important find, maybe one that would put a lot of things in perspective.

But the *real* discovery came in midafternoon, while he and the older men were cleaning the demolished living room. "This fireplace is still in pretty good order," one of the older workers surmised. "Look! The grate is still in place, and there is still a working damper. Take a look at this."

Don paused, weary from the day's labor. He dragged the push-broom behind him as he sought to respond to the excited request. After all, those two had hung in there all day, and they deserved a little respect.

The man spoke with real authority. "I seen a lot of fireplaces in my day, and this is a damned good one." He motioned Don to crouch down and take a look. "See that?" The weathered finger was pointing up at the damper. "That's quality, mister, that's stuff that will last forever."

Don pretended to take a close look. "Hey, I believe you're right. Look at that, it still flips back and forth…"

The soot hit him hard in the face, covering the handkerchief so thickly that he pulled it off, just to breathe, but it fell into the rubble of the hearth, raising a puff of ash. Mr. Collins sat back on his haunches, letting the other two enjoy the gleeful mishap. Then, knowing he still needed that covering for his face, he pulled the dirt-laden thing out, intending to give it a bit of a shake before putting in back over his face.

And there it was, under a thick layer of litter — the camera.

He noted there was a spent flash bulb in the reflector. It had to be the photographic evidence of the Fortuna symbol. The handkerchief was dropped quickly back down. "Hey, guys, could you get me some water? I have a lot of crap in my eyes."

"Oh, for Pete's sake, Don. We're so sorry." There was a scramble as the two went to the rescue.

Don wiped his eyes with the damp rags the two brought, then ambled slowly out to his car, still wiping and blinking. He had to sit there for a few minutes, of course, to recover.

At four o'clock that afternoon, Don had to leave, for his eyes were "bothering" him. Once home, he contacted Inspector McDonald.

"Sure, I can drop them off, if you're still in the office at five-thirty or so. Connie and I will be going up to the hospital to pray with the Bigelow family."

***

By sundown, the last plywood panel was in place, and all blown-out windows had been covered with heavy plastic or tarps, bringing the Suree house back to somewhat livable status. Mickey thanked the crew as they packed up, before rumbling slowly down the icy road, heading home from a long day's work.

Leo looked at his mentor. "Heidi has been cooking up a storm all day. She wants you to join us for supper."

"Oh, that would be so nice, Leo."

She didn't really want the man to join them for dinner, but went through the motions, anyway. Time was needed for the two men to shower and change into clean clothes, so the meal was served at six-thirty or so, on a small table in the guest house. Leo said a perfunctory prayer over the food.

"I love pot roast, Heidi," the weary leader smiled. "Thanks so much for inviting me."

"Not at all, Mickey. You've had a rough day." She carefully placed the brimming gravy boat in its place beside the platter of beef and vegetables.

"More like 'a few rough weeks,'" her husband concluded. "I don't know too many people who could handle all that *you* have, in such a short time, and still be standing strong."

"Thanks. It has been quite a ride, what with the transfer of leadership at the church, and Rita's passing, and then Paul, and now, the other two boys."

She handed him the serving fork for the platter. "How *are* the boys, Mickey?"

He lifted a slice of roast beef and a large chunk of carrot onto his plate. "It's rough for them, right now." The potato and onion were scraped off onto the empty spot beside the meat on his plate. "But, life is not easy, and the sooner they learn that, the better."

"Sadly, that is so true," the would-be pastor commiserated, as he passed the gravy. "But still, if there is anything Heidi and I can do, please let us know. We will help in any way we can."

Heidi nodded in agreement, but her attention seemed to be on offering the homemade applesauce to her husband.

The remainder of the meal was filled with comments on how well the work crew had functioned over the course of the day, and ideas on how to complete the repairs, including — if the insurance coverage allowed it — some improvements, like better office space and more security, maybe even more fire-prevention measures. The two men tossed ideas around, until the last bite of ice cream was devoured, and then it was time for Mickey to go home.

"Well," he said as he left, "at least I have a couple of other bedrooms I can use… smoky, though they may be."

"Oh, hey!" Leo blurted out, "you can always bunk down here in the second bedroom. We'd only need to move some of the junk out of the way."

"No-no. I'll be fine. I have some things I need to work on, and I wouldn't want to keep you up all night." He pulled his jacket close across his chest, and disappeared into the night.

He was helping her do up the dishes, even though he was physically at the end of his strength. Manual labor was not his style, since leaving Maine. He shook his shoulders to loosen the muscles, once the last plate was back into the cupboard. "Man, I need to hit the hay, sweetheart." He bent close to kiss the blush of her cheek, but she pulled back, turning those huge eyes toward him. He stiffened. "What???"

"I know you're tired, Leo, but how could you have missed it?"

"What?" he repeated.

She slapped the dishcloth into the sink. "That man has ice water in his veins, I swear." His mouth dropped open, but there were no words. "Leo! For heaven's sake, the man talks about the death of his wife and son like there was a change in the weather!" She blinked an "Are you listening?"

"Uh… I didn't see that, Heidi."

"Look again!" There was a sharpness in her voice this time. "The first thing on his list of trials, was the 'transfer of leadership' in our church, *not* the deaths of his wife and oldest son." Her look intensified. "What does that tell you?"

"Oh no, hon, — just a slip of the tongue. The man is in a temporary slump."

"But not so devastated that he has a real concern about his other two sons, who are conveniently stashed away in some school that is too far away for them to even see their father on a normal weekend." This time, there was a glare. "Would *you* do that to our children, Pastor Leo Spencer? Hmm?" She was clearly angry. "Because, if you would, I don't want to even be around you, any more, *ever*."

He followed her to the bedroom door, head spinning. "Wait a minute. Where did all this come from?"

"It comes from a gut feeling. It comes from what I keep hearing from that man's mouth." She pulled the bedspread back from the pillows. "In your whole conversation over this supper, did he even mention Willis Bigelow? Hmmm? No, he did *not*." Her fist punched a pillow. "That man has a freezing-cold heart; he doesn't really *love* anybody… not even himself."

He needed to take control. "Okay, Heidi, you need to stop this nonsense. It's not your place to pass judgment here."

"Really?" She yanked the spread to a half-fold, and threw it onto the floor. "How about if I avoid making judgments, and just use plain, old, spiritual discernment?" She kicked the rumpled bedspread toward the door, before she threw one of the pillows at it. "And how about if you take a long, hard look at the facts, before you get back into the marriage bed, mister?"

He was speechless.

One last kick sent the bedding all the way through the doorway, almost knocking him off his feet. Before ending the conversation, she gave him one more thing to think about: "How about the possibility that your wonderful mentor is nothing less than a cold-blooded murderer?"

"What are you talking about?"

"He killed his wife, Leo. That's what I'm talking about."

Then she slammed the door, and locked it.

"We're not supposed to go to our marriage bed angry," the man moaned through the door jamb.

"No problem," she called back, "you're out there, and I'm in here, and so we're definitely *not* going to the marriage bed."

***

"I have to say," Jessie commented as he crawled under the covers, "that was a hard-working bunch of guys."

Laura's heart warmed.

"But Michael Suree is one focused, business-like character."

"Oh?"

"Ay-yuh." He scratched his mid-drift. "Never told us how it happened, or how the Bigelow family was doing." There was a prolonged yawn. "Just took charge and got things done."

"Oh?"

"Mmmm. Like he was in charge of a hurricane mop-up, or something." He turned to look at her. "So how *is* Mr. Bigelow, anyway?"

"In a lot of pain, but it could have been much worse, you know?"

"Who's taking care of the chickens?"

"One of the neighbors has a couple of teenage-ish girls, old enough to cover things for the weekend,"

"That's good." He yawned again, turned onto his side, and scrunched the pillow. "'Night, Missus Dairyman."

"'Night, Mister Dairyman." She cuddled down, smiling. *"One inch at a time, right, Lord?"*

***

The camera was dirty, but a quick wipe with a moist finger showed there was film inside. Slowly, he wound the remaining length onto the receiving spindle, until it stopped. Liam McDonald opened the Kodak Hawkeye Brownie carefully, without removing the flash attachment, not wanting to destroy evidence, just in case. The detective slipped the exposed film and the camera into separate plastic containers and set them aside.

It was the worn booklet on Greek gods that interested him.

"I'll need coffee," he told himself.

The evening passed, and it was finally the last page of the instruction booklet, when Liam looked up at the clock. "Okay, I need to get out of here." On the spur of the moment, he tucked the booklet inside his overcoat, before stepping out into the winter night.

The short walk to his bachelor's apartment on King Street woke him, the cold air whipping against his face. A motive for murder emerged, as the brain fog dissipated. When he finally slipped into the comfort of home, he was feeling quite satisfied. "He knew very well, he was in Maine when she got pregnant."

It was now clear that Mr. Michael Suree was familiar with the fundamentals of this Greek goddess thing. Further, if Inspector McDonald's hunch was right all along, that knowledge was exactly what that crafty killer had to have. Still, before proceeding any further, he needed to confer once again with the professor.

CHAPTER EIGHTEEN

Oddities

The three of them were walking along the snowy edge of the Jericho Center green. Greta's mother had been living at Maude's Nursing Home for over a year. She was still physically quite strong and loved these walks when Greta and Gerald came up to visit. She could have lived alone back there in Burlington, but loss of her short-term memory resulted in too many dish towels burned on the stove, and so something had to be done. Her long-term recollection, however, was excellent. On more than one occasion, her schoolteacher background helped her relate an interesting tidbit from the past. "Historical records show that this was called the Congregational Church green, way back in nineteen-thirteen," she informed the couple.

"Is that right, Mother? And how do we know that?" Greta asked.

"Read some of the town history once."

"Wow! That goes back pretty far, Millie," Gerald remarked. "What makes it so special that you remembered it?"

"They were having some kind of celebration about prohibition or something, right here in this park... I mean, green." She smiled. "They must have had a lot of trees around, because some of the young men cut down a whole bunch of them and stuck them into the ground, for shade around the picnic tables. Can you imagine?"

"Outlandish," Greta commented, as they ambled slowly by a driveway just past the historic Congregational Church. Anna's eyes focused on a little house, halfway up the drive. It was surrounded by a white picket fence. "Those are two very odd people."

The other two zeroed in on the dwelling.

"What do you mean?" He was puzzled, for the place appeared neat and clean.

"Something going on there, if I was to make a guess about those two. Brother and sister, somebody said."

They strolled farther along, waiting for the rest of her assessment. "He works somewhere, but she mostly sits on the back porch and paints pictures... mostly landscapes, I think, but I'm not sure... can't remember. But they're weird people, just the same."

"Why do you say that, Mother?"

The little woman stopped and turned around, to point at the back of the nursing home. "See that top row of windows at the home?" They nodded. "Well, my window is the one closest to us. I can see those folks' whole backyard from there."

"Oh, my goodness. I bet you can." Gerald mentally measured the distance between the window and the backyard of the small house. "So, tell us why you think things are not normal over there."

"Some curious things going on, whenever they have a visit from that little woman with the curly black hair. Blue lights in the backyard at night, and even some kind of praying and singing, if you can imagine, even in the dead of winter." She shook her head before turning to continue the walk. The other two bent closer to hear the rest of it. "Most people can't see it, but I can. Angela's — I think that's her name — Angela's room is right next to mine, and she could see it, if she could even see, but she can't. I'm probably the only one in — uh — what's the name of this town?"

"Jericho Center," they replied in unison.

"Anyway, I can see it very well, and there's nothing wrong with my hearing either."

The rest of the stroll was made in relative silence. When they got back to the large front porch, she wanted to sit out on the porch swing, even though it was still February. Greta grabbed a heavy throw from off one of the rocking chairs and slid onto the swing beside the rosy-cheeked lady.

Gerald signaled he was going inside to the office, where they always made the monthly payment. The warmth touched his nose as he entered the office, off to the right of the main entrance. No one was there, but he pulled out his checkbook, tapped it lightly on his other hand, and looked around. The office was the picture of busyness, with papers overflowing from the in and out boxes on the cluttered desk. Still, it was rather a pleasant atmosphere. He attributed that pleasantness, in part, to a lovely painting on the wall, to the right of the door.

It was an autumn landscape, featuring a field of wild grasses bending in the wind. Dark clouds moved across the top of the picture, parting just enough to let a shaft of transparent blue light descend boldly toward something just over the hill. It was as intriguing as it was beautiful. Curious, he rose to peer closely at the signature. It was written in small script, on the lower right corner: "E. Schwarz."

The home director bustled into the room. "Oh, Mr. Short, I see you're admiring our painting."

"I am," he replied as casually as he could. "Do you happen to know where it came from?"

"From right up the hill. Edith donated that painting last year."

They sat with Millie a while longer on the porch, while she told them more about the prohibition celebration, and how there were whole roasted pigs served, along with big tubs of rice pudding, and there was even a special committee for the music. At length, she wound down, silently watching the traffic pass by.

"Are you ready to go inside and get warm?" Greta asked.

"I think so." She stood up with barely a wobble, casting one last look at the vehicles rattling by at twenty miles per hour. "My land," she said, "look at those things go lickety-split!"

***

Don Collins got two phone calls that night: one from Gerald Short, and one from Harold Taylor, the seer.

"I have a feeling Edith is involved in some kind of witchcraft," Gerald said softly. He went on to tell of the visit to Jericho Center. "I urge you to look into the matter, or at least let the authorities know." He cleared his throat. "Just so you know, Greta and I suspected something under that bedroom rug, all along. When we were cleaning up after the fire, I did see remnants of brightly painted wood, so I'm assuming there was a hidden message or something. Anyway, it was probably not just redoing the bedroom floor, like Mickey said."

"By the way, Gerald, I want to commend you for coming out to help. After the way that man treated you, you had plenty of reason to not be there."

"Sure. No problem." He needed to get back to the subject. "I am also concerned that if Edith is involved in some kind of cult, or whatever, then it would also make sense that Sammy would be in — probably up to his neck. You know, he seems to be more of a follower, than a leader."

"You may have a point there."

"It bothers Greta and me… this long delay of finding out what happened to Rita." Drawing on a hidden boldness, he dropped the information into Don's lap. "We've seen too many odd things with Mickey and Rita. Something has been very, very wrong, for a long time… and… we feel there is intense demonic activity in this whole situation."

"I see." Don took in a breath, but decided not to comment on the Jezebel thing. "I guess you two aren't the only ones."

He needed to draw this talk to a close. "Well, keep in touch with me, would you, Gerald? Inspector McDonald will probably want to talk with you two."

"Of course. Have him call, whenever he's ready."

Don was making some quick notes, when Harold's call came.

"You got a few minutes?" The tone was tentative.

"Sure, Harold." He put down the pencil and waited.

"Is Connie around?"

"No, she's not. Do you need to talk with her also?"

"Nope. Don't want to talk about this, if she's there."

"No problem, she's at the grocery store."

"Okay." Don heard the deep breath. "I guess I'll just come right out with it, then." Another breath. "Had a vision two nights ago; I think you should know about it." This time it was a short sigh. "Have to let *somebody* know, and figured you would at least listen to me."

Don picked up the pencil again. "Sure, Harold. Just go ahead."

"I think this could help in the investigation about Rita, okay?"

"Sure." He flipped the notebook open. "You know I respect your gift, Harold."

"I mean, I was right about Paul… as awful as that was."

"Right. You were right on the mark. I believe it was from God."

"Okay," the relieved fellow replied. "So, I woke up in the middle of the night, like it's happened before, and I knew I was awake, because it made me sit right up in bed. But I saw it all, like it was a dream."

"Okay."

"Rita was lying in the center of a bright-colored circle, wrapped like a bride in some kind of shiny, white sheet, with a crown of white flowers over her hair — you remember she had that shiny, black hair. She had her eyes closed and she was smiling. Then suddenly, this huge thing, I think it was human — a really big guy, dropped down on the circle near her, for some kind of dance or something. I couldn't see the face of the thing, but it was huge and powerful, and masculine. Then it suddenly dropped all the way down, like… like it was taking advantage of her, if you know what I mean. Rita screamed, but the thing would not stop, and all the while she was screaming, this horrible, mocking laughter was coming from the darkness around them. I opened my mouth, but couldn't find my voice, or the words, so I put my hands over my ears and closed my eyes. The vision stopped, but when I lay back in my bed, I was covered with a cold sweat." He let it sink in for a couple of seconds. "I guess you get the picture, Don."

"Ay-yuh," came the reluctant confirmation.

"I guess you'll have to take it from here, my friend. All I do, is deliver the message."

"Right." The counselor wasn't quite sure how much Harold knew, so he spoke carefully. "So… so, this was a rape, for sure?"

"More like a kind of religious… uh… what do you call that?"

"A ritual?"

"That's exactly right, Don. And she didn't come out of that encounter, without consequences."

"Can you be more specific, Harold?"

The seer measured his words. "What often happens, unfortunately: a pregnancy."

"You think so?"

"I *know* so."

Although Don knew he had to pass this information to the Snoops — whether or not they believed it — he realized it was even *more* important to get in touch with George White. There was no more room for delay.

***

It was a rainy afternoon, the late February thaw being in full mode, and Ma Bigelow thought it would be a nice bright spot in Willis's day, if they would take a break from all the pain and dread of the upcoming finger amputations. "It's one of your favorites, Willis: *Bud Abbot and Lou Costello Meet Frankenstein*." She patted him on the shoulder. "You go ahead and take your pill, and off we go, just like we always do, only this time, I'll drive."

There was no line in front of Burlington's Flynn Theater, it being a Monday and most kids were in school, so the tickets were in her hands before she knew it. As she turned to smile at her husband, however, a familiar face filled that space.

"Greta! Hey!" The two ladies hugged.

"Taking a break, I see. Good for you." The peachy complexion glowed in the early afternoon drizzle, as she turned to Willis. "Good for you, my friend."

Gerald nodded a smiling greeting as he spoke. "Glad to see you out and about, Willis. That's great."

"Oh, the pills are a big help," Willis slurred back.

"Whatever it takes… at least for now." He stepped forward to the ticket window. "Two adults, please."

"What a treat to see you two," Greta crooned. "We should sit together. Would that be alright with you?"

"Absolutely," Ma grinned. "We haven't seen you in so long. Let's do that."

The movie was as good as they all remembered it, with Lou Costello playing the usual clueless bumbler and Bud Abbot coming to the rescue in one hilarious stunt after another. It was an uplifting ninety minutes or so, at the end of which, the four of them decided to go next door for milkshakes at Main Street Burgers. Halfway through his milkshake, however, Willis needed to use the restroom.

"Oh-oh," Ma said, "I didn't figure on that. At home, I usually help him, what with the bandaged hands, and all, but this is a public men's room."

"I can help, if it's okay with you, Willis." Gerald made the humble offer.

"Aw, jeez… I guess so. Got no choice."

"I promise you, I will be most discreet," the gentleman whispered.

As the two men left the booth, Ma shook her head. "Boy-oh-boy, who would'a thought we'd all be doing this stuff… ever."

"Ay-yuh, and it's all through our little church, one disaster after another." Greta took another sip on her straw. "Started when Pastor James stepped down, really. Wasn't only a couple of weeks after that, Rita was… Rita died."

Ma leaned back against the padded Naugahyde. "That poor woman. It's hard to say what really happened to her, ya know? I mean, she knew what Mickey had in mind for this church, and what that would do to her own family, I imagine, plus, she was pregnant." She wiped her mouth with the flimsy white paper napkin. "Yeah, she had a full plate, fer sure."

It was hours later, and Gerald was apologetic. "I don't want to keep bothering you, Don, but I think this is important." He took one of his little breaths. "Did you, uh, were you aware that Rita was expecting?" There was an uncomfortable silence on the other end.

"It is something we have been pretty quiet about. Didn't seem like it needed to be broadcasted, if you know what I mean."

"Alright, then I will honor that, sir."

"Thanks, my friend." More silence passed before he asked the question: "Mind telling me how you found this out?"

CHAPTER NINETEEN

Clues

"Okay, let's add it all up," Inspector McDonald commanded the men around the table. "For a few minutes, ignore your previous notes, turn to a fresh page, and start over." Pages flipped and pens were drawn forth. The Snoop Squad was ready for action.

"For a few minutes, I would like to concentrate on one suspect: *Mister Suree*." He relaxed in his chair. "So, think about it. And don't even *look* at the string picture up there on the bulletin board. Just look at the following facts about our obsessive personality, Michael 'Mickey' Suree." He glanced at the four men. "Are you ready?" The nods were accompanied by soft grunts.

"Number one: He has a shady background." He tapped the ever-present cigarette on the ash tray. "Which of you can fill us in on that information?"

"Probably all of us," the quiet one answered. "Bad past, full of brushes with the law and the mafia, and don't forget the shady real estate deals. He had to leave New York State for some pretty significant reasons — and we have a pretty good idea what they were." There was a ripple of sarcastic chuckles around the table.

Liam went on: "Number two; He usually gets what he wants."

"No doubt about that, according to the folks we've interviewed. This guy doesn't take no for an answer." Three other heads waggled in agreement as they scribbled away.

"Three: He controls everything, or else — public image, whatever."

"Roger that one." More scribbling.

"Four: He is obviously queer, or bi-sexual — a whole new set of possibilities."

"Are we just taking Bigelow's word for that?"

"Maybe… but Mr. Bigelow *did* exhibit the usual signs of incredulousness — remember his face?"

"Yeah, you told us. Thought he was gonna pee his pants," the smart-aleck quipped.

"Shut up, man," the sensitive one murmured.

"Get some balls, will ya?"

"Knock it off, both of you." Then the inspector continued: "Five: Wife was pregnant with someone else's child."

"Right. She got knoc — she got pregnant while he was in Maine, if my notes are correct."

"They are," his boss affirmed. "So, six: Very familiar with Greek god myths. In fact, it appears he and Rita were involved with satanic rituals. A book was found in his desk, during the cleanup after the fire. Furthermore, we have sketches, witnesses (including their own two younger sons), and even a poor-but-acceptable photo showing the Fortuna symbol on their bedroom floor — by the way, we know that satanic symbol had been deliberately hidden from the public."

Four sets of eyes cast a knowing look toward their leader.

"And then, number seven: Sammy Black is employed by him, and apparently is his queer lover. Also, it is Black's sister who painted the symbol on the bedroom floor, according to information coming from Mr. Suree, who claims *Rita* commissioned that lady to do the actual painting. So, there is a real connection between the four of them." He took another draw from the stub of tobacco. "Anybody got anything to add to that?" He waited the right amount of time before he drew it to a close. "Any conclusions, gentlemen?"

"That gawdim S.O.B. killed his chippy wife," the wiseacre surmised.

"Oh-ho, *man!*" the offended one whined. "Can't you even 'make a call' without being a potty-mouth?"

***

Deputy Smith maneuvered the official vehicle carefully inside the deep muddy ruts of the road, which were quickly disappearing in the twilight. As he switched on the headlights, Sheriff Max Duncan, riding shotgun, caught the glint of taillights off the right side of the road. The ruts were nudging their tires right toward them. "Some cowboy in a truck, off the road, of course," he muttered to his driver. The thought of getting his shiny boots dirty crossed his mind, and then he moaned in recognition. "That dumb Bigelow kid again," he snorted. As Smith pulled over slowly into a dwindling patch of snow, the door to the truck swung wide and Bud came bounding out. He slammed it shut before hurrying toward the sheriff.

The two men immediately went on alert; they'd seen this behavior, before. Their exit was swift, two doors slamming before the duo took defensive postures on both sides of the glaring headlights. Sure enough, the youngster had a moment of uncertainty, nervously glanced back at the truck, and then the yapping began… the familiar claptrap of somebody who's hiding something. Max's eyes never left the back window of the stranded truck, even as Bud offered up the all-too-cheerful greeting.

"Wow, Sheriff, am I glad to see you." He forced a laugh. "Yeah, yeah, it's me again… in the ditch again." He came to a stop in front of the man, attempting to make eye contact. When that didn't work, he followed the sheriff's gaze toward the truck. "Yeah, it's a mess. I'll have to get my pa to come and pull it out." He licked his dry grin. "I don't want to bother ya, but if ya could just let my pa know."

A movement in the window confirmed the lawman's suspicions, so he nodded for Smith to move in, then turned to speak directly to the kid. "Your pa? You want me to send your pa out here to get you?" He folded his arms. "Have you forgotten that your pa has no use of his hands?" He could see the lad's face deepen in color, even in the fading light. He looked to Smith for an answer.

"Girl," the deputy smirked.

"So, how about I go get *her* pa, instead?" When there was no answer forthcoming, the sheriff continued: "Not a good idea, I take it." The boy's head lowered as he nodded in agreement. Max sighed. "Alright, Bud, who is she?"

"Next-door neighbor."

"One of Walt's girls?"

"Yeah…"

"Which one?"

A foot kicked at the edge of the snow. "Patsy."

The lawman was trying to remember which one she was. "The blonde one with the pigtails?"

"No, that's her older sister."

"Older?" He frowned. "Wait a minute. How old is this Patsy?"

The boy shrugged.

"Don't start lying to me, boy. You've always been on the up-and-up with me; don't start lying now."

"Yeah, okay… she'll be twelve next month."

The hands went to the hips as he bent close to Bud's sweaty face. "Are you kidding me? You dumb kid! You been messing around with an eleven-year-old girl?" His head went back, the words directed toward the dark clouds. "Aw, for ga-awd's sake."

"No! Wait-wait-wait! It's not like *that!*"

The head came back down. "Well, it *looks* like 'that.' Sometimes you don't have to actually do something… it still *looks* like you did it, anyway, and no matter how much you deny it, it will *always* look like 'that.'"

"Huh?" The youngster was clueless; Max drew back mentally.

"Just tell me this: Where have you two been for the past few hours?"

"Patsy came over to help with the chickens, and when we finished, I offered to drive her home."

"It's not that far."

"No, but it turned out, she wanted me to show her where Sam's Place was."

"Because…?"

"Some of the kids at school told her that their fathers saw *her* pa there, more than once… and doin' crazy stuff or somethin'."

"Hmmm." He pushed the hat back on his head, making a strategic decision. "And does her mother know about those little trips?"

"Don't sound like it." He shifted his weight onto the other foot. "Anyways, that's where we've been, and then we slid off the road because of the mud."

Max moved toward the truck. "Any damage?"

"Nope. It's an old truck, anyway." He was following the man around the rear end, toward the passenger door at the front. The deputy stepped back. When the sheriff peered in, Patsy was sitting stiffly, hands folded in her lap.

"Roll down the window, please," he instructed her. She complied immediately. "You Patsy?" She affirmed it softly. "Okay, Patsy, here's the deal: I'm going to pull this truck back up onto the road, and then Bud is going to take you home. He is going to go into the house with you, and tell your folks about wanting to see that bar. Hopefully, your father will not want to discuss this with you, and will simply give you a verbal reprimand for not coming right home. You will apologize, right?" She nodded. "And then you'll never do this again, right?" Another nod. The lawman straightened up. "Of course, you will always have some leverage when it comes to future dealings with your father, since he will certainly not want you to bring up the subject again. But," he scowled, "you will be honest and dependable in every way, from that moment on, right?"

Finished with her, he turned to the boy. "As for you, as soon as you drop her off and apologize to her father, you'll drive over to Ralph's Diner on Shelburne Road. You know where that is, right?" Bud acknowledged the order. "Good, because you and I are going to have a long talk. Got that?"

It was dark by the time the two met in the diner's parking lot. The sheriff motioned for Bud to join him inside, leaving Smith to keep an ear out for any radio contacts from dispatch. The two of them took the booth closest to the restroom, where their voices were naturally muted by the bustle behind the counter. He started the conversation with a reference to the baseball bat incident of several years ago.

"How's your pa doing these days? Still having those relapses every fall?"

"He's still fightin' something."

"What?"

"Don't rightly know, but..."

"But what?"

Bud scratched his head. "Well, Ma... she seems to be keeping up with a few things."

"Why do you say that?"

"I don't know. It's like, she asked to borrow my truck and wouldn't tell me why. And then things settled down for a while."

"Got any idea where she went with that truck?"

"Not really. I can only guess."

"So, what would you guess? Is she meeting somebody, or what?"

"Don't know."

"Does this happen a lot?"

"Mmmm, nope. Just once, so far."

Max pulled a packet of Wrigley's spearmint chewing gum from his shirt pocket. Drawing a stick from that, he took a slightly different tactic. "So maybe she was just checking to see if your pa was over at the bar. What do you think?"

"I wouldn't be surprised. She has that thing about investigatin', gettin' down to the nitty-gritty, you know. Just into the books all the time."

He offered a stick of gum to the boy. "Yeah? What kind of books?"

"Mostly all them Greek gods and stuff," he said, as he slid the flat stick from the package.

Sheriff Max Duncan thought he had finally hit the jackpot: Greek gods and goddesses could very well go along with the weird goings-on over at Sam's Place.

"Wow! I'm impressed. Never knew she was so intellectual. You know, she seems like a sweet little country gal." The forced chuckle went unnoticed by the boy. "I bet she's pretty much up-to-snuff, when it comes to all the stuff that's going on around here."

"Oh, I don't know about that, Sheriff. She don't know everything."

"Oh yeah?" He finished chewing the stick into a soft cud. "I bet she knows just about everything that's been going on. Maybe even knows what happened to Rita Suree."

He shoved the stick of gum into his mouth. "Nope," Bud sputtered between bites. "She don't know everything, that's fer shore."

"Sounds like you know something, Bud, that your ma isn't in on. Am I right?"

"Maybe."

The sheriff signaled for two coffees, 'to go.' "So, this stuff that your ma doesn't know… is it important, or just gossip, or what?"

"Well, it ain't gossip, that's fer shore. I heard it myself."

"Is that right?" He smiled. "Tell you what… you need to convince *me*, mister, or nobody — and I do mean *nobody* — is going to believe you." He switched the gum to the other side of his mouth. "Are you listening?"

The head bowed, eyelids lowered. "Prob'ly won't believe me, anyways."

"Hey, here's your chance. Try me."

Buddy swished his tongue around and swallowed the sweet saliva. "Why should I?"

"'Cause I'm the one who could spill the beans to your folks about you having the hots for Patsy."

"I don't… I don't have…"

There was a long silence, while both of them chewed and stared at the restroom doors.

"It's kinda embarrassing."

"Hey, I'm a law officer. I've heard it all." He sniffed lightly. "I don't think you're going to shock me… not one bit."

A pudgy waitress poked her face between them. "Did-ja want those coffees black, or what?"

"Black, for sure." His eyes never left Bud's face. "Let's see if you can surprise me, Buddy."

The lad stared hard at his folded hands on the table in front of him. The fingers twisted as he started to speak. "I'm kinda big for my age, you know?" It was more of a cough, than a laugh. "In more ways than one, if you know what I mean." Another small cough. "So, I don't like using the men's room at the church. No privacy, you know? Kinda embarrassing… like it's some kind of a contest, you know?"

"Gotcha."

"So, I usually go around back, near the church office, where there's bushes, when I need to."

"Sure."

"So, I was out there, in the dark — we had a late prayer meeting that Sunday night — and suddenly there's footsteps, and 'course, I didn't want anybody to know I was out there, so I just scrunched down where I was." The hands loosened a bit. "Turned out, there was two of 'em — my pa and Mrs. Suree."

"Rita Suree?"

"Ay-yuh."

"Were they necking?"

"What?" The hands spread and lifted as though to erase that picture. "Nah-nah-nah. Nothing like that." He almost smiled. "They were arguing. Yeah. Like a couple of kids, whispering loud at each other in the dark."

"Mad at each other?"

"Yeah, I think so. He was telling her he wasn't going to do something, and she was saying he *had* to, 'cause if he didn't somebody was going to be mad, and they would do something bad to her."

"Bad? What do you… I mean, can you remember whether she was more specific?" The boy looked lost. "Or, can you remember her exact words?"

Bud cradled his chin in his hand. "Um, I think she said something about a sacrifice." The hand dropped. "That was it. She said, 'They will sacrifice me.'"

"Mmm, probably just a loose sense of the word, but, by the way, when did this little conversation take place? Was it summer, or spring, or what?"

"Okay, uh, school was still going, so it was last spring."

The waitress set the two covered cups on the table and waited while Max drew out a dollar. "Keep the change, Betty."

"Hey, thanks, Sheriff!" Her eyes sparkled as she tucked it into her ruffled apron pocket.

"Sure," he said, as he rose to leave.

Outside, the man stopped at Bud's truck. "Was there anything else that those two talked about, son?"

"No, sir, but my pa got ticked off and walked away. She yelled once, but I guess she was afraid somebody would hear her. Stood there a minute, then blew her nose." He shrugged. "Then she left."

"Have you told anybody else about this?"

"Nope."

"Keep it that way, unless I tell you otherwise. Got that?"

"Yessir."

CHAPTER TWENTY

Tendrils

Heidi was cleaning up after the picnic lunch she had brought up to Leo and Mickey, who were overseeing that Saturday's installation of new plumbing and wiring in the reconstructed Suree kitchen. Conversation between the two men was pocketed in the brief spaces between the banter of the workmen, so it was short and to the point: Mickey was complaining about the mess Willis had caused by his negligence. "How stupid could a guy be, not to vent a work area as dangerous as that?" There was a contemptuous snort. "Last time I employ a doofus like that." Heidi glanced over at her husband, hoping for some form of excuse on behalf of Mr. Bigelow, but there was none. She grabbed the picnic basket and marched out the new front door, onto the patio. To her surprise, Crusty arose from where he was curled upon a bench, as though to say, "I've been waiting for you."

"Hey, kiddo!" she whispered. "Whatcha doing all the way up here?"

He meowed as he dropped into pace with her quick stride down the road. She adjusted the handle over her arm, taking in the scene in front of her. Patches of snow remained here and there, but mostly, yellow field grasses lay partly buried in fragrant mud. Overhead, puffy clouds moved slowly across the noonday sky, casting mobile shadows across the fields, the road, and even the big blue spruce.

The tree, itself, seemed to be vibrating with life. "Look at that, Crusty," she said aloud, "I think it's that time of year." She moved the handle farther up on her arm. "I think they're nesting." For a few more steps, she focused on the fluttering forms moving in and out of the branches. Then she looked down. "See that you keep your distance, mister. They don't take lightly to disturbances at a time like this."

Still, the early spring-like weather beckoned, and so it was that the lady shoved the dishes into the sink, ditched her jacket for a warm sweater, and headed out the door for a walk. "Tell you what, Crusty-cat," she whispered, "let's take a walk around the whole pond today." She breathed in the earthy scent of the fields. "We need to have a little talk with God."

They started at the north end, about where they had found Rita's body, and headed south on the east side of the expanse of thin, broken ice. The long grass crinkled beneath her steady tread for a few minutes. When she drew to a stop, her little friend kept going.

"Hey! We need to stand still for a minute. Crusty? Hey!" When the sleek fellow kept padding ahead, she turned her attention to the task at hand.

"Okay, Father." Her lips pursed, then she let it out. "We've been here over six months. Next week it will be March. So I have a question: Where have You been? I mean, You promised You would never leave us, and yet..." There was a hard swallow. "Look at this mess, Lord. Just look at this mess." From where she stood, she could see the big log house. "That man is just plain evil. Surely, You have noticed, and surely, I don't have to recite the whole, long list of hateful stuff he's been doing — to Your own people, no less." Her eyes lifted. "I know I'm not You, but would You mind if I just asked, *'Why?'* Why are You letting people, including my husband, get bruised and battered by this guy? Didn't You want us to come down here to Vermont? Or were we jumping the gun on this thing?" That thought dropped like lead into the pit of her stomach. For a moment, she could not get another word out; she froze there at the edge of the water, hoping that the two of them had not been, after all, chasing a dream that had nothing to do with God's plan for them.

Crusty announced his return with a soft yowl. "I don't know, little buddy. Do you think Leo and I created our own mess?" The striped one moved a few feet away and sat down, as though he were waiting for her to get this thing done, and get on with the adventures ahead. A wry smile crossed her face. "Easy for you to say, mister."

Steadily, they approached the south end of the pond, taking in the view across the glimmering expanse to the west bank. She smiled again, as they passed the frozen form of the resting boxer, who was still keeping watch over his right shoulder, out there in the middle of that fragile ice rink. As they moved south, the rink became a mirror, reflecting the blue February sky. It was a perfect "sugaring off" day for Vermont maple syrup makers.

At length they came to the canoe rack where a thin layer of snow covered the corrugated roof. She stopped there, contemplating how Rita could have pulled one of those things off, then dragged it over to the water all by herself. "I guess it's possible, but not likely, in my opinion." She looked for the footprints, but there was too much snow still on that sandy area. Then, becoming a bit more inventive, the lady looked back at the imprints from her own steps. She noted there were ten of them.

"Ten," she murmured. "Only ten." She racked her brain, trying to recall what Leo had told her. "Yes," she exclaimed as she remembered: the investigation's report had said that. "Ten steps. That was it." She folded her arms and worked it through.

"Okay, I am taller and my stride is a lot longer than that petite woman's, for sure. If that is so, then it couldn't have been Rita who dragged that canoe over to the water; it had to be somebody with a longer stride. Somebody who was quite a bit taller, more long-legged." She felt the warmth move up her throat. "So it wasn't her who pulled that thing over there." A sudden thought stopped her cold. "But the shoes were her size; they have that documented." Her brows pulled together. "I wonder if somebody my size could squeeze into shoes two sizes smaller, I mean, maybe not get all the way into them or whatever, and walk across that small space, dragging a canoe?" She stood there looking at the imaginary picture. "It would be more likely, that bigger person would have to have kind of skinny feet, so they could slide in without drooping over the sides." She blinked. "Why not? Why couldn't that have happened?"

Crusty was getting impatient, rubbing a soft circle around her legs.

"Sorry, buddy, but we need to get back to the house. I need to make a phone call before Leo gets home."

By the time she stepped into the warmth of the guest house, she had decided whom she needed to call. It had to be someone who would not be talking to Mickey, or to Leo, for that matter. It also had to be somebody who would respect her judgment, and would likely agree with her suspicions, and of course, it would most likely have to be another woman. Surely, it had to be Greta Short. Greta's connections would make certain Inspector McDonald was informed about this discovery, and finally — she smiled to herself — nobody could say that Heidi Spencer had "called the cops" on that skinny, pointy-toed rat, Mickey Suree. No, Greta would get the credit for pointing out this critical clue, and that rascal would be caught in his own carefully woven scheme, at least, that's what she hoped.

***

The Snoop Squad was not autonomous; Inspector McDonald was answerable to the chief of the Burlington Police Department, and there had already been two meetings concerning, amongst other community matters, the death of Rita Suree. The Chittenden County Sheriff, Max Duncan, would be offering his own consultation, of course, on the same day. Liam was not looking forward to this event, which was scheduled two short weeks away and that was, alarmingly, into March already. Little wonder, then, that he pulled a few strings to get a private meeting room at a lawyer-friend's office on College Street. The place was often surrounded by city vehicles, including police and sheriff's department types, so no special attention would be attracted by this unusual group's assemblage.

And it *was* a rather unusual group: This time, Sheriff Max Duncan was included in the meeting with Professor George White, and Christian counselor Don Collins. The inspector started the discussion by attempting to build a case for Mickey's guilt, running down the list he had established with his team of detectives. "The man has a shady past, with numerous brushes with the law. He's abnormally focused on success, won't take no for an answer, and is extremely controlling. Granted, that doesn't make him a murderer, but listen to this: We have a witness that he is queer, and probably bisexual, since he had children with Rita, but either way, that opens up a whole new area for a motive. Add to that, this guy with the big ego discovers his wife is pregnant with another guy's kid. So we have still another motive." He tapped the paper in front of him. "And that's not all. He and Rita were mixed up in worship of Greek gods, and participating in satanic rituals. But not by themselves. Edith Schwarz and her brother, Sammy Black may have been in on that little party."

Don raised a hand to interject. "We know Edith painted the Fortuna symbol on the bedroom floor, and was doing some weird kind of ceremonies whenever Rita visited up at her place in Jericho Center."

"Wait a minute," George interrupted, "Edith was doing rituals with Rita, up there in the Center?"

"Greta's mother saw them from her window at the nursing home. More than once," Don replied.

"Oh, for Pete's sake," the professor declared, "that's it! Edith is the Aunt Tykie Rita would go to visit."

"Yeah," the counselor murmured, "and I'm relieved that I'm not the only one who thinks that."

Liam made a quick note. "Very good, gentlemen." He looked up. "So we have more information that those four were probably in cahoots, but it still looks like our man is Mister Suree."

"Because…?" the sheriff wanted to know.

"He had the most to lose. Why would Edith or Sammy want her dead? After all, the woman was probably an important part of their ceremonies."

The detective put a toothpick in his mouth and waited. When nobody came up with a motive for the two siblings, he went on to press the point. "Remember, this is a guy who doesn't take no for an answer, and on the night of the murder, he and Rita had a fight that was loud enough for their boys upstairs to hear. And we have no alibi for Michael Suree for that whole night. The boys all stated that they didn't see him until early the next morning at breakfast."

"Hmm," George mused, "so, putting the personality traits aside, what do we have for hard evidence against him?"

Inspector Liam McDonald shook the paper out and read them off: "Had a big fight with his wife the night she was murdered, and has no alibi. Also, wife had been unfaithful." Suddenly, he remembered something else. "Also, these fights had been going on for some time, according to the children, and she would leave for a few days to visit an aunt, who, it turns out, was not really an aunt, but somebody who did satanic rituals with her. Anyway, she stayed until she was ready to return home, and both Michael and Rita lied to their sons about this so-called aunt."

"Conjecture?" Max didn't want any loopholes.

"*Why* were they lying?" The toothpick wobbled. "*What* were they hiding?"

"Well, for one thing, he would have certainly been kicked out of the church." Don was emphatic. "He may yet be."

"What if Rita was tired of playing games and wanted out — regardless of what that would mean to the others?"

George proposed. "I mean, she was beginning to show, for goodness sake — she had to do something — even get an abortion, maybe."

"Okay, then Edith and Sammy would become suspects, as well." Max replied, "Even if she just wanted out, those two *and* her husband would have worried that she might spill the beans."

"Aw, jeez," the inspector moaned, realizing Mickey was *not* the only suspect, after all.

"Right. Now listen to this." Sheriff Duncan continued, "I have a witness who overheard Rita and Willis Bigelow arguing out behind the church one late night last spring. Seems he wanted out of something, and she wasn't having it. Said if he didn't cooperate, that, quote, 'They will sacrifice me.'" He tilted his chair onto its back legs. "What do you gentlemen think of that?"

The silence was brief. "I think we might have a small complication, here," Don grunted. "And there's still another little something we all need to address, as well." His lips firmed, then relaxed. "Got a call from somebody, letting me know that *Mrs.* Bigelow — 'Ma' — has been aware, for some time, that Rita was expecting."

The toothpick moved with the annoyed grumble. Was this still another suspect?

"I'm afraid there's more, Inspector," Don went on, "It seems there is some doubt that those footprints at the canoe rack were Rita's. Seems like the stride was too long for that petite lady."

"What? No! She was probably hurrying or something. That would be like, like she was running." He pulled the pick out and waved it as he spoke. "Those were her shoes, a size six, and she was wearing them when we found her."

"Did you say 'a size six'?" The sheriff bent forward to make sure he was hearing right. "Well now, isn't that interesting. You know who else wears a size six?" The men waited. "Ma Bigelow."

"How do you know that?"

"She used to borrow shoes from Rita."

"And how do you know *that*?" Liam was clearly upset.

"Betty, one of the waitresses at Ralph's Diner. She knows all the gossip, and I'm a good tipper," he grinned.

"You know, now that I think about it, we don't know a whole lot about that little lady, do we?" George suggested. "Maybe we need to check her out. We might even come up with a motive."

"Maybe, just maybe, it has something to do with that argument out behind the church between her husband and Rita." The eyebrows went up. "You think that might be it?"

"Aw, jeez..." The toothpick snapped in two. "Is there anything else you guys got for me?"

Don wiped his hand across his mouth. "Maybe I should let you know about the dream that this fellow had. A fellow in our church, who is a seer. He prophesied the death of Paul Suree, and about a suicide next spring." He wiped his mouth again. "I know it may seem weird to you, but I think I should bring it up."

"You're talking about Harold, right?" The professor was all ears. Turning to the other two, he cautioned that this was probably important. "Listen up, my friends."

Don related Harold's phone call as briefly and clearly as he could. "He saw a large, muscular male perform a ceremonial — what I would call a rape — of Rita." After he had given the details, he bowed his head. "You can believe that Harold saw this, or you can rack it up to a bunch of nonsense, but this man did predict Paul's death, and I would remind you that he has predicted a coming suicide in our church body."

The sheriff and the detective sat silently, inspecting the tabletop.

"Okay," Don said, "I've done what I'm supposed to do. You folks will have to deal with it, one way or the other."

"Tell you what," the frustrated detective offered, "I'll do some checking on Mrs. Bigelow, then get back to you."

The meeting was over.

***

Late that same night, the inspector opened the tattered booklet on Greek gods, trying to find a clue, a ritual, anything that might pin it all down. It took a little time, but he found it — some kind of fertility ritual — and it was almost identical to that described by the 'seer.' The idea that this might be part of the mystery of Rita's demise, set him back on his heels. All those strings on the office bulletin board suddenly meant nothing. New strings were evolving, for the picture no longer covered only those who were thought to be on the property the night she died. There was, instead, a whole new dimension to the puzzle.

"It's like a frickin' octopus," he muttered. "Every time you turn around, there's another tentacle."

He stepped into a warm shower, and then, putting out the last cigarette of the day, he slid into the rumpled bed and fell into a fitful sleep.

CHAPTER TWENTY-ONE

Changes

Willis P. Bigelow was a lucky man; he lost only the little fingers on both hands. The surgery went well, and as soon as the upcoming skin grafting was done, the future looked promising. There would be some loss of dexterity, of course, and it would never be a pretty sight, but he was a rugged Vermonter, and a little thing like that wouldn't bother him… not in the slightest. Meanwhile, he needed to get better before the next procedure. Ma drove her groggy husband home, keeping an eye on him as he leaned against the car door, the noonday sun warming his bright red hair.

"I'm gonna be jus' fine," he murmured through the drugs. "Jus' fine."

"Ay-yuh. Got a ways to go yet, but you'll be good."

"I guess that stuff works, ya know?"

"What, the medicine?"

"Ay-uh, that too." He wiped his nose with a bandaged hand. "Ow…"

"So, what else you talkin' about? Besides the medicine, I mean?"

"You know," he said.

"Know what? The bandages?"

"Nah, you know, what them two done."

She had to think a minute, before she got the picture. "You talking about the Collinses?" He smiled and nodded. "So, what works, Willis?"

"What they done." He opened his eyes to get her reaction. "You know. Okay, what I know is that they was there a lot, helpin' and even prayin'."

She glanced quickly at the man. "Oh! Is that what yer talkin' about? Them prayers?" Seeing his nod, she continued: "Ay-yuh, that stuff works. I guess you and me should know that, after all we just been through."

"Ay-yuh. I guess we should." He smiled and closed his eyes. "That prayer stuff really works. Too bad we didn't know that before. It might-a kept her alive."

"Rita?"

"Ay-yuh. Maybe we could have scared off them stinkin' devils."

"What devils, Willis?" She was careful about how she inquired. "Was there some devils botherin' her, or somethin'?" He did not answer, so she glanced over to catch, just perchance, a telling expression on his face.

But he was asleep.

***

Professor George White moved lightly down the steps outside the historic Billings Library, leaving the handsome redstone building after almost four hours of scouring references on Greek gods. He turned right to walk along College Way, past Ira Allen Chapel. The clock in its tower informed him it was four thirty-three. Pulling his overcoat closer over his chest, the man bent gently into the persistent March breeze moving across the green of the University of Vermont.

At Colchester Avenue, he paused.

"Nah," he whispered, "I think I'll skip the bus this time. It's not more than a couple of miles to the house, and I need to clear my mind."

It was a fairly easy trek to Winooski, mostly downhill, and the sky was a live backdrop of swirling clouds behind a variety of trees, most of which were royally crowned with tiny buds of glowing vermillion reds, vibrant chartreuse greens, and smoldering golds. Spring was not far away.

He passed the Dewey building and was coming up to the sidewalk in front of the Fletcher Museum, when the deep red buds of the shrubs along the front also caught his attention.

"This place features showings on a regular basis, for native Vermont artists — they're always quite pleasant farms, barns, or snow scenes." He smiled. "And no wonder." He glanced around at the natural beauty, again. "They have so much to work with, even a mediocre painter can look good."

"Maybe even this Edith Schwarz person."

That thought brought him back to his research, and how that woman might, just maybe, fit into the mystery of Rita's death. He wondered if she'd ever done any painting, besides ancient symbols on people's bedroom floors.

"Nobody makes a living as an artist, let alone, at finding water. There has to be more to her than we've all been thinking." He pulled the coat together and slipped a couple of buttons snuggly through their matching, solidly stitched holes. The hairy head bent forward for a couple of minutes, as the heavy overshoes sloshed rhythmically through the drizzle of the sidewalk.

"Okay, who would know something about her? Or about her queer brother?" He slid his bare hands into the warm pockets. *"Oh, yeah, maybe the caretakers at the poorhouse over there at Burlington's north end district. What was the name of that road again?"* He glanced up to his right, where the Mary Fletcher Hospital perched at the top of a hill, caused a temporary distraction. *"That place was so pristine — pure Victorian Gothic — before they put the new addition on. But still, they did the best they could, I guess."* He dug his hands more deeply into the folds of the coat. *"Things don't just stay the same, that's for sure. In fact, those poor farm caretakers have probably long departed both the job and this mortal soil."* Once again, he glanced up at the historic hospital, and then, he drew to a stop. *"I wonder how many folks can say they were born there? Probably hundreds, or maybe even thousands. Born under the most ideal conditions, with a*

doctor at hand, if there were any problems. So unlike much of the rest of the world."

And then, he was whispering to God, right out of the blue… just standing there in the middle of a sidewalk, on a windy March afternoon.

"Of all the places I've been in the world, there wasn't even one — not one — that offered this kind of care." That statement enlarged, even as he spoke: "In fact, babies born in ages past, in those ancient archaeological digs never had this level of care. The mothers suffered greatly, I'm sure." Then it hit him: "Oh my Lord, oh, my Lord. How did the mothers of nephilim ever manage to deliver those huge, giant newborns?" His eyes blinked repeatedly. "It must have killed them." Immediately, there came a picture of human women screaming in agony, as tendons, bones and flesh were torn in the bloody birthing of these oversized babies. "My god, no wonder Rita Suree wanted out." A shiver passed over his body. "Of course, there was the possibility of a caesarean birth." He quickly negated that thought. "It probably would have injured or even killed those poor women, just going through the heaviness of the pregnancy."

He heard the footsteps before the voice.

"Hey there, Professor!" Don Collins's smile beamed brightly. "I was hitching a ride home on the bus, spotted you walking, and decided to join you. Hope you don't mind."

"I don't mind, Don," came the relieved reply. "I'm having an unpleasant encounter with reality." He proceeded to explain as the two took up a steady stride toward Winooski. By the time they had discussed this horrific probability, they were passing Green Mount Cemetery, where Ethan Allen was buried. They came to a stop outside the open gates, welcoming the change of subject.

"I never get tired of this place." Don pointed toward the tall memorial deep inside the entrance and to the left. "That's a forty-two foot tall Tuscan pillar, and the statue of Ethan Allen is about eight feet tall. Have you ever seen it up close?"

"Yes, I have, and the square fence at the base is made up of cast-iron muskets and cannons. Quite impressive."

Don grinned. "So then, you probably already know that he and his brother are credited largely with establishing the state of Vermont."

"Oh yes, and there's a smaller statue of Ira, his brother, right there on the UVM campus green."

"Well, here's a fact you're probably not familiar with..." The man was still grinning. "Lots of folks around here figure the real burial site is actually located some forty feet away."

The archeologist laughed. "Well, if they want some answers, I'd be happy to do a dig for them."

The walkers resumed their pace, now descending at a steeper angle. A cooler breeze indicated they were getting closer to the Winooski River. The bridge was already in sight, though several minutes away. Don stopped to zip up his jacket.

"It's been a while since I thought about that gravesite thing." He shoved his bare hands into his pockets and pulled the garment down snugly over his buttocks.

"Funny how the mind works, Professor, but I am suddenly aware of how we all could be off the mark, with this Rita Suree murder."

"How so?"

He sniffed back the cold dribble at the end of his nose. "Well, what if she was attacked somewhere else, and then dumped into the pond, the killer thinking she was already dead? She would have been unconscious, breathing that water into her lungs. Even then, she was not dead, because the coroner's report stated she died of suffocation in the mud."

"Okay, then it would have to have been someone strong enough to attack, then haul the body to the pond, and then get it to the shore and pack it tightly in the mud." The scholar took a quick mental inventory. "Maybe Mickey, or maybe

Sammy Black. Edith would be a long shot, and so would little Ma Bigelow."

"Don't forget Willis Bigelow, who had the argument with her."

"Mmmm. Somehow, he doesn't fit the picture, you know?" But George offered another theory: "What if it was two people? Partners in crime, quite literally?"

Don latched onto the idea immediately. "Of course! It could be Mickey and Sammy... or Edith and Sammy... or even Willis and Ma Bigelow." He glanced at George. "Or, even Willis and Bud, father and son?"

"Bud?" There was some doubt in his reply. "I don't think the lad has any real knowledge about Greek gods and rituals, and — come to think of it — neither does his father, Willis." His head wobbled a negative. "Nope, I think we need to stick with only the ones who definitely knew something about those rituals."

"Are you thinking she was killed in one of those rituals, then?"

"I'd be willing to put money on it," George stated.

Suddenly, they were approaching the Winooski Bridge, striding along through what once had been known as the Burlington-Winooski Mills District.

Don nodded to a wide driveway to their right. It sloped down to an old brick building. "Hey! That's where my grandma lost the tip of her middle finger in one of those machines."

"No kidding?"

"Ay-yuh. One of those happy boyhood memories, I guess." As George laughed, the native Vermonter pointed across the avenue at a triangular piece of land. "And before all those shrubs grew in, that patch of real estate boasted a grist mill, and I think there was also a lumber mill for a while, not to mention a bunch of other businesses. There were all kinds of buildings on both ends of that bridge, constructed on the rock outcroppings. But they finally quit doing that, after a couple of bad floods and a half-dozen fires kept destroying the whole lot of them." He looked back over his left shoulder as they stepped onto the bridge. "Not a good place to build a business, for sure."

"I imagine it was the water power source that kept them trying," the professor mused.

"That, and some of us are just slow learners." Don had to raise his voice, what with the crashing and rumbling falls below. He came to a halt, bending over the rail just far enough to view the turmoil below. George joined him in a moment of silent admiration. Finally, Don looked up and across to the Winooski side of the river, where a large smokestack kept vigilance over a multi-floored brick building. "You know that's the Chace Mill over there, right?" he called out.

Professor White nodded, but Don wasn't finished. He gently touched his friend's shoulder, to steer him the rest of the way across the bridge. As they stepped off onto Winooski, he pointed left, to a huge building with row-upon-row of windows. "And this is the old Woolen Mill, George. You probably already know that, too, but I have a point to make: All of these mills are closed, the buildings are empty. What we have here, are ghostly remains of more prosperous times." He saw the confirmation in the archeologist's eyes. "It's another reminder, that everything on this earth is temporary, you know? Even our very lives."

"For sure, Don."

The hike up East Allen Street was a strenuous change from the previous downhill romp. Halfway up, Don unzipped his coat and wiped the sweat from his brow. Still, the view was impressive, for the two could see the whole, sweeping bulk of the Chace Mill, nearly uninterrupted. The teacher stopped for a few seconds, to take in the arresting sight.

"History, right in front of our eyes," Don wheezed.

"And some of that history… not so great," his friend murmured.

"Like what, Professor?"

"Like how much of their work force were just young children, some of them only eight or nine years old." He stared at the dead structure. "I can't help but wonder how many of those poor little kids had *their* fingers cut off." For a brief second, he considered confiding in Don, about his plan to adopt David and Matt, but thought better of it.

The conversation ceased, the two men, breathing hard as they finally shuffled onto Florida Avenue. There, George said goodbye to this kind Christian counselor, and headed for his own place of refuge. It had been a good walk.

An hour later, his phone rang. He was surprised to hear Don's voice.

"I'm so sorry to bother you, Professor, but I thought you would want to know this." It was a pregnant pause.

"Sure. Go ahead, Don."

"Okay, well, I just got a call from Gerald Short, and, uh, the Chittenden County Sheriff's Department arrested Edith Schwarz early this morning."

CHAPTER TWENTY-TWO

Trust

"She was *what?*" The Burlington Chief of Police looked up from Sheriff Max Duncan's report.

"Just like it says: She was standing in a half-full washtub, naked, singing at the top of her voice."

"Was she taking a bath?"

"No, sir. No soap, no washcloth, towel, or anything else — just water."

"On a cold March morning."

"Well, sir, apparently she had been at it for most of the night before, off and on, with the singing, and then the neighbors finally saw it all in broad daylight and called it in."

"So you and Deputy Smith took the call." He laid the report down and waited for the oral version.

"We did." Max cleared his throat. "Arrived at six in the morning, found her like that in her backyard. Tried to cover her with a car blanket, but she was out of it — eyes all glazed over, still singing something like a chant, over and over. So of course we called for medics and they took her to the Fanny Allen. We followed, then issued an indecent exposure and public nuisance, and waited long enough to see what the doctor had to say. He committed her to Waterbury, of course. Said he wasn't sure what was going on, but she was unresponsive. Had to put her under, so's she'd stop the chanting."

"Whoa! Hold it right there, for a minute." Inspector McDonald leaned forward in his chair. "That sounds like the 'si-reen' Mrs. Bigelow saw out near Sam's Place on Halloween night."

"I don't have the details on that incident," Max remarked. "Although it took place in my jurisdiction. I would have appreciated that information, before now, Inspector." When Liam did not reply, he pushed it further. "So, how do we know there was a 'si-reen' that night? Is this some kind of ritual? Can you prove that?"

"Actually, I can." He pulled the toothpick from his pocket. "It's in the booklet on Greek gods that came from Mickey Suree's desk."

The sheriff's jaw went hard. "A booklet? When did that happen? And why wasn't that information shared with my department?"

The police chief spoke up. "I'm sure that was just an oversight, Sheriff. We will get a copy printed up for you this afternoon." He turned to the inspector. "I'm sure you can do that, Liam."

"Of course, and I do apologize, Max. It's been a helluva ride for my guys. I'm sure you understand."

"Fine. But if you would also include the details of what Ma Bigelow saw that night, I would be a lot more understanding."

The police chief shook out the report, scanning it quickly. "Any sign of drugs in the medical report?

"No." Max tilted his head as if suddenly remembering. "They thought it might be some kind of hypnosis, or something like that." He shrugged. "Actually, I think they're just grasping at straws in the wind. It's weird."

Liam removed the pick from his mouth. "Doesn't she live with her brother?"

"Ay-yuh. He was gone overnight. Got him at work about nine in the morning. He came to the hospital, then followed them up to the psycho ward at Waterbury." Max leaned his weary body back into the chair. "Okay, if nothing else, we've removed at least one suspect in the murder of Rita Suree."

"Mmm, maybe, maybe not," Liam murmured.

"What's that mean? You got something on the brother, uh, Sammy Black?"

"Willis Bigelow caught him in the shower with Mickey Suree — and they weren't playing patty-cake."

Sheriff Duncan exploded. "Gawdim you, McDonald! You've been holding out on me this whole, frickin' time!" His fist rattled the table. "I oughtta beat your sorry —"

"Knock it off, Max!" The chief turned to shoot an angry reprimand at his head detective. "You know the protocol, mister. If I see this one more time, it'll go on your record, you understand me?"

The toothpick wiggled acknowledgment, but that wasn't enough for Max.

"I want to see that Bigelow statement, and the copy of that booklet on my desk by the end of today, understand?" He looked at the police chief. "If there's anything else that you folks haven't shared with me, I will file a complaint." He glowered at Liam as he rose to leave. "So, make sure *anything else* you know is *also* on my desk today, you hear?"

***

George White knew he would have to wait for the details of Edith's arrest; after all, he was only a witness on matters pertaining to Mickey's activities in the stealing of another church for the OECA. There was only a vague connection between the murder investigation and his advisory position because of his educational background, so there was no obligation on the part of Inspector McDonald and the Snoop Squad to keep him informed. Still, lying in his bed that night, he couldn't stop pondering the mystery of Rita's murder, and the rape.

The events of Harold Taylor's dream, or vision, or whatever it was, kept replaying in his head: Rita, dressed in a satin-like wrap, white flowers crowning her glistening black hair. His own sister, who had hung onto his hand during family hikes, sung soprano during the many songfests, the little sister smiling through a marshmallow mustache in front of the campfires. *"How could this have happened?"* He turned over, sliding the pillow into a more comfortable position.

"God, You know. You knew what he was when he came into her life. How could You let this happen?" He knew better than to ask that, but the heaviness overruled the common sense. The picture of her lying on that circle — smiling, the seer had reported — presented a mystery, in itself. *"Why would she be smiling? People only smile when they're happy, content, at peace."* He lay silent, thinking that one through. *"So, she was expecting something wonderful. That had to be it. She probably had no idea of what was going to happen."* His thoughts froze on that fact: His sister had been deceived. That had to be it. Nobody looks forward to being raped, and his sister had been horribly raped. Horribly. She had screamed in terror and pain.

He sat up and wiped his wet temples. Again, he accused God. "How could You let that happen?" But no answer came from the darkened room.

"Well, the least thing You could do, is tell us who it was. Who raped her?" He remembered Harold's description. "Yeah, that's right; a huge male. Did some kind of dance around her, then dropped down on her." He tried to draw back from the agony of her terror, trying to picture the monster, the huge thing that would not stop, and left her pregnant with an oversized baby."

"Oh, Lord." He shook his head and swung his legs over the side of the bed. "No. No. There are no Greek gods, no fallen Watcher angels on earth today. There are only demons, who can do nothing but fake being Greek gods, or whatever, and they're not able to procreate with human women. No. No. This can't be the answer." Still, he sat on the side of the bed, frozen in the thought.

"It has to be just a really big human being. That's all it could be. The real fallen Watcher angels are in Tartarus. The only thing left are the legions of dead nephilim, the demons, who are 'shades' referred to in the Bible, and all they can do, is to pretend to be gods, unless they take over a human body, or something like that."

There came a sudden urge to urinate. When he came back from the bathroom, he slipped into the bed, pulling the covers up close under his chin. He needed to get some sleep and try to figure this out tomorrow.

"Yeah, tomorrow I'll be more alert. And maybe God will help me. Maybe Jesus will help. Maybe the Holy Spirit... yeah, I just need to trust... just trust."

***

It was six o'clock, so there would be time for at least one more load of trash to burn in the metal barrel the Bigelows used as an incinerator. Lou made her way out to the smoldering container, located a safe distance away between the house and chicken coops. The task had been put off too long, with bags of throw-aways finally becoming a cumbersome pile on the back porch. She struggled with the torn grocery bag as she made her way down the worn path. Something dropped through the wet hole in the bottom of the large paper sack, before she could catch it.

"Aw, crap," she muttered.

A raven swooped by her, looking for a last morsel of the day.

"Help yerself," she called out. It was only a few more feet, so she sped up and tossed the thing into the fiery glow, drawing back quickly, to escape the shower of bursting coals rising up from the impact.

"Aw, crap." She brushed the burning particles from her jacket, then waited to see that the trash was catching fire properly. The flutter of new flames filled the quiet evening. As she turned to go back to the house, the raven rose from the fallen trash on the path, issuing a raspy declaration of disappointment.

"Better luck next time," she sassed it back. Then, realizing she needed to pick it up and drop it into the burn barrel, she went quickly to retrieve the odiferous pile.

"Aw, nuts. I should have brought gloves." But, in the dusk, the items seemed to be quite compact, like a couple of white bundles, so she waited for a few seconds for her eyes to adjust from the brightness of the fire.

"Hey, what the heck?"

Entering the house, she found Ma in the kitchen, frying chicken.

"Mmm, that smells so good, Ma."

"You always say that, girl."

"It's 'cause it always smells good." She held up her dropped trash. "But look what I found in the trash, will ya?" She wiggled a pair of soiled tennis shoes in the air. "Ain't these yours?"

Ma squinted. "Looks like it."

"Ain't nothing wrong with them, is there?" She inspected the muddy-looking soles of the dangling duo. "Gosh, I wonder how they ended up in the bottom of a trash bag?"

The mother shrugged. "They wasn't supposed to. I was goin' to wash 'em after scraping out the henhouse. Maybe we can save em... I don't know. So, whatever." She flipped a chicken leg in the grease. "Go wash yer hands for supper."

"Sure, Ma."

***

Back at office the next day, Liam ordered his team to take down the colored strings. The overall picture no longer involved only those who were thought to be on the property the night Rita died. There had first been a ritual, weeks before — at least, according to Harold Taylor — that involved, most likely, Edith and her brother, Sammy. Mickey had been in

Maine, and the boys, it turned out, had all been at summer camp that same week, Paul being one of Camp Abnaki's favorite counselors. So, Mickey was not involved — at least, not in the actual ritual.

"Here's where we are," he explained to the Snoop Squad. "Some new suspects, and let's see where you guys can go with that." He lit up, watching their faces. "I'm going to be gone for an hour or so. Try to come up with something by the time I get back."

"And if somebody asks where you are?"

"Clearing up some details about this satanic ritual thing."

They met at the Lincoln Inn at the five-cornered intersection in Essex Junction, a convenient spot for the Collinses; Connie could come over from the high school during her lunch hour, and Don was scheduled for a three o'clock swing shift in Burlington, The noon meeting was perfect.

"Thanks for coming," Liam spoke to the two, as he slid into the coffee shop booth. He glanced around at the bustle of the lunch crowd. "We gonna be okay here?" He was thinking of the delicate nature of the conversation about to take place.

Don's impish grin was reassuring. "These folks are too busy getting their orders. They could care less what we're talking about."

"You sure?"

The grin continued. "Trust me."

Connie bent forward to address the head detective. "I guess you want to talk about the rituals, huh?" When he nodded, she blinked slowly. "They won't have a clue what we're even talking about, believe me."

The couple ordered egg salad sandwiches; Liam ordered a black coffee.

"So," he said, as the waitress moved away, "my first question is about these nephilim things. What are they, again?"

"The giant children fathered by Watcher angels," she answered quickly.

"Born of human women," Don added.

"So, half-angel, half-human, right?"

"Right. See, the plan was for the Devil to foul up the human lineage that would lead to the birth of the Messiah, Jesus Christ. The aim of those fallen Watcher angels was to keep God from carrying out a plan of salvation for His children."

"In other words, no Messiah, no pure blood to wash away the sins of all believers," Connie added.

"Sure. Got that part, but…" He looked up, waited for the waitress to place three coffees on the table and leave. "So, did these giants, um, *nephilim* have children, too?"

"Probably not." Don wasn't sure of this. "They were *hybrids*, right?"

"Yeah, but," Liam squirmed in his seat, "didn't you tell us that there were whole settlements of giants mentioned in the Bible? How could that be?"

The grin was back. "I figure those Watchers were pretty busy, procreating all those hybrids."

"Does that mean there were female nephilim, too?"

"Oh brother!" Don gently slapped his own forehead. "I really don't know the answer to that." The look on the inspector's face brought him back to the point. "Why are you wondering about that?"

A quick glance toward the buzzing crowd, then eye-to-eye contact. "I'm wondering if both Edith and Sammy are nephilim." Seeing their surprise, he hastened to explain. "I was wondering about *him*, first, because you also told us that he had six toes, at least, according to Mr. Bigelow, who saw, you know…" He deferred to Connie's presence. "Uh, you remember Professor White's remarks about the six-toed giants in the desert?" He remembered the rest. "And the same stuff found over in the Mediterranean and other parts of the world?"

"Hmmm," Don softly acknowledged.

"And have you noticed that Edith and Sammy are both very tall?"

"Ah-ay-yuh," the man answered slowly.

"So, I was wondering about the possibility that…" he shrugged lightly, "that it was Sammy who raped Rita." He tossed an apologetic look to Connie. "Because, if that was true, then maybe *both of them,* the brother and sister, took part in that ritual."

"Well, Inspector, just what would Edith have done to take part?" Connie's glinting gray stare demanded an answer.

"She could have been the one who talked Rita into it, and then, there was what Mr. Taylor described as 'mean laughter' in the background, as it was all happening."

"I hate to admit it, but you may have something there, Inspector." The thought rattled around in his brain. "After all, we know Edith is the mysterious Aunt Tykie who had been 'advising' Rita for quite some time. So the woman had *some* kind of influence over her."

"And the both of them were doing some 'weird' rituals in her backyard," Connie mused.

The egg sandwiches arrived, along with the order receipts.

"Let me take care of that," the inspector insisted, slipping the tickets into his shirt pocket.

"Hey, we'll get it next time." Don smiled. He took the first bite before he continued. "And now," he murmured through the egg salad, "here's Edith doing weird stuff all by herself." He paused for a quick sip of coffee. "I guess she was pretty much out of it, chanting and naked and unresponsive. They had to call the ambulance."

"If I were to make a guess," Connie said as she licked the mayonnaise off her lower lip, "I would think she got in too deep. You know, you can chant yourself into a kind of hypnosis, fooling around with that stuff."

"That's what the hospital guy told Sheriff Duncan! I think he called it 'self-hypnosis' or something like that." Liam's voice reflected a tiny glimpse of hope.

"Oh boy, I don't know about all this, Inspector." The man tugged at the knot of his bus driver's tie. "You know, there is this medical term for having extra digits on the hands or feet. It's called polydactyl syndrome. Not common, but not all that rare, either."

"Are these people also tall?"

"Don't know, sir." He took another bite, stalling for time.

Inspector McDonald leaned back slowly. "Aw, nuts. Maybe I'm chasing my own tail here." His head hung down as he went on. "I've been trying to make something out of nothing. That's how lost we are, concerning this case." He laughed softly at himself. "Never thought I'd get so desperate that I'd start believing in angels and demons and satanic powers." He laughed again. "I think I need to get back to reality." He drew a fresh toothpick out and slipped it into his mouth. "Even if there were such things as giant nephilim on the earth at one time, who's to say there are any of those things around anymore?" He picked something out from between his front teeth, looked at it, then sucked it back in, swallowing it down with a final slurp of the coffee. "I need to get back to reality, for sure."

Don put down what was left of his sandwich and quickly wiped his mouth. "Let me tell you something, Inspector: I believe you are very good at your profession. Not too many people would have even delved into this whole area." He sat up straight, as though to emphasize the point. "The truth is, the spiritual world is *very* real — probably more than the worldly realm, since it continues forever, while the earthly dimension does not — not by a long shot." He wrapped both hands around the warm cup in front of him. "So, what are we *really* dealing with, here?"

"You tell me," the weary fellow said.

"What we have to remember, is that these rituals, and even the books about them, are the product of demonic influences, and as such, full of lies and false formulae. Not one of those rituals can be trusted. Furthermore, all of those fallen angel 'gods' are in Tartarus. They are not allowed to walk the earth.

Not that they can't still influence those disembodied shades we call demons."

"Yeah, those evil things are getting their marching orders from *somewhere*," Connie asserted.

"Right," Don agreed. "Now listen, the Watchers who fathered the nephilim, are the ones in chains in Tartarus, until the Great White Throne judgment, but there is still a good chance they may still be able to direct the demonic activity up on the earth. After all, God can summon Satan into His presence at any time — there are scriptures to prove that. And there are scriptures to prove that there is communication between Hell and the rest of the spiritual world, as well. So, it's not beyond possibility that these fallen Watcher angels still have some clout on the spiritual level."

"Like what kind of clout?" the inspector queried.

"Just enough to make them think they can do some real damage. Remember, it was their goal to foul God's plan of redemption, but they're really too late, so all they can do is take as many humans to Hell with them as possible."

The head of detectives held up his hands to stop the onslaught of information. "Man, I'm really in over my head, here."

"Okay, the reality here, is that these demonic beings are at work and will continue to work in this world. There will be rituals and spells and all kinds of wicked goings-on, as long as gullible people continue to open themselves up to those creatures through pride, greed, lust, and the whole slimy gamut of sins."

Connie held up a teaching finger. "And it will continue until Jesus, Himself, comes back."

It was like a small light blinked on.

"Alright, you two, I see the facts, and they're sad, but they're also, unfortunately, very real." He stood to leave, drawing the lunch tickets from the pocket. "So now I kind of know what I'm working with, but nobody, in law enforcement or otherwise, is going to believe it. How the heck do I work this thing?"

"It's pretty simple, sir," Don replied. "You just have to see if it was a human being who got used by those demons, to kill Rita Suree." He rose to shake the man's hand. "That's all the worldly realm requires of you, Inspector." The reassuring grin was back. "You probably need to ask God to help you with that."

CHAPTER TWENTY-THREE

Evangelizing

Ten days had passed since Edith was admitted to the state hospital at Waterbury. Heidi was helping Leo in the church office on an almost daily basis. Today, she licked the stamp for the last envelope, pressing it smoothly into place. "So, okay," she called out to Leo in Mickey's office, "I have the bills ready."

"Great. That's a big help, hon."

"So, do I take them out to the mailbox, or to the post office?"

"Mailbox. Don't forget to raise the red flag."

She pulled on a sweater, knowing it was still chilly on this late March afternoon, and the mailbox was all the way out there at the side of the road.

"Anything else to go out there?" she spoke over the ring of the telephone. "I've got it," she called out.

"Ah-ha! That's where you are." Laura Wilson's voice was a welcome surprise. "I tried to get you at home, at least twice this week, and now I see you're probably helping in the office."

"Right."

"So, is Mickey still working on the house, or what?"

"That, and keeping up with the Sammy Black situation."

"Mmmm. And how *is* his sister?"

"Not so good, I'm afraid."

"Darn." She took a few seconds to get the proper words. "Is this something we can help Sammy with, or are we supposed to not gossip, and that's it?"

Heidi was amused at the lady's flimsy attempt at diplomacy. "Okay, it doesn't appear Sammy needs anybody's help, except for Mickey, and yes, we aren't to gossip."

Laura chuckled. "Yeah, he probably has every last detail, all nicely scribbled down on his trusty clipboard, and nobody else is to be involved."

"Well said," the temporary help confirmed. Then, seeing her husband appear in the inner office doorway, she waved him off. "It's for me," she whispered.

"Okay, kiddo," Laura said, "just letting you know, I won't be at crafts this Sunday afternoon." Heidi could almost see the smile. "My Jessie and my son, and I are all going to a family wedding that day at a church in Burlington."

"Super!"

"I know!" Hope shot through the telephone line. "So, pray, just pray, that there is somebody or something."

"I will, Laura. Have you called the other ladies?"

"Connie, and Ma and Lou, of course. If you think of anybody else…"

"You bet. You can count on me."

"Thanks. I'll let you all know how it goes."

"Promise, promise, young lady? If your family gets saved, we all want to know!"

"Promise, promise, my friend!"

She picked up the mail to leave, but stopped when Leo reappeared in the office doorway. "Who was that? Is everything alright, hon?"

"It was Laura Wilson. You remember her, don't you? She's one of our crafters." He nodded. "And she is so excited. Her husband and son will be in church on Sunday."

"Here?"

"Oh, no. No, it's a family wedding in Burlington." She held up a staying hand. "*But,* if something opens their eyes to

Jesus, they will probably… very well might… start attending *here*." She blinked in anticipation. "Wouldn't that just be great, Leo?"

"Oh course," he agreed, even though there was disappointment in his eyes.

"Well, we both know, it doesn't matter where they get saved; it only matters that they're going to Heaven." She approached him, touching his arm. "Am I right?"

"I guess."

"You know what your problem is, my man?" She tapped him lightly on the nose. "*You* are an *evangelist*. You would rather tell somebody about Jesus and lead them into the kingdom, than to preach a dozen sermons in a big church, or even pastor the biggest congregation in the whole world." She shifted her weight. "I truly believe that, Leo. You are not so much a pastor or a preacher — although you have a little of both — as you are, an evangelist." Her blonde eyebrows arched.

He took that in. "I never thought of that," he murmured.

"Okay, let me give you a little 'fer instance' here." She turned toward the outer office desk, where the mail sat waiting for her to take it to the mailbox with the red metal flag. "Now, when I just told you that the Wilson men might get saved by going to another church, or another person, or whatever, I saw. Yes, I *saw* the envy in your eyes." There was a confident tilt of her head. "*You* wanted to do that. *You* wanted to be the one, or at least *one of the people* who would lead those two guys to the Lord."

"Well," he replied defensively, "I certainly do want people to get saved, but it doesn't actually require my own participation. I know that, Heidi."

"But it tugged at something way down deep in your spirit, Leo Spencer." There was that tilt of the head again. "I saw it. And it's not the first time." Her voice softened. "You need to address this, hon. You really do."

When she got back from the mailbox, Leo was standing in front of the outer office desk, where she had spent most of the day. The somber countenance brought her to a quick stop.

"What's the matter, Leo?"

He took a deep breath. "Just got off the phone with Mickey." He shook his head. "It's not good."

"Oh-ka-ay."

He pointed her to the wobbly desk chair, and she complied.

"Edith is not doing well. Mickey has been keeping close tabs on her progress, accompanying Sammy on every visit, even participating in the doctor's updates and all medications… you know… the whole thing." He slipped his bottom onto the top of the desk, balancing with one foot on the floor. "The poor woman is staring wildly into space, not eating on her own, and barely able to control her own bowels. She's not responding to daily sessions of psychotherapy, does not know her own name, let alone her own *brother's* name." He wiped his trembling mouth. "Heidi, this poor woman is in deep confusion and extreme anxiety. Her doctor has noted that she is suffering from intermittent, but severe heart palpitations."

"Is she getting medication for that?"

"Apparently not. Mickey says her doctor doesn't have much confidence in them. He feels they would have to be a last-resort treatment." He shrugged, and pushed the balancing foot into a more solid stance. "This doctor told Mickey these drugs were too dangerous, in his opinion."

"That's what Mickey said?"

"Yeah, pretty much. Why?"

"Just wondering, hon." She crossed her long legs and leaned into the chair. "You know, Mickey has a way of getting people to see things his way; look at what happened with Paul and his rock-and-roll band."

"You know I don't agree with you on that subject. No good father would do that to his own kid."

"Right, no *good* father."

Leo bolted to his feet. "Listen, Heidi, I've had about enough of your attitude toward Mickey Suree. You have pronounced yourself judge and jury over a man who has done nothing less than to step in, over and over, to protect and guide the sheep of this church. He has spent endless hours of prayerful study, in order to give his flock the best of the best, and here you are, dismissing him as some kind of charlatan, a fake, a manipulator, and a tool of the devil." His stance became combative. "Well, that's just about all I'm going to take from you." A self-righteous fury drove the blood to his face. "For your information, Sammy Black is under extreme duress, and Mickey is extremely frightened about that."

She frowned. "Oh?" She crossed the other leg over this time. "And since when has Mickey Suree been 'extremely frightened' about folks who *don't* threaten his own agenda?" It was a huff. "Not ever." She sniffed back the huff. "He is only 'frightened' by folks who *get in his way*." She stood up and slapped the top of the desk. "You know what I think? I think he's trying to make sure Edith doesn't start talking about a lot of stuff that you and I don't even know about. It's the only thing I can figure out right now. Why would he neglect the church business and the insurance business, and even the reconstruction of his burned-out home, just to 'watch over' Edith and even, Sammy?" She sat back down. "I have prayed and prayed, and I have to tell you, Leo, that I have no peace. Are you hearing me? I have no *faith* in this man's leadership!"

"How can you say that? Look at all he's done, for so many people, and for us, Heidi. Don't you realize he came to Maine and 'saved our bacon'?"

"I wonder why he did that?"

"Because he cared."

She fell silent.

Thinking he had made his point, he softened his voice. "We need to close up. It's four-thirty."

They quietly put things away for the day, then started out the door. Halfway through, she turned around and spoke firmly: "You know what, Leo? You *really are* an evangelist. Trouble is, you're touting the *wrong savior*."

***

Willis's hands were healing quite well, except for one spot over the right center knuckle. If left to heal naturally, the scarring would be so extensive he wouldn't be able to bend that finger.

"But we can do something about that," the doctor had said. "It won't look all that good, but the tissue and skin right there should be a lot more supple." He had smiled. "And if you agree to let med students at the University of Vermont perform the procedure, it won't cost you a penny."

So, Ma Bigelow found herself in a surgery waiting room on an early spring morning. But she was not alone.

"It's the least we could do," Inspector McDonald said, as he handed her a cup of stout coffee, "what with him losing fingers, and now this, just to get evidence of that floor painting."

"But, isn't this your day off?" She balanced the cup on her knee.

He laughed. "I don't remember the last time I had a day off. It's part of the job, you know?"

"Sort of like having a poultry farm," she murmured.

"Point taken, Mrs. Bigelow." He looked at the black brew. "Is this stuff drinkable?" When she chuckled, he thought she might be ready for some real conversation. He took a sip. "Ooo-oo, that's bad."

She tried it, and shrugged. "I've had worse."

He leaned back. "I imagine you have. My staff tells me you're quite the legend over there in Hinesburg — a real pioneer woman." Her eyelids dropped in ladylike humility. "No-no. I'm serious." He got a big grin on his face. "Is it true you can split rocks?" She giggled a confirmation. "Really? I mean, how did you learn to do that? You're so small and dainty."

"Oh, pshaw," she objected, "I may be a little short on one end, but I ain't… I'm *not* dainty."

"Yeah? Well, okay, you know how to plow a field, and haul those things over to make a fence, right? And it's the ones that are too big to haul — those are the ones you had to split, right?"

She nodded. "Had to cut them down to size, so's we could move 'em."

He set the coffee cup on the floor beside his chair. "So, how did you *do* that?"

Well, there's a trick to it." She looked around to make sure the room was still empty, then leaned forward. "You have to look real close and find the layers. Every rock is put together in layers, and if you look close enough, you can see the seams of them things." Another quick look around. "Then you get a big chisel and an even bigger hammer, and you jest start working at that seam, and pretty soon," she winked, "it starts splitting apart."

"Well, I'll be darned."

"Mind ya, it don't happen without workin' up a good sweat."

"That's amazing." He leaned forward, elbows on his knees. "Another thing I heard about you; that you and your husband dug the same well that you have on your property in just a few days. Is that true?"

"It shore is."

"So, did you two find the water, first, or what?"

"Oh, heck, no. We hired a water witch." She took another small sip. "Shore sorry I ever put up with *that* one."

"Um, are we talking about a lady named Edith?"

A noisy grunt signaled a bull's-eye for the detective. "If ya wanta call her a lady."

"Um," he repeated himself, "are we talking about the same Edith who was taken to Waterbury a short while ago?"

"And who the heck is surprised by that?" She rolled her eyes in disdain. "With all the voodoo crap she's been mixed up in?"

"Really?" He hoped he looked innocent.

"Oh, I could tell ya…"

He struggled to keep that clueless look. "What? What could you tell me?"

"I ain't about to get into all that."

This time, it was he who surveyed the room. "Okay, I read you loud and clear. This is stuff you probably don't need to spread around the neighborhood. But, there's nobody in here but you and me, and this is not an official interview — just two people talking in a waiting room." He kept the elbows on the knees, moving toward a more personal conversation, one which would draw the lady in to eventually recognizing and verbalizing the truth. "Listen, Ma, if you can do anything, *anything*, to help me understand that strange woman, I would appreciate it, and this would not be official — just two friends talking, okay?" She seemed reluctant. "Please. I will do everything in my power to keep this conversation private." The hesitation was still there. "Okay, it really is okay. I respect your feelings on this matter. I will not press you any further." He sat back and let the silence do its job. A few seconds passed.

"I caught her spreading something like sugary gold dust onto our well." She went on to tell about the only other time that happened was during the 'blessing' of Walt's well, and how, of all the other dowsing jobs she had witnessed Edith performing, these were the only two that had the gold dust treatment. And then, it was only logical that she tell about how both Willis and Walt had suddenly started going to Sam's Place, and especially around Halloween, which led naturally into the repeat of her story of the 'si-reen'. But this time, there was a twist: "I got to thinkin' about that, and I would bet my bottom dollar that it was her, Edith, in that funnel of water, singin' and reelin' in that poor, stupid Walt." A couple of sympathetic clucks of the tongue brought her to the next revelation. "All I can think, now, is that if I hadn't bounced a rock off his head, he woulda taken part in some kind of... I don't know what to call it." She shook her head in disbelief. "It's only by chance, that my Willis never got took in, like that."

"How do you know that?"

"Well," she took a sip and set the cup on the floor beside her own chair. "I can only think of one thing that was different between Walt's well 'blessing' and ours." Again, she seemed to be in awe of the situation. "Before Willis and me slid that cover over the well, I stuck all three of them fresh willow dowsin' branches into the underside of it." Her face reflected incredulity. "I'm thinkin' that might have broken the 'spell', or whatever."

"Willow branches, eh?" He wanted her to feel affirmed. "That does seem to make sense, in a spiritual context."

"What?"

"You may be right on the mark with that." He carefully chose his next words. "Hmmm. Kind of makes you wonder, though." His feet tapped the floor lightly, as he appeared to think it through. "Was Edith able to make that column of water happen, or was she being a phony goddess, or what? I mean, *something* was making that water form a hollow enclosure, a tube, you know?" He took a breath as though he'd just had a new thought. "Or was Edith actually being possessed by a goddess from way back in the Greek times?"

A glint of relief sparkled in the little pioneer woman's eyes. "I don't know, Inspector, the perfesser and the Collinses seem to think them gods are in some part of Hell, and can't get out to do anythin' to anybody. What do *you* think?"

"I was hoping *you* could enlighten me on these Greek gods and all that. I understand you've become somewhat of an expert on the subject. You read a lot, right?"

"I read, for shore, but that don't make me an expert, Inspector." She had a sudden thought. "You know what? You need to talk to Don and the perfesser! They'll keep you pretty straight on them things. Yeah, that's who you need to talk to."

A darkness appeared in her eyes. "'Course, they could be wrong, too."

It was time to pull back, and get to other things. "You're probably right, Ma." He looked at the clock. "What time did Willis go in?"

"They said it was scheduled for seven o'clock."

"How long did they estimate?"

"A couple of hours, or so." She looked at her watch. "Should be gettin' back to us pretty soon, unless there's a problem." Worry furrowed her brow. "Hope we didn't make a mistake, lettin' them college kids work on him like that."

"Oh, they're almost doctors, Ma, and they have a real surgeon working with them." He reached over and patted her hand.

"Yeah, that's right. That's right, Inspector."

"So, what do you say? Shall we talk about something else?"

"Prob'ly a good ideer..." She gave him a hard look. "How long you been a detective, anyways?"

"Let's see, four years in Albany and going on my fifth year with Burlington. Why do you ask?"

"Jes' wondering how much you really know about things, that's all."

"You mean, about Rita Suree's murder?" He could almost see her ears perk up. "Well, I'll tell you, it's been a wild ride, as we say in the business. We could use all the help we can get, that's for sure."

"Like what?"

"Like, who would drown somebody, and then jam the body face-down into five inches of mud?" He folded his arms. "I can tell you, it had to be somebody who was of pretty good size. You know, pretty strong and heavy, themselves. Would you agree with that?" She hummed a yes. "Got any ideas on that one?"

"Somebody big and strong, eh?"

"Right. You know anybody like that?"

"Prob'ly quite a few, as a matter of fact. But they have to have a reason to kill that poor lady, ya know."

"How about this one: To hide a pregnancy." He saw that she was aware, nodding knowingly. "So you knew about that, right from the beginning?" She nodded again. "How did you find out? It's my understanding that she was hiding it."

"Walked in on her in the ladies' room at the church. She was retchin' and coughin' in the other stall, right next to me." The faded eyebrows came together. "I didn't say nothing, jes' washed my hands and left. But when she come out a few minutes later, I saw the pale face, and sure enough, the baby bump she was trying to hide under that loose blouse."

"Oh."

"Then she went over and said something to Mickey, and he motioned for Deacon Black to come over, and then Sammy took her home." She blinked. "Yeah, she was expectin', for shore, but it wasn't my place to say anythin'."

"That was very respectful, Ma. But then, you and Rita were pretty friendly, weren't you? Somebody said you used to wear each other's shoes… had a lot of fun with that."

"We did." Suddenly, there was a new sadness. "I forgot about that, with all the shock of her being killed." She tapped her fingers lightly on her knees. "Anyways, we had to quit doin' that, 'cause she was so pigeon-toed, all of my left shoes were run over on the outer side." A soft laugh. "Kinda funny, huh?"

"I'm sorry." He sat up straight. "This whole thing has taken quite a toll on all of us." He seemed to comfort her. "But you may have prevented a whole lot more in this tragedy, than you know."

"Really?"

"Really. But it has to do more with the spiritual side of the situation." She frowned. "Bear with me, here." He pictured an imaginary scene on the ceiling. "So, here we have two special well 'blessings' by Edith Schwarz, both being doused with some kind of sugary gold dustings, and — what do you know — only one of them makes the husband strip naked and walk into some kind of ritual in that particular spot on Lewis Creek." He made a square with the fingers of his two hands.

"Only *one* of those two husbands." He caught her eye. "Got the picture?" She looked doubtful. "No, really, only one of those two husbands was drawn into that seductive 'si-reen' song: Walt, with all the kids!" He waited for her to absorb that. "Why do you think that happened? Why wasn't Willis, your husband, drawn into that seductive scenario?"

"Uh, you tell me."

"Alright, just putting it out there, but have you ever considered that it *really* might have been those willow branches you stuck under the well cover?" He challenged her. "Think about it, one more time. It's the only difference between the two well blessings."

She drew her hands slowly up to the opposite shoulders, shielding her heart from something unseen. "What're you gettin' at?"

"I'm getting at the fact that the spell-breaker in the water witch's plan, was the presence of fresh willow branches." He waited for that to sink in. "But, in *your case*, there was a double barrier, wasn't there?"

"What are you talkin' about, mister?"

"I'm not sure how it all works out, but if willow branches stop the spell of a water witch, what does the name of the wife of the targeted husband do to that evil plan?" He leaned forward and touched her hand. "Can you even *think* what that would do, in the spiritual realm, Willow?"

Her voice was barely audible. "So, you know my given name?"

"Willow. Yes. And, I don't think this is a mere coincidence, dear lady. If all this spiritual stuff is real, your name may have had some kind of influence. Although, I must admit, I don't really know."

Her head was bowed low. "Mmmm. So, I guess you know my background."

"Yes, ma'am. Illegitimate —"

"Bastard child," she interrupted. "Up there in Canada. Didn't want my kids to know." She sniffed quietly. "Even Willis don't know about that."

"And it is not my intention to reveal any of that, Willow. I just had to let you know that my office is aware of all that, okay?" He noted the slight acknowledging nod, before he went back into inspector mode. "Alright, Mrs. Bigelow, I appreciate your honesty."

The operation was a success, so Liam McDonald followed up on a few leads on a couple of other cases, and was back in his office by three that afternoon. The overall events of the day seemed quite successful, but as he strolled back to his apartment on King Street, he felt a small jostle in his soul about the Hinesburg pioneer lady: Even though she seemed to explain away the shoes and the hidden pregnancy, and so very much more, in the end, neither Ma "Willow" Bigelow, nor her husband, Willis, had an alibi for the night of Rita Suree's murder.

"And, oh yes — there was the fact that Willis drank the water before the ten days were up."

CHAPTER TWENTY-FOUR

Traps

Mickey Suree was being very careful about what he spoke out loud, and what he wrote down. His lifestyle had taken a definite turn since he ordered the destruction of the Tyche symbol on the bedroom floor. No longer was it comfortable to make notes or to even mutter orders under his breath. Things had to be done differently now, because there were others who could hear and read and figure out his plans. Up until recently, there had been friends and coworkers in all of his shady endeavors. He had enjoyed the power and invisibility of these entities, for certain. But today, they were no longer in his corner. The fight was his alone, and it was not against a clueless human opponent; it was against what he believed to be descendants of pankratiasts, ancient warriors — boxers and wrestlers — who fought without rules of combat. No wonder that he had little room for church matters or reconstruction projects. It was time for this little pugilist to go into full battle mode. Indeed, he was backed into a corner, and he had to "do or die."

The man immediately nurtured his relationship with Edith's doctor, with much input about her delusionary lifestyle, and how her brother had been under such stress to keep her under control. He emphasized how he had urged the man to change his last name from Schwarz to Black in order to set some space between her lifestyle and his. Then, presenting himself as Sammy's mentor, Mickey expressed concern over the heaviness of this sibling relationship on the poor fellow. "I worry about his own mental stability, to be honest. What should I do for this guy, Doc?"

If the doctor had any suspicions about the motor-mouthed friend of his patient, he did not reveal them. In fact, he drew back a bit, occasionally allowing Mickey to be alone with Edith during those first three weeks. Sammy would have these rare solitary updates with the doctor, while Mickey spent time in the visiting room of the asylum, conversing with the helpless Edith. He would draw her close and whisper into her ear, all the time stroking her arm as though to comfort her.

"They've got you, Edith. Can you feel them gnawing at your innards? Can you feel them nibbling at your gut? Can you? Because that's what they want, you know. They want you in deep pain. And, guess what? Nobody can stop them. That's right." He would kiss her on the temple. "Because they want to experience your fear, and your suffering, and your actual death. Yeah." He would pull her closer in a grip-like hug. "And you can't do anything about it. Nope, you can't." He would rock her like a small child. "Can't do anything, can't do anything, can't do anything, but suffer, until they finally eat your whole insides away." He would chuckle softly into her ear, before another steely hug. "And that's what they are doing, Edith. And you should be very, very afraid."

Then, Sammy would come into the visiting room, and it would be time for applying more pressure to the grieving brother on the drive back to the big log house, where Mickey would say something like, "Listen, Sammy, you've had a tough day. You should have a long, hot shower, and stay the night."

***

Greta Short walked into the church office on Friday morning, intent on demanding her last paycheck of three hundred and forty-three dollars, "...which is two months overdue."

Heidi looked up. "Hey, it's nice to see you." She smiled. "We're alone, Greta. Leo has a dental appointment."

"Don't know whether I'm glad about that, or not." She pulled a straight chair up beside her old desk and sat down. "Although, I wasn't looking forward to standing up to that rascal Mickey, again." She placed her felt purse squarely on her lap.

"He *is* a rascal, that's for sure. Leo and I go around about that a lot."

"Do you, Heidi? That's got to be hard." She patted her purse. "But, don't worry, girl, I won't be telling anybody about that."

"Greta, you have turned out to be a good friend, and I so appreciate it. Thanks for passing the word about the ten footprints."

"Well, it may be only a theory, but I think it's a good one." She looked at the pile of paperwork on the desk. "Looks like they can't keep up with all that, those two."

"Yeah, Leo is overwhelmed, and Mickey is up to his neck trying to manage the Edith Schwarz situation."

"Mmmm. Makes you wonder why he's dropped everything else to, as you say, 'manage' that situation." She leaned closer. "Makes you think he's trying to hide something." She pulled back, then leaned in, again. "...like how our Rita died."

"You're already aware of my feelings about that, and I tell you, Greta, it has started to keep me awake at night." She tapped the eraser end of a pencil on the desk, to emphasize her words. "I tell you, the man is *not* a Christian. He has a heart of stone! He doesn't mourn the deaths of his wife and oldest son, and the other two boys are shoved off into a boarding school. He is more interested in micro-managing everything else in his life. That's... that's..."

"Sick?"

"Lord help us, we need to find a way to stop him. No, get *rid* of him, is more like it." She quickly clarified that remark: "The man needs to be fired, plain and simple."

"Hah! That guy won't go down without a fight."

"True. The man is still a champion boxer, so to speak."

"Yeah, well, if you get right down to it, that kind of behavior is ungodly in every sense of the word. You know, Pastor James had a name for folks like that: 'Demon-possessed.'"

"Oh, boy, you know who else thinks that about Mickey? The Collinses. They let it slip during one of our meetings. I remember thinking they were probably right on. Now I'm sure of it." Suddenly, she got it. "Oh my goodness, Greta. Oh my goodness." She looked directly at her friend. "They said something else, or, at least somebody else made the remark, about a Jezebel spirit, and the only way to get rid of one of those was to remove their source of power."

"What?"

Heidi repeated herself, then added a conclusion: "And the only way we can get rid of Mickey Suree, is to dissolve this church." She blinked twice. "Right?"

Greta drew in a slow breath, then nodded. "Right. You're exactly right, girl." She drew the purse closer to her ample tummy. "We could disband, and then, when he moves on, reorganize."

"*If* he moves on. Otherwise, he may try to take over the property and start a whole new denomination, or whatever." Heidi laughed. "Oh my goodness. Isn't that exactly what he's doing?"

"Is it?"

"He wants an elder-run church. Leo told me."

"But this has always been a democratically run fellowship," Greta objected. "What does he think he's doing?" She pulled the purse up close to her bosom. "And why does he think he can steal that from Swift Street Pentecostal?"

For a minute, the tapping pencil kept an erratic beat.

"Ooo-oo, think about this," Greta almost whispered, "if Mr. Suree is charged with a crime, he certainly would have to step down, and he wouldn't get back into *this* particular pulpit, for sure, not ever. The church wouldn't even have to go away!"

"Of course!" The pencil tap was more controlled. "Unless, he didn't kill her."

"Ay-yuh, so, there would have to be some other charge like, mismanaging funds, or something like that."

"Nah, that man knows how to cover his rear end, like nobody I've ever known before." Heidi sighed. "It would have to be something he had no idea that he was doing wrong, like breaking a nonprofit rule, or something."

"Or some kind of lawsuit that would probably keep him out of leadership for a bit." A smirk brought color to the beautiful peachy complexion. "How about I sue him for defamation of character and nonpayment of back wages?"

"Ha!" Heidi shook her head. "He would chop you and Gerald into little pieces and eat you in a salad!" They shared an ironic snicker.

"So I guess what we need, is somebody who knows stuff about this guy, that we don't know." She caressed the brass clip on her purse. "Maybe his boys?"

"Hey! A relative!" The blonde head bobbed. "Of course! So, what family member do we know, who might be willing to, uh, pull the rug out from under this tyrant? And remember, we have all of Rita's folks, as well."

Greta rose up slowly from her chair. "Oh my gosh, girl. I think we need to talk to Don Collins."

When Don got around to calling George White, he had no idea there were some other important things happening.

"Prof, I got a call from Greta Short a few minutes ago. She's been trying to reach me for hours, but I just got home from work. Anyway, I don't know how much she knows, but she's insisting that you, as a relative, probably have something on Mickey, that we could use to vote him out of business, there at Swift Street Pentecostal." He tossed his tie onto the bed, then started to work on the top button of his bus driver's shirt. "Like I say, I don't know what she knows, if anything."

"Doesn't matter, Don. Gerald is one of the witnesses, and he will fill her in, in a few days."

"What does that mean?" The buttonhole released its chokehold.

"Remember when Mickey hired me to do that survey? Well, I rigged it so I knew who had information, then went back later and got them to sign affidavits. Sent them and my whole report in a month ago. Today, I heard back from the big boys, and they're all in. Inspector McDonald was in touch with them, as well, by late this afternoon," He sounded like a school boy at a ball game. "It's going down!"

"You… you mean, the investigation is complete? They're going after the OECA and Mickey?"

"We can serve warrants the first thing Monday morning. Everybody's been waiting for the go-ahead. It looks like everything is in place." He laughed. "Well, it should be. We've been working on all these angles for months."

"So, exactly how will all of this work, Professor?"

"Probably better if you don't know, Don. Just stand back, and wait for my phone call." There was a small sigh of relief. "This is the haymaker that's gonna send that phony to the mat, and it's been a long time coming."

Don acknowledged George's soft groan of relief. "So, it's finally happening."

"Looks like it." The professor went on to the next thing. "Um, I guess I should let you in on something else."

"Okay…"

"Well, I've been working on getting custody of the two boys, in case Mickey is arrested."

"Matt and David. Yes! Well, that was a good move, Professor."

"You know, I've been over there almost every weekend. We have grown pretty close." When Don didn't respond, he went on. "Those guys need a family, and so do I." He let another silent moment pass. "I have all these brothers, sisters, aunts, and uncles for these two great kids to enjoy." A short breath was expelled through his nostrils. "Am I making any sense, Don?"

"Absolutely, Professor." The affirmation was gentle. "I think this is probably one of the best ideas you've ever had."

George's relief was almost palpable. "So, okay, the biggest concern I have, is that he will pin Rita's death on that brother and sister team, Sammy and Edith. And it looks like he's been up there at Waterbury working all the angles. He hasn't been in the church office more than three times in these last few weeks, not to mention paying any attention to the insurance business. This is a sign of someone in *frantic mode*, trying to keep everything under control."

"I have to agree. Leo has been trying to keep things going at the church, both from the preaching and business ends, and it has been pretty sad." The tone changed to one of encouragement. "But, if all goes well with this thing on Monday, we'll be able to make some recovery moves, right? Some healing measures for this little congregation, for sure."

"Those folks at Waterbury need to know about the satanic stuff. That will tip the scales in our favor, for sure."

"All that will eventually be revealed, I'm thinking." Don had a sudden thought. "Of course, we've all been praying about this whole situation, so I can't help but think that, God, Himself, is working. We need to be careful not to jump the gun; He needs to do what He needs to do."

"I have no doubt God is right in the middle of this, but let's not forget that we are His hands and feet. There are things *we* need to do." The suggestion was offered carefully. "Don, you need to call a congregational meeting as soon as that man is under house arrest, or whatever, and vote him off the board of deacons. The sooner, the better."

"Oh boy. I know you're right, but this could be a problem. Some folks won't like it, I'm sure."

"If you knew how many of them have signed witness documents for me in this investigation, you would not hesitate to go forward with this move."

"Really? I had no idea."

"Of course not. You're a nice guy, and I sure wouldn't want to compromise you in any way." He thought to thank the man, again. "And I appreciate all the incidents you witnessed, as well. You know, all the evidence collected from these folks is collaborated by multiple witnesses, and I have a good feeling about this." A happy note shot through the line. "And, the big boys are so confident about this case, too. It has taken a long time to nail somebody in action, and it was Mickey who finally filled the bill."

"I guess there's something to be said for having an obsessive personality."

"For sure. I doubt that he can wiggle out of this one." Another thought. "Of course, there is also a good chance he'll be charged in the murder of his wife."

"Think so?"

"Between the two of us, Don, Inspector McDonald is hot on the trail of that one." A small grunt of approval slipped out. "No, I think we've got this guy out of your church, one way or another, or *both*, for Pete's sake."

***

Because the authorities were closing in on his chief murder suspect — not for killing his wife, but for stealing church properties and other assets — Inspector McDonald felt he needed to protect his own investigation. After all, he reasoned, the man might escape the OECA thing, and all the current evidence concerning Rita's death could get lost in the fray, maybe for years. Mickey's involvement in his wife's demise, and even with the satanic rituals, if not established as facts, could either distract from the church investigation, or get relegated to a dusty file cabinet in the basement of the Burlington Police Department. He needed to get this thing nailed down.

So it was, that Inspector McDonald showed up at Sammy's house in Jericho Center on the next morning. He parked in front of the property, just up the rise from the center's village green. Birds chirped softly as the Saturday sunrise rose, a soft glow on the clear, pale blue horizon. It illuminated the picket fence that marked the territory of the town's most peculiar siblings — by now regarded as a crazy lady and her clumsy brother.

"Okay," he thought, *"I'm early, but that's okay, too. I want to know if that guy so much as takes a six o'clock dip in a bird bath in the morning. I want to see if he sends smoke signals to aliens, or performs rituals in the backyard."* He laughed softly. *"If it's out there, I need to find it. It has to be there. These two are definitely disturbed people and they had to be manipulated by Mickey, because, that is what he does. He had to be in charge of* them, *because he would never have allowed them to be in charge of him."* An affirmation rumbled from within. *"That's the truth, and Mr. Black needs to get real."*

He waited until seven-fifteen before he left the car making his way up the hard clay path to the front door. There, he took a big breath, then pounded on the peeling white paint. In an instant, he heard a movement inside. Somebody would be peeking out the window, he knew, so he allowed some time for that, and then he pounded insistently on the door once again. It creaked gently to a six-inch opening.

"Yeah?"

"Good morning. I'm Liam McDonald. I'm here to see Mr. Sammy Black."

"Yeah? What for?"

He strained to get a look at the half-hidden face. "Are you Mr. Black?"

"What do you want?"

"A little private conversation, sir. That's why I'm here at your house, so early on a Saturday morning. Needed to catch you at home, hopefully, alone." He squinted at the shadowed head moving slowly behind the crack. "You are Sammy Black, aren't you?"

Slowly, the door opened a bit wider. Disheveled dark hair topped a long, angular face, as pale eyes peered from the dark hollows beneath a massive brow. "What do you want?"

"Just a few minutes of your time, Mr. Black."

"You with the insurance patrol?"

"Insurance?" He quickly took note that this guy was wary of being caught by some kind of policing organization. "Um, no. Nothing like that, sir."

"So, what *do* you want?"

"I, uh, need to talk about Rita Suree and satanic rituals."

"What? What did you say?" He opened the door and stepped toward the man. "Who the hell are you, anyway?"

Liam noted the fellow's one free hand was formed into a massive fist. "I'm probably the guy who's going to save your butt, so let's not be too hasty, Mr. Black." The fist loosened. "I'm a detective from the Burlington Police Department, but," he raised a cautionary hand, "I'm here on unofficial business. This conversation is to be strictly between you and me, and it will go no further."

Sammy's face relaxed somewhat. "If you could please allow me to sit down and have a little time with you, I think I can keep you out of this, uh, *murder*, and, in return, maybe you could help steer me in the right direction."

"What makes you so sure it was murder?"

"Please, Mr. Black. Could we just sit down and talk about it?"

The lanky fellow, it turned out, was dressed in rumpled gray and white striped pajamas, and wearing some worn-out moccasin slippers. He sat down heavily into a faded overstuffed chair. Liam took a seat on the sofa, close enough to talk pretty much into the man's face.

"I hear Mickey has been going to Waterbury with you, on a regular basis, talking with the doctor and even with your sister, in private, hugging her and whispering into her ear. Is that true?"

"I guess so." His jaw twitched. "She's not with it, anyway. It doesn't matter."

"Oh, I think it does matter; it matters very much, Mr. Black."

"I don't know what you're talking about."

"Mr. Black, may I call you 'Sammy'?" The nod allowed him to continue. "Sammy, your boss is in deep trouble. He's trying to cover his butt, and it's not working, because he has no idea how deep into crap he really is." He waved away the curiosity in the man's eyes. "Can't go into details right now, but I'm here to warn you and your sister, that you're both in real *danger*, here."

"What kind of danger?"

"Mickey is trying to *set you* up, and *shut her* up. He doesn't want you two spilling the beans about those satanic rituals. Yeah, we know all about it, what with the symbol on the bedroom floor, and oh, the hot showers." The long face went pale. "Yeah, we know about that, too, but that's not the point, here." His hands spread wide, palms up. "Can't you see how Mickey is maneuvering to look like your great mentor, when, in fact, he wants to accuse you, you ungrateful S.O.B., of lying about the rituals and trying to pin Rita's murder on *him*?" He brought both hands down hard on his knees. "He wants you to take the dive for him, Sammy. He's setting you up. As for Edith, well, she could suddenly, conveniently, 'pass away.' Yeah, that's what I think." He leaned back. "Now, what do *you* think?"

The large head drooped. "I… don't know."

"Mickey has no alibi for that night. Do you know where he was?"

"Who says he was even there?"

"Wait a minute! Were you at the scene of the murder?"

"I'm not saying that."

"Okay, um, you and Edith vouched for each other, saying you were both here at home." He hunched forward. "Look, he could say you're both lying. He could find some way to prove it, too. That's the way this guy works, Sammy, you *know* that! You need to wake up, man!"

Stress was beginning to manifest in the big, knobby hands. They flexed repeatedly as Sammy Black spoke. "I… can't even answer all of this stuff, Detective. It's too much. It's too much."

"Okay, let me say this: I'm just a phone call away. Here." He pulled out a business card. "Call me if you need me. Call me if you can help me nail this phony. And remember, he's *not* your friend, and," he stood slowly to his feet, "he's not in love with you, either, Sammy. He's just a lustful, self-centered bastard."

He was almost all the way to the door before he made a last, big jab at the man's delusional bubble. "By the way, Sammy, we also know you have a condition called polydactyl syndrome. Thought you should know that."

CHAPTER TWENTY-FIVE

Portals

Al, being the sharp lawyer he was, had Mickey out on bail by Monday night.

Nevertheless, the shock of the situation threw the little manipulator into a panic; the clipboard appeared again, and there were scurrying walks about the Suree property and the insurance office, accompanied by low mutterings and short bursts of exasperation. Leo, stunned into reality, kept his head low and spent longer hours at the church office, making sure Heidi was with him as much as possible. It was a complicated — and yet, sudden — change, but the Spencers were finally in lock-step about Mickey Suree's true character.

Meanwhile, Don, Harold-the-seer, and even the former deacon, Gerald Short, began to notify church members that there would be an emergency meeting after the usual service on Sunday. Leo stayed out of that, to build an appropriate sermon for that day, and Sammy Black was busy with the situation in Waterbury. Still, by the weekend, word had gotten out about the meeting. Indeed, extra seating was required to accommodate the overflowing attendance.

A lady in a pink dress led worship from the upright piano, and there were hymns of joyful hope, specially selected to help alleviate the tension in this gathering of troubled believers. No mention of the situation at hand was even made during announcements and the worship service, but there was, it seemed, a whole new Leo who stepped up to the pulpit. He prayed briefly, then opened with a simple statement. "Anybody can say they are a Christian, but it's not what they *say*, it's what they *do*." The brethren sat still, as he slowly opened his Bible.

"Our Bible verses for today's sermon are Romans twelve, verses two through five, and later, First Corinthians twelve, verses twelve through fourteen. You may want to mark these two places in your Bible." He let the rustle of paper settle down a bit before he read the passage from Paul's letter to the Romans, verbatim: "And be not conformed to this world: but be ye transformed by the renewing of your mind, that you may prove what is that good, and acceptable, and perfect will of God.

"For I say, through the grace given unto me, to every man that is among you, not to think of himself more highly than he ought to think; but to think soberly, accordingly as God hath dealt to every man the measure of faith.

"For as we have many members in one body, and all members have not the same office.

"So we, being many, are one body in Christ, and every one members of one of another."

Before he launched into the meat of the message, he stepped away from the podium a bit, his eyes fixed on an imaginary scene being played out on the back wall of the humble sanctuary.

"My mom, before she got saved, used to keep us in line with some pretty raw wisdom. Whenever we got too big for our britches, she would chew us up one side and down the other, and it always ended with this remark: 'If I didn't give a damn about you, I wouldn't give a damn about what you did.'"

Heidi, sitting on the front row, visibly cringed. "*Oh no, he didn't really say that.*"

Leo continued. "Then she would say, 'But I *do* give a damn, because I love you, you hear me?' And then there was always the clincher, at the end of the speech: 'You don't live in this world alone, you know that? There are a whole bunch of people in your life who love you, and every time you make an ass of yourself, you break their hearts.'" He gazed across the congregation, to let that sink in, before continuing: "Then she would wipe her eyes and leave the room."

A collective hum moved through the place.

He locked his hands behind his back and scanned the little crowd again. "Yeah. I hear you, friends. My mom was right. We don't live in this world all by ourselves — everything we do affects somebody else — or even a whole bunch of somebody elses." He took a couple of steps to his right. "I realize these verses are pointing out the various gifts in the Body of Christ, but if we draw back to another perspective, we see how intricately we are interconnected, by the consequences of our attitudes and choices." He referred quickly to the verses of First Corinthians, which largely echoed those in Romans, chapter twelve. "If you take the time to read it, you'll see how the same message applies here as well. Are we learning anything, here? We are all so connected!" He moved toward the front of the platform. "We need to work together, or we can drag a whole bunch of other people into… hey, I'm going to say it right out… the depths of an eternal Hell." His body bent forward. "We need to get real, folks. This is serious stuff!" His torso straightened with the thrust of his hands toward the heavens. "Life is full of deadly, hidden crevasses — *giant* ones — and there is no way that we, alone, can avoid them. We can be swallowed alive at any moment." His visage reflected the horror of such a thing. "I'm not kidding, folks. These deep, dark openings — these portals — of temptation are out there and, other than our own willpower, we have no human defense against them." The hands went to the hips. "And since when do we trust our own willpower, one hundred percent?"

He went on to present several examples of folks falling into various forms of temptation, some of them tragic, others downright funny. He added a few actual Bible characters, like Cain, King David, and Samson, and at the end of fifteen minutes, he had raised the human frailty factor to a higher level of reality. "And we still deal with this stuff — every single day."

He lowered his head as he moved once more to stand near the podium.

"Hey, whether we like it or not, we have to deal with these temptations — these portals — and the fact is, we can't simply leap over them, nor can we avoid falling into *all* of them, and, when we *do* fall into them, heaven knows, we don't have the human strength to climb up *out* of them. We are truly in need of rescue — over and over and over. It behooves us to recognize this fact, and to wise up: Our *only* rescuer is Jesus Christ, and His Blood, and we had darned well better recognize that, or we'll surely spend forever, down deep in a literal hell-hole." He let them get that as he shuffled his notes into a neat stack.

"One more thing about my mom: When us guys were going to hang out with our friends, she'd come on with a bit more gentleness, giving us advice as we went out the door: 'Remember, you are answerable to everyone else in this world who loves you. What you do with your life, affects them very deeply. Don't be stupid!'"

As the congregation laughed, he moved back to lean casually on the side of the pulpit. He took a few seconds to enjoy the humor with them, before winding down. Then he signaled the lady in the pink dress, who began to play softly on the piano as he made the final point.

"Well, I don't know how many of us need that advice, but maybe we should be trying harder to think about the other loving folks in the Body of Christ. So, my questions for you today are these: Are you actually even a part of the Body of Christ, or are you just hanging out there? Can we actually depend on you, or will you fall away when the going gets rough — when you're faced with the next portal, the next test? If that's the case, then maybe it's time for you to learn how to make the leap across that gaping crevasse, or, if you do fall in, how to escape the deadly consequences. Listen, you can't do either of those things without the Blood of Jesus.

"My friend, let me invite you to make *another* giant leap today. You only need to step forward and give your heart and soul to the Savior. You, too, can be rescued from the bottomless pit."

The music continued, as he pulled it all together.

"Listen, my friend, there are people in the Body of Christ who love you. There is a Savior who loves you. The Holy Spirit loves you. Your Heavenly Father loves you. You have nothing to lose but your worldly pride. That's it."

Willis P. Bigelow sprinted down that aisle and came to a tipsy stop. "Pastor," he whispered, "I'm tired of bein' a stupid ass!"

***

"I just found her like this," the young man in white told the head nurse.

"Does she have a pulse? My gosh, she's positively purple."

"Ay-yuh, she has a pulse. Just unconscious, right?"

The woman picked up Edith's wrist and counted the movements on her own nurse's watch. "Uh-huh, it's weak, but it's there." She turned to the aide. "Did she eat breakfast this morning?" He nodded that she had. "Then you got her out here into the day room, and what happened after that?"

"I came back a few minutes ago to give her some water, and she was passed out, just like this."

"Lord god, we finally get her to eat something, and she chokes on it."

"Um, I don't think so, ma'am. She swallowed the Jell-O just fine. No choking or nothing. Really."

"Stand in front of her and grab her arms." She stepped behind Edith's chair and pushed her forward. "Lift!" she commanded, and as the arms went up, she pounded firmly between the woman's shoulder blades.

"Drop!" she ordered. When the hands rested on the knees, she counted to five.

"Lift!" she repeated.

By the third time, there was a short cough and orange liquid dribbled from the patient's lips. Then she drew a gurgling breath. "Wow! I've never seen anybody use that method before," the young man marveled.

"And you didn't see me do that just now, either, mister."

"What?"

"I know it's not protocol, but I have three kids, and it works every time."

"Oh."

"Keep an eye on her for a few minutes."

"Yes, ma'am, but, I mean, who chokes on Jell-O, for Pete's sake?"

"Somebody with a blockage, or a murderous thumb on their esophagus."

"What?"

The nurse laughed. "Something is choking her, kiddo. I'll schedule her for an exam tomorrow morning. Meanwhile, don't feed her orally, okay?"

"Yes, ma'am, and thanks for your help. You enjoy the rest of this sunny Sunday morning."

Neither one of them saw the terror in Edith's eyes.

***

The back porch had been cleared of trash to be burned, so Ma had swept it off and mopped up, and put two folding chairs out there so she and Willis could have some quiet time together. Now that he had accepted Jesus and she had come back into that holy relationship, this husband and wife were determined to get back what they had when they were first married — only with the Lord included this time. He was already sitting out there, when she brought out the bowls of ice cream.

"Here ya go," she said, handing him the gleaming, icy treat.

"Oh yeah, that sure looks good."

The clink of spoons against the glass bowls prefaced the continuation of a conversation that had been taking place for the last few nights. Ma swished a creamy bite and then swallowed before she spoke.

"I was wonderin', why do you suppose Rita asked you, of all people, to do that ritual thing?"

He hummed through the smoothness. "You know, I think she thought I was just plain stupid." He dug into the vanilla-flavored clump. "Do you know, Ma, that if I got her pregnant, I could have been the number one suspect in her murder?" The spoon brought up a bite, which he held precipitously in front of his mouth. "Imagine that. I guess God was lookin' out for me." He waved the full spoon slightly. "Besides, I figured my family was worth a whole lot more than a hundred dollars."

She nearly dropped her spoon. "A hundred dollars? She was gonna pay you a hundred dollars to do that?" Her hands trembled as she turned the bowl around for no good reason. "My, goodness, Willis. I had no ideer." For a few minutes, she enjoyed the concept of being worth more than a hundred dollars, before it occurred to her to ask about the stuff that happened over at Sam's Place. She set the cold dish down on her lap, bowing her head before asking. "So, was that make-believe si-reen, Edith Schwarz, was she offerin' you money, too?"

He laughed out loud. "Gawd, no!" He leaned forward over the dish. "It was some kind of... I don't know... thing that I couldn't shake. I almost did it, Willow. I almost went for it, and I can't even tell you why." He shook his head in shame. "I am so sorry, that I even went over there."

But she knew. It was the breaking of the gold dust spell on the well. Like the inspector had suggested... the willow branches, and then drinking the water before the ten days were up. Her hand reached over to touch his. "That's okay,

Willis. You ain't... you haven't done anything wrong. That's what counts. That's what counts. In your right mind, you never would-a hurt anybody, that's for sure."

His shoulders slumped. "You're something else, Willow, and that's why I know the same about you." His spoon dinged lightly against the glass. "It just ain't yer nature to smother somebody in mud. No, it ain't, and never will be."

Her smile was actually shy. "Well, ain't... I mean, *isn't* that jes' the nicest thing... jes' the nicest thing, Willis, that you've ever said to me?"

"Aw, Willow, when're you gonna learn?"

"What?"

"You don't have to correct your English in front of me; I like you, just the way you are." He reached over and took the bowl from her, then slid the two unfinished treats off to the side. "What do you think about takin' a little walk with me out behind the henhouse, where the neighbors got no business bein'?"

It was one of the best nights of Willow Bigelow's life.

CHAPTER TWENTY-SIX

Decisions

Meanwhile, back at Swift Street Pentecostal Church, no potluck was scheduled on this Sunday morning because of the meeting. Instead, folks kept their seats by leaving Bibles and sweaters on them, then sauntered up to the coffee and cookie table along one side of the sanctuary, where they made small talk.

At half-past noon, a car pulled into the parking lot, and heads turned to watch Mickey Suree, accompanied by two U.S. Marshals, walk into the church, taking seats at the rear of the building.

"What the heck?" somebody remarked. "Why the law?"

"Probably under house arrest," someone else theorized. "They must have given him permission to come to defend himself. See, he can't go anywhere except on his own property, if I'm right about this."

That arrival signaled the beginning of the meeting, so folks took their seats and waited for Don Collins to call it to order. A long table had been lifted onto the platform, for what was left of the board of deacons: Don, Harold Taylor, and Sammy Black. Don stood up. "Thank you all for coming to this meeting today. I'm sure every one of you is aware of the situation, namely, that we have lost accessibility to our head deacon, due to circumstances beyond our control." He checked his notes, to stay carefully within the narrative, not wanting to accuse or defame Mickey Suree. After all, this was a Christian group, and the leadership — or what was left of it — had the responsibility to set the proper, godly tone.

"So, what we need to do here today, is to elect a new head deacon, and if possible, at least two more new ones, so we have a total of five. We need five, in order to function properly, meeting quorums and things like that." He looked over the crowd. "Are there any concerns or questions about this?"

It was like waiting for a bomb to hit the building.

"May I speak, Don?" Mickey's request sounded more like a command.

"Uh," the counselor caught the eye of the other two at the dais. Both men shrugged. "Uh, if you would please be brief, Mickey. I'm sure you know that the rules of conduct have been broken here, and we have no choice but to elect a new head deacon."

"I will be brief," he said as he pranced up the aisle, "even though, I beg to differ as to rules of conduct being broken." He turned to speak to the crowd, a humble smile on his lips. "Folks, you have known me for a long time. You have watched as Rita and I and the boys took great delight in being part of this church, and you have loved us and thanked us, so many times for so many things. But the truth is, we could not have done any of it — the picnics, the camp-outs, the weddings, none of it — without the love and cooperation of this wonderful, loving congregation." The smile twitched a tiny bit. "I want to thank you for being our friends — our friends in the Lord, as we worked together to serve Him." He wiped something from the edge of one eye. "You know, I was just an old fighter, slugging my way through life 'til I met Jesus." There was another light touch to the corner of the other eye. "And you also know, if it hadn't been for Pastor James, I don't know where I would have been today." The mouth quivered. "He showed me how to love and serve people; how to do the work of the Lord."

Suddenly, Heidi stood up from her front row seat. Leo pulled at her arm, but she pushed it away. "So, just tell us this, Mickey: If you have to lie and cheat to do the work of the Lord, there must be something wrong with that, don't you think?"

His eyes went dark as she spoke, but before he could answer, the murmur of the crowd filled the room. His face reddened as he spewed it out: "After all I've done for you, you have the nerve to talk to me like that?!" He moved toward her, even as the murmuring increased, but the two marshals dashed forward to take him by both arms. They were out the door in seconds.

"Don?" It was Sammy. "Don?" He jumped to his feet, calling over his shoulder as he rushed to that same exit, "Brief recess! Brief recess!"

Some of those folks rushed to the windows to see what was up.

"He's talking to Mickey."

"Wow! Don't know what he said, but Mickey's so mad he's yelling."

"Oh my gosh, look at that! Sammy's standing up to him."

"Whoa! The marshals are pushing him into the car, but he's still yelling at Sammy."

"He's firing him! I heard it: *You're fired!* Just like that!"

"Ladies and gentlemen," Don called out, "please return to your seats. We need to have order in this room. We need to have order, right now!"

"He's coming back in," somebody warned, and there was a flurry of bodies returning to their places.

When Sammy returned to the platform, his face was white and shiny with sweat. He nodded a thank-you to Don, and everyone got back to business.

It was probably one of the most efficiently and decisively run meetings that little church had ever conducted. To begin with, because of the bylaws concerning rules of conduct, Mickey was voted off the board of deacons. The motion was made and passed that Gerald Short be reinstated as a church member, and onto the board once again. A young man named Bernard, who had just come back from Bible School, was voted in as the fifth deacon, and then Don was elected head deacon. At this point, the crowd was happy to put off lunch, so they could vote Greta back in as church secretary, and make Leo Spencer their temporary pastor. Those two shook hands and promised a smooth-running office. After that, the date for the next congregational meeting was set, and Don prayed a closing blessing over them. When they were dismissed at two-thirty, most folks thought they had set a record. Everybody was feeling pretty good, and all the cookies had disappeared.

***

Mickey slammed the door behind him and threw his jacket across the great room. He had hardly been able to control himself during the ride home from the meeting, but the continuous glare of those professional lawmen kept him from going off the deep end.

He was angry — so angry that he was bawling like a baby. "After all I've done for them — all of them. No, especially for Sammy, and the Spencers." As he plopped down into his winged chair in front of the fireplace, he zeroed in on those three. "That ugly, six-toed jerk. Nothing but a big, dumb queer. I should never have put out for him like that. He would've done anything I asked, anyway. What a sad-sack loser. Good riddance."

Not normally a drinking man, the thought came to him unexpectedly. A secret bottle of brandy had escaped the explosion and fire, hidden in a floor safe in the front restroom of the office. Now seemed like a good time to get it out, so he made a beeline for it. When he passed Sammy's newly redone office, he realized there was a big problem: That man knew way too much.

He stopped in his tracks. "Knows about the rituals, about Rita, about Edith, about, oh hell, about everything." There was a sinking feeling. "What can I do about all that?" Another deeper sinking feeling. "And none of that had anything to with the OECA. I need to take care of this." He continued toward the restroom. "Well, Edith is so far gone, all I have to do is prove that Sammy is just as nuts as she is."

At the floor safe, he struggled to remember the combination, but got it right on the third try. Dropping the floor covering back into place, he gazed at the golden bottle. "Okay, let's see whether this stuff is still any good."

As he once again passed Sammy's old office, another ghastly thought caught up with him: "Oh shee-it. The rug thing. Heidi and Lou, and even Willis." He was back into the kitchen before he started to solve that one.

"Alright, I've already explained to Willis that it was Rita who ordered that thing painted on our floor. He will take care of that, getting it straight with his family; otherwise, I'll threaten to sue him for the damage he caused. Not that I really would, but if I mention big enough numbers and a good team of lawyers, I do believe that doofus will fold and go back to chicken farming."

But Heidi, he realized, was a whole different matter. "She would have to be discredited, big-time. A light went on. "Of course. A good-looking blonde, all alone out there in the guest house. Nothing to do but make trouble for the man who rejected her advances."

He sat down in the wing-backed chair and took a sip of the brandy. "Of course," he whispered to himself, "that'll have to happen before they move into the church parsonage."

CHAPTER TWENTY-SEVEN

Choices

The next Sunday, two announcements were made at the end of the usual eleven o'clock service: Ma Bigelow gave her "testimony," as she called it. It was short and to the point, which everybody appreciated, because there was potluck a few minutes away. The nervous lady gave her witness, rapid-fire: "I want you all to know that I am rededicating my life to Jesus — I have been studying too much about Greek gods and magic spells and all that stuff, and not enough about the Bible — that was wrong." She took a breath. "Of course, I could say there's a couple of good things that come out of all that, you know — I learned that demons are real, and there is a real Hell, and I do mean *real*, because that's where those Watcher angels are."

Another breath. "Of course, the Bible tells us they're in a special section of Hell, called Tartarus, and they are in chains, but maybe they can still command the demons that are floating all around us, trying to get us to sin."

There was a slight hesitation as she sucked in the final lung-full. "So anyways, I jes' want to make a public dee-claration, and also say that I am proud of my kids, and my wonderful husband, Willis P. Bigelow."

Hearty handclapping ushered her quickly to her chair, right in front of where Laura Wilson and Connie Collins were seated.

"Wow!" Laura murmured to Connie. "There's hope for my guys yet!"

Leo moved from behind the pulpit to bring the second announcement. He motioned for Heidi to join him. When she stood beside him, he put his arm around her. "Heidi and I have something to tell you all. I hope you will receive it with as much joy as we two have about this." He returned her smile and gave her a gentle squeeze. "After some very long talks this past week, we have decided that, even though you all have been so kind as to ask us to fill in this pastorate, we are called to go to the mission field."

The brethren reacted with a soft murmur.

"We want you to know we love you, but we know now that my real calling is as an evangelist. We'll return to Bible school for some refresher courses, and then, well, God will lead us to wherever we are needed. We hope you'll send us off with your blessings."

"Oh my goodness," Greta called out. "We've never sponsored a missionary family before. Maybe it's time we did!"

Several voices agreed.

"We love you guys," one of the other ladies shouted. It brought the congregation to its feet, some applauding, other folks moving forward to hug the couple. The rest started to set up tables and haul food over from the parsonage. They were hungry.

***

It was several days before people realized Sammy Black had not been in church that Sunday. In fact, it was Tuesday night's regular deacon board meeting at the parsonage, when his absence was noted.

"We probably should have called him at his home," Gerald Short said. "He's probably been looking for a job, you know?"

"Yes, that, and looking after Edith," Harold suggested. "All those trips to Waterbury take time."

"Not to mention," the young Bernard added, "all the stress of that situation."

"If you all can wait for a couple of minutes, I'll make a call from the church office." Don rose to leave.

"No-no," Gerald objected. "Let me do it. You go ahead and get started."

Don thanked him and opened the meeting with prayer. It was longer and more heartfelt than usual, for the men were about to start on a whole new program, differing greatly from the dictatorial structure so long imposed by Mickey. When they lifted their heads, Gerald was standing inside the door, a troubled look on his face. "We got a letter," he said, "from Sammy." He handed it to Don, then took a seat across the table.

"Oh boy," Bernard worried, "I hope he's not resigning."

Don took the business-sized envelope and opened it carefully. Slowly, he undid the triple fold, shaking it out flat. "'To whom it may concern.'" He stopped and looked up at the men. "Oh no…"

Harold's face was white. "Oh, Lord God, please tell me that isn't what I think it is."

Don lowered his head and began to read it aloud:

"To whom it may concern,

"Please forgive me, but I have come to the end of my rope. Despite our years of faithful devotion to them, the gods have turned on us. First, they sacrificed Rita in a fertility rite because Bigelow would not cooperate in a play-acted one — something which was supposed to honor Tyche on her special day. Edith told her Willis had changed his mind, so Rita lay drugged on the symbol of that Titan witch, while that wretched son of Hercules impregnated her. Only the drugs weren't enough, and she went through it, wide awake.

"I believe they killed Rita when she tried to end the pregnancy. Edith and I went to the pond to help her perform the ritual, but she wouldn't get into the water, insisting instead, on using one of the canoes. We waited on the bank while she ran around to the other side, then pushed the thing into the water. We saw her jump into it, but she forgot the paddle. She was hurrying because Mickey showed up, looking for her. She saw him coming up behind me and Edith, so she used her hands to steer the canoe toward the center of the pond. It was moving right along, but then, for a couple of seconds, she disappeared behind the boxer statue. There was no sound, no hint. The canoe just reappeared from behind the statue, empty, floating on its side.

"I jumped into the water to search for her. Then Mickey and then Edith joined me. It was a long time before we found her body jammed into the mud at the north end of the pond. It was glowing with that certain greenish color, so we knew not to touch it. Instead, we cleaned up everything and left.

"The gods are getting revenge for us trying to help Rita. We interfered with their plans for the new seeding of nephilim. Mickey is cornered like a terrified rat. And now, they have Edith. She is totally possessed. A living Hell.

"And they are coming for me, too. I feel them just one step behind me. But I will not live with that same punishment. I will keep my own mind. They will not feast off my emotions.

"Learn from this. These heartless gods are real. Stay away from them.

"I'm done.

Sammy Black"

The four men sat quietly in their chairs, tears falling silently. "My God, please have mercy on our brother," Gerald prayed.

"He wasn't serving our God, Gerald," the seer reminded him. "That was the problem."

"Uh, gentlemen," the newest deacon ventured, "shouldn't we notify somebody?"

"Of course," Don replied. "I'll call the sheriff's department to do a couple of site checks."

Forty-five minutes later, Max Duncan found Sammy's car parked outside his house in Jericho Center. It was locked up, and the cottage windows were dark.

The sheriff pounded on the front door. When there was no stirring within, he tried one more time.

"You got a key that fits this frickin' door?" he asked Deputy Smith.

"Yessir, I probably do." It took four tries before the lock moved, and the knob turned in the deputy's hand. He pushed open the door slowly and stepped back.

Sheriff Duncan listened carefully before he stepped inside. He found the light switch to the right of the door, and the parlor was illuminated under the glow of an etched-glass ceiling light. The men looked around, then moved slowly into the center of the room.

"Hey! Anybody home?" Max waited, not expecting an answer. Turning to his partner, he chided him. "So, Smith, you know how these things work. Go check out that bathroom. I'll see what's in the bedroom."

Lights turned on as the two moved through the home, checking each room. Finally, there was a quick shuffle of footsteps, and Smith came into the hallway.

"In here!"

Sammy Black had planned things as carefully as he could so there would be no gross messes or an immodest corpse, just the simple discovery of a body, dressed in a bathing suit, floating in bloody water, the kitchen knife placed carefully on the bathmat on the floor near the old bathtub's clawed legs. Finally, a note was taped carefully to the mirror so it would not be missed.

But there was one factor the man had not considered. No doubt, the water had been very, very hot, to deaden the pain of deeply slit wrists, but now, several days later, it was icy cold and crusted over, and the odor was overwhelming.

Deputy Smith went outside and puked.

It took a few hours for the whole incident to get legally processed, much to the delight of the neighbors, but when Sheriff Max Duncan finally slipped back into the front seat of his vehicle, he was more perplexed than ever. "I can't help but wonder," he said to his driver, "why the man had two suicide notes."

"Yeah?"

"Yeah, and from what the guys at the church showed me, the two notes were exactly the same."

Smith turned on the ignition and the engine hummed. "Maybe he was just a really meticulous person," he suggested.

A sudden sharp rap on the passenger window jolted Max into action. He shot backward in the seat, his hand on his holster.

"Hey! Back off, Max!" Inspector McDonald's face pressed close to the glass.

As he rolled the window down, the sheriff had a few choice words for the detective.

The man took a draw on the stub of a cigarette. "Relax, man. You told me to let you in on stuff, and that's what I'm trying to do, okay?" He stood up straight, dropped the glowing butt to the ground and stomped it. "So, this note? What do you think? You believe it, about the gods?"

"Hell, no."

"Well, I wouldn't be too hasty, Max. Remember, these two were involved in some pretty weird stuff, some of which we can't explain, I might add."

"What? You telling me there are real witches and bogeymen on this planet?"

"That's not exactly what I'm trying to say. I think you'd better sit back and try pulling it all together. You know, there have been a whole lot of people in this murder case, all talking about demons and angels and rituals and God only knows what else. A *lot* of them, Max."

"So? Ever heard of crowd hypnosis, Liam? Ever think of that?"

"Heard of it. Don't think it applies here."

"So what *does* apply here?"

"We're all — the whole bunch of law enforcement agencies in the state of Vermont — probably in over our heads, this time."

The sheriff guffawed, slapping his thigh. "Man, you need to take a sabbatical or something, you know that? Hey, if I was you, I wouldn't let your bosses hear that."

"Right. Well, I promised I would keep you informed, Sheriff." He touched his brow in a phony salute. "And I have done just that. Do with it, whatever you will."

Max laughed again, then signaled Smith to move on out. As the vehicle turned and headed down the slope toward the green, Liam McDonald stood quietly, the night settling silently around him.

"If Mickey *was* there the night of the murder, neither Sammy nor Edith can testify of that." He coughed deeply, the usual raw throat being worse in the cool night air. "On the other hand, if Sammy is telling the truth, the gods killed her... if there really are such things." He strode over to his car and slid behind the wheel. Slowly, he lit another cigarette. "This case is closed, as far as I'm concerned. I don't care what the justice system calls it, a 'cold case,' or what. I can't prove Mickey Suree killed his wife. Period."

He coughed again, bringing up a whole lot more phlegm than usual. "Damn! This stuff is getting to be a nuisance."

CHAPTER TWENTY-EIGHT

Murderers

The same afternoon they made their announcement to the church, the Spencers stopped by Mickey's to give notice that they would be vacating the guest house, to take up temporary residence in the church parsonage.

"Well, I would certainly hope so," the mouse snapped from his open front door. "You two have taken advantage of me long enough."

"We won't get into a discussion of who took advantage of whom," Leo replied. "But we have appreciated the lodging, that's for sure." He took Heidi's hand. "We'll be packed and out of here in a few days. In the meantime, I'm sure you understand when I ask you to give us our privacy. We will be extremely busy, and we intend to leave everything in tip-top shape."

"You'd damned well better, or you'll get a bill in the mail."

The couple exchanged a knowing look. "We thought you might say that," Leo answered. "But we never signed a contract, so that's probably a moot point."

"The hell it is; I'm not a 'moot point' kind of guy."

"Right." They turned, heading for the '36 Ford truck.

"And you need to get control over that sassy-mouthed woman you married!"

As they entered the vehicle, he fired one final shot: "You don't measure up to this pastorate, or any other pastorate, *anywhere*; you can't even be a *deacon*, you know that?"

He shut out the squealing tires and the cloud of dust, returning to his chair near the fireplace. The half-empty glass offered a bit of comfort, and he went for it. As he wiped his mouth, he settled into a plan. "Packing, huh? Well, all I have to do is wait for the right moment."

A couple of days later, he got word of Sammy Black's suicide. He received it with a great sigh of relief. "That's one less thing I have to deal with, and Edith will be no problem, either." A bit of a smile caressed his lips. "She's already scared to death, so I can probably back off from that troublesome duo, for good."

He rose from the kitchen counter, to view the bright Wednesday morning sunrise. From where he stood, the top of the blue spruce jutted up from behind the slope of the hill, against the golden sky. He knew Heidi would be feeding the birds at her usual time of eight in the morning, maybe for the last time. "Wonder what those things will do, after she's moved out?" He snorted softly. "Been too damned many freeloaders around here, for sure. Well, that's going to end."

Suddenly, Leo's truck appeared on the roadway, heading for town. As it passed, Mickey could see plainly that the man was alone. He swallowed hard. So Heidi was alone also... finally. A quick check of his watch told him it would be eight o'clock in fifteen minutes. It was now, or maybe never.

He pulled on his tennis shoes, sprayed some deodorant inside his T-shirt, and headed out the door. When he got to the bend in the drive where the front door to the guest house was visible, he paused, then crouched down beside a shrub. Another glance showed him it was two minutes to eight. He sat back on his haunches and watched.

Little did he know, others were watching as well.

It seemed like it took forever before she came out, carrying a half-empty sack of bird seed. He could see she was dressed in shorts and a halter, and her hair was swept back in a ponytail, ready for another day of packing and cleaning. He grinned widely. "Perfect. If you want to seduce a man, you put on something like that." He watched as she stepped down from the little porch, followed by the ever-present Crusty. When she turned her back and headed for the feeding trays under the tree, he stood up and moved quietly down the road.

She was talking to the birds, her eyes searching the branches. "Hey, little friends, here it is probably the last time." There seemed to be a twittering reply, which brought a bit of moisture to her eyes. "Oh my goodness, how sweet," the woman whispered. She stood there, the bag cradled in the bend of both elbows. "I don't know what to do, except maybe leave what's left of the bag." Crusty's insistent yowl made her turn, and she froze at the sight of Mickey, less than four feet behind her.

"W-what do you want?" she said, as she managed to move backward.

He took a couple of smaller steps toward her. "Just taking a walk. It's a beautiful morning."

"Oh, well, don't let me stop you. Enjoy yourself."

A sly smile spread across his mouth. "You, uh, you want me to enjoy myself? Really?" He took a long, slow look, starting at her ankles and stopping at her mouth. "Well now, Heidi Spencer, look at you." He moved a step closer. "You sure know how to turn a guy on. You're doing this on purpose, right?"

"I'm doing no such thing. You just go take your walk, and leave me alone." She glanced at the road behind him. "Leo will be right back. He just went to check yesterday's mail at the mailbox," she lied.

Unfortunately, this expert fabricator knew a fabrication, when he heard one. He moved in. "That bag looks heavy. Here, let me help you with that…"

"No!" She tried to throw the bag at him as she turned toward the cottage, but the supple sack dropped in front of her own feet, and his swift grasp of her arm spun her around, on the spot.

"Let go of me!" she commanded.

He laughed and grabbed her other wrist. As he yanked her to the ground, the yellow cat split for the bushes.

"Stop it!" She moved her face away as he fell upon her, but his mouth bit into her neck, anyway. "Ow!"

"Oh, does that hurt?" he muttered in her ear. "Does it? Huh?"

Her knee lifted hard into his crotch, and he rolled over with a yelp. "You bitch!" As she rolled away, he brought his clenched fists down on the back of her head, and then she lay very still. He clutched his painful groin, and struggled to his feet. "You ungrateful bitch..." he muttered, as he kicked her in the ribs. He stumbled backward in pain, then lifted his foot for another strike.

But he had not heard the rising din in the tree above him, and the first swooping scrape almost knocked him off his feet. "What?" He hardly got the word out before the second blow, and then he was ducking and cringing and trying to run toward the big log house.

If it hadn't been for the manila envelope with the Bible school's return address on it, Leo would *not* have been right back from the mailbox. Instead of continuing on to the church office, he had taken time to open and read the application forms, then turned the truck around and headed back to give his wife the exciting news. As he approached the big house, he spotted the diving birds and brought his truck to a slow pace. Over the rise in front of him, lay the writhing focus of what he recognized as a "murder of crows" attack.

"I... I don't know what to do," he whispered to himself. And then he thought of Heidi. "No, not her, not her, Lord." He hit the gas pedal and sped through the attack, sending the birds into a dark flurry of retreat. "Oh thank God, that wasn't her, but, Heidi, where are you?" The answer came quickly, as he spotted her body under the big blue spruce.

Sheriff Max Duncan stood at the side of the hospital bed where Heidi lay, her husband holding her hand. "You know, I've never liked that ponytail hair style on women… makes them look like the south end of a fat horse, if you know what I mean. But I have to agree with the doctor you just saw, that thing probably kept you from getting your neck broken. The guy hit too high up!"

"Thank God, because Mickey could have killed her. That little fighter always had a killer punch."

"Hmph. It may be that very factor that will keep him going from now on. You know, that need to be a champion, a winner. But it will be a whole new scenario, I can tell ya."

"So, what did the doctor say about him?"

"Looks pretty bad. I've never seen so much blood, and the victim still alive. He has serious punctures all over his head and back and arms, but especially on his hands, because he was protecting his eyes, of course." The lawman shrugged. "Still, there was a lot of damage. He may be pretty much a blind man, after this." He signaled to Deputy Smith. "We've gotta get out of here." An ironic smile stretched across his face. "An emergency room is the last place I want to spend the rest of my shift." Then he touched the bill of his hat, and went out into the warmth of that June afternoon.

The sheriff's prediction proved to be accurate; Mickey was left with a heavily scarred body, and very little vision — to the point that he was declared legally blind. Ironically, this proved to be the deciding factor in George White's petition to adopt David and Matt. The archeologist finished his visiting professor stint at UVM, a week after the boys got back from their annual outing at Camp Abnaki, and the three of them headed for his new teaching assignment, a few miles from several aunts and uncles in the state of Virginia.

***

Inspector Liam McDonald was truly sick. It had been months since the suicide of Sammy Black, and the appearance of too much phlegm in that searing cough out there in the middle of that dark, cool night. A visit to the doctor two weeks later, had confirmed that all was not well. "You've got emphysema there," the physician had said. But further tests had confirmed the more serious diagnosis of lung cancer. "Stage four," the report had read. It was a shock that sent him into a spin.

"It's a death sentence," he declared to the only person he trusted. "I'm a dead man."

"Not as dead as you might think," Don Collins stated. "Remember, all human beings are made up of body, soul, and spirit."

"I don't know what that means."

"It means your body will die, but your soul and spirit will keep on living."

"Okay, I'm having trouble believing all of that."

"Yeah, that can happen, when you first hear about it." He switched the phone to his other ear. "Say, Liam, I'm on my way to the Suree property this afternoon. Mickey has decided to sell everything and move into Burlington, where there are more conveniences for the blind."

"That scoundrel."

"I know, but since he's agreed to testify against OECA, he'll probably get off with a slap on the wrist. I agree, it doesn't seem fair, but you have to admit, the man has lost a lot in the last few weeks, including most of his eyesight."

"I suppose. So what makes you think I would want to go up to the Suree property with you?"

"Okay, here's the deal: Mickey has also decided to donate the canoes and paddles to Camp Abnaki, really, I think, to make points with his sons."

"Good luck with that one," the man laughed. "I have a feeling it's going to take a whole lot more than that." He coughed gently. "So, why did you think I would even go up there, again?"

"Probably would help settle a few things. If you're really getting ready to graduate to Heaven, you need to let go of all that frustration and unforgiveness."

"Yeah? Well, good luck with *that* one, too!"

"Okay, fine, but why don't you come along, anyway? I could use the company."

The borrowed flatbed truck rattled along Route 7, making a left down the slope of Swift Street, past the church and on toward Hinesburg. The conversation was lively as the two men enjoyed the summer sunshine.

"You were right. I needed to get out and get some fresh air," Liam remarked. "Thanks for twisting my arm."

"No problem." Don slowed the truck down a bit, thinking to reduce the plume of dust behind them. "I love my wife dearly, but she's not much help when it comes to hauling canoes." He glanced at his friend. "Not that they're so heavy, really, it's just a matter of leverage, and then they tip right into place. That's where you come in, sir. I need that extra pair of hands to tilt them onto the trailer, once I get them in position."

"Piece o' cake," Liam joked. "Might as well do things, while I still can."

"Oh, you're going to be doing things, alright." Don cast an encouraging grin his way. "You have some big surprises coming, my friend, once you slip out of that body."

"I don't know, it's kind of creepy."

"Don't let it be. Don't let it be scary, Liam. You have so much great stuff ahead of you. Heaven is such a wonderful place — no pain, no worry, no fear." He waved a reassuring hand across the dashboard. "You'll see."

"Aw, I don't know, Don. I can't even make sense of all this... nephilim, demons, Watcher angels... whatever else." He coughed gently into one hand. I mean, did you even understand what Sammy was talking about? 'They' killed Rita? Really? If you ask me, Mickey was on the other side of that statue, and he dumped her and held her under water."

He drew out a handkerchief to wipe his mouth. "And who the heck impregnated her, you know?" He continued with that thought. "It had to be Sammy, you know it? I'm ninety-nine percent sure of it."

The frustration increased as he went on. "But then, I have to ask myself, 'Why would Sammy want the abortion ritual, and why would Edith help with that?' And while I'm at it, I have to wonder why those two didn't bump into Mickey as he dragged Rita's body up to the north end of the pond and pounded it into the mud?"

"According to Sammy's suicide note," Don reminded him, "Mickey didn't do that."

He turned to look at the driver. "You know, it's damned hard to be a detective, sometimes."

"Ay-yuh, Liam, I can see that. But you definitely have a gift to solve those mysteries."

"Only this time, I have been a miserable failure."

"Maybe not. It's not over yet. God has it all under control."

It was a laugh that turned into a cough. "Um, well," he murmured as he used the soiled cloth again, "if God really is in charge, I wish He would let me see the solution to this puzzle." He blew his nose, wiping it gently before he finished the challenge. "Maybe then, I could, at least die in peace."

Don steered the truck off the main road and onto the Suree property's driveway, approaching the lower end of the pond along the stubbled area of what used to be the camping road. The boxing ring rose like an abandoned site, its weathered ropes hanging limply from faded, tilted posts. He drew the vehicle to a stop on the sandy part of the beach, right in front of the boat storage rack.

It took only a short time to load the first two canoes, Liam being exactly the help that Don needed, but then, the Christian counselor had a sudden notion.

"You know what, Liam?" He looked out at the placid pond. "I have an urge to take one last boat ride out on the water." His brows lifted with the question: "What do you say? Are you up for that?"

"Aw-w-w, I don't know. What for?"

"How about, just for the heck of it? What harm can it do?" Noting the lingering reluctance, he went for the bait. "Maybe, if you take one more look at the murder scene, you might find some answers. What do you think about that?"

The detective went for it.

They slid the canoe into the water, each taking up a paddle to move the featherweight pod northward. It skimmed along, until they dragged paddles to a stop, a few feet from where Rita's body was found. Neither man spoke, as they pondered the poignancy of that situation. At length, Liam put his paddle in the water, signaling departure, and before long, the craft was sliding through the glassy surface toward the center of the former campground's swimming area. Don pointed toward the large statue. "Let's take a look; I've never seen it up close, have you?"

They slid to a stop at the back of the seated figure. Liam peered up into the face that looked fiercely over the right shoulder of the boxer-body. "Wow! Look at the intensity of that expression, Don. That's some nice artwork."

"Yeah?" He back-paddled far enough to get a better look. "Oh yeah, this guy means business, my friend." They laughed together as they inched the canoe through the water, moving slowly around to the front.

"Hey, take a look at those boxing gloves, and the muscles on those arms, will ya?" Liam was even more impressed with the detail in this pugilistic icon.

But Don did not respond with the same enthusiasm; instead, his voice was solemn and subdued: "Hey, Liam."

"What?" The inspector was still marveling over the details of the artwork.

"I'm just noticing something. This whole property, the whole Suree property." Don's head was turning slowly as he made the observation. "It's shaped like a big soup bowl. I mean, it's like somebody tilted it, and this pond is the last of the soup."

The inspector laughed, but looked up at the panorama. "Hey, you're right."

Don smiled and gave another little push with his paddle. "Whoa!" He steadied the canoe to a stop. "What's this?"

"What's what?"

"There's an inscription on this statue, see it?" Don was pointing at a short line of chiseled letters that was being gently bathed in the ripples from their canoe.

The detective corrected him. "Looks more like a title, than an inscription. Statues have titles. I can't quite see it, Don. Move ahead a bit, would you?"

But the man was suddenly looking around at the landscape, again. "Oh my goodness, Liam. This whole property is a portal."

"What? Why would you even think such a thing?" He leaned forward as his friend moved the craft closer to the title.

"Take a look, buddy. I think maybe this thing just answered both your questions: Who impregnated her, and who killed her?"

A mossy-green waterline ran through the carved lettering, making it difficult for Liam McDonald to see the whole title, but after a moment, he gasped.

It read, THE WATCHER.

"Nah, not possible," the detective asserted. "Watchers are in chains, according to your Bible."

"True, but we don't understand all the details." A shadow fell over the pixie face. "In this case, we know the rapist was a giant, or something like that."

Liam noted the darkness on his friend's face. "What are you saying? We still have those nephilim things around?"

"I don't know, Liam. I just don't have a decisive answer for that, but Rita was the victim of something with supernatural power, for sure."

Liam McDonald's quick breath brought on a hard, cleansing cough. "Oh my gawd," he choked, as he dug the paddle deeply into the deceptively placid pond, "we need to get the hell out of here!"

THE END

From L. E. Fleury's *Junctions Murder Mystery Series*:

Book One: LOST

Book Two: HAUNTED

Book Three: PORTALS

Book Four: HEROES

Book Five: DAMAGED

Stay tuned for more to come!